W9-BUE-408

SPLIT SECOND

Also available from MIRA Books and
ALEX KAVA

A PERFECT EVIL

Watch for Agent Maggie O'Dell's next appearance
Coming August 2002
in hardcover

ALEX KAVA

SPLIT SECOND

MIRA

KAV

ISBN 1-55166-835-1

SPLIT SECOND

Visit us at www.mirabooks.com

Printed in U.S.A.

For Amy Moore-Benson, Dianne Moggy and Philip Spitzer,
an incredible team that makes dreams come true.
One book was a privilege; two, an honor.

Special thanks to:

Patricia Sierra, fellow author and friend—
I'm not sure this one would have been completed without your tender,
gentle nagging. Thanks for seeing me through all the anxiety attacks.

The amazing crew at MIRA Books for their enthusiasm,
hard work and dedication, especially Valerie Gray, Craig Swinwood,
Krystyna de Duleba, Alex Osuszek and the best sales force in the business.
Perhaps there is a reason we call them publishing houses—
you've certainly made me feel as if I've found a home.

Megan Underwood and the gang at Goldberg McDuffie Communications, Inc.
for their expertise and hard work.

Annie Belatti, the only person I know who gets excited
about describing gunshot wounds over dinner.
Thanks for your patience, medical expertise and friendship.

Sharon Car, fellow writer and friend, who listens
and encourages through the good and the bad.

Marilyn and John Cooney and Mary Means for taking such
loving care of my kids when I need to be on the road.

Patti El-Kachouti for your unconditional friendship and encouragement.

Nicole Friend, who has often been my sounding board and voice of reason.

Tony Friend for sharing information,
images and ideas that only you can provide.

Ellen Jacobs for telling the truth, first as a reader, then as a friend.

LaDonna Tworek for reminding me that some friendships are forever.

For their inspiration, enthusiasm and loving support,
many thanks to Kenny and Connie Kava, Jeanie Shoemaker Mezger
and John Mezger, Natalie and Rich Cummings, Marlene Haney,
Sandy Rockwood, my mom and dad—Patricia and Edward Kava—
Mac Payne and the Movie Club group: Lyn Belitz, Mary Michaelsen,
Jo Ellen Shoemaker and Becky Thomson.

Also, I want to thank the many book buyers and booksellers
for making room on your lists and on your shelves for a new voice.

And to the readers. With all the wonderful fiction available, thank you
for choosing mine to be a part of your escape and entertainment.

Finally, thanks to Philip Spitzer, Amy Moore-Benson and Dianne Moggy.
None of this would be possible without Philip taking a chance on me,
without Amy being my personal crusader and without Dianne's patient,
steady guidance and support. Together the three of you
are truly a writer's dream team.

PRO**L**OGUE

North Dade County Detention Center
Miami, Florida
Halloween—Friday, October 31

Del Macomb wiped the sweat from his forehead with the sleeve of his shirt. The stiff cotton of his uniform stuck to his back, and it was only nine in the morning. How could it be this hot and humid in October?

He had grown up just north of Hope, Minnesota. Back home, ice would be forming at the edges of Silver Lake. His daddy would be writing his sermons while watching the last of the snow geese pass overhead. Del pushed wet strands off his brow. Thinking about his daddy reminded him that he needed a haircut. Crazy stuff to be thinking about. Even crazier that it was stuff that could still make him homesick.

"So who's the fucking asshole we're chaperoning today?"

Del's partner startled him. He winced at Benny Zeeks's language, then glanced over at the barrel-chested ex-marine to see if he had noticed. He certainly didn't need another lecture—not that he didn't have a lot to learn from Benny.

"Guys said his name is Stucky." He wondered if Benny had heard him. He seemed preoccupied.

At North Dade County Detention Center Benny Zeeks was somewhat of a legend, not only because he was a twenty-five-year veteran, but because he had spent most of that time working up in Starke on death row and even on X Wing. Del had seen his partner's scars from scuffles he'd won over X Wingers trying to avoid the coffinlike solitary confinement.

He watched Benny shove his shirtsleeves up over his veiny forearms, not bothering to fold or roll them, revealing one of those legendary scars. It intersected a tattoo, a Polynesian dancer who now had a jagged red line across her abdomen as if she had been sliced in half. Benny could still make the dancer dance, flexing his arm and sending the lower half of her into a slow, sexy sway while the other half—the top half—froze in place, disconnected. The tattoo fascinated Del, intriguing and repulsing him at the same time.

Now his partner climbed into the armored truck's passenger seat, concentrating on negotiating the narrow steps up into the cab. The man moved slower than usual this morning, and Del immediately knew his partner had another hangover. He swung up into the driver's seat, buckling himself in and pretending, once again, not to notice.

"Who'd you say this asshole is?" Benny asked, while he twisted his thermos lid, the short stubby fingers desperate to get at the coffee. Del wanted to tell him the caffeine would only compound his problem, but after four short weeks on the job, he knew better than to try to tell Benny Zeeks anything.

"We're taking Brice and Webber's run today."

"What the hell for?"

"Webber's got the flu and Brice broke his hand last night."

"How the fuck do you break a hand?"

"All I heard was that he broke it. I don't know how. Look, I thought you hated the monotony of our regular route. Plus, all the traffic just to get to the courthouse."

"Yeah, well, there better not be more paperwork," Benny shifted restlessly as if anticipating the dreaded change in his routine. "And if this is Brice and Webber's run, that means this asshole's headed up to Glades, right? Puttin' him in close custody until his fucking hearing. Means he's some big-time fuckup they don't want down here in our wussy detention lockup."

"Hector said the guy's name is Albert Stucky. Said he's not such a bad guy, pretty intelligent and friendly. Hector says he's even accepted Jesus Christ as his savior."

Del could feel Benny scowling at him. He turned the key in the ignition and let the truck vibrate, then rumble to a slow start while he braced himself for Benny's sarcasm. He turned the air-conditioning on, blasting them with hot air. Benny reached over and punched it off.

"Give the engine some time, first. We don't need that goddamn hot air in our faces."

Del felt his face grow red. He wondered if there would ever be anything he could do to win the respect of his partner. He ignored his simmering anger and rolled down the window. He pulled out the travel log and jotted down the truck's odometer and gas tank readings, letting the routine calm him.

"Wait a minute," Benny said. "Albert Stucky? I've been reading about this guy in the *Miami Herald*. Feebies nicknamed him The Collector."

"Feebies?"

"Yeah, FBI. Jesus, kid, don't you know anything?"

This time Del could feel the prickle of red at his ears. He turned his head and pretended to be checking the side mirror.

"This Stucky guy," Benny continued, "he carved up and slaughtered three or four women, and not just here in Florida. If he's the guy I'm thinking of, he's one badass motherfucker. And if he's claiming he's found Jesus Christ, you can bet it's because he wants to save his sorry ass from being fried by Old Sparky."

"People can change. Don't you believe people can change?" Del glanced at Benny. The older man's brow was beaded with sweat and the bloodshot eyes glared at him.

"Jesus, kid. I bet you still believe in Santa Claus, too." Benny shook his head. "They don't send guys to wait for their trial in close custody because they think he's found Jesus-fucking-Christ."

Benny turned to stare out the window and sip his coffee. In doing so, he missed Del wince again. He couldn't help it. Twenty-two years with a daddy for a preacher made it an instant reaction, like scratching an itch. Sometimes he did it without even knowing.

Del slipped the travel log into the side pocket and shifted the truck into gear. He watched the concrete prison in his side-view mirror. The sun beat down on the yard where several prisoners milled around, bumming cigarettes off each other and enduring the morning heat. How could they enjoy being outside if there was no shade? He added it to his mental list of unfair treatment. Back in Minnesota, he had been quite the activist for prison reform. Lately he'd been too busy with the move and starting his new job, but he kept a running list for when he had more time. Little by little he'd work his way up to battling causes like eliminating Starke's X Wing.

As they approached the final checkpoint he glanced at the rearview mirror. He almost jumped, startled to find their prisoner staring back at him. All Del could see through the thick slit of glass were the piercing black eyes, and they were looking directly at him in the mirror.

Del recognized something in the prisoner's eyes, and a knot tightened in his stomach. He had seen that look years ago as a boy, on one of his trips accompanying his father. They had visited a condemned prisoner, who Del's father had met at one of his prison fellowship meetings. During that visit, the prisoner had confessed all the horrible, unimaginable things he had done to his own family before he murdered them—a wife, five children and even the family dog.

As a boy, the details Del heard that day had been traumatizing, but even worse was the evil pleasure the prisoner seemed to get from retelling each detail and watching the impact on a ten-year-old boy. Now Del saw that same look in the eyes of the man in the back of the armored truck. For the first time in twelve years, he felt as if he was looking straight into the eyes of pure evil.

He made himself look away and avoided the temptation to

glance back. He pulled out from the last checkpoint and onto the highway. Once they got on the open road, he could relax. He enjoyed driving. It gave him time to think. But when he took a quick left, Benny, who had appeared to be lost in his thoughts, suddenly became agitated.

"Where the hell you going? I-95's the other direction."

"I thought we'd take a shortcut. Highway 45 has less traffic, and it's a much nicer drive."

"You think I fucking care about nice?"

"It's shorter by about thirty minutes. We get the prisoner delivered, and then we'll have an extra half hour for lunch."

He knew his partner wouldn't argue with an extended lunch hour. In fact, he had hoped Benny would be impressed. Del was right. Benny leaned back in his seat and poured another cup of coffee. He reached over and punched the AC. This time, cool air began filling the cab, and Benny rewarded Del with a rare smile. Finally, he had done something right. Del sat back and relaxed.

They had left Miami's traffic and had been on the road only thirty minutes when a thump rattled the back of the truck. At first Del thought they had dropped a muffler, but the thumping continued. It came from the back of the truck but inside, not underneath.

Benny slammed his fist against the steel partition behind them. "Shut the fuck up."

He twisted around to look through the small rectangle of glass that separated the cab from the back. "Can't see a damned thing."

The noise grew louder, sending vibrations under the seat. It felt to Del as though a baseball bat were being swung against the truck's metal sides. Ridiculous, really. No chance the prisoner would have anything remotely like a baseball bat. Each blast sent Benny reeling, grabbing at his temples. Del glanced over and saw the Polynesian dancer swinging her hips with each slam of Benny's fist against the partition.

"Hey, cut it out," Del yelled, adding his voice to the noisy din that was beginning to make his head pound.

Obviously, the prisoner had not been completely restrained and was ramming himself against the walls of the truck. Even if it didn't drive them crazy during the rest of the trip, it could cause some serious damage to the prisoner. He certainly didn't want to be responsible for delivering a battered prisoner. He slowed down, pulled the truck to the side of the two-lane highway and stopped.

"What the hell you doing?" Benny demanded.

"We can't have this going on for the rest of the trip. The guys obviously didn't completely restrain him."

"Why would they? He's found Jesus Christ."

Del only shook his head. As he climbed out of the truck it occurred to him that he had no idea what to do with a prisoner who had gotten an arm or leg loose from one of the leather restraints.

"Now hold on, kid," Benny yelled after him, scrambling out from the passenger side. "I'll take care of this bastard."

It took Benny too long to come around the truck. When he did, Del noticed a stagger in his walk.

"You're still drunk!"

"The hell I am."

Del reached into the cab and pulled out the thermos, jerking it away when Benny grabbed for it. He twisted off the top and in one whiff could smell the alcohol-laced coffee.

"You son of a bitch." Del's words surprised him as much as they did Benny. Instead of apologizing, he threw the thermos and watched it explode against a nearby fence post.

"Shit! That was my only thermos, kid." Benny looked as though he might head into the overgrown ditch to retrieve the pieces. But he turned and stomped toward the back of the truck. "Let's make this fucker shut up."

The banging continued, louder, now rocking the truck.

"You think you're up for this?" Del asked, feeling angry and betrayed enough to allow the sarcasm.

"Hell, yes. I was shutting up assholes like this when you were still suckin' at your momma's tit." Benny grabbed at his service revolver, fumbling with the holster's snap before pulling the gun free.

Del wondered how much alcohol Benny Zeeks had in his system. Could he still aim his gun? Was the gun even loaded? Up until today, Brice and Webber transported the hard-core criminals, making the trips up to Glade and Charlotte, while he and Benny were assigned petty thieves and white-collar criminals, escorting them in the other direction to the county courthouse in Miami. Del unbuckled the strap on his holster, his hand shaking, the butt of his gun feeling awkward and unfamiliar.

The noise stopped as soon as Del started sliding the locks open on the heavy rear door. He looked to Benny who stood beside him with his revolver drawn. Immediately, Del noticed the slight tremor in Benny's hand. It sent a wave of nausea loose in Del's stomach. His back was soaked, his forehead dripping. Wet pools under his armpits soiled his once-crisp uniform. His heart pounded against his rib cage, and now in the silence, he wondered if Benny could hear it.

He took a deep breath and tightened his hold on the handle. Then he flung the door open, jumping aside and letting Benny have a full view of the dark inside. Benny stood, legs apart, arms extended in front of him, both hands gripping the gun as he tilted his head, ready to take aim.

Nothing happened. The door slammed back and forth, hitting against the side of the truck. The sound of metal clanking against metal was amplified by the peaceful surroundings and the deserted highway. Del and Benny stared into the darkness, squinting to see the corner bench where the prisoner usually sat, restrained by thick straps that snaked out of the wall and floor.

"What on earth?" Del could see the leather straps, cut and hanging from the wall of the truck.

"What the fuck?" Benny mumbled as he slowly approached the open truck.

Without warning, a tall, dark figure flew out at Benny, knocking him and the gun to the ground. Albert Stucky clamped his teeth onto Benny's ear like a rabid dog. Benny's scream dismantled Del. He stood paralyzed. His limbs refused to react. His heart knocked against his chest. He couldn't breathe. He couldn't think. By the time he pulled out his service revolver, the prisoner was on his feet. He ran straight at Del, colliding with him and shoving something sharp and smooth and hard into Del's stomach.

Pain exploded throughout his body. His hands were useless, and the gun slid from his fingers like water. He forced himself to look into Albert Stucky's eyes, and instantly he saw the evil staring back at him, cold and black, an entity of its own. Del felt the demon's hot breath on his face. When he glanced down, he saw the large hand still gripping the dagger. He looked up just in time to see Stucky's smile as he shoved the dagger deeper.

Del slipped to his knees. His eyes blurred as he watched the tall stranger split into several images. He could see the truck and a sprawling Benny. Everything began to spin and blur. Then he slammed hard against the pavement. The steaming concrete sizzled up through his wet back, but it wasn't as hot as his insides. A wildfire spread through his stomach, catching each of his organs on fire. Now, on his back, he saw nothing but the clouds swirling above him, brilliant white against solid blue. The morning sun blinded him. Yet, it was all so beautiful. Why hadn't he noticed before how beautiful the sky was?

Behind him a single gun shot blasted the silence. Del managed a weak smile. Finally. He couldn't see him but good ole' Benny, the legend, had come through, after all. The alcohol had just slowed him down a bit.

Del pulled himself up, just enough to look at the damage to his stomach. He was startled to find himself staring down at the bloody carved image of Jesus. The dagger causing his insides to spill onto the deserted highway was actually a mahogany crucifix. Suddenly, he couldn't feel the pain anymore. That had to be a good sign, didn't it? Maybe he'd be okay.

"Hey, Benny," he called out, laying his head on the pavement. He still wasn't able to see his partner behind him. "My daddy's gonna make a sermon out of this when I tell him I was stabbed with a crucifix."

A long, black shadow blocked the sky.

Once again Del found himself looking into those empty, dark eyes. Albert Stucky loomed above him, tall and straight, a lean, muscular man with sharp features. He reminded Del of a vulture, perched with black wings pressed patiently against its sides, cocking its head, staring, waiting for its prey to stop struggling, to give in to the inevitable. Then, Stucky smiled as though pleased with what he saw. He raised and pointed Benny's service revolver at Del's head.

"You won't be telling your daddy anything," Albert Stucky promised in a deep, calm voice. "Tell it to Saint Peter, instead."

The metal slammed into Del's skull. A blast of brilliant light swirled together with oceans of blue and yellow and white and then finally...black.

CHAPTER 1

Northeast Virginia
(just outside Washington, D.C.)
Five months later—Friday, March 27

Maggie O'Dell jerked and twisted, trying to make herself more comfortable, only now realizing she had fallen asleep in the recliner again. Her skin felt damp with perspiration and her ribs ached. The air in the room was stale and warm, making it difficult to breathe. She fumbled in the dark, reaching for the brass floor lamp, clicking the switch but getting no light. Damn! She hated waking to complete darkness. Usually she took precautions to prevent it.

Her eyes adjusted slowly, squinting and searching behind and around the stacks of boxes she had spent the day packing. Evidently Greg had not bothered to come home. She couldn't have slept through one of his noisy entrances. It was just as well he didn't come home. His temper tantrums would only annoy the movers.

She tried to get out of the recliner but stopped when a sharp pain raced along her abdomen. She grabbed at it, as if she could catch the pain and keep it from spreading. Her fingers felt something warm and sticky soaking through her T-shirt. Jesus! What the hell was going on? Carefully, she pulled up the hem and even in the dark she could see it. A chill slipped down her back and the nausea washed over her. A slit in her skin ran from below her left breast across her abdomen. It was bleeding, soaking into her T-shirt and dripping down into the fabric of the recliner.

Maggie bolted from the chair. She covered the wound and pressed her shirt against it, hoping to stop the bleeding. She needed to call 911. Where the hell was the phone? How could this have happened? The scar was over eight months old, and yet it was bleeding as profusely as the day Albert Stucky had cut her.

She knocked over boxes, searching. Lids popped open as cartons fell, scattering crime scene photos, toiletries, newspaper clippings, underwear and socks and sending pieces of her life bouncing off the floor and walls. Everything she had taken such care to pack suddenly flew, rolled, skidded and crashed around her.

Then, she heard a whimpering sound.

She stopped and listened, trying to hold her breath. Already her pulse beat too rapidly. Steady. She needed to stay calm. She turned slowly, cocking her head and straining to hear. She checked the desktop, the surface of the coffee table, the bookshelf. Oh dear God! Where the hell had she left her gun?

Finally, she saw the holster lying at the foot of the recliner. Of course, she would have kept it close by as she slept.

The whimpering grew louder, a high-pitched whine like a wounded animal's. Or was it a trick?

Maggie edged her way back to the recliner, eyes darting, watching all around her. The sound came from the kitchen. And now she could smell a foul odor seeping in from that direction, too. She picked up the holster and tiptoed toward the kitchen. The closer she got, the easier it was to recognize the smell. It was blood. The acrid scent stung her nostrils and burned her lungs. It was the kind of stench that came only from massive amounts of blood.

She crouched low and eased through the doorway. Despite the warning smell, Maggie gasped at the sight of it. In the moonlit kitchen, blood had sprayed the white walls and pooled on the ceramic tile. It was everywhere, splattered across the countertops and dripping down the appliances. In the far corner of the room stood Albert Stucky. His tall, sleek shadow hovered over a whimpering woman who was down on her knees.

Maggie felt the prickling start at the back of her neck. Dear God, how had he been able to get inside her house? And yet, she wasn't surprised to see him. Hadn't she expected him to come? Hadn't she been waiting for this?

Stucky yanked the woman's hair in one hand and in the other he held a butcher knife to the woman's throat. Maggie prevented another gasp. He hadn't seen her yet, and she pressed herself against the wall, into the shadows.

Steady. Calm. She repeated the mantra in her head. She had prepared herself for this very moment. Had dreaded and dreamed and anticipated it for months. Now was not a time to let fear and panic unravel her nerve. She leaned against the wall, strengthening her position, though her back ached and her squatting knees trembled. From this angle, she could get a clean shot. But she knew she'd be allowed only one. One was all she needed.

Maggie gripped the holster, reaching for her gun. The holster was empty. How could it be empty? She spun around, searching the floor. Had the gun dropped out? Why hadn't she noticed?

Then suddenly, she realized her startled reaction had just blown her cover. When she looked up, the woman was reaching out to her, pleading with her. But Maggie looked past the woman, her eyes meeting Albert Stucky's. He smiled. Then, in one swift motion, he slit the woman's throat.

"No!"

Maggie woke up with a violent jolt, nearly falling out of the recliner. Her fingers groped along the floor. Her heart pounded. She was drenched in sweat. She found her holster and this time ripped the gun out, jumping to her feet and swinging her outstretched arms back and forth, ready to spray the stacked cartons with bullets. Sunlight had only begun to seep into the room, but it was enough to show that she was alone.

She slumped down into the chair. The gun still clenched in her hand, she wiped the perspiration from her forehead and dug the sleep from her eyes with trembling fingers. Still not convinced it was a dream, she clawed at the hem of her T-shirt, pulling it up and twisting to see the bloody cut across her abdomen. Yes, the scar was there, a slight pucker of skin. But no, it was not bleeding.

She leaned back in the chair and raked her fingers through her tangled, short hair. Dear God! How much longer could she put up with the nightmares? It had been over eight months since Albert Stucky had trapped her in an abandoned Miami warehouse. She had chased him for almost two years, learning his patterns, studying his depraved habits, performing autopsies on the corpses he left behind and deciphering the bizarre messages for the game he, alone, had decided the two of them would play. But that hot, August evening, he had won, trapping her and making her watch. He had no intention of killing her. He simply wanted her to watch.

Maggie shook her head, willing the images to stay away. She knew she'd be successful as long as she remained awake. They had captured Albert Stucky that bloody night in August, only to have him escape from prison on Halloween. Her boss, FBI Assistant Director Kyle Cunningham, had immediately taken her out of the field. She was one of the Bureau's top criminal profilers, and yet Cunningham had stuck her behind a desk. He had exiled her to teaching at law enforcement conferences, as if complete boredom would be some sort of protection from the madman. Instead it felt like punishment. And she didn't deserve to be punished.

Maggie stood, immediately annoyed at her wobbly knees. She weaved through the maze of cartons to the cabinet in the corner. She checked the clock on the desktop and saw that she had almost two hours before the movers arrived. She laid her gun close by, sorted through the cabinet and brought out a bottle of Scotch. She poured herself a glass, noticing that already her hands were more steady, her heartbeat almost back to normal.

Just then she heard a high-pitched whine coming from the kitchen. Jesus! She dug her fingernails into her arm, feeling the sting and finding no comfort in the fact that she was, indeed, awake this time. She grabbed for her gun and tried to steady her pulse, already racing out of control. She slid against the wall, making her way to the kitchen, trying to listen and sniffing the air. The whining stopped as she got to the doorway.

She prepared herself, arms secure and close to her chest. Her finger pressed against the trigger. This time she was ready. She took a deep breath and swung into the kitchen, her gun pointed directly at Greg's back. He spun around, dropping the freshly opened can of coffee, jumping backward as it crashed to the floor.

"Damn it, Maggie!" He wore only silk boxers. His normally styled blond hair stuck up, and he looked as if he had just gotten out of bed.

"Sorry," Maggie said, desperately trying to keep the panic from her voice. "I didn't hear you come in last night." She tucked the Smith & Wesson .38 into the back waistband of her jeans in an easy, casual motion, as if this was a part of her regular morning routine.

"I didn't want to wake you," he snapped through gritted teeth. Already he had a broom and dustpan and was sweeping up the mess. Gently, he lifted the tipped can, rescuing as much of his precious gourmet coffee as possible. "One of these days, Maggie, you're gonna shoot me by mistake." Then he stopped and looked up at her. "Or maybe it wouldn't be a mistake."

She ignored his sarcasm and walked past him. At the sink, she splashed cold water on her face and the back of her neck, hoping he didn't notice that her hands were still shaking. Though she needn't worry. Greg saw only what he wanted to see.

"I'm sorry," she said again, keeping her back to him. "This would never happen if we had gotten a security system."

"And we would never need a security system if you'd quit your job."

She was so tired of this old argument. She found a dishcloth and wiped the coffee grounds from the counter. "I'd never ask you to quit being a lawyer, Greg."

"It's not the same thing."

"Being a lawyer means just as much to you as being an FBI agent means to me."

"But being a lawyer doesn't get me cut up and almost killed. It doesn't have me stalking around my own house with a loaded gun and almost shooting my spouse." He returned the broom, slamming it into the utility closet.

"Well, after today I guess it won't be an issue," she said quietly.

He stopped. His gray eyes met hers and for a brief moment he looked sad, almost apologetic. Then he looked away, snatching the dishcloth Maggie had set aside. He wiped the counter again in careful, deliberate swipes as though she had disappointed him even in this small task.

"So when are the guys from United getting here?" he wanted to know, as if it were a move they had planned together.

She glanced at the wall clock. "They'll be here at eight. But I didn't hire United."

"Maggie, you have to be careful about movers. They'll rip you off. You should know..." He stopped, as if reminding himself it was no longer any of his business. "Suit yourself." He started filling the coffeemaker with level, precise scoops, pursing his lips to confine the scolding he normally would have unleashed on her.

Maggie watched him, predicting his movements, knowing he'd fill the pot to the three-cup line and that he'd squat to eye level to make certain it was exact. She recognized the familiar routine and wondered when they had become strangers. After almost ten years of marriage, they couldn't even afford each other the courtesies of friendship. Instead, every conversation seemed to be through clenched teeth.

Maggie turned and went back to the spare room, waiting, but hoping he wouldn't follow her. Not this time. She wouldn't get through this day if he continued to scold and pout or worse, if he resorted to telling her he still loved her. Those words should have been a comfort; instead, they had come to feel like a sharp knife, especially when he followed them with, "And if you loved me you would quit your job."

She returned to the liquor cabinet where she had left the glass of Scotch. The sun had barely risen and already she needed her daily dose of liquid bravery to get her through the day. Her mother would be proud. The two of them finally had something in common.

She glanced around the room while she sipped. How could this stack of cartons be the sum of her life? She rubbed a hand over her face, feeling the exhaustion as though it had taken up permanent residence in her bones. How long had it been since she had slept through an entire night? When was the last time she had felt safe? She was so tired of feeling as though she was trapped on a ledge, coming closer and closer to falling.

Assistant Director Cunningham was fooling himself if he believed he could protect her. There was nothing he could do to stop her nightmares, and there was no place he could send her that would be out of Albert Stucky's reach. Eventually, she knew Stucky would come for her. Although it had been five months since Stucky's escape, she knew it with certainty. It could be another month or it could be another five months. It didn't matter how long it took. He would come.

CHAPTER 2

Tess McGowan wished she had worn different shoes. These pinched and the heels were too tall. Every nerve ending in her body concentrated on not tripping as she walked up the winding sidewalk, all the while pretending not to notice the eyes that followed her. The movers had stopped unloading the truck as soon as her black Miata pulled into the drive. Sofa ends stayed in midair. Handtrucks remained tipped. Boxes were ignored while the men in sweaty, blue uniforms stopped to watch her.

She hated the attention and cringed at the possibility of a wolf whistle. Especially in this well-manicured neighborhood where the sanctuary-like silence would make the whistles even more obscene.

This was ridiculous; her silk blouse stuck to her, and her skin crawled. She wasn't close to being stunning or beautiful. At best, she had a decent figure, one for which she sweated hours at the gym, and she still needed to monitor her cravings for cheeseburgers. She was far from being *Playboy*-centerfold material, so why did she suddenly feel naked though dressed in a conservative suit?

It wasn't the men's fault. It wasn't even their primal instinct to watch that bothered her as much as what seemed to be her involuntary reflex to put on a show for them. The annoying habit clung to her from her past, like the scent of cigarette smoke and whiskey. Too easily she found herself reminded of Elvis tunes coming from a corner jukebox, always followed by cheap hotel rooms.

But that had been a lifetime ago, certainly too many years ago to trip her up now. After all, she was on her way to becoming a successful businesswoman. So why the hell did the past have such a hold on her? And how could something as harmless as a few indiscreet stares, from men she didn't know, dismantle her poise and make her question her hard-earned respectability? They made her feel like a fraud. As if, once again, she was masquerading as something she was not. By the time she reached the front entrance, she wanted to turn and run. Instead, she took a deep breath and knocked on the heavy oak door that had been left half-open.

"Come on in," a woman's voice called from behind the door.

Tess found Maggie O'Dell at the panel of buttons and blinking lights that made up the house's newly installed security system.

"Oh, hi, Ms. McGowan. Did we forget to sign some papers?" Maggie only glanced at Tess while she punched the small keyboard and continued to program the device.

"Please, you really must call me Tess." She hesitated in case Maggie wanted to say the same, but wasn't surprised when there was no such invitation. Tess knew it wasn't that Maggie was rude, just that she liked to keep her distance. It was something Tess could relate to, something she understood and respected. "No, there aren't any more papers. I promise. I knew today was the big move. Just wanted to see how things were going.

"Take a look around, I'm almost finished with this."

Tess walked from the foyer into the living room. The afternoon sunlight filled the room, but thankfully all the windows were open, a cool south breeze replacing the stale warm air. Tess wiped at her forehead, disappointed to find it damp. She examined her client out of the corner of her eyes.

Now, this was a woman who deserved to be ogled by men. Tess

knew Maggie was close to her own age, somewhere in her early thirties. But without the usual power suit, Maggie could easily pass for a college student. Dressed in a ratty University of Virginia T-shirt and threadbare jeans, she failed to hide her shapely athletic figure. She had a natural beauty no one could manufacture. Her skin was smooth and creamy. Her short dark hair shone even though it was mussed and tangled. She possessed rich brown eyes and high cheekbones that Tess would kill for. Yet, Tess knew that the men who had stopped in their tracks just moments before to stare at her would not dare do the same to Maggie O'Dell, though they would definitely want to and it would take tremendous effort not to.

Yes, there was something about this woman. Something Tess had noticed the very first day they had met. She couldn't quite describe it. It was the way Maggie carried herself, the way she appeared, at times, to be oblivious to the outside world. The way she seemed totally unaware of her effect on people. It was something that invoked—no, demanded, respect. Despite her designer suits and expensive car, Tess would never capture that ability, that power. Yet for all their differences, Tess had felt an immediate kinship with Maggie O'Dell. They both seemed so alone.

"Sorry," Maggie said, finally joining Tess who had moved to the windows overlooking the backyard. "I'm staying here tonight," she explained, "and I want to make certain the alarm system is up and running."

"Of course," Tess nodded and smiled.

Maggie had been more concerned about the security system than the square footage or the seller's price of any of the houses Tess had shown her. In the beginning, Tess chalked it up to the nature of her client's profession. Of course FBI agents would be more sensitive to security matters than the average home buyer. But Tess had witnessed a look in Maggie's eyes, a glimpse of something that Tess recognized as vulnerability. She couldn't help wondering what the confident, independent agent hoped to lock herself away from. Even as they stood side by side, Maggie O'Dell seemed far away, her eyes examining her new backyard like a woman looking for and expecting an intruder, rather than a new home owner admiring the foliage.

Tess glanced around the room. There were plenty of stacked boxes, but very little furniture. Perhaps the movers had only begun to bring in the heavy stuff. She wondered how much Maggie was able to take from the condo she and her husband owned. Tess knew the divorce proceedings were growing messy. Not that her client had shared any of this with her.

Everything Tess knew of Maggie O'Dell, she had learned from a mutual friend, Maggie's attorney, who had recommended Tess. It was this mutual friend, Teresa Ramairez, who had told Tess about Maggie O'Dell's bitter lawyer husband, and how Maggie needed to invest in a substantial piece of real estate or risk sharing—maybe even losing—a large trust left in her name. In fact, Maggie O'Dell had confided nothing in Tess, other than those necessities required for the business transaction. She wondered if Maggie's secrecy and her aloof manner were an occupational hazard that carried over into her personal life.

It didn't matter—Tess was used to just the opposite. Usually clients confided in her as if she was Dear Abby. Being a real estate agent had proven to be a little like being a bartender. Perhaps part of her colorful past had been good preparation, after all. That Maggie O'Dell didn't wish to bare her soul was perfectly fine with Tess. She certainly didn't take it personally. Instead, she could relate. It was exactly the way she handled her own life, her own secrets. Yes, the less people knew, the better.

"So, have you met any of your new neighbors?"

"Not yet." Maggie answered while she stared out at the huge pine trees lining her property like a fortress. "Only the one you and I met last week."

"Oh sure, Rachel...um...I can't remember her last name. I'm usually very good with names."

"Endicott," Maggie supplied without effort.

"She seemed very nice," Tess added, though what little she had gleaned from the brief introduction made her wonder how Special Agent O'Dell would fit into this neighborhood of doctors, congressmen, Ph.D.'s and their stay-at-home society-conscious wives. She remembered seeing Rachel Endicott out for a jog with her pure white Labrador, while dressed in a designer jogging suit, expensive running shoes and not a blond hair out of place nor a single bead of sweat on her brow. And in contrast, here was Agent O'Dell in a stretched-out T-shirt, worn jeans and a pair of gray Nikes that should have been thrown out ages ago.

Two men grunted their way through the front entrance with a huge rolltop desk. Immediately, Maggie's attention transferred to the desk, which looked incredibly heavy and was quite possibly an antique.

"Where ya want this, ma'am?"

"Over against that wall."

"Sorta centered?"

"Yes, please."

Maggie O'Dell's eyes never left them until the piece was carefully set down.

"Dat good?"

"Perfect."

Both men seemed pleased. The older one smiled. The tall, thin one avoided looking at the women, slouching not from pain but as though he wasn't comfortable being tall. They unwrapped the tape and unlatched the plastic fasteners from the desk's many nooks. The tall man tested the drawers, then stopped suddenly, snapping his hand back as though he had been stung.

"Um...ma'am. Did you know you had this in here?"

Maggie crossed the room to look inside the drawer. She reached in and pulled out a black pistol encased in some kind of holster.

"Sorry. I forgot about this one."

This one? Tess wondered how many the agent had stashed. Maybe the obsession with security was a bit over the top, even for an FBI agent.

"We should be done in a bit," the older man told her, and he followed his partner out as though there was nothing unusual about hauling loaded guns.

"Do you have anyone coming to help you unpack?" Tess tried to disguise her mistrust, her distaste for guns. No, why kid herself? It was more than a simple distaste, it was a genuine fear.

"I really don't have much."

Tess glanced around the room, and when she looked back, Maggie was watching her. Tess's cheeks grew hot. She felt as though she had been caught, because that was exactly what she had been thinking—that Maggie O'Dell really didn't have much. How could she possibly fill the huge rooms that made up this two-story Tudor?

"It's just that...well, I remember you mentioning that your mother lives in Richmond," Tess tried to explain.

"Yes, she does," she said in a way that told Tess there would be no further conversation on the topic.

"Well, I'll let you get back to work." Tess suddenly felt awkward and anxious to leave. "I need to finish up the paperwork."

She extended her hand, and Maggie politely shook it with a strong, firm grip that again took Tess off guard. The woman exuded strength and confidence, but unless Tess was imagining things, Maggie's obsession with security sprung from some vulnerability, some deep-seated fear. Having dealt with her own vulnerabilities and fears for so many years, Tess could sense them in others.

"If you need anything, anything at all, please don't hesitate to call me, okay?"

"Thanks, Tess, I will."

But Tess knew she would not.

As Tess backed her car down the driveway, she wondered whether Special Agent Maggie O'Dell was simply cautious or paranoid, careful or obsessive. At the corner of the intersection, she noticed a van parked along the curb, an oddity in this neighborhood where the houses were set far back from the street and the long driveways afforded plenty of parking space for several cars or utility vehicles.

The man in dark glasses and a uniform sat behind the wheel, absorbed in a newspaper. Tess's first thought was how odd to be reading a newspaper with sunglasses on, especially with the sun setting behind him. As she drove by, she recognized the logo on the side of the van: Northeastern Bell Telephone. Immediately, she found herself suspicious. Why was the guy so far out of his territory? Then suddenly, she shrugged and laughed out loud. Perhaps her client's paranoia was contagious.

She shook her head, pulled out onto the highway and left the secluded neighborhood to return to her office. As she glanced back at the stately houses tucked away between huge oaks, dogwoods and armies of pine trees, Tess hoped Maggie O'Dell would finally feel safe.

CHAPTER 3

Maggie juggled the boxes that filled her arms. As usual she had taken on more than she should have. Her fingers searched the door, grasping for a knob she couldn't see, yet she refused to put anything down. Why in the world did she own so many CDs and books when she had no time to listen to music or read?

The movers had finally left, after a thorough search for one lost carton, or as they insisted—one misplaced carton. She hated to think of it still at the condo, and hated even more the thought of asking Greg to check. He would remind her that she should have listened to him and hired United Movers. And knowing Greg, if the carton was still at the condo, his anger and curiosity would not leave it alone. She imagined him ripping off the packing tape as though he had discovered some hidden treasure, which to him it would be. Because, of course, it would be the one container with items she'd rather have no one thumb through, items like her personal journal, appointment calendar and memorabilia from her childhood.

She had torn her car's trunk apart, looking through the few boxes she had loaded on her own. But these were the last. Perhaps the movers had honestly misplaced the carton. She hoped that was the case. She tried not to worry about it, tried not to think how exhausting it was to be on alert twenty-four hours a day, to be constantly looking over her shoulder.

She set the boxes on the handrail, balancing one with her hip, while she freed a hand to grab at the tightening knot in the back of her neck. At the same time, her eyes darted around her. Dear God, why couldn't she just relax and enjoy her first night in her new home? Why couldn't she concentrate on simple things, stupid everyday things, like her sudden and unfamiliar hunger?

As if on cue, her mouth began to water for pizza, and immediately she promised herself one as a reward. Her appetite had long been gone, making this craving a novelty, one she needed to relish. Yes, she would stuff herself with pizza garnished with spicy Italian sausage, green peppers and extra Romano cheese. That is, after she drank several gallons of water.

Maggie's T-shirt stuck to her skin. Before she ordered the pizza, she'd take a quick, cool shower. Ms. McGowan—Tess—had promised to call all the utility companies. Now Maggie wished she had double-checked with her to make certain she had done so. She hated depending on other people, having recently found herself with a full cast of them in her life, from movers and real estate agents, to lawyers and bankers. Hopefully the water would, indeed, be on. Tess's word had been good so far. In all fairness, there was no need to question it now. The woman had gone out of her way to make this accelerated sale go as smoothly as possible.

Maggie repositioned the boxes to her other hip. Her fingers found the knob. She pushed the door open, carefully maneuvering her way in, but still sending several loose CDs and books crashing onto the doorstep. She bent just enough to look down at Frank Sinatra smiling up at her through his cracked plastic window. Greg had given her the CD several birthdays ago, although he knew she hated Sinatra. Why did that gift suddenly feel like some prophetic microcosm of their entire marriage?

She shook her head and the thought out of her mind. The memory of their brief morning exchange stayed annoyingly fresh in her mind. Thankfully, he had left for work early, mumbling about all the construction on the interstate. But tonight he would be having his last laugh, sifting through her personal things. He would see it as his right. Legally she was still his wife, and she had given up long ago arguing with him when he shifted into lawyer mode.

Inside her new home, the wood floors' recent varnish glowed in the late-afternoon sunshine. Maggie had made certain there wasn't a stitch of carpet in the entire house. Footsteps were too easily muffled by floor coverings. Yet, the wall of windows had cinched the deal for Maggie, despite them being a security nightmare. Okay, so even FBI agents weren't always practical. But each individual window was set in a narrow frame that not even Houdini could squeeze through. The bedroom windows were another story, but reaching the second floor from outside would require a tall ladder. Besides, she had made certain that both security systems, inside and outside, rivaled those at Fort Knox.

The living room opened into a sunroom with more windows. These stretched from the ceiling almost to the floor, and though they were also thin and narrow, they made up three walls in the room. The sunroom extended into and looked out over the lush green backyard. It was a colorful, wooded fairyland with cherry and apple blossoms, sturdy dogwoods, a blanket of tulips, daffodils and crocus. It was a backyard she had fantasized about since she was twelve.

Back then, when she and her mother had moved to Richmond, they could afford only a tiny, suffocating third-floor apartment that reeked of stale air, cigarette smoke and the body odor of the strange men her mother invited overnight. This house was more like the one Maggie remembered of her real childhood, their house in Wisconsin, where they had lived before her father was killed, before Maggie was forced to grow up quickly and become her mother's caretaker. For years, she had longed for someplace like this with lots of fresh air and open spaces, but most importantly—plenty of seclusion.

The backyard sloped down only to be met by a dense wooded area that lined a steep ridge. Below, a shallow stream trickled over rocks. Though she couldn't see the stream from the house, Maggie had checked it out at great length. It made her feel safe, as if it were her own personal moat. It provided a natural boundary, a perfect barrier that was reinforced by a line of huge pine trees standing guard like sentries, tall and straight, shoulder to shoulder.

That same stream had been a nightmare for the previous owners who had two small children. Fences of any kind were against the development's covenant. Tess McGowan had told Maggie that the owners simply realized they couldn't keep two curious kids from being enticed or lured by such a dangerous adventure. Their problem became Maggie's safeguard, her potential trap. And their impulsive purchase became Maggie's bargain. Otherwise, she would never have been able to afford this neighborhood where her little red Toyota Corolla looked out of place next to BMWs and Mercedeses.

Of course, she still would never have been able to afford the house had she not used the money from her father's trust. Having received scholarships, grants, fellowships and then working her way through college and graduate school, Maggie had been able to leave most of the trust alone. When she and Greg got married, he was adamant about not touching the money. In the beginning, she had wanted to use it to buy them a modest home. But Greg insisted he would never touch what he called her father's blood money.

The trust had been set up by fellow firefighters and the city of Green Bay to show appreciation for her father's heroism, and probably to assuage their guilt as well. Maybe that was part of the reason she had never been able to bring herself to use the money. In fact, she had almost forgotten about the trust until the divorce proceedings began and until her lawyer highly recommended she invest the money in something not so easily divided.

Maggie remembered laughing at Teresa Ramairez's suggestion. It was ridiculous, after all, knowing the way Greg had always felt about the money. Only it wasn't ridiculous when the trust showed up on an assets sheet, which Greg had shoved at her several weeks ago. What for years Greg had called "her father's blood money," he was now calling community property. The following day she asked Teresa Ramairez to recommend a real estate agent.

Maggie added the boxes to those already arranged and stacked in the corner. She glanced over the labels one last time, hoping the missing one would miraculously show itself. Then, with hands on her hips, she turned slowly around, admiring the spacious rooms decorated for the time being in Early American corrugated brown. She had brought very few pieces of furniture with her, but more than she had expected to extract from Greg's lawyerly clutches. She wondered if it was financial suicide for anyone to ask for a divorce from a lawyer spouse. Greg had handled all of their joint financial and legal affairs for almost ten years. When Teresa Ramairez had started showing Maggie documents and spreadsheets, Maggie hadn't even recognized some of the accounts.

She and Greg had married as college seniors. Every appliance, every piece of linen, everything they owned had been a joint purchase. When they moved from their small Richmond apartment to the expensive condominium in the Crest Ridge area, they had bought new furniture, and all of it went together. It seemed wrong to split up sets. Maggie smiled at that and wondered why she couldn't bring herself to split up furniture but could do so with their ten-year marriage?

She did manage to take with her the pieces of furniture which mattered most. Her father's antique rolltop desk had made the trip without a scratch. She patted the back of her comfortable La-Z-Boy recliner. It and the brass reading lamp had been exiled long ago to the condo's den, because Greg said it didn't match the leather sofa and chairs in the living room. Maggie couldn't recall much living having ever occurred on them.

She remembered when they had first bought the set. She had tried to break it in with some passionate memories. Instead of letting his body respond to her flirtatious suggestions, Greg had been horrified and angered by the idea.

"Do you know how easily leather stains?" He had scolded her as though she was a child spilling Kool-Aid instead of a grown woman initiating sex with her husband.

No, it was easy to leave those pieces behind. As long as the memory of their crumbling marriage stayed with them. She pulled out a small duffel bag from the pile in the corner and set it on the desk next to her laptop. Earlier she had opened all the windows to remove the stale, warm air. As the sun set behind the line of trees, a moist but cool breeze swirled into the room.

She unzipped the duffel bag and carefully removed her holstered Smith & Wesson .38 revolver. She liked the way the pistol fit in her hands. There was a familiarity and ease, like the touch of an old friend. While other agents had upgraded to more powerful and automatic weapons, Maggie drew comfort from the gun she knew best. The same gun with which she had learned.

She had depended on it numerous times, and though it had only six rounds compared to an automatic's sixteen, she knew she could count on all six without any jamming. As a newbie—as FBI recruits were called—she had watched an agent go down, helpless with a Sig-Sauer 9 mm and a magazine half-full, but jammed and useless.

She pulled out of the bag her FBI badge in its leather holder. She laid both it and the Smith & Wesson on the desk, almost reverently, alongside the Glock 40 caliber found earlier in the desk drawer. Also in the duffel bag was her forensic kit, a small black pouch that included an odd assortment of things she had learned over the years never to be without.

She left the forensic kit safely tucked in place, zipped the duffel bag and slid it under the desk. For some reason, having these things close by—her guns and badge—made her feel secure, complete. They had become symbols of who she was. They made this feel more like home than any of the possessions she and Greg had spent their adult lives collecting. Ironically, these things that meant so much to her were also the reasons she could no longer be married to her husband. Greg had made it quite clear that Maggie needed to choose either him or the FBI. How could he not realize that what he was asking her to do was like asking her to cut off her right arm?

She traced a finger over the leather case of her badge, waiting for some sign of regret. But when none came, it didn't necessarily make her feel any better. The impending divorce brought sadness, but no regret. She and Greg had become strangers. Why hadn't she seen that a year ago when she lost her wedding ring and hadn't felt compelled to replace it?

Maggie swiped at strands of hair that stuck to her forehead and the back of her neck. Its dampness reminded her that she needed a shower. The front of her T-shirt was dirty and stained. Her arms were marred with black and purple scuffs. She rubbed at one to discover a bruise instead of dirt. Just as she began to search for her newly installed phone, she noticed a police cruiser whiz by.

She found the phone under a stack of papers. She dialed from memory and waited patiently, knowing it would take more than five or six rings.

"Dr. Patterson."

"Gwen, it's Maggie."

"Hey, how the hell are you? Did you get moved in?"

"Let's just say my stuff is moved." She noticed the Stafford County Coroner's van drive past. She went to the window and watched the van curve to the left until it was out of sight. The street had no outlet. "I know you're swamped, Gwen, but I was wondering if you had a chance to check on what we talked about last week?"

"Maggie, I really wish you'd leave the Stucky case alone."

"Look, Gwen, if you don't have time, all you need to say is that you don't have time," she snapped, and immediately wished she could take her words back. But she was tired of everyone trying to protect her.

"You know that's not what I meant, Maggie. Why do you always make it so goddamn hard for people to care about you?"

She let the silence hang between them. She knew her friend was right. Suddenly in the distance, Maggie heard a fire engine's siren, and her stomach turned to knots. What was happening just around the corner? Her knees threatened to buckle at the thought of a possible fire. She sniffed the breeze coming in through the window. She couldn't smell or see smoke. Thank God. If it was a fire, she would be incredibly useless. The thought alone scared the hell out of her, reviving memories of her father's death.

"How about I stop over tonight?"

Gwen's voice startled Maggie. She had forgotten she was still on the phone.

"The place is a mess. I haven't even started to unpack."

"It doesn't bother me if it doesn't bother you. Why don't I pick up a pizza and some beer? We can picnic on the floor. Come on, it'll be fun. Sort of a housewarming party. A prelude to your new independence."

The fire engine's siren began to grow distant, and Maggie realized it was not on its way to her neighborhood. Her shoulders relaxed, and she sighed in relief.

"You can pick up some beer, but don't worry about the pizza. I'll have it delivered."

"Just remember, no Italian sausage on my side. Some of us need to watch our weight. I'll see you around seven."

"Fine. Sure. That'll work." But Maggie was already distracted as another police cruiser sped by. Without a second thought, she put down the phone and grabbed her badge. She quickly reset the security system. Then she tucked her revolver in her back waistband and headed out the front door. So much for seclusion.

CHAPTER 4

Maggie hurried past three of her new neighbors who politely stayed in the street, a safe distance from the house flanked with police cruisers. The coroner's van sat in the driveway, already empty. She ignored a police officer on his hands and knees who had gotten a roll of crime scene tape tangled in a rosebush. Instead of tearing it and starting over, he took on the thorns and kept snapping his hand back with each prick.

"Hey," he finally yelled when he realized Maggie was headed for the door. "You can't go in there."

When his voice didn't slow her down, he scrambled to his feet, dropping the roll of tape and sending it unraveling down the slope of the lawn. For a minute he looked as though he'd go for the tape instead of Maggie. She almost laughed, but kept her face serious as she held up her badge.

"I'm with the FBI."

"Yeah, right. And this is what the FBI is wearing these days." He snatched the leather case from her, but his eyes took their time making their way down her body.

Instinctively, Maggie stood up straight and crossed her arms over her sweat-drenched chest. Ordinarily, she paid close attention to her presentation and attire. She had always been self-conscious and aware that her hundred-and-fifteen-pounds, five-foot-five stature did not live up to the FBI's authoritarian image. In a navy blazer and trousers, her aloof, cold attitude could pull it off. In a T-shirt and faded jeans, she realized she might not be able to.

Finally, the officer took a closer look at her credentials. The smirk slid off his narrow face as he realized she was not a reporter or a curious neighbor playing around with him.

"Son of a bitch. You're on the level."

She held out her hand for the badge. Now a bit embarrassed, he quickly handed it back.

"I didn't realize this was something the FBI would be in on."

It probably was not. She failed to mention that she was just in the neighborhood. Instead, she asked, "Who's the lead detective?"

"Excuse me?"

She pointed to the house.

"Who's leading the investigation?"

"Oh, that would be Detective Manx."

She headed for the entrance, feeling his eyes follow her. Before she closed the door behind her, he hurried after the tangled ribbon of tape that now trailed over much of the front lawn.

No one greeted Maggie at the door. In fact, no one was in sight. The house's foyer was almost as large as Maggie's new living room. She took her time, peeking into each room, stepping carefully and touching nothing. The house looked impeccable, not a speck of dust, until she got to the kitchen. Scattered across the butcher-block island were all the makings for a sandwich, now dried up, wilted and crusty. A head of lettuce sat on a cutting board amongst the remnants of tomato seeds and bits and pieces of green pepper. Several candy bar wrappers, containers left on their sides and an open mayonnaise jar waited to be cleaned up and put away. In the middle of the table sat the sandwich, thick with its contents spilling over the wheat bread. Only one bite taken from it.

Maggie's eyes examined the rest of the kitchen, shiny countertops, sparkling appliances and a spotless ceramic floor, marred only by three more candy bar wrappers. Whoever made this mess didn't live here.

She could hear voices now, muffled and coming from above. She climbed the stairs while avoiding contact with the oak handrail. She wondered if the detectives had been as careful. On one of the steps she noticed a clump of mud, left perhaps by one of the officers. There was something unusual in it that glittered. She resisted the urge to pick it up. It wasn't as though she carried evidence bags in her back pocket. Though at one time it wouldn't have been odd to find a stray in one of her jacket pockets. These days the only evidence she came across was in books.

She followed the voices down the long, carpeted hall. There was no longer a need to scrounge for evidence. At the doorway to the master bedroom a puddle of blood greeted her, the imprint of a shoe stamped at one edge, while the other edge soaked into an expensive Persian rug. With little effort, Maggie could see a spatter pattern on the oak door. Oddly, the spatter reached only to about knee level.

Maggie was lost in thought and hadn't entered the room when the detective in a bright blue sports jacket and wrinkled chinos yelled at her.

"Hey, lady. How the hell did you get in here?"

The two other men stopped their work in opposite corners of the room and stared at her. Maggie's first impression of the detective was that he looked like a wrinkled advertisement for the Gap.

"My name's Maggie O'Dell. I'm with the FBI." She opened her badge to him, but her eyes were examining the rest of the room.

"The FBI?"

The men exchanged looks while Maggie took a careful step around the puddle and into the room. More blood speckled the white down comforter on the four-poster bed. Despite the spatter of blood, the bedcovers remained neatly spread with no indentations. Whatever struggle took place did not make it to the bed.

"What's the FBI's interest in this?" the man in the bright sports jacket demanded.

He scraped a hand over his head, and Maggie wondered if the buzz cut was recent. His dark eyes slid down her body, and again she was reminded of her inappropriate attire. She glanced at the other two men. One was in uniform. The other, an older gentleman—who Maggie guessed was the medical examiner—was dressed in a well-pressed suit and a silk tie held down by an expensive gold collar bar.

"Are you Detective Manx?" she asked the buzz cut.

His eyes shot up to hers, the look not only registering surprise but alarm that she knew his name. Was he worried that his superiors were checking up on him? He looked young, and Maggie guessed he was close to her age—somewhere in his early thirties. Perhaps this was his first lead in a homicide.

"Yeah, I'm Manx. Who the hell called you?"

It was time to confess.

"I live down the street. I thought I might be able to help."

"Christ!" The same hand swiped over his face as he glanced at the other two men. They quietly watched as though observing a standoff. "Just because you've got a fucking badge, you think you can barge in here?"

"I'm a forensic psychologist and a profiler. I'm used to examining scenes like this. I thought I could—"

"Well, we don't need any help. I've got everything under control."

"Hey, Detective." The yellow-tape officer from outside walked into the room and immediately all eyes watched him step into the puddle. He jerked his foot up and awkwardly stepped back into the hall, holding up the dripping toe of his shoe.

"Hell, I can't believe I did that again," he muttered.

Just then Maggie realized the intruder had been more careful. The toe print she had seen was worthless. When she looked back at Manx, his eyes darted away. He shook his head, disguising the embarrassment as disdain for the young officer.

"What is it, Officer Kramer?"

Kramer looked desperately for somewhere to place his foot. He glanced up apologetically as he rubbed the sole on the hall carpet. This time Manx avoided looking at Maggie. Instead, he shoved his large hands into his jacket pockets as if needing to restrain them from strangling the young rookie.

"What the hell do you need, Kramer?"

"It's just...there are a few neighbors out front asking questions. I wondered if maybe I should start questioning them. You know, see if anybody saw something."

"Get names and addresses. We'll talk to them later."

"Yes, sir." The officer seemed relieved to escape the new stain he had created.

Maggie waited. The other two men stared at Manx.

"So tell me, O'Donnell. What's your take of this mess?"

"O'Dell."

"Excuse me?"

"The name's O'Dell," she said, but she wouldn't wait for another invitation. "Is the body in the bathroom?"

"There's a whirlpool bath with more blood, but no body. In fact, we seem to be missing that small detail."

"The blood seems to be confined to this room," the medical examiner told her.

Maggie noticed he was the only one wearing latex gloves.

"If someone ran out, but was injured, you'd think there'd be some drips, some scuffs, something. But the house is fucking clean enough to eat off the floors." Manx swiped at his new hairdo again.

"The kitchen's not so clean," Maggie contradicted him.

He scowled at her. "How goddamn long have you been sneaking around here?"

She ignored him and kneeled down to get a closer look at the blood on the floor. Most of it was congealed, some dried. She guessed it had been here since morning.

"Maybe she didn't have time to clean up after lunch," Manx continued instead of waiting for her to answer his question.

"How do you know the victim is a woman?"

"A neighbor called us when she couldn't get her on the phone. Said they were supposed to go shopping. She saw the car in the garage, but no one answered the door. See, I'm thinking the guy— whoever he was—must have interrupted her lunch."

"What makes you think the sandwich was hers?"

The three of them stopped simultaneously. Again, they exchanged looks, then stared at Maggie, like foreign diplomats relying on each other for interpretation.

"What the hell are you saying, O'Donnell?"

"The name is O'Dell, Detective Manx." She let him hear her irritation this time. His blatant disregard was a small but familiar and annoying way to discredit her. "The victim's house is impeccable. She wouldn't have left a mess like that, let alone sit down to eat before she cleaned it up."

"Maybe she was interrupted."

"Perhaps. But there's no sign of a struggle in the kitchen. And the alarm system was off, right?"

Manx looked annoyed that she had guessed correctly. "Yeah, it was off, so maybe it was someone she knew."

"That's possible." Maggie stood and let her eyes take in the rest of the room. "If he did interrupt or surprise her, that didn't happen until they were up here. She may have been waiting for him, or perhaps she invited him up. That's probably why there's no signs of a struggle until we get into the bedroom. She may have changed her mind. Didn't want to go through with whatever they had agreed to. This spatter pattern here on the door is strange." She pointed to it, careful not to touch. "It's so far down, one of them would need to be on the floor when this wound was inflicted."

She walked to the window, feeling the men's eyes follow her. Suddenly she had their attention. Through the sheer curtains she could see the backyard, similar to her own, spacious and secluded by flowering dogwoods and huge pines. None of the neighbors' houses were even visible, all hidden by the foliage and trees. No one would see an intruder come or go back here. But how would he maneuver the steep ridge and the stream? Had she overestimated the strength of that natural barrier?

"There really is not much blood," she continued. "Unless there's a lot more in the bathroom. Perhaps there's not a body simply because the victim left on her own."

She heard Manx snort. "You think they had a nice little lunch, he beat the shit out of her because she decided not to fuck him, but then she left willingly with this guy? And in the meantime, the whole goddamn neighborhood didn't notice?" Manx laughed.

Maggie ignored his sarcasm. "I didn't say she left willingly.

Also, this blood is much too congealed and dry to have happened a few hours ago during lunch. I'm guessing it happened early this morning. She glanced at the medical examiner for confirmation.

"She's right about that." He nodded in agreement.

"I don't think they had lunch together. He probably fixed the sandwich for himself. You should bag the sandwich. If you can't get a dental imprint, there may be some saliva for a DNA test."

When she finally turned to face him, Manx stared at her. Only now his frustration had turned to wonder and the crinkles at his eyes became more pronounced. Maggie realized he was older than her initial assessment. Which meant the clothes and the hair might be part of a midlife crisis rather than a youthful indiscretion. She recognized Manx's stunned look. It was the same look that often followed her on-the-spot, blunt profiles. At times, that look made her feel like a cheap fortune-teller or a psychic. But always beneath their skepticism lay just enough amazement and respect to vindicate that initial reaction.

"Mind if I check out the bathroom?" she asked.

"Be my guest." Manx shook his head and waved her through.

Before Maggie got to the bathroom door, she stopped. On the bureau was a photograph. She recognized the beautiful blond-haired woman who smiled out at her, one arm wrapped around a dark-haired man and the other around a panting white Labrador retriever. It was the same woman she and Tess McGowan had met the first day Maggie looked at her new house.

"What is it?" Manx asked, now standing directly behind her.

"I've met this woman before. Last week. Her name's Rachel Endicott. She was out jogging."

Just then, in the bureau mirror, she saw more blood. Only this was smeared on the bottom of the bed ruffle. She stopped and turned, hesitating. Was it possible that whoever had been bleeding was still under the bed?

CHAPTER 5

Maggie stared at the bloodied ruffle then slowly walked to the bed.

"Actually she was walking," she said, keeping the excitement from her voice. "She had a dog with her, a white Lab."

"We haven't found any fucking dog," Manx said. "Unless he's out in the backyard or the garage."

Carefully, Maggie got down on one knee. There was blood in the grooves of the hardwood floor, too. Here the intruder must have taken the time to mop it up. Why would he do that, unless some of it was his own?

The room grew silent as the men finally noticed the blood on the hem of the bed ruffle. Maggie felt them standing over her, waiting. Even Manx stood quietly, though out of the corner of her eye she could see the toe of his loafer tapping impatiently.

She lifted the ruffled material, avoiding the bloodied area. Before she could get a closer look underneath, a deep-throated growl caused her to jerk her hand away.

"Shit!" Manx spat, jumping back with such force he sent a nightstand scraping into the wall.

Maggie saw the glint of metal in his hand and realized he had drawn his service revolver.

"Move out of the way." He was next to her, shoving her shoulder and almost knocking her over.

She grabbed his arm as he recklessly took aim, ready to fire at anything that moved underneath the bed even though he couldn't see it.

"What the hell are you doing?" she yelled at him.

"What the fuck do you think I'm doing?"

"Calm down, Detective." The medical examiner took hold of Manx's other arm and gently pulled him back.

"This dog might be your only witness," Maggie said, getting down on her knees again but staying back a safe distance.

"Oh right. Like a dog's gonna tell us what happened."

"She's right," the M.E.'s voice was amazingly calm. "Dogs can tell us a lot. Let's see if we can get this one under control."

Then he looked to Maggie as if waiting for her instructions.

"Most likely, he's wounded," she said.

"And in shock," the M.E. added.

She stood and looked around the room. What the hell did she know about dogs, let alone how to subdue one?

"Check the closet and grab a couple of jackets," she told him. "Preferably thick, something like wool and something that's been worn and not laundered. Maybe there are some clothes on the floor."

She found a tennis racket leaning against the wall. She rummaged through the bureau's drawers then noticed a tie rack on the back of the closet door. She snatched a silk pinstripe and knotted one end of the tie to the handle of the racket. She made a slipknot at the other end.

The medical examiner came back with several jackets.

"Officer Hillguard," he instructed. "See if you can find some blankets. Detective Manx, get at the end of the bed. We'll have you lift up the bedspread when we're ready.

Maggie noticed Manx's impatience did not extend to the doctor. In fact, he seemed to regard the older man as an authority figure and willingly took his post at the end of the bed.

The medical examiner handed Maggie one of the jackets, an expensive wool tweed. She sniffed the sleeve. Excellent. There was still the faint scent of perfume. She pulled the jacket on backward, pushing the sleeves over her bare arms but keeping enough at the end to ball up in her fists. Then she grabbed the tennis racket and kneeled about two feet from the bed. The doctor kneeled next to her as Officer Hillguard set a quilt and two blankets on the floor beside them.

"Are we ready?" The medical examiner glanced at all of them. "Okay, Detective Manx. Lift the bedspread up, but slowly."

This time the dog was prepared, his eyes glazed, teeth bared, the growl deep and low. But he didn't lunge at them. He couldn't. Underneath the bloody mess of fur that was once white, Maggie spotted the main wound, a gash just above the shoulder and barely missing the throat. The matted fur must have temporarily stopped the bleeding.

"It's okay, boy," Maggie told the dog in a quiet, calm voice. "We're going to help you. Just relax."

She scooted closer, extending a part of the sleeve and letting it hang beyond her hand. He snapped at it, and Maggie jerked backward, almost losing her balance.

"Jesus!" she muttered. Had she completely lost her mind? She tried not to think of her aversion to needles, yet found herself wondering if the treatment for rabies was still six shots.

Maggie steadied herself. She needed to stay focused. She tried again, more slowly this time. The dog sniffed at the dangling sleeve, possibly recognizing the scent of his owner. His growl turned into a whine and then a whimper.

"It's okay," Maggie promised in a hushed tone, uncertain whether she was trying to convince the dog or herself. She inched closer with the tennis racket in her other hand, the tie's loop hanging down, moving in while the dog watched and continued to whimper. She let the dog sniff the tie. He didn't resist when she slipped it over his snout. Gently, she tightened the knot.

"How're we gonna get him out from under there?" Officer Hillguard was now on his knees on the other side of Maggie.

"Let's unfold one of those blankets and get it next to him."

But as soon as Officer Hillguard's hands got close, the dog

snapped and snarled, growling and struggling against the makeshift muzzle. He jumped toward the officer, and Maggie used the opportunity to grab the dog's collar from behind. She yanked him forward onto the blanket, all the while holding the tennis racket and keeping the muzzle tight. The dog yipped, and immediately Maggie worried that she had opened one of the wounds.

"Holy shit," she heard Detective Manx say, but this time he kept his revolver in its holster.

"We got him." The medical examiner stood and waved Officer Hillguard over to his side. The two men tugged on the blanket corners and pulled the dog out from under the bed. "We can use my van to transport him to Riley's Clinic."

Maggie sat back on her feet, only now noticing that she was soaked with perspiration.

"Shit." Manx was back to his belligerent mood. "That means all the blood by the door and in the bathtub is probably the fucking dog's blood, and we don't have a damn thing."

"I wouldn't count on that," Maggie said. "Something violent happened here, and the dog's owner may have suffered the brunt of it." She watched the doctor and officer cover the trembling dog and secure their blanket stretcher, grateful they were too busy to notice how much effort it took for her to stand.

"I'm guessing this guy—" she pointed to the Lab "—tried to stop whatever happened. He may have gotten in a couple of good bites. There's a chance some of the blood, especially here by the bed, may be the intruder's. Your forensics people should be able to get a sampling even though it's been wiped up."

"You think you can allow me to do my own investigation?" Manx shot her a look of contempt.

Maggie wiped strands of hair off her forehead. Jesus! Couldn't this guy give her a break? Just then she realized she had blood on her hands and now had blood on her forehead and in her hair. When she glanced at the medical examiner, he was shaking his head at Manx and giving him a warning look as though he, too, was fed up with Manx's arrogance.

"Yes, of course, the investigation is all yours," Maggie finally said, and grabbed a corner of the blanket to help the men move the swaddled dog. "I'm sure the whole neighborhood will sleep soundly tonight, knowing you're on the case."

Manx seemed surprised by her sarcasm, then turned red when he noticed the two men would not be coming to his defense. Maggie caught the medical examiner smiling. She didn't turn to see if Manx had caught it, too.

"Just keep your big FBI badge and your pretty little butt out of my investigation," he said to her back, determined to get in the last word. "You got that, O'Donnell?"

She didn't bother to look at him or answer, the ungrateful son of a bitch. He wouldn't have even found the dog if it wasn't for her. Now she wondered if he would bother to take blood samples, simply because it had been her suggestion.

She held her corner of the blanket tight and followed Officer Hillguard and the medical examiner. As they reached the landing, Maggie turned to look at Manx, who had stayed in the bedroom's doorway.

"Oh, Detective Manx," she called to him. "One more thing. You might want to check out this mud here on the steps. Unless, of course, you're the one who tracked it in and contaminated your own crime scene."

Instinctively, Manx lifted his right foot, taking a look at the sole before he realized his defensive reaction. The M.E. laughed out loud. Officer Hillguard knew better and confined himself to a smile. Manx's face went red again. Maggie simply turned, concentrating on keeping their patient steady and calm while they hauled him down the stairs.

CHAPTER 6

Tess McGowan stuffed a copy of the closing papers into her leather briefcase, ignoring its worn sheen and cracked handle. A couple more sales and just maybe she could afford a new briefcase instead of the hand-me-down she had bought at the thrift store.

She jotted a note on her desk blotter, "Joyce and Bill Saunders: a dozen long-stemmed chocolate chip cookies." The Saunderses kids would get a kick out of them, and Joyce was a chocoholic. Then, she wrote, "Maggie O'Dell: a garden bouquet." Quickly, she scratched out the notation. No, it was too simple, and Tess liked to customize her thank-yous to her customers. They had become one of her trademarks and paid off big-time in referrals. But what would O'Dell like? Hey, even FBI agents liked flowers, and O'Dell seemed nuts about her huge backyard, but a bouquet didn't seem right. No, what seemed right for Agent O'Dell was a killer Doberman. Tess smiled and jotted down "a potted azalea" instead.

Pleased with herself, Tess switched off her computer and slipped on her jacket. The other offices had gone silent hours ago. She was the only one nuts enough to be working this late. Though it didn't matter. Daniel would be at his office until eight or nine and not ready to think about her for several more hours. But she wouldn't dwell on his inattentiveness. After all, she'd be running in the other direction if Daniel was constantly calling her, infringing on her independence or pushing for a commitment. No, she liked things just the way they were—safe and uncomplicated with very little emotional investment. It was the perfect relationship for a woman who couldn't handle any real commitments.

She passed by the copier room but stopped when she heard shuffling. Her eyes darted to the front door at the end of the hall, making certain nothing obstructed her path in case she needed to run. She leaned against the wall and peeked around the door to the room where a copy machine buzzed into action.

"Girl, I thought you went home hours ago." Delores Heston's voice startled Tess as the woman stood up from behind the machine and shoved a tray of paper into the mouth of the copier. Finally, she looked at Tess and her face registered concern. "Good Lord! I'm sorry, Tess. I didn't mean to scare you. You okay?"

Tess's heart pounded in her ears. Immediately she was embarrassed at being so jumpy. The paranoia was a leftover from her old life. She smiled at Delores while she leaned against the doorjamb and waited for her pulse to return to normal.

"I'm fine. I thought everyone else was gone. What are you still doing here? Aren't you supposed to be taking the Greeleys to dinner?"

Delores punched some buttons, and the machine whizzed to life with a soft, almost comforting, hum. Then she looked at Tess, hands on her ample hips.

"They had to reschedule, so I'm catching up on some paperwork. And please don't tell Verna. She'll scream at me for messing with her precious baby." The machine beeped as if on cue.

"Holy Toledo! What did I do now?" Delores turned and began punching buttons again.

Tess laughed. The truth was, Delores owned the machine just like she owned every last chair and paper clip. Delores Heston started Heston Realty nearly ten years ago and had made quite a name for herself in Newburgh Heights and the surrounding area. Quite an accomplishment for a black woman who had grown up poor. Tess admired her mentor who, at six o'clock in the evening after a full day of work, still looked impeccable in her deep purple custom-made suit. Delores's silky, black hair was swept up into a compact bun, not a strand out of place. The only indication that she was finished for the day were her stocking feet.

In contrast, Tess's suit was wrinkled from too many hours of sitting. Her thick, wavy hair frizzled from the humidity, strands breaking free from the clasp she used to tie it back. She was probably the only woman alive who dyed her naturally blond hair a nondescript brown in order to buy herself more credibility and to avoid sexual advances. Even the eyeglasses, which dangled from a designer cord around her neck, were a prop. Tess wore contact lenses, but didn't young, attractive women always look more intelligent when they wore glasses?

Finally, the machine stopped beeping and started spitting out copies. Delores turned to Tess and rolled her eyes.

"Verna's smart not to let me touch this thing."

"Looks like you've got it under control."

"So, girl, what are you doing here so late? Don't you have a handsome man you should be home snuggling with on a Friday evening?"

"Just wanted to finish all the paperwork on the Saunders' house."

"That's right. I forgot you closed this week. Excellent job, by the way. I know the Saunderses were in a hell of a hurry to sell. How much of a beating did we take?"

"Actually, it turned out quite well for everyone involved. Plus, we beat their two-week deadline, so on top of our commission we'll also be receiving the selling bonus they tacked on."

"Ooooh, I do so love to hear that. There's no better advertising than surpassing a customer's expectations. But that selling bonus is all yours, dearie."

Tess wasn't sure she heard her boss correctly.

"Excuse me?"

"You heard me. You're keeping that selling bonus for yourself. You deserve it."

For a minute Tess didn't know what to say. The bonus was almost ten thousand dollars. That was almost six months' pay back when she had been bartending. Her look of surprise sent Delores into gales of laughter.

"Girl, I wish you could see the look on your face."

Tess waited quietly. She managed a weak smile. She was embarrassed to ask if her boss was joking. It would be a cruel joke. But then, it wouldn't be the first time Tess had experienced such cruelty. In fact, she expected it, accepted it, almost more readily than kindness.

Delores was staring at her again, with a look of concern.

"Tess, I am serious. I want you to have the selling bonus. You worked your ass off to move that property in two weeks. I know it's a beautiful house and the asking price was a steal, but with all the paperwork and hedging and negotiating—selling anything right now that quickly, and especially in that price range, is nothing less than a miracle."

"It's...well, it's just an awful lot of money. Are you sure you want to—"

"Absolutely. I know what I'm doing, girlfriend. I'm investing in you, Tess. I want you to stick around. Don't need you going out on your own and becoming my competition. Besides, I'm making a nice piece of change off that property, as it is. Now go home and celebrate with that handsome man of yours."

On the way home Tess wondered if it was possible, the part about celebrating with her "handsome man." Daniel had been so angry with her last week when she'd refused to move in with him. She wasn't sure she blamed him. Why was it that every time a man wanted to get close to her, she pushed him away?

Jesus, she wasn't a kid anymore. In a couple of weeks she'd be thirty-five. She was becoming a successful and respected businesswoman. So why couldn't she get her personal life right? Was she destined to fail at every damn relationship she attempted? No matter what she did, the past seemed to follow her around, sucking her back into its old, comfortable, but destructive, cocoon.

The last five years had been a constant battle, but finally she was making progress. And this last sale had proven that she was actually good at this. She could make a living without conning anyone. Even Daniel had become a sort of trophy, with his refined handsome features, his educated and cultured background. He was sophisticated and ambitious and so completely unlike any man she had ever been with. So what if he was a little arrogant, or that they had so few things in common. He was good for her. She winced at the thought. It made Daniel sound like cod liver oil.

Tess found herself pulling her leased Miata into the back-alley parking lot of Louie's Bar and Grill. She decided to pick up a bottle of wine. Then she'd call Daniel, apologize for last week and invite him over for a late dinner to help her celebrate. Surely he would be excited for her. He had said he liked her independence and determination, and Daniel was stingy with compliments, even the halfhearted ones.

She sat back in the leather seat and tried to remember why she felt she needed to apologize to him again. Oh well. It didn't matter, as long as they put it behind them and moved forward. She was getting good at putting things in the past. Yet, if that were true, what was she doing back here at Louie's? Shep's Liquor Mart was only three blocks down the street and on her way home. What in the world did she need to prove to anyone? Or rather, what was it she still needed to prove to herself?

She reached for the key in the ignition and was just about to start the car and leave when the back door swung open, startling her. A stocky, middle-aged man came out, his hands filled with trash bags, his apron grimy and his balding head glistening with sweat. A cigarette hung from his lips. Without removing it, he heaved the bags into the Dumpster and wiped the sweat from his forehead with the sleeve of his shirt. As he turned to go back in, he saw her, and then it was too late.

He grabbed the cigarette—one last puff—and tossed it to the ground without stomping it out. He strolled up to the car, carrying his bulk with a swagger Tess knew he imitated from the professional wrestlers he idolized. He thought he looked cool. When, in fact, he simply looked like a pathetic, overweight, balding, middle-aged man. Despite all that, she found him endearing, the closest thing she had to an old friend.

"Tessy," he said, then waited as the window hummed opened. "What the hell you doin' here?"

She noticed the beginning of a smile before he wiped at it, pretending instead to scratch the five o'clock shadow.

"Hi, Louie." She got out of the car.

"Fuckin' nice ride ya got here, Tessy," he said, checking out the shiny black Miata.

She let him examine and admire it, neglecting to tell him it was a company car and not her own. One of Delores's mottoes was that to be successful you must first look successful.

Finally, Louie turned his sights on Tess. She felt his eyes slide down her designer suit and his whistle made her blush. She should have felt proud. Instead, his attention made her feel like a fraud for a second time in the same day.

"So whatcha doin' here? Slummin'?"

Immediately, her face grew hot.

"Of course not," she snapped.

"Hey, I'm just jokin' with ya, Tessy."

"I know that." She smiled, hoping she sounded convincing and not defensive. She turned to the car and pretended to lock the door, though the remote could do it from ten feet away. "I need to pick up a bottle of wine. Just thought I'd give you the business rather than Shep's."

"Oh really?" He stared at her, his eyebrow raised, but quickly gave in to a smile. "Well, I appreciate it. And you never need no excuse to come see us, Tessy. You know you're always welcome."

"Thanks, Louie."

Suddenly she felt like that restless, going-nowhere bartender she had left here five years ago. Would she ever be rid of her past?

"Come on," Louie said as he swung a muscular arm up around her shoulder.

Wearing heels, Tess was a couple inches taller, making the dragon tattooed on his arm stretch its neck. The smell of body odor and French fries made her stomach turn, only she was surprised to find it was homesickness she was feeling instead of nausea. Then she thought of Daniel. Later, he would smell the cigarette smoke and the greasy burgers. She realized that would be enough to ruin the celebration.

"You know what, Louie. I just remembered something I forgot back at the office." She turned and slipped out from under his arm.

"What? It can't wait a few minutes?"

"No, sorry. My boss will have my ass in a sling if I don't take care of it right now." She bleeped her car door open and climbed inside before Louie had a chance to do any more objecting. "I'll stop in later," she said through the half-opened window, knowing full well she would not. The window was already on its way up again when she said, "I promise."

She shifted the car into gear and carefully maneuvered the narrow alley, watching Louie in the rearview mirror. He looked more confused than pissed. That was good. She didn't want Louie pissed at her. Then immediately wondered why it mattered. She didn't want it to matter.

She turned the car onto the street, and when she knew she was safely out of sight, she gunned the engine. But it took several miles before she felt like she could breathe and before she could hear the car radio instead of the pounding of her heart. Then she remembered that she had passed Shep's Liquor Mart. She didn't care. She no longer felt as if she deserved a celebration, yet she tried to concentrate on her recent successes and not the past. In fact, she remained so focused, she hardly noticed the dark sedan following her.

CHAPTER 7

Before the pizza or Gwen arrived, Maggie poured a second Scotch. She had forgotten about the bottle until she discovered it staring up at her, safely stored in the box—a necessary antidote accompanying the contents of horror. The box was labeled #34666, the number that had been assigned to Albert Stucky. Perhaps it was no accident that his file number would end in 666.

Assistant Director Cunningham would be furious if he knew she had copied every last piece of paper from Stucky's official file. She would have felt guilty if each report, each document, each note had been recorded by someone other than herself. For almost two years Maggie had tracked Stucky. She had viewed every one of his scenes of torture and dissection, scanning his handiwork for fibers, hairs, missing organs, anything that would tell her how to catch him. She had a right to his file, considering it some strange documentation of a portion of her own life.

She had taken a quick shower after her unexpected trip to the vet. Her UVA T-shirt soaked in the bathroom sink. She might never be able to remove the bloodstains. The T-shirt was old, stretched and faded, but she had an odd attachment to it. Some people kept scrapbooks, Maggie kept T-shirts.

Her years at the University of Virginia had been good ones. It was there she discovered a life of her own outside of being her mother's caretaker. It was where she had met Greg. She glanced at her watch, then checked her cellular phone to make certain it was on. He still hadn't returned her call about the missing carton. He'd make her wait, but she wouldn't let herself get angry. Not tonight. She was simply too exhausted to take on one more emotion.

The doorbell chimed. Maggie glanced at her watch again. As usual, Gwen was ten minutes late. She tugged at her shirttail, making certain it hid the bulging Smith & Wesson tucked into her waistband. Lately, the gun had become as common an accessory as her wristwatch.

"I know I'm late," Gwen said before the door was fully open. "Traffic was a bitch. Friday night and everyone's trying to get the hell out of D.C. for the weekend."

"Good to see you, too."

She smiled and pulled Maggie in for a one-armed hug. For a brief moment Maggie was surprised by how soft and fragile the older woman felt. Despite Gwen's petite and feminine stature, Maggie thought of her as her own personal Rock of Gibraltor. She had leaned on Gwen and depended on her strength and character and words of wisdom many times during their friendship.

When Gwen pulled away, she cupped Maggie's cheek in the palm of her hand, attempting to get a good look at her.

"You look like hell," was her gentle assessment.

"Gee, thanks!"

She smiled again and handed Maggie the carton of long-necked Bud Light she carried in her other hand. The bottles were cold and dripping with condensation. Maggie took them and used the action as an excuse to keep her eyes away from Gwen's. It had been almost a month since the two women had seen each other, though they talked on the phone regularly. On the phone, however, Maggie could keep Gwen from seeing the panic and vulnerability that seemed to lie so close to the surface during these past several weeks.

"Pizza should be here any minute," Maggie told her as she reset the security system.

"No Italian sausage on my half."

"Extra mushrooms, instead."

"Oh, bless you." Gwen didn't wait for an invitation to come in. She took off to roam through the rooms.

"My God, Maggie, this house is wonderful."

"You like my designer?"

"Hmm...I'd say brown cardboard is you, simple and unpretentious. May I check out the second floor?" Gwen asked, already making her way up the stairs.

"Can I stop you?" Maggie laughed. How was it possible for this woman to sweep into a place and bring a trail of energy as well as such warmth and delight?

She and Gwen had met when Maggie had first arrived at Quantico for her forensic fellowship. Maggie had been a young, naive newbie who hadn't yet seen blood except in a test tube, and had never fired a gun except during training on the firing range.

Gwen had been one of the local psychologists brought in by Assistant Director Cunningham to act as a private consultant and to help profile several important cases. Even back then she had a successful practice in D.C. Many of her patients were some of the elite of Washington—bored wives of congressmen, suicidal generals and even one manic-depressed White House cabinet member.

However it was Gwen's research, the many articles she had written and her remarkable insight into the criminal mind that had attracted Assistant Director Cunningham when he first asked her to be an independent consultant for the FBI's Investigative Support Unit. Though Maggie learned quickly that the assistant director had been attracted to Dr. Gwen Patterson in other ways as well. A person would have to be blind not to see the ongoing chemistry between the two, though Maggie knew firsthand that neither had acted upon it, nor ever intended to.

"We respect our professional relationship," Gwen explained to Maggie once, making it clear she didn't want the subject brought up again, though this was long after Gwen's stint as a consultant had ended. Maggie knew that Assistant Director Cunningham's estranged marriage probably had more to do with their hands-off policy than any attempt to remain professional.

From the first time Maggie met Gwen, she had admired the woman's vibrancy, her keen intellect and her dry sense of humor. Gwen refused to think inside the box and didn't hesitate to break any of the rules while still appearing to be respectful of authority. Maggie had seen her win over diplomats as well as criminals with her sophisticated but charming manner. Gwen was fifteen years older than Maggie, but the woman had instantly become a best friend as well as a mentor.

The doorbell chimed again, and Maggie's hand reached back and grabbed her revolver before she could stop herself. She glanced up the stairs to see if Gwen had witnessed her knee-jerk reaction. She smoothed her shirttail over her jeans and checked the portico from the side window before she disarmed the alarm system. She stopped and looked out the peephole, examining the fish-eye view of the street, then she opened the door.

"Large pizza for O'Dell." The young girl handed Maggie the warm box. Already she could smell the Romano cheese and Italian sausage.

"It smells wonderful."

The girl grinned as though she had prepared it herself.

"It comes to $18.59, please."

Maggie handed her a twenty and a five. "Keep the change."

"Gee, thanks."

The girl bounced down the circular drive, her blond ponytail waving out the back of her blue baseball cap.

Maggie set the pizza down in the middle of the living room. She returned to the door to reset the security system just as Gwen came rushing down the steps.

"Maggie, what the hell happened?" she asked, holding up the dripping T-shirt, splattered with blood.

"What is this? Did you hurt yourself?" Gwen demanded.

"Oh, that."

"Yes, oh that. What the hell happened?"

Maggie quickly cupped a hand under the dripping T-shirt and grabbed it away, racing up the stairs to drop it back into the sink.

She drained the red, murky water, tossed in more detergent and ran fresh water over the fabric. When she looked up in the mirror, Gwen was standing behind her, watching.

"If you're hurt, please don't try to take care of it yourself," Gwen said in a soft but stern voice.

Maggie met her friend's eyes in the mirror and knew that she was referring to the cut Albert Stucky had sliced into her abdomen. Maggie had slipped away into the night, after all the commotion had ended, and tried to discreetly dress her own wound. But an infection had landed her in the emergency room a few days later.

"It's nothing, Gwen. My neighbor's dog was injured. I helped take it to the vet. This is the dog's blood. Not mine."

"You're kidding." It took a minute for relief to wash over Gwen's face. "Jesus, Maggie, you just can't keep your nose out of anything that involves blood, can you?"

Maggie smiled. "I'll tell you about it later. We need to eat, because I am starving."

"That's new and different."

Maggie grabbed a towel, wiped her hands and led the way back downstairs.

"You know," Gwen said from behind her, "you need to put on some weight. Do you ever eat regular meals anymore?"

"I hope this isn't going to be a lecture on nutrition."

She heard Gwen sigh, but knew she wouldn't push it. They went into the kitchen, and Maggie pulled out paper plates and napkins from a carton on the counter. Each grabbed a cold bottle of beer and returned to the living-room floor. Already Gwen had kicked out of her expensive black pumps and thrown her suit jacket over the arm of the recliner. Maggie scooped up pizza as she noticed Gwen examining the open carton next to the rolltop desk.

"This is Stucky's, isn't it?"

"Are you going to rat me out to Cunningham?"

"Of course not. You know me better than that. But I am concerned about you obsessing over him."

"I'm not obsessing."

"Really? Then what would you call it?"

Maggie took a bite of pizza. She didn't want to think about Stucky, or her appetite would be ruined again. Yet that was one of the reasons Gwen was here.

"I simply want him caught," Maggie finally said. She could feel Gwen's eyes examining her, looking for signs, watching for underlying tones. Maggie hated it when her friend tried psychoanalyzing her, but she knew it was a simple instinct with Gwen.

"And only you can catch him? Is that it?"

"I know him best."

Gwen stared at her a few more moments then picked up her bottle by its neck and twisted off the cap. She took a sip and put the drink aside.

"I did some checking." She reached for a slice of pizza, and Maggie tried not to show her eagerness. She had asked Gwen to use her connections to find out where the Stucky case was stalled. When Assistant Director Cunningham exiled Maggie to the teaching circuit, he had also made it impossible for her to find out any information about the investigation.

Gwen took her time chewing. Another sip while Maggie waited. She wondered if Gwen had called Cunningham directly. No, that would have been too obvious. He knew the two of them were close friends.

"And?" She couldn't stand it any longer.

"Cunningham has brought in a new profiler, but the task force has been dismantled."

"Why the hell would he do that?"

"Because he has nothing, Maggie. It's been, what? Over five months? There's no sign of Albert Stucky. It's like he's fallen off the face of the earth."

"I know. I've been checking VICAP almost weekly." Initiated by the FBI, the Violent Criminal Apprehension Program recorded violent crimes across the country, categorizing them by distinguishing features. Nothing close to Stucky's M.O. had shown up. "What about in Europe? Stucky has enough money stashed. He could go anywhere."

"I checked my sources at Interpol." Gwen paused for another sip. "There's been nothing that looks like Stucky."

"Maybe he's changed his M.O."

"Maybe he's stopped, Maggie. Sometimes serial killers do that. They just stop. No one can explain it, but you know it happens."

"Not Stucky."

"Don't you think he'd be in touch with you? Try to start his sick game all over again? After all, you're the one who got him thrown in jail. If nothing else, he'd be mad as hell."

Maggie had been the one who had finally identified the madman the FBI had nicknamed The Collector. Her profile, and a lucky discovery of an almost indistinguishable set of fingerprints—arrogantly and recklessly left behind at a crime scene—were what led to the unveiling of The Collector as a man named Albert Stucky, a self-made millionaire from Massachusetts.

Like most serial killers, Stucky seemed pleased by the exposure, enjoying the attention and wanting to take the credit. When his obsession turned to Maggie, no one was really surprised. But the game that followed was anything but ordinary. A game that included clues to catch him, only the clues came as personal notes with a token finger, a dissected birthmark, and once, a severed nipple slipped into an envelope.

That was about eight or nine months ago. Almost a year had passed and Maggie still struggled to remember what her life had been like before the game. She couldn't remember sleep without nightmares. She couldn't remember not feeling the constant need to look over her shoulder. She had nearly lost her life capturing Albert Stucky, and he had escaped before she could remember what feeling safe felt like.

Gwen reached over and pulled a stack of crime scene photos from the box. She laid them out while she continued eating her pizza. She was one of the few people Maggie knew who wasn't a member of the FBI and who was able to eat and look at crime scene photos at the same time. Without looking up, she said, "You need to let this go, Maggie. He's chopping away pieces of you, and he isn't even around."

The images from the scattered photos stared out at Maggie, just as horrific in black and white as they had been in color. There were close-ups of slashed throats, chewed-off nipples, mutilated vaginas and an assortment of extracted organs. Earlier, with only a glance, she had discovered how many of the reports she still knew by heart. God, that was annoying.

Greg had recently accused her of remembering more details about entry wounds and killers' signatures than she remembered about the events and anniversaries in their life together. There had been no point in arguing with him. She knew he was right. Perhaps she didn't deserve a husband or a family or a life. How could any female FBI agent expect a man to understand her job, let alone something like this...this obsession? Was it an obsession? Was Gwen right?

She set the pizza aside and realized that her hands had a slight tremble. When she looked up, she saw that Gwen noticed the tremor, too.

"When was the last time you slept through the night?" Her friend's brow crinkled with concern.

She chose to ignore the question and avoided Gwen's green Irish eyes as well. "Just because there hasn't been a murder doesn't mean he hasn't started his collection again."

"And if he has, Kyle will be watching." Gwen rarely slipped, using Assistant Director Cunningham's first name, except times like now, when she seemed genuinely concerned and worried. "Let it go, Maggie. Let it go before it destroys you."

"It's not going to destroy me. I'm pretty damn tough, remember?" But she couldn't meet her friend's eyes for fear that Gwen would see the lie.

"Ah, tough," Gwen said, sitting back. "So that's why you're walking around your own home with a gun stashed in the back of your pants."

Maggie winced. Gwen caught it and smiled.

"Now, see, instead of tough," she told Maggie, "I think I would have called it stubborn."

CHAPTER 8

He couldn't remember pizza delivery girls being so cute back in his younger days when he had worked at the local pizza place. Hell, he couldn't remember there being delivery girls back then.

He watched her hurry up the sidewalk, strands of long blond hair trailing behind her. She had her hair in a cute ponytail—sticking out the back of her blue baseball cap, a Chicago Cubs cap. He wondered if she was a fan. Or maybe her boyfriend was. Surely she had a boyfriend somewhere.

It was too dark now to depend on the streetlights. His eyes were already stinging and a bit blurred. He slipped on the night goggles and adjusted the magnification. Yes, this was good.

He saw her check her watch as she waited on the front porch. This time another man answered the door. Of course, the guy would give her that dumb-ass look of astonishment. The man fished bills out of the pockets of his blue jeans, jeans that sagged at his bulging waist. He was a slob, grimy with sweat stains under the armpits of his T-shirt and a tuft of hair sticking up out the neckline. And yet...yep, there it was, another wiseass remark about how cute she was or what he wouldn't mind tipping her with. But again, she smiled politely, despite the color rising in her cheeks.

Just once he'd like to see her kick one of these idiots in the groin. Maybe that was a lesson he could teach her. If things worked out as he planned, he'd have plenty of time with her.

She hurried away along the winding sidewalk, and the cheap bastard who had tipped her only a dollar, watched her ass the whole trip back to her shiny little Dodge Dart. That sight alone was worth much more than a dollar. The cheap son of a bitch. How the hell was she supposed to put herself through college on dollar tips?

He decided that women were better tippers when it came to delivery services. Maybe they felt some odd sense of guilt for not having prepared the meal themselves. Who knew. Women were complicated, fascinating creatures, and he wouldn't change that if he could.

He replaced the goggles with dark sunglasses, simply out of habit now, and because the oncoming headlights burned his eyes. He waited for the Dodge Dart to reach the intersection before he turned around and followed. She was finished with this batch. He recognized the route back to the pizza place, Mama Mia's on Fifty-ninth and Archer Drive. The cozy joint took up the corner of a neighborhood strip mall. A Pump-N-Go occupied the other entrance. In between were a half-dozen smaller shops, including Mr. Magoo's Videos and Shep's Liquor Mart.

Newburgh Heights was such a friendly little suburb it gagged him. Not much of a challenge. Nor much challenge in the cute pizza delivery girl either. But this wasn't about challenge, it was simply for show.

The girl parked behind the building, near the door, and gathered up the stack of red insulators. She'd be back in a few minutes with another load ready to deliver.

The neon sign for Mama Mia's included a delivery number. He flipped open the cellular phone and dialed the number while he unfolded a real estate flyer. The description promised a four-bedroom colonial with a whirlpool bath and skylight in the master bedroom. How romantic, he mused, just as a woman barked in his ear.

"Mama Mia's."

"I'd like two large pepperoni pizzas delivered."

"Phone number."

"555-4545," he read off the flyer.

"Name and address."

"Heston," he continued reading, "at 5349 Archer Drive."

"Would you like some breadsticks and soda with that?"

"No, just the pizza."

"It'll be about twenty minutes, Mr. Heston."

"Fine." He snapped the phone shut. Twenty minutes would be plenty of time. He pulled on his black leather driving gloves, and then he wiped the phone with a corner of his shirt. As he drove by the Dumpster, he tossed the phone.

He headed south on Archer Drive, thinking about pizza, a moonlit bath and that cute delivery girl with the polite smile and the tight ass.

CHAPTER 9

Maggie's eyes begged to close. Her shoulders slouched from exhaustion. It was almost midnight by the time Gwen left. Maggie knew she'd never be able to sleep. She had already checked every window latch twice, leaving only a choice few open to keep the wonderful chilly breeze flowing through the main floor. Likewise, she had double-checked the security system several times after Gwen's departure. Now she paced, dreading the night hours, hating the dark and vowing to put up drapes and blinds tomorrow.

Finally she sat back down cross-legged in the middle of the pile created from the contents of Stucky's personal box of horror. She pulled out the folder with newspaper clippings and articles she had downloaded. Ever since Stucky's escape five months ago, she had watched newspaper headlines across the country by using the Internet.

She still couldn't believe how easily Albert Stucky had escaped. On his way to a maximum-security facility—a simple trip that should have taken a couple of hours—Stucky killed two transport guards. Then he disappeared into the Florida Everglades, never to be seen again.

Anyone else may not have been able to survive, having become a nifty snack for some alligator. But knowing Stucky, Maggie imagined him emerging from the Everglades in a three-piece suit and a briefcase made of alligator skin. Yes, Albert Stucky was intelligent and crafty and savvy enough to charm an alligator out of its own skin, and then reward it by slicing it up and feeding it to the other alligators.

She sorted through the most recent articles. Last week, the *Philadelphia Journal* had an article about a woman's torso found in the river, her head and feet found in a Dumpster. It was the closest thing she had seen in months to Stucky's M.O., yet it still didn't feel like him. It was too much. It was overkill. Stucky's handiwork, though inconceivably horrible, had never included chopping away a victim's identity. No, Stucky enjoyed doing that with subtle psychological and mental tricks. Even his extraction of an organ from the victim was not a statement about the victim but rather his attempt to continue the game. Maggie imagined him watching and laughing as some unsuspecting diner found Stucky's appalling surprise, often tucked into an ordinary take-out container and abandoned on an outside café table. It was all a game to Stucky, a morbid, twisted game.

The articles that frightened Maggie more than the ones with missing body parts were the ones of women who had disappeared. Women like her missing neighbor, Rachel Endicott. Intelligent, successful women, some with families, all attractive, and all described as women who would not suddenly leave their lives without telling a soul. Maggie couldn't help wondering if any of them had become part of Stucky's collection. By now he had surely found somewhere isolated, somewhere to start all over again. He had the money and the means. All he needed was time.

She knew Cunningham and his defunct task force, and now his new profiler, were waiting for a body. But if, and when, the bodies did start showing up, they were the ones Stucky killed only for fun. No, the ones they should be looking for were the women he collected. These were the women he tortured—who ended up in remote graves deep in the woods, only after he was completely finished playing his sick games with them. Games that would drag on for days, maybe weeks. The women Stucky chose were never young or naive. No, Stucky enjoyed a challenge. He carefully chose intelligent, mature women. Women who would fight back, not those easily broken. Women he could torture psychologically as well as physically.

Maggie rubbed her eyes. She wanted another Scotch. The two earlier, added to the beer, were already making her head buzz and her vision blur. Though she had brewed a pot of coffee earlier for Gwen, she hated the stuff and stayed away from it. Now she wished she had something to help her stay alert. Something like the Scotch, which she knew was becoming a dangerous anesthetic.

She lifted another file folder and a page fell out. Seeing his handwriting still sent chills down her spine. She picked it up by its corner as though its evil would contaminate her. It had been the first of many notes in the sick game Albert Stucky had played with her. He had written in careful script:

What challenge is there in breaking a horse without spirit? The challenge is to replace that spirit with fear, raw animal fear that makes one feel alive. Are you ready to feel alive, Margaret O'Dell?

It had been their first insight into the intellect of Albert Stucky, a man whose father had been a prominent doctor. A man who had been afforded all the best schools, all the privileges money could buy. Yet he was thrown out of Yale for almost burning down a women's dormitory. There were other offenses: attempted rape, assault, petty theft. All charges had been either dropped or were never pressed, due to lack of evidence. Stucky had been questioned in the accidental death of his father, a freak boating accident though the man had supposedly been an expert yachtsman.

Then, about six or seven years ago, Albert Stucky took up a business partner, and the two of them succeeded in creating one of the Internet's first stock-market trading sites. Stucky became a respectable businessman, and a multimillionaire.

Despite all of Maggie's research, she never felt certain about what had set Stucky off in the first place. What had been the event, the precursor? Usually with serial killers, their crimes were precipitated by some stressor. An event, a death, a rejection, an abuse that one day made them decide to kill. She didn't know what that had been for Stucky. Perhaps evil simply couldn't be harnessed. And Stucky's evil was especially terrifying.

Most serial killers murdered because it gave them pleasure, some form of gratification. It was a choice, not necessarily a sickness of the mind. But for Albert Stucky, the kill was not enough. His pleasure came from psychologically breaking down his victims, turning them into sniveling, pleading wretches— owning them body, mind and soul. He enjoyed breaking their spirit, turning it into fear. Then he rewarded his victims with a slow, torturous death. Ironically, those he killed immediately, those whose throats he slashed and whose bodies he discarded in Dumpsters—only after extracting a token organ—those were the lucky ones.

The phone startled her. She grabbed the Smith & Wesson .38 that sat by her side. Again, it was a simple reflex. It was late, and few people had her new number. She had refused to give it to the pizza place. She had even insisted Greg use her cell phone number. Maybe Gwen had forgotten something. From the floor, she reached up to the desktop and pulled the phone down.

"Yes?" she said, her muscles tense. She wondered when she had stopped answering hello.

"Agent O'Dell?"

She recognized Assistant Director Cunningham's matter-of-fact tone, but the tension did not leave her.

"Yes, sir."

"I couldn't remember if you were already using the new number."

"I just moved in today."

She glanced at her wristwatch. It was now after midnight. They spoke infrequently these days, ever since he had taken her out of the field and assigned her to training duty. Was it possible he had some information on Stucky? She sat up with an unexpected flutter of hope.

"Is there something wrong?"

"I'm sorry, Agent O'Dell. I just realized how late it is."

She imagined him still at this desk at Quantico, never mind that it was Friday night.

"That's quite all right, sir. You didn't wake me."

"I thought you might be leaving for Kansas City tomorrow, and I didn't want to miss you."

"I leave on Sunday." She kept the question, the anticipation from her voice as best she could. If he needed her to stay, she knew Stewart was able to fill in for her at the law enforcement conference. "Does there need to be a change to my schedule?"

"No, not at all. I just wanted to make sure. I did, however, receive a phone call earlier this evening that gave me great concern."

Maggie imagined a body, sliced and left for some unsuspecting person to find beneath the trash. She waited for him to give her the details.

"A Detective Manx from the Newburgh Heights Police Department called me."

Maggie's anticipation quickly dissipated.

"He told me that you interfered with a crime scene investigation this afternoon. Is that true?"

Maggie reached to rub her eyes again, only now realizing she still gripped the revolver. She put it aside and sat back, feeling defeated. Damn that prick, Manx.

"Agent O'Dell? Is that true?"

"I just moved into the neighborhood this afternoon. I noticed police cruisers at the end of the block. I thought perhaps I could help."

"So you did barge in uninvited on a crime scene."

"I did not barge in. I offered my help."

"That's not the way Detective Manx described it."

"No, I don't imagine it is."

"I want you to stay out of the field, Agent O'Dell."

"But I was able to—"

"Out of the field means you don't go using your credentials to walk onto crime scenes. Even if they are in your own neighborhood. Is that understood?"

She ran her fingers through her tangled hair. How dare Manx. He wouldn't have discovered the dog, had it not been for her.

"Agent O'Dell, is that clear?"

"Yes. Yes, it's perfectly clear," she said, almost expecting an additional reprimand for the sarcasm in her voice.

"Have a safe trip," he said in his usual abrupt manner and then hung up.

She threw the phone onto the desktop and began rifling through the files. The tension tightened in her back, her neck and shoulders. She stood up and stretched, noticing the anger still slamming in her chest. Damn Manx! Damn Cunningham! How long did he think he could keep her out of the field? How long did he intend to punish her for being vulnerable? And how could he ever expect to catch Stucky without her help?

Maggie reset the security system a third time, double-checking the red On light, even though the mechanical voice told her each time, "Alarm system has been activated." The hell with the buzz in her head. She poured another Scotch and convinced herself that one more would surely relieve the tension.

The mess stayed scattered on the living-room floor. It seemed appropriate that her new home be initiated with a pile of blood and horror. She retreated to the sunroom, grabbing her revolver and snatching an afghan from a box in the corner, wrapping it around her shoulders. She shut off all the lights, except the one on the desk. Then she curled into the recliner that now faced the wall of windows.

She cradled and sipped the Scotch as she watched the moon slip in and out of the clouds, making shadows dance in her new backyard. In her other hand she gripped the revolver resting in her lap, tucked under the cover. Despite the progressive blur behind her eyes, she would be ready. Perhaps Assistant Director Cunningham couldn't stop Albert Stucky from coming for her, but she sure as hell would. And this time, it would be Stucky's turn for a surprise.

CHAPTER 10

Reston, Virginia
Saturday evening
March 28

R. J. Tully peeled off another ten-dollar bill and slid it under the ticket window. When had movie tickets started costing $8.50 each? He tried to remember the last time he had been to a movie theater on a Saturday night. He tried to remember when he had last been to a movie theater, period. Surely he and Caroline had gone some time during their thirteen-year marriage. Though it would have been early on—before she began preferring her co-workers to him.

He glanced around to find Emma dawdling far behind him, off to the side and at least three moviegoers back. Sometimes he wondered who the hell this person was. This beautiful, tall fourteen-year-old with silky blond hair and the beginnings of a shapely body she blatantly emphasized with tight jeans and a tight knit sweater. She looked more and more like her mother every day. God, he missed the days when this same girl held his hand and jumped into his arms, anxious to go anywhere with him. But just like her mother, that too had changed.

He waited for her at the ticket taker and wondered how she'd be able to sit next to him for two hours. He saw her eyes dart around the crowded lobby. Immediately, his heart sank. She didn't want any of her new friends to see her on a Saturday night, going to a movie with her dad. Was she really that embarrassed by him? He couldn't remember ever feeling that way about either of his parents. No wonder he spent so many hours at work. At the moment, understanding serial killers seemed much easier than understanding fourteen-year-old girls.

"How 'bout some popcorn?" he offered.

"Popcorn has, like, tons of fat."

"I don't think you have a thing to worry about, Sweet Pea."

"Oh my God, Dad!"

He stopped abruptly, checking to see if he had stepped on her toes. She sounded so pained.

"Don't call me that," she whispered.

He smiled down at her, which seemed to embarrass her more.

"Okay, so no popcorn for you. How about a Pepsi?"

"Diet Pepsi," she corrected him.

Surprisingly, she waited next to him in line at the concession stand, but her eyes still roamed the crowded lobby. It had been almost two months since Emma had come to live with him full-time. The truth was, he saw even less of her than when they were all back in Cleveland, and he was only a weekend dad. At least then they did things together, trying to make up for lost time.

When they first moved to Virginia he had tried to make sure they had dinner together every night, but he was the first to break that routine. His new job at Quantico had swallowed up much more of his time than he realized. So in addition to he and Emma settling into a new home, a new job, a new school and a new city, she also had to get used to not having her mother.

He still couldn't believe that Caroline had agreed to the arrangement. Maybe when she got tired of playing CEO by day, and the dating game by night, she would want her daughter back in her life full-time.

He watched Emma's quick, nervous swipes at the misbehaving strands of her long hair. Her eyes were still casing the theater. He wondered if fighting for full custody had been a mistake. He knew she missed her mother, even if her mother had been less available to her than he was. Damn it! Why did this parenting thing have to be so damn hard?

He almost ordered buttered popcorn, but stopped himself and ordered plain, hoping Emma might change her mind and snitch some.

"And two medium Diet Pepsis."

He looked to see if she was impressed by her influence on him. Instead, her light complexion paled, as discomfort converted to panic.

"Oh my God! It's Josh Reynolds."

Now she stood so close, Tully had to take a step back to collect their sodas and popcorn.

"Oh God! I hope he didn't see me."

"Who's Josh Reynolds?"

"Just one of the coolest kids in the junior class."

"Let's say hi."

"Dad! Oh God, maybe he didn't see me."

She stood facing Tully, her back to the young, dark-haired boy who was making his way toward them, his destination definitely Emma. And why shouldn't it be? His daughter was a knockout. Tully wondered if Emma was really panicked or if this was part of the game. He honestly had no clue. He didn't understand women, so how could he possibly expect to understand their predecessors?

"Emma? Emma Tully?"

The boy was closing in. Tully watched in amazement as his daughter manufactured a nervous but glowing smile from the twisted panic that had existed just seconds before. She turned just as Josh Reynolds squeezed through the concession line.

"Hi, Josh."

Tully glanced down to check if some impostor had replaced his obstinate daughter. Because this girl's voice was much too cheerful.

"What movie you seeing?"

"Ace of Hearts," she admitted reluctantly though it had been her choice.

"Me too. My mom wants to see it," he added much too quickly.

Tully found himself sympathizing with the boy, who shoved his hands into his pockets. What Emma called cool visibly took effort. Or was Tully the only one who could see the boy nervously tapping his foot and fidgeting? After an awkward silence and them ignoring his presence, Tully said, "Hi, Josh, I'm R. J. Tully, Emma's father."

"Hi, Mr. Tully."

"I'd offer you a hand, but they're both filled."

Out of the corner of his eye he could see Emma roll her eyes. How could that possibly embarrass her? He was being polite. Just then his pager began shrieking. Josh offered to take the sodas before it even occurred to Emma. Tully snapped the noise off, but not before getting several irritated stares. Emma turned a lovely shade of red. At a glance, he recognized the phone number. Of all nights, why tonight?

"I need to make a phone call."

"Are you a doctor or something, Mr. Tully?"

"No, Josh. I'm an FBI agent."

"You're kidding? That is so cool."

The boy's face brightened, and Tully saw that Emma noticed. Instead of heading directly for the phone bank, Tully stalled.

"I work at Quantico, in the Investigative Support Unit. I'm what you'd call a criminal profiler."

"Wow! That is so cool," Josh repeated.

Without looking at her, Tully saw Emma's face change as she watched Josh's reaction.

"So do you track serial killers just like in the movies?"

"I'm afraid the movies make it look more glamorous than it is."

"Geez! I bet you've seen some pretty weird stuff, though, huh?"

"Unfortunately, yes, I have. I really need to make a phone call. Josh, would you mind keeping Emma company for a few minutes?"

"Oh sure. No, problem, Mr. Tully."

He didn't look at Emma again until he was safely at the pay phone. Suddenly, his belligerent daughter was full of smiles, genuine this time. He watched the two teenagers talk and laugh while he dialed the number. For the first time in a long time, he felt happy and glad that Emma was with him. For a few minutes, he had almost forgotten that the world could be cruel and violent, then he heard Assistant Director Cunningham's voice.

"It's Tully, sir. You paged me?"

"Looks like we may have one of Stucky's."

Tully felt instant nausea. He had been anticipating and dreading this call for the last couple of months.

"Where at, sir?"

"Right under our noses. About thirty to forty-five minutes from here. Can you pick me up in about an hour? We can go to the site together."

Without asking, Tully knew Cunningham meant picking him up at Quantico. He wondered if the man ever went home.

"Sure. I'll be there."

"I'll see you in an hour."

This was it. After years of sitting behind a desk in Cleveland and profiling killers from afar, this was his chance to prove himself and join the real hunters. So why did he feel sick to his stomach?

Tully made his way back to his daughter and her friend, anticipating her disappointment.

"I'm sorry, Emma, I've got to leave."

Immediately, her eyes grew dark, her smile slid off her face.

"Josh, did you say you were here with your mom?"

"Yeah, she's getting us popcorn." He pointed to an attractive redhead in the line. When she noticed Josh pointing, she smiled at him and shrugged at the stagnant line in front of her.

"Josh, Emma, would you mind if I ask Josh's mom if Emma could join you for the movie?" Tully steeled himself for his daughter's panic and horror.

"No, that would be cool," Josh said without hesitating, and Emma immediately seemed pleased.

"Sure, Dad," she said.

Tully wondered if she knew how cool she was pretending to be right now.

CHAPTER 11

Tully followed Cunningham's directions and turned at the intersection. Immediately, he saw spotlights in the back alley of a small strip mall. Police cruisers blocked the street, and Tully pulled up beside one, flashed his badge and drove through the maze. He tried to take a lesson from his daughter's new friend Josh by pretending to be cool. Fact was, his stomach felt hollow and perspiration slid down his back.

Tully had seen plenty of crime scenes, severed limbs, bloodied walls, mutilated bodies and sick, disgusting killer signatures that ranged from a single long-stemmed rose to a decapitated corpse. But all those scenes, up until now, had been only in photographs, digital scans and illustrations sent to him at the FBI Cleveland Field Office. He had become one of the Midwest's experts in developing precise criminal profiles from the bits and pieces law enforcement officers sent him. It was his accuracy that had prompted Assistant Director Kyle Cunningham to offer Tully a position at Quantico in the Investigative Support Unit. In one phone call and

When he introduced himself to Jennifer Reynolds, she also seemed pleased to help him out. He offered to repay her another night by treating all of them to another movie. Then he kicked himself when he noticed her wedding band. But Jennifer Reynolds accepted his offer without hesitation, and with a flirtatious look that even an out-of-practice, newly single guy didn't need to decipher. Despite his curiosity, he couldn't help feeling a bit excited.

He smiled all the way to his car, greeting people in the parking lot and jingling his car keys. The evening was still warm and the moon promised to be brilliant despite wisps of clouds. He slid behind the steering wheel and checked his reflection in the rearview mirror, as though he had forgotten the configuration of his face when it was happy. What an unusual feeling, happiness and excitement, and all in the same evening. Two things he hadn't felt in years, though he knew both would be short-lived. He drove out of the theater's parking lot feeling he could take on anything and anyone. Maybe even Albert Stucky.

without ever having met him, Cunningham had offered Tully a chance to work out in the field, starting with the hunt for one of the FBI's most infamous fugitives—Albert Stucky.

Tully knew Cunningham had been forced to dismantle the task force after months of nothing to show for their time and expense. He also knew he owed his good fortune to the agent he had replaced, an agent who had been temporarily assigned to teaching at law enforcement conferences. Without much digging, he discovered the agent was Margaret O'Dell, whom he had never met but knew by reputation. She was one of the youngest and one of the best profilers in the country.

The unofficial word was that O'Dell had burned out and needed a break. Rumors suggested that she had lost her edge, that she was combative and reckless, that she had become paranoid and obsessed with recapturing Albert Stucky. Of course, there were also rumors that Assistant Director Cunningham had sidelined Margaret O'Dell to protect her from Stucky. The two had played a dangerous game of cat and mouse about eight months ago that had eventually led to Stucky's capture, but only after he had tortured and almost killed O'Dell. Now after months of studying, searching and waiting, Tully would finally meet the man nicknamed The Collector, if only through his handiwork.

Tully pulled the car as close to the barricades as he could. Cunningham jumped out before Tully had it in park. He almost forgot to turn off the lights. He noticed his palms were sweaty when he pulled the key from the ignition. His legs seemed stiff, his knee suddenly reminding him of an old injury as he hurried to catch up with his boss. Tully stood four inches taller than the assistant director, and his strides were long, yet it took an effort to keep up. He guessed Cunningham to be at least ten years his senior, but the man had a lean, athletic body, and Tully had witnessed him bench-pressing twice the weight the academy recruits started at.

"Where is she?" Cunningham wasted no time asking a police detective who looked to be in charge.

"She's still in the Dumpster. We haven't moved a thing, except the pizza box."

The detective had a neck as thick as a linebacker's and the seams of his sports jacket bulged. He was treating this like an everyday traffic check. Tully wondered which big city the detective had come from, because he definitely had developed his no-nonsense manner somewhere other than Newburgh Heights. He and the assistant director seemed to know one another and took no time for introductions.

"Where is the pizza box?" Cunningham wanted to know.

"Officer McClusky gave it to the doc. The kid who found it sorta dropped it, and the stuff got all jostled."

Suddenly the smell of stale pizza and the sounds of police radios made Tully's head hurt. During the drive, the adrenaline had pumped him into action. Now the reality was a bit overwhelming. He ran unsteady fingers through his hair. Okay, this couldn't be that much different than looking at photos. He could do this, and he ignored the recurring nausea as he followed his boss to the Dumpster where three uniformed officers stood guard. Even the officers stood a good ten feet away to avoid the stench.

The first thing Tully noticed was the young woman's long blond hair. Immediately, he thought of Emma. He could see over the Dumpster's edge easily, but waited as Cunningham pulled up a crate. His boss's face remained emotionless.

Though covered in garbage, Tully could tell the woman had been young, not much older than Emma. And she had been beautiful. Discarded lettuce and spoiled tomatoes clung to her naked breasts. The rest of her was buried in garbage, but Tully saw glimpses of thigh, and then realized she wore only a blue baseball cap. He could also see that her throat had been slashed from ear to ear, and there was an open wound in her side, almost at her lower back. But that was all. There were no severed limbs, no bloody mutilation. He wasn't sure what he had expected.

"She looks like she's in one piece," Cunningham said as though reading Tully's thoughts. He stepped off the crate and then addressed the detective again. "What was in the box?"

"Not sure. Looked like a bloody glob to me. Doc can probably tell you. He's over in the van."

He pointed to a dusty silver van marked with the Stafford County emblem on the side. The doors were open and a distinguished gray-haired man in a well-pressed suit sat in the back with a clipboard.

"Doc, these gentlemen from the FBI need to see that special delivery."

The detective turned and started to leave just as a media van pulled into an adjacent parking lot.

"Excuse me, gentlemen. Looks like the zoo visitors have arrived."

Cunningham stepped up into the van, and Tully followed, though it seemed crowded with the three of them. Or was Tully the only one having problems breathing? Already he could smell the contents of the box, which sat in the middle of the floor. He sat on one of the benches before his stomach started to churn.

"Hello, Frank." Assistant Director Cunningham knew the medical examiner, too. "This is Special Agent R. J. Tully. Agent Tully, Dr. Frank Holmes, deputy chief medical examiner for Stafford County."

"I don't know if this is your man, Kyle, but when Detective Rosen called me, he seemed to think you might be interested."

"Rosen worked in Boston when Stucky kidnapped Councilwoman Brenda Carson."

"I remember that. What was that two, three years ago?"

"Not quite two."

"Thankfully, I was on vacation. Fishing up in Canada." The doctor cocked his head as though trying to remember some sporting event. Tully found everyone's ease, all the casualness, a bit unnerving. He sat still, hoping no one could hear his heart pounding. The doctor continued. "But now if I remember right, Carson's body was buried in a shallow grave in some woods. Outside Richmond, wasn't it? Certainly not in some Dumpster."

"This guy's complicated, Frank. The ones he collects are the ones we rarely find. These women...these are his rejects. They're simply for sport—for show-and-tell." Cunningham sat forward, leaning his elbows on his knees, the balls of his feet rocking as though ready to jump into action at any moment. Everything about Cunningham telescoped his constant energy, his immediacy. Yet, his face, his voice remained calm, almost soothing.

Tully stared at the pizza box on the floor of the van. Despite the scent of pizza dough and pepperoni, he recognized the acrid scent as blood. So much for eating pizza ever again.

"Nothing happens in this quiet little suburb," Dr. Holmes said while continuing to jot details on the forms he had clipped to his board. "Then two homicides in one day."

"Two?" Cunningham's patience seemed to wear thin with the doctor's slow, deliberate manner. He stared at the pizza box, and Tully knew his boss wouldn't touch it without first being invited to do so by Dr. Holmes. Tully had discovered early on that despite the director's authority, he showed great respect for those he worked with, as well as for rules, policy and protocol.

"I'm not aware of another homicide, Frank," he said when the doctor took too long to offer an explanation.

"Well, I'm not sure the other one is a homicide, yet. We never did find a body." Dr. Holmes finally put the clipboard aside. "We had an agent on the scene. Maybe one of yours?"

"Excuse me?"

"Yesterday afternoon. Not far from here in the nice quiet neighborhood of Newburgh Heights. Said she was a forensic psychologist. Just moved into the victim's neighborhood. Very impressive young woman."

Tully watched Cunningham's face and saw the transformation from calm to agitated.

"Yes, I did hear about that. I had forgotten her new neighborhood was in Newburgh Heights. I apologize if she got in the way."

"Oh, no apology necessary, Kyle. On the contrary, she proved very helpful. I think the arrogant bastard who was supposed to be investigating the scene may have even learned a thing or two."

Tully caught the assistant director with a smile at the corner of his lips, before he realized he was being watched. He turned to Tully and explained, "Agent O'Dell, your predecessor, just bought a new home in this area."

"Agent Margaret O'Dell?" Tully held his boss's eyes until he saw that Cunningham had now made the same connection Tully had just made. Both of them stared at Dr. Holmes as he slid the pizza box closer. Suddenly, Tully knew it didn't matter what they found in the box. Whatever had been discarded, neither of them needed to see the bloody mess to confirm that this was most likely the work of Albert Stucky. And Tully knew it was no coincidence that he had chosen to start again, close to Agent Margaret O'Dell's new home.

CHAPTER 12

Exhaustion seeped into his bones and threatened to incapacitate him by the time he returned to the safety of his room. He shed his clothes with minimal movement, letting the fabric slide off his lean body, though what he really wanted to do was rip and tear. His body disgusted him. It had taken almost twice as long for him to come this time. Of all the fucking things he had to deal with, that one was the most annoying.

His fingers fumbled through his duffel bag, searching frantically, tossing items haphazardly to the floor. Suddenly, he stopped when he felt the smooth cylinder. Relief washed over him, chilling his sweat-drenched body.

The fatigue had moved to his fingers. It took three attempts to snap off the plastic cap and poke the needle into the orange rubber top of the vial. He hated not having complete control. The anger and the irritability only added to his nausea. He steadied his hands as best he could and watched the syringe suck the liquid from the vial.

He sat on the edge of the bed, his knees weak and perspiration sliding down his naked back. In one quick motion he stuck the needle into his thigh, forcing the colorless liquid into his bloodstream. Then he lay back and waited, closing his eyes against the red lines that jetted across his field of vision. In his mind he could hear the blood vessels popping—pop, pop, pop! The thought might drive him completely mad before it drove him completely blind.

Through closed eyelids he was aware of the flickers of lightning that invaded his dimly lit room. A rumble of thunder vibrated the window. Then the rain began again, soft and gentle, tapping out a lullaby.

Yes, his body disgusted him. He had pushed it to be strong and lean, using weights, steel machines and gut-wrenching wind sprints. He ate nutritious meals high in protein and vitamins. He had freed himself of all toxins including caffeine, alcohol and nicotine. Yet, his body still failed him, screaming out its limitations and reminding him of its imperfections.

It had only been three short months since he had noticed any of the symptoms. The first ones were simply annoying, the eternal thirst and the constant urge to piss. Who knew how long this damn thing had been lying dormant inside him, ready to strike at just the right moment.

Of course, it would be this one abnormality that would eventually do him in, a gift from his greedy mother whom he had never even known. The bitch would have to give him something that could destroy him.

He sat up, ignoring the slight dizziness in his head, his vision still blurred. The lapses came more often and were getting harder and harder to predict. Whatever the limitations, he refused to let them interfere with the game.

The rain tapped more persistently now. The lightning came in constant flickers. It made the room crawl with movement. Dusty objects sprang to life, jerky miniature robots. The whole frickin' room jumped and jerked.

He grabbed the lamp on the bedstand and twisted it on, making the movement halt in the yellow glow. In the light, he could see the heap from his spilled duffel bag. Socks, shaving kit, T-shirts, several knives, a scalpel and a Glock 9 mm lay scattered on the plush carpet. He ignored the familiar buzz that had begun to invade his head, and rifled through the mess, stopping when he found the pink panties. He rubbed the soft silk against his bristled jaw, then breathed in their scent, a lovely combination of talcum powder, come and pizza.

He noticed the real estate flyer crumpled under the pile and pulled it out, unfolding it and smoothing its wrinkles. The eight-and-half-by-eleven sheet of paper included a color photo of the beautiful colonial house, a detailed description of its amenities and the shiny blue logo of Heston Realty. The house had definitely lived up to its promises, and he was sure it would continue to do so.

At the bottom corner of the flyer was a small photo of an attractive woman, trying to look professional despite something...what was it in her eyes? There was an insecurity, something that made her look uncomfortable in her cute conservative white blouse and navy blue suit. His thumb rubbed over her face, smudging the ink and dragging a trail of black and blue over her skin. That looked better. Yes, already he could feel her vulnerability. Perhaps he could see and feel it only because he had spent so much time watching her, had taken time to study and examine her. He wondered what it was that Tess McGowan was trying so hard to hide.

He walked across the room, taking slow, deliberate steps deciding not to get angry because his knees were still weak. He tacked the flyer to the bulletin board. Then, as if the memory of Tess and those shapely legs of hers had reminded him, he slid a box out from under the table. Unfortunately, movers were so negligent these days. Going off and taking breaks without tending to the precious possessions left in their care. He smiled as he broke the packaging tape and then flipped off the lid that was marked "M. O'Dell."

He took out the yellowed newspaper clippings: Firefighter Sacrifices Life, Trust Fund Established for Hero. What a horrible way for her to lose her father, in a hellish fire.

"Do you dream about him, Maggie O'Dell?" he whispered. "Do you imagine the flames licking off his skin?"

He wondered if he had finally found an Achilles' heel to the brave, unflinching Special Agent O'Dell.

He set the articles aside. Underneath, he discovered a bigger treasure—a leather appointment book. He flipped to the upcoming week, immediately disappointed. The anger returned as he double-checked the penciled notation. She would be in Kansas City at a law enforcement conference. Then he calmed himself and smiled again. Maybe it was better this way. Still, what a shame Agent O'Dell would miss his debut in Newburgh Heights.

CHAPTER 13

Sunday, March 29

Maggie unpacked the last of the boxes labeled Kitchen, carefully washing, drying and placing the crystal goblets on the top cupboard shelf. It still surprised her that Greg had allowed her the set of eight. He claimed they had been a wedding gift from one of her relatives, though Maggie didn't know anyone remotely related to her who could afford such an expensive gift or have such elegant taste. Her own mother had given them a toaster oven, a practical gift void of sentiment, which more likely reflected the characteristics of the O'Dells she knew.

The goblets reminded her that she needed to call her mother and give her the new phone number. Immediately, she felt the familiar tightness in her chest. Of course, there would be no need for the new address. Her mother rarely left Richmond and wouldn't be visiting any time soon. Maggie cringed at the mere thought of her mother invading this new sanctuary. Even the obligatory phone call felt obtrusive to her quiet Sunday. But she should call before leaving for the airport. After years, flying still unhinged her, so why not take her mind off being out of control at thirty thousand feet with a conversation that was sure to clench her teeth?

Her fingers moved reluctantly over the numbers. How could this woman still make her feel like a twelve-year-old caretaker, vulnerable and anxious? Yet, Maggie had been more mature and competent at twelve than her mother ever was.

The phone rang six, seven times, and Maggie was ready to hang up when a low, raspy voice muttered something incomprehensible.

"Mom? It's Maggie," she said in place of a greeting.

"Mag-pie, I was just going to call you."

Maggie grimaced, hearing her mother use the nickname her father had given her. The only time her mother called her Mag-pie was when she was drunk. Now Maggie wished she could just hang up. Her mother couldn't call her without the new number. Maybe she wouldn't even remember this call.

"You wouldn't have gotten me, Mom. I just moved."

"Mag-pie, I want you to tell your father to stop calling me."

Maggie's knees buckled. She leaned against the counter.

"What are you talking about, Mom?"

"Your father keeps calling me, saying stuff and then just hanging up."

The counter wasn't good enough. Maggie made it to the step stool and sat down. The sudden nausea and chill surprised and annoyed her. She placed her palm against her stomach as if that would calm it.

"Mom, Dad's gone. He's been dead for over twenty years." She gripped a kitchen towel, the nearest thing she could lay her hands on. My God, could this be some new dementia brought on by the drinking?

"Oh, I know that, sweetie." Her mother giggled.

Maggie couldn't ever remember her mother giggling. Was this a sick joke? She closed her eyes and waited, not sure there would be an explanation, but certain she had no idea how to continue this conversation.

"Reverend Everett says it's because your father still has something he needs to tell me. But hell, he keeps hanging up. Oh, I shouldn't swear," and she giggled, again.

"Mom, who's Reverend Everett?"

"Reverend Joseph Everett. I told you about him, Mag-pie."

"No, you haven't told me anything about him."

"I'm sure I have. Oh, Emily and Steven are here. I've got to go."

"Mom, wait. Mom..." But it was too late. Her mother had already hung up.

Maggie dragged her fingers through her short hair, resisting the urge to yank. It had only been a week...okay, maybe two weeks, since she had talked to her last. How could she be making so little sense? She thought about calling her back. She hadn't even given her the new phone number. But then her mother wasn't in any condition to remember it. Maybe Emily and Steven or Reverend Everett—whoever the hell these people were—maybe they could take care of her. Maggie had been taking care of her mother for far too long. Maybe it was finally someone else's turn.

The fact her mother was drinking again didn't surprise Maggie. Years ago, she had accepted the compromise. At least when her mother was drinking she wasn't attempting suicide. But that her mother thought she was talking to her dead husband disturbed Maggie. Plus, she hated the reminder that the one person who had truly loved her, loved her unconditionally, had been dead for more than twenty years.

Maggie tugged the chain around her neck and brought out the medallion from under her shirt collar. Her father had given her the silver cross for her First Holy Communion, claiming it would protect her from evil. Yet, Maggie couldn't help remembering that his own identical cross had not saved him when he ran into that burning building. She often wondered if he had honestly believed it would protect him.

Since then Maggie had witnessed enough evil to know that a body armor of silver crosses would never be enough to protect her. Instead, she wore the medallion out of remembrance for her brave father. The medal against her chest dangled between her breasts and often felt as cool and hard as a knife blade. She let it remind her that there was a fine line between good and evil.

In the last nine years she had learned plenty about evil, its power to destroy completely, to leave behind empty shells that once were warm, breathing individuals. All those lessons were meant to train her to fight it, to control it, to eventually annihilate it. But in doing so, it was necessary to follow evil, to live as evil lives, to think as evil thinks. Was it possible that somewhere along the way evil had invaded her without her realizing it? Was that why she felt so much hatred, so much need for vengeance? Was that why she felt so hollow?

The doorbell rang, and again Maggie had her Smith & Wesson in her hand before she realized it. She tucked the revolver into what was becoming its regular spot, the back waistband of her jeans. Absentmindedly, she pulled down her T-shirt to conceal it.

She didn't recognize the petite brunette standing on her front portico. Maggie's eyes searched the street, the expanse between houses, the shadows created by trees and bushes before she moved to disarm the security system. She wasn't sure what she expected. Did she honestly believe Albert Stucky would have followed her to her new house?

"Yes?" she asked, opening the door only wide enough to place her body in the space.

"Hi!" the woman said with a false cheerfulness.

Dressed in a black-and-white knit cardigan and matching skirt, she looked ready for an evening out. Her dark shoulder-length hair didn't dare move in the breeze. Her makeup enhanced thin lips and concealed laugh lines. The diamond necklace, earrings and wedding ring were modest and tasteful, but Maggie recognized how expensive they were. Okay, so at least the woman wasn't trying to sell anything. Still, Maggie waited while the woman's eyes darted around her, hoping for a glimpse beyond the front door.

"I'm Susan Lyndell. I live next door." She pointed to the split-timber house, only a corner of its front roof visible from Maggie's portico.

"Hello, Ms. Lyndell."

"Oh, please call me Susan."

"I'm Maggie O'Dell."

Maggie opened the door a few inches more and offered her hand, but stayed solidly in the doorway. Surely the woman didn't expect an invitation inside. Then she caught her new neighbor glance toward her own house and back at the street. It was a nervous, anxious look, as though she was afraid of being seen.

"I saw you on Friday." She sounded uncomfortable, and it was obvious she wasn't here to welcome Maggie to the neighborhood. There was something else on her mind.

"Yes, I moved in on Friday."

"Actually I didn't see you move in," she said, quick to make the distinction. "I mean at Rachel's. I saw you at Rachel Endicott's house." The woman stepped closer and kept her voice soft and calm even though her hands were now gripping the hem of her cardigan.

"Oh."

"I'm a friend of Rachel's. I know that the police..." She stopped and glanced this time in both directions. "I know they're saying Rachel may have just left on her own, but I don't think she would do that."

"Did you tell Detective Manx that?"

"Detective Manx?"

"He's in charge of the investigation, Ms. Lyndell. I was simply there trying to lend a hand as a concerned neighbor."

"But you're with the FBI, right? I thought I heard someone say that."

"Yes, but I wasn't there in an official capacity. If you have any information, I suggest you talk to Detective Manx."

All Maggie needed was to step on Manx's toes again. Cunningham had already questioned her competency, her judgment. She wouldn't let some prick like Manx make matters worse. However, Susan Lyndell didn't seem pleased with Maggie's advice. Instead, she stalled, fidgeting, her eyes darting around while she seemed to become more and more agitated.

"I know this is an awkward introduction, and I certainly apologize, but if I could just talk to you for a few minutes. May I come in?"

Her gut told her to send Susan Lyndell home, to insist she call the police and talk to Manx. Yet, for some reason she found herself letting the woman into her foyer, but no farther.

"I have a flight to catch later this afternoon," Maggie allowed impatience to show in her voice. "As you can see I haven't had time to unpack, let alone pack for a business trip."

"Yes, I understand. It's quite possible I'm simply being paranoid."

"You don't believe Ms. Endicott just left town for a couple of days? Maybe to get away?

Susan Lyndell's eyes met Maggie's and held her.

"I know there was something...something in the house that suggests Rachel didn't do that."

"Ms. Lyndell, I don't know what you've heard—"

"It's okay." She stopped Maggie with a wave of a small hand, long slender fingers that reminded Maggie of a bird's wing. "I know you can't divulge anything you may have seen." She fidgeted again, shifting her weight from one foot to another as though her high-heeled pumps were the cause of her discomfort. "Look, I don't have to be a rocket scientist to know that it's not routine for three police cruisers and the county medical examiner to come rescue an injured dog. Even if it belongs to the wife of Sidney Endicott."

Maggie didn't recognize the man's name nor did she care. The less she knew about the Endicotts, the easier it would be to keep out of this case. She crossed her arms over her chest and waited. Susan Lyndell seemed to interpret it as having Maggie's full attention.

"I think Rachel was meeting someone. I think this someone may have taken her against her will."

"Why do you say that?"

"Rachel met a man last week."

"What do you mean she met a man?"

"I don't want you to get the wrong impression. It's not something she's in the habit of doing." She said this quickly, as if needing to justify her friend's actions. "It just sort of happened. You know how that is." She waited for some sign of agreement from Maggie. When there was none, she hurried on. "Rachel said there was this...well, she described the guy as wild and exciting. It was

strictly a physical attraction. I'm sure she had no intention of ever leaving Sidney," she added as though needing to convince herself.

"Ms. Endicott was having an affair?"

"Oh God, no, but I think she was tempted. As far as I know, it was just some heavy-duty flirting."

"How do you know all this?"

Susan avoided Maggie's eyes, pretending to watch outside the window.

"Rachel and I were friends."

Maggie didn't point out that Susan had suddenly switched to past tense. "How did she meet him?" she asked, instead.

"He's been working in the area for the last week or so. On the phone lines. Something to do with new cable that's going to be laid. I haven't heard much about it. It seems like they're constantly putting in something new and different in this area."

"Why do think this man may have taken Rachel against her will?"

"It sounded like he was getting serious, trying to escalate their flirting. You know how guys like that can be. They really just want one thing. And for some reason they always seem to think us lonely, rich wives are more than ready to let them—" She stopped herself, realizing she may have revealed more than she intended. Immediately, she looked away, her face a bit flushed, and Maggie knew Susan Lyndell was no longer talking about her friend, but speaking from experience. "Well, let's just say," she continued, "that I have a hunch this guy wanted more from Rachel than she meant to give him."

The image of the bedroom came to Maggie. Had Rachel Endicott invited a telephone repairman to her bedroom and then changed her mind?

"So you think she may have invited him in and that things got carried away?"

"Isn't there something in the house that makes it look that way?"

Maggie hesitated. Were Susan Lyndell and Rachel Endicott really friends, or was Susan simply looking for some juicy gossip to share with the other neighbors?

Finally Maggie said, "Yes, there is something that makes it look like Rachel was taken from the house. That's all I can tell you."

Susan paled beneath the carefully applied makeup and leaned against the wall as though needing the support. This time, her response seemed genuine.

"I think you need to tell the police," Maggie told her again.

"No," she said quickly, and immediately her face grew scarlet. "I mean, I...I'm not even sure she met him. I wouldn't want Rachel to get in trouble with Sid."

"Then you need to at least tell them about the telephone repairman so they can question him. Have you seen him in the area?"

"Actually, I've never seen him. Just his van once—Northeastern Bell Telephone Company. I'd hate to have him lose his job because of my hunch."

Maggie studied the woman who clutched and wrung the hem of her cardigan. Susan Lyndell didn't care about some nameless repairman's job.

"Then why are you telling me all this, Ms. Lyndell? What do you expect me to do?"

"I just thought...well..." She leaned against the wall again, and seemed flustered that she had no clue what she expected. Yet, she made a weak effort to continue. "You're with the FBI. I thought maybe you could find out or do a check...you know, discreetly without...well, I guess I don't know."

Maggie let the silence hang between them as she examined the woman's discomfort, her embarrassment.

"Rachel's not the only one who's flirted with a repairman, is she, Ms. Lyndell? Are you afraid of your husband finding out? Is that it?"

She didn't need to answer. The anguished look in Susan Lyndell's eyes told Maggie she was right. And she wondered if Ms. Lyndell would even call Detective Manx, though she promised to as she turned and left, hurrying away, her head pivoting with worried glances.

CHAPTER 14

Tess McGowan smiled at the wine steward who waited patiently. Daniel had rambled on into the cellular phone the whole time the tall young man had uncorked the bottle and poured the obligatory amount for the taste test. At first, when he noticed Daniel on the phone, he had offered the glass to Tess. She quickly shook her head. Without a word, she directed the steward to Daniel with her eyes, so as not to embarrass the inexperienced man, whose smooth, boyish face still blushed.

Now they both waited. She hated all the interruptions. It was bad enough they were having an unusually late Sunday dinner because of Daniel's business dealings. Why couldn't he, at least, take Sundays off? She fingered the long-stemmed rose he had brought her, and found herself wishing that just once he could be more creative. Why not some violets or a clump of daisies?

Finally, Daniel firmly, but calmly, called the person on the other end of the line "an incompetent asshole." Fortunately for Tess and the wine steward, that was his closing.

He snapped the cellular phone in half and slipped it into his breast pocket. Without looking up, he grabbed the glass, sipped then spit the wine back without giving it a swirl in his mouth.

"This is sewer water. I asked for a 1984 Bordeaux. What the hell is this crap?"

Tess felt her nerves tense in anticipation. Not again. Why couldn't they ever go out without Daniel making a scene. She watched the poor wine steward twist the bottle around, desperate to read the label.

"It *is* a 1984 Bordeaux, sir."

Daniel snatched the bottle from the young man's hands and took a look. Immediately, he snorted under his breath and handed it back.

"I don't want a goddamn California wine."

"But you said domestic, sir."

"Yes, and as far as I remember, New York is still in the United States."

"Yes, of course, sir. I'll bring another bottle."

"So," Daniel said, letting her know he was ready to talk to her though his hands rearranged his silverware and folded the napkin in his lap. "You said we had something to celebrate?"

She pushed up her dress strap, wondering why she had spent two hundred and fifty dollars on a dress that wouldn't stay up on her. A sexy, black dress that Daniel hadn't noticed. Even when he looked up at her, he raised an eyebrow at her fumbling instead of at the dress, and instantly he frowned at her. Dear God, she didn't need another lecture about fidgeting in public. The man spent more time rearranging his dinnerware than he did eating, and yet, he felt he could lecture her about fidgeting. She pretended not to notice his frown and launched into her good news. If she kept enthusiastic, he couldn't possibly ruin this night for her. Could he?

"I sold the Saunders' house last week."

His brow furrowed, reminding her that he didn't have time to remember where the hell each of her clients lived.

"It's the huge Tudor on the north side. But the best part is that Delores is letting me keep the entire selling bonus."

"Well, that *is* good news, Tess. We should be having champagne and not wine." He turned in his chair, going into what looked like a search-and-destroy mode. "Where the hell is that incompetent imbecile?"

"No, Daniel, don't."

He scowled at her for squelching his noble gesture, and she hurried to correct it.

"You know I enjoy wine much more than champagne. Please, let's have wine."

He raised his hands in mock defeat. "Whatever pleases you. Tonight is your night."

He began to sip from his water glass but stopped, grabbed his napkin and wiped at the water spots. Tess braced herself for another scene, but Daniel managed to get the glass in satisfactory condition on his own. He replaced his napkin and the glass without taking a sip.

"So, how much is this selling bonus? I hope you didn't spend it all on that overpriced frock that won't stay on your shoulders."

She felt the heat crawl up her neck before she had a chance to contain it.

"Of course not." She kept her voice strong and managed a quick smile, pretending to enjoy his savage attempt at what he called dry humor.

"So? How much?" he wanted to know.

"Almost ten thousand dollars," she said, holding up her chin proudly.

"Well, that is a nice little chunk of change for you, isn't it?"

This time he sipped his water without cleaning the glass. Already his eyes darted around the room, looking for familiar faces. She knew it was a sort of professional habit and not meant to be rude, but each time, she felt as though he was hoping to be rescued from a mundane conversation with her.

"Do you think I should invest it?" she asked, hoping to bring his attention back to her with the one topic he loved to discuss.

"What's that, sweetie?" His eyes only glanced at her. He had spotted a couple he seemed to know at the reservation stand, waiting for their table.

"The bonus. Do you think I should invest it in the stock market?"

This time he looked back at her with that smile she immediately recognized as the beginning of another lesson.

"Tess, ten thousand dollars really isn't enough for you to be getting into the market. Maybe a nice little CD or less risky mutual fund. You really don't want to mess with something you don't understand."

Before she could protest, his cellular phone started ringing. Daniel quickly flipped it out of his pocket as though it were the most important thing in the room. Tess pushed up her strap. Why kid herself. The damn phone *was* the most important thing in the room.

The wine steward returned, glanced at Daniel on the phone again, and Tess wanted to laugh at the young man's pained expression.

"Why the hell is it so hard to fucking get this right?" Daniel barked into the phone loud enough for other diners to look over. "No, no, forget it. I'll do it myself."

He slapped the phone shut and was on his feet before he had it tucked back into his pocket.

"Tess, sweetie, I need to go take care of something. These idiots can't seem to get one fucking thing right." He pulled out a credit card and slipped out two hundred-dollar bills from his money clip. "Please have a shamefully expensive dinner to celebrate your bonus. And you don't mind taking a cab home, do you?"

He handed her the credit card and the folded bills. He pecked her on the cheek and then left before she could object. But she noticed he had enough time to stop at the door and talk to the couple he had seen earlier.

Suddenly, she realized the wine steward was still at the table and now staring at her, stunned and waiting for her instructions.

"I think I'd like the bill, please.

He continued to stare, then held up the uncorked bottle. "I didn't even pour one glass."

"Enjoy it later with the other waiters."

"Are you serious?"

"I'm serious. On me. Really. Oh, and before you bring the bill, would you add two of the most expensive entrées you have on the menu."

"You want them as takeout?"

"Oh no. I don't want them at all. I just want to pay for them." She smiled and held up the credit card. Finally, he seemed to get the message, smiled back and hurried off to take care of it.

If Daniel insisted on treating her like a hooker, she could certainly accommodate him. Maybe her silly little mind couldn't possibly comprehend something as complex as the stock market, but there were plenty of other things she knew about that Daniel didn't have a clue about.

She signed the bill for the wine steward, making sure to add a hefty tip for him. Then she took her two hundred dollars and hailed a cab, hoping the anger would burn off by the time she got home. How could he ruin this for her? She had been looking forward to a celebration. Maybe ten thousand dollars was a drop in the bucket for Daniel, but for her it was a tremendous accomplishment in a long journey uphill. She deserved a pat on the back. She deserved a celebration. Instead, she had a long, lonely cab ride home from D.C.

"Excuse me," she said, leaning forward in the stale-smelling cab. "When we get to Newburgh Heights, forget the address I gave you. Take me to Louie's Bar and Grill on Fifty-fifth and Laurel."

CHAPTER 15

Kansas City, Missouri
Sunday evening

It was almost midnight when Agents Preston Turner and Richard Delaney knocked on Maggie's hotel-room door.

"How 'bout a nightcap, O'Dell?"

Turner wore blue jeans and a purple golf shirt that enhanced the rich brown of his skin. Delaney, on the other hand, still wore a suit, his lopsided tie and open collar the only indications that he was no longer on duty.

"I don't know, guys. It's late." Not that sleep mattered. She knew she wouldn't be going to bed for hours.

"It's not even midnight." Turner grinned at her. "Party's just gettin' started. Besides, I'm starved." He glanced back at Delaney for reassurance. Delaney only shrugged. Five years older than both Turner and Maggie, Delaney had a wife and two kids. Maggie imagined Delaney had been a conservative Southern gentleman even when he was ten years old, but somehow Turner managed to bring out a reckless competitive side.

Both men noticed that Maggie had answered the door with her Smith & Wesson gripped firmly in her right hand, dropped at her side. However, neither mentioned it. Suddenly it felt extra heavy. She wondered why they put up with her, though she knew Cunningham purposely assigned the three of them to the same conferences. They had been her shadows since Stucky had escaped last October. When she complained to Cunningham, he had been insulted by her accusation that he was providing watchdogs to make certain she didn't go after Stucky on her own. Only later did it occur to her that her boss might do so in an attempt to protect her. Which was ridiculous. If Albert Stucky wanted to hurt her, no show of force would stop him.

"You know you guys don't need to baby-sit me."

Turner pretended to be wounded and said, "Come on, Maggie, you know us better than that."

Yes, she did. Despite their mission, Turner and Delaney had never singled her out as some damsel in distress. Maggie had spent years working to be treated like one of the guys. Perhaps that's why Cunningham's motive, however honorable or well intentioned, still angered her.

"Ah, come on, Maggie," Delaney finally joined in. "Knowing you, your presentation is all ready for tomorrow."

Delaney politely stayed in the hallway while Turner leaned against the door frame as though taking up permanent residence until she agreed.

"Let me get my jacket."

She closed the door enough to make Turner retreat into the hall and give her some privacy. She strapped on her holster, looping the leather contraption over her shoulder and buckling it tight against her side. Then she slid her revolver in and put on a navy blazer to hide the bulge.

Turner was right. The nearby bar and grill in what was called Westport buzzed with late-night conventioneers. Turner explained that the midtown Bohemian district, which still showed quaint signs of its early days as a trading post, was "KC's nightlife hub." How Turner always knew these details Maggie had never bothered to find out. It did seem as if Turner quickly became the expert at finding the hot spots in every city they visited.

Delaney led the way, squeezing through the crowd along the bar and finding a table in a dark corner. Only when he and Maggie sat down did they realize they had lost Turner, who had stopped to talk to a couple of young women perched on bar stools. From their tight knit dresses and shiny dangling earrings, Maggie took a wild guess that they weren't law enforcement officers, but rather a couple of single women looking to meet a man with a badge.

"How does he do that so easily?" Delaney asked, watching and admiring.

Maggie glanced around while she scooted her chair against the wall so she could see the entire room. She hated having her back to a crowd. Actually, she hated crowds. Clouds of cigarette smoke hung over the room like fog settled in for the evening. The din of voices and laughter blended together, making it necessary to speak louder than comfortable. And though she would be with Turner and Delaney, she hated the looks thrown her way, some of which reminded her of vultures waiting for their prey to be left alone and vulnerable.

"You know, even when I was single, I hated dating," Delaney confessed, still watching his buddy. "But Turner makes it all look so easy." He twisted his chair closer to the table and leaned in as though ready to give Maggie his full attention. "So what about you? Are you thinking about getting back into the game?"

"The game?" She had no idea what he was talking about.

"The dating game. What's it been? Three, four months?"

"The divorce isn't final yet. I just moved out of the condo on Friday."

"I didn't realize the two of you were still living together. I thought you broke up months ago."

"We did. It was more practical for both of us to live there until things were settled. Neither one of us is hardly ever there."

"Shoot! For a minute there I thought maybe the two of you were thinking about giving it another shot." He looked hopeful. She knew Delaney was a firm believer in marriage. Despite admiring his partner's finesse at dating, Delaney seemed to love being married.

"I don't think reconciliation is possible."

"You sure?"

"What would you do if Karen made you choose between her and being in the FBI?"

He shook his head, and before he answered she was sorry she'd asked. He pulled his chair closer and his face got serious. "Part of the reason I became an instructor was because I know Karen gets nervous about me being in the middle of hostage negotiations. That last one in Philly, she had to watch most of it on TV. Some sacrifices are worth making."

She didn't want to have this conversation. Discussing her failed marriage accomplished nothing these days except to remind her of the hollowness in her gut.

"So I'm the bad guy because I'm not willing to sacrifice my career to make my husband feel better?" The anger in her voice surprised her. "I would never ask Greg to stop being a lawyer."

"Relax, Maggie. You're not the bad guy." Delaney remained calm and sympathetic. "There's a big difference between asking and expecting. Karen would never have asked. *I* made the decision. Besides, Greg's got some major screws loose if he would let you get away, period."

Her eyes met his, and he smiled, then quickly looked back around to see that Turner was still with his new friends. Though Delaney, Turner and Maggie spent hours together, week after week, there were usually no emotional revelations or personal discussions.

"Do you miss it?"

He glanced back at her and laughed. "What's to miss? Standing in freezing-cold or stinking-hot weather for hours, trying to talk some asshole out of blowing away innocent people?" He rested his elbows on the table and scratched his jaw, his eyes serious again. "Yeah, I do miss it. But I get called in on a case every now and then."

"What can I get you two?" a waitress asked as she squeezed between two diners to get to their table.

Immediately, Maggie felt a wave of relief, welcoming the interruption. She saw Delaney's face relax, too.

"Just Diet Coke for me." He smiled up at the pretty redhead.

Maggie was impressed with his unconscious flirting. Had it simply become a habit from hanging around Turner so long?

"Scotch, neat," she said when the waitress looked her way.

"Oh, and that guy over at the end of the bar—" Delaney pointed "—it doesn't look like it now, but he will eventually be joining us. Is your grill still on?"

The waitress checked her watch. A small beauty mark above her upper lip twitched as she scrunched her eyes to make out the time. In the dim light, Maggie could see the lines of exhaustion in the woman's attractive face.

"They're supposed to close down at midnight." She kept her voice friendly though Maggie could tell it was an effort. "There are still a few minutes if I get it in now." Her offer was genuine. "Any idea what he wants?"

"A burger and fries," Delaney said without hesitation.

"Medium rare," Maggie added.

"With pickles and onion."

"And a bottle of A.1 sauce, if you have it."

"Oh, and cheddar cheese on the burger, too."

The waitress smiled at them. Maggie glanced at Delaney, and they burst out laughing.

"God, I wonder if Turner realizes how predictable he is?" Maggie said while wondering if there was anyone who paid as much attention to her habits and quirks.

"It sounds like the three of you are very good friends." The waitress had relaxed, looking a little less fatigued. "I don't suppose you know what he'll be drinking?"

"Do you have Boulevard Wheat?" Delaney asked.

"Of course. Actually, it's a Kansas City brew."

"Okay. Well, that's what he'll want."

"I'll get his order in and bring back your drinks. Sure I can't get either of you something to eat?"

"Maggie?" Delaney waited for her to shake her head. "Maybe some fries for me."

"You got it."

"Thanks, Rita," Delaney added as though they were old friends.

As soon as she left their table, Maggie gave Delaney's shoulder a shove. "I thought you said you weren't good at this stuff?"

"What stuff?"

"This flirting stuff. Usually Turner's doing it, so I don't get to see the real master at work."

"I don't have any idea what you're talking about." But it was obvious from his grin that he was enjoying the attention.

"'Thanks, Rita'?"

"That's her name, Maggie. That's why they wear those name tags, so we can all share a friendly meal."

"Oh, right, only she never gets to know our names or sit down and eat with us. How friendly is that?"

"Hey, guys." Turner slid into the last chair. "Lots of attorneys here this time."

"Those two women are attorneys?" Delaney craned his neck to get a better look.

"You betcha." He waved a piece of paper with their phone numbers before tucking it into his pocket. "And I never know when I might need an attorney."

"Yeah, right. Like the three of you were talking legal matters."

Maggie ignored their banter and simply asked, "What conference is this anyway?"

Both men stopped and stared at her as if waiting for the punch line.

"You're serious?" Turner finally asked.

"Hey, I make the same presentation every time, whether I'm in Kansas City or Chicago or L.A."

"You really don't get into these things, do you?"

"It's definitely not why I joined the FBI." Suddenly she felt uncomfortable with both of them studying her as if she had slipped and said something wrong. "Besides, Cunningham keeps my name off the program roster, so it's not like anyone is coming specifically to hear me and my words of wisdom."

She had interrupted their jovial moods, reminding them why she was really here. Not because she longed to teach profiling to a bunch of cops, but to keep her out of the field, away from Albert Stucky. Rita returned, relieving Maggie once again, this time with a tray of drinks. Turner immediately raised his eyebrows at her when she placed the bottle of beer and a glass in front of him.

"Rita, you're a mind reader." He wasted no time using her name just as Delaney had, as if they, too, were old friends.

The pretty waitress blushed, and Maggie watched Delaney, searching for signs of rivalry. Instead, he seemed pleased to leave the flirting to his single friend.

"Your burger and fries should be ready in about ten minutes."

"Oh my God! Rita, will you marry me?"

"Actually, you should thank your friends. They got the order in just before Carl closed the grill." She smiled at Maggie and Delaney this time. "I'll bring out the rest of the order as soon as it's ready." Then she hurried away.

Maggie couldn't help thinking that Rita was a seasoned waitress who already knew which of her customers were the big tippers. Turner rewarded his waiters and waitresses with attention and familiarity, but it was Maggie or Delaney who remembered to leave a substantial tip.

"So, Turner," Delaney said. "Why are there attorneys at this conference?"

"Mostly prosecutors. Sounds like they're all here for that computer workshop. You know, the database thing the Bureau's been setting up. Lots of D.A. offices are finally getting connected. At least in the bigger cities. And since they're all *sooooo* very busy, and can never spare an experienced attorney, it looks like they've sent their fresh young things." He sat back and surveyed the room.

Maggie and Delaney shook their heads at each other. Just as Maggie tipped back her glass, she saw a familiar figure in the long mirror that stretched behind the bar. She slammed her glass down and stood, sending the table rocking and her chair screeching. She looked over in the direction from where she thought the mirror had reflected the image.

"Maggie, what is it?"

Turner and Delaney stared at her as she stretched to see over the bar patrons. Was it her imagination?

"Maggie?"

She checked the mirror again. The figure in the black leather jacket was gone.

"What's going on, Maggie?"

"Nothing," she said quickly. "I'm fine." Of course she was fine. Yet her eyes searched for and found the door. There was no man in a long, black leather jacket coming or going.

She sat down, pulling her chair in and avoiding her friends' eyes. They were getting used to her jumpy, erratic behavior. Soon, she'd be like the little boy who cried wolf, and no one would pay any attention. Maybe that was exactly what he wanted.

She grabbed her glass and watched the amber liquid swirl. Had it only been her imagination? Had she really seen Albert Stucky or was she simply losing her mind?

CHAPTER 16

He waited for her at the rear exit, knowing this was the door she would use when she was finally ready to leave. The alley was dark. The brick buildings stood tall enough to block out any moonlight. A few bare lightbulbs glowed above some of the back doors. The bulbs were dull, covered with bug shit and swarmed by moths, but still his eyes stung when he looked at them directly. He tucked his sunglasses into his jacket pocket and checked his watch.

Only three cars remained in the small parking lot. One was his, and he knew neither of the other two belonged to her. He knew she wouldn't be driving this night. He had decided to offer her a ride, but would she accept?

He knew how to be charming. That was simply a part of the game, a part of his disguise. If he was to take on this new identity, he would need to play the role that came with it. And out of the two of them, women always preferred him to Albert.

Yes, he knew what women liked to hear, and he didn't mind telling them. In fact, he enjoyed it. It was part of the manipulation, an integral piece of the puzzle to gaining complete control. He had discovered that even strong, independent women didn't mind giving up control to a man they found charming. What silly, wonderful creatures. Maybe he would give her his sad story about his failing eyesight. Women loved being caretakers. They loved to play roles of their own.

The challenge excited him, and he could feel his erection swelling. He would have no trouble tonight. Now, if he could just wait. He must be patient—patient and charming. Could he be charming enough to get her to invite him home with her? Already, he tried to imagine what her bedroom looked like.

A door screeched open halfway down the alley, and he stepped into the shadows. A short, burly guy in a stained apron came out to toss several trash bags into the Dumpster. He lingered, lighting a cigarette and sucking in several quick drags before stomping it out and going back in.

Most of the other places had closed. He didn't worry about being seen. If anyone noticed him, he could tell them almost anything, and they would believe it. People heard what they wanted to hear. Sometimes it was too easy. Though if he had guessed right, she would be a bit of a challenge. She was much older, much more street savvy than the cute little pizza girl. He would need to do some serious talking to get her to trust him. He would need to pour on the charm, compliment her and make her laugh. Again, he could feel his erection as he thought of winning her over, wondering how far he could go.

Perhaps he would start with a gentle touch, a simple caress of her face. He'd pretend he was getting a strand of her lovely hair out of her eyes or tell her she had an eyelash on her cheek. She would think him concerned, attentive and sensitive to her needs. Women loved that crap.

Suddenly the door opened, and there she was. She hesitated, looking around first. She checked the sky. A light mist had begun about fifteen minutes ago. She popped open a bright red umbrella and started walking quickly toward the street. Red was definitely her color.

He waited, giving her a head start, while he reached down and checked the scalpel, safe in its custom-made, leather sheath, and tucked inside his boot. He caressed its handle, his fingers lingering, but he left it there. Then he followed her down the alley.

CHAPTER 17

Monday, March 30

Tess McGowan awoke with a splitting headache. Sunlight streamed through her bedroom blinds like lasers. Damn it! She had gone to bed again without removing her contact lenses. She threw her arm over her eyes. Why hadn't she gotten the type she could leave in forever? She hated this recent reminder of her age. Thirty-five was not old. Okay, so she had squandered her twenties. She wasn't doing the same with her thirties.

Suddenly she realized she was naked beneath the covers. And then she felt the sticky mess beside her. Alarmed, she pushed herself up, keeping the bedsheets to her breasts, searching the room through blurred vision for clues.

Why couldn't she remember Daniel being here? He never stayed over at her house. He said it was too quaint. She noticed her clothes in a tangled mess on the chair across the room. Heaped on the floor next to the chair were what looked like men's trousers, the tips of shoes peeking out from underneath. A black leather bomber jacket hung from the doorknob. She didn't recognize it as anything Daniel would wear. That's when she heard the shower, aware of its sound only as the water stopped. Her pulse quickened as she tried to remember something, anything, from last night.

She checked the bedside stand. It was eight forty-five. Somehow she remembered it was Monday morning. She knew she didn't have any appointments on Mondays, but Daniel would. Why couldn't she remember him coming over? Why couldn't she remember herself coming home?

Think, Tess! She rubbed her temples.

Daniel had left the restaurant and she had taken a cab home, but of course she hadn't gone straight home. The last thing she did remember was doing tequila shooters at Louie's. Had she called Daniel to pick her up? Why couldn't she remember? And would he be furious if she asked him to fill in the blanks? Obviously he hadn't been angry with her last night, and she shifted away from the damp spot.

She laid her head back on the pillows, squeezing her eyes shut and wishing the throbbing would stop threatening to split her head open.

"Good morning, Tess," a rich, deep voice came into the room.

Before she could open her eyes, she knew the voice didn't belong to Daniel. In a panic she sat up again and pushed her back against the headboard. The tall, lean stranger with only a blue towel wrapped around his waist looked startled and concerned.

"Tess?" he said softly. "You okay?"

Then she remembered, as if a dam broke loose in her brain, releasing the memories in a flood. He had been at Louie's, watching her from the corner table, handsome and quiet, so very unlike anyone who frequented Louie's. How could she have brought him into her home?

"Tess, you're starting to scare me."

His concern seemed genuine. At least she hadn't brought home a mass murderer. But then, how in the world did she think she'd know the difference? With his hair still wet, he looked harmless, wrapped in only a towel. Immediately she noticed his hard, firm body and realized he would be strong enough to overpower her without much effort. How could she have been so foolish?

"I'm sorry. I...you startled me." She tried to keep the alarm from her voice.

He grabbed his trousers from the floor but stopped suddenly before putting them on as if something had just occurred to him.

"Oh Christ! You don't remember, do you?"

Beneath the morning bristles, his boyish face looked embarrassed. He fumbled into his trousers, stumbling once and accidentally dropping the towel before the trousers were all the way up. Tess watched, flustered and annoyed that his muscular body was turning her on, despite her confusion. She should be worried he could hurt her, instead she found herself wondering how young he was. And dear God, why couldn't she remember his name?

"I should have known you had too much to drink," he apologized as he frantically searched for his shirt, going through her things and carefully folding them as he put them back on the chair. He stopped at her bra, and his embarrassment only grew. His distraught politeness made her smile. When he glanced over at her, he did a double take, startled by her expression. He sank into the chair, now ignoring her clothes and absently wringing his hands and her bra without realizing it.

"I'm a complete idiot, aren't I?"

"No, not at all." She smiled again, and his obvious discomfort relaxed her. She sat up, keeping the sheet carefully pressed against her as she drew her knees up to her chest and placed her arms on top to rest her chin.

"It's just that I don't do this sort of thing," she tried to explain. "At least, not anymore."

"I don't usually do this sort of thing at all." He noticed her bra in his hands, folded it and set it on the nearby bookcase. "So you really don't remember any of last night?"

"I remember you watching me. I remember being very attracted to you." Her revelation surprised her almost as much as it surprised him.

"That's it?" He looked wounded.

"Sorry."

Finally, he grinned and shrugged. She couldn't believe how comfortable she felt with him. There was no more panic, no more alarm. The only tension seemed to be the obvious sexual attraction, which she tried to ignore. He didn't look as if he was even thirty. And he was a stranger, for heaven's sake. She wanted to kick herself. Dear God! How could she have been so reckless? Had she not changed at all after all this time?

"If I ever find my shirt, could I maybe take you to lunch?"

Then she remembered Daniel. How would she explain any of this to Daniel? She felt the sapphire ring he had given her stabbing into the soft underside of her chin, like some painful reminder. What was wrong with her? Daniel was a mature, respectable businessman. Sure, he was arrogant and self-absorbed sometimes, but at least he wasn't some kid she had picked up in a bar.

Still, she watched the handsome young stranger put on socks and shoes while he waited for her answer. He glanced around the room in search of the missing shirt. Her toes felt a wad at the end of the bed. She reached beneath the covers, unearthing a pale blue, wrinkled oxford shirt. She held it up to him and instantly remembered having worn the shirt. The memory of him taking it off her made her cheeks flush.

"Is it salvageable?" he asked, stretching to take it from her while keeping a safe distance.

He was being a gentleman, pretending he hadn't had access to every inch of her body only hours ago. The thought should have repulsed or terrified her. It didn't. Instead, she continued to watch him, enjoying his nervous but fluid motions, yet at the same time annoyed with herself. She should not be noticing that the color in his shirt brought out the blue flecks in his otherwise green eyes. How had she been so certain he wouldn't hurt her? One of these days a stranger's eyes might not be a safe way to judge his character.

"So what about lunch?" he asked, looking as though he was steeling himself for further rejection. He had trouble buttoning the shirt, had it almost finished when he realized he was off a button and started all over again.

"I don't even remember your name," Tess finally admitted.

"It's Will. William Finley." There was a glance and a hesitant smile. "I'm twenty-six, never been married. I'm a lawyer. Just moved to Boston, but I'm visiting a friend here in Newburgh Heights. His name's Bennet Cartland. His father has a law practice here. Pretty high-profile one, actually. You can check it out if you want." He hesitated. "Probably more than you wanted to know, right?" When she rewarded him with a smile, he continued. "What else? I have no diseases, except I did have the mumps when I was, like, eleven, but then so did my buddy, Billy Watts, and he has three kids. Oh, but don't worry, I used protection last night."

"Um...there's a damp spot," she said quietly.

When he met her eyes, the embarrassment seemed to be replaced by a flicker of desire that his memory must have triggered.

"I had only two condoms, but the third time I...well, I pulled out before, well, you know."

Suddenly she remembered the intensity, could feel it fill her body. The unfamiliar rush surprised her, frightened her. She couldn't allow herself to slip back into her old habits. She wouldn't. Not now when she had worked so hard.

"I think maybe you better leave, Will."

He opened his mouth to say something, maybe to try to change her mind. He hesitated, staring at his feet. She wondered if he wanted to touch her. Did he have the urge to kiss her goodbye or to convince her to let him stay? Maybe she even wanted him to. Instead, Will Finley found his jacket on the doorknob and left.

She lay back into the pillows, now noticing remnants of his aftershave, a subtle scent, not like Daniel's overpowering musk. Dear God, twenty-six fucking years old! Almost ten years her junior. How could she be such an idiot? Yet, this time when she closed her eyes, their night together started coming back to her in clear, crisp sights and sounds and sensations. She could feel his body rubbing against hers, his tongue and hands playing her like some delicate instrument, knowing just where and when to touch her and how to send her to places she hadn't been in a long time.

The memories that embarrassed her more were those of her own urgency, her own hunger, her own fingers and mouth devouring him. They had taken turns ravishing each other as if they had been starving. The passion, the urgency, the desires were nothing new. She had experienced plenty in her sordid past. What was new, what was different had been Will's gentle caresses, what seemed to be a genuine concern that she feel the same pleasure, the same sensations he was experiencing. What was new and different was that she and Will Finley hadn't just had sex last night, but that Will Finley had actually made love to her. Perhaps she should have taken some comfort in that realization. Instead, it stirred up an unsettling restlessness within her.

Tess rolled onto her side, twisting her pillow and hugging it to her. She couldn't let someone like Will Finley sidetrack her. Not now. Not when she had worked so hard for what she had. She needed to remain focused. She needed to think of Daniel. Despite their differences, Daniel gave her credibility in a community where credibility was everything. He was good for her in all the ways that were necessary for her to become a respected, successful businesswoman. So why did she feel as though she had let something valuable slip from her fingers when she asked Will Finley to leave?

CHAPTER 18

Will slammed the front door, rattling its beveled glass. For a brief moment, his anger gave way to concern while he checked to make sure he hadn't cracked or broken anything. The door looked old but solid. The glass looked custom-made, maybe antique. Not that he would know such things. But he had noticed that Tess Mc-Gowan had a taste for antiques. Her small cottage was decorated with an eclectic mix, creating a soothing, comfortable environment. He had felt incredibly warm and cozy waking up and being surrounded by lavender sheets and wallpaper with tiny little violets.

Last night when she invited him in, he had initially been surprised. He would never have guessed that the wild, passionate woman who had shamelessly hustled him at pool while throwing back tequila shooters would surround herself with old lace, hand-carved mahogany and what looked like original watercolors. But after only one night, he knew Tess McGowan's home was a reflection of a woman who was as passionate and independent as she was sensitive and vulnerable.

It was that unexpected vulnerability that had made it difficult to leave. It had surprised him last night—or was it already early this morning—when he held her in his arms. She had curled into his body as though finding some long-sought-after shelter.

He scraped a sleeve over his face in an attempt to wake up to reality. Christ! Where did he come up with this crap? Vulnerability and finding shelter. He sounded like something out of a fucking chick flick.

He got into his car and immediately glanced up at what he knew to be the bedroom window. Hell, maybe he expected her to be standing there, watching him. But it was easy to see no one was standing behind the sheer curtain.

He felt angry again, used. It was ridiculous. He was the one who had picked her up. His friends had dared him, goaded him into one last fling before his impending wedding. A wedding that at one time seemed far into the future was now suddenly less than a month away.

At first he did it simply to shock his friends. They'd never expect good ole' Will, the eternal choirboy, to flirt with any woman, let alone a woman like Tess. Geez, maybe he needed some new friends, ones whose maturity levels weren't stuck back in college. But he couldn't blame them for his stupidity last night, nor for his going as far as he had. Nor could he say he'd had too much to drink, because unlike Tess, he had known exactly what he was doing from start to finish.

He had never met anyone like Tess McGowan. Even before she shed her conservative black shawl and started shooting pool with the bar's owner, Will thought she was the sexiest woman he had seen. It wasn't like she was a knockout or centerfold-sexy. She was definitely attractive, with thick, wavy hair she wore loose and down to her shoulders. And she had a good body, not like some bulimic model, but with plenty of curves and amazing shapely legs. God, he got hot just thinking about her. Just thinking about running his hands over the curve of her hips and the swell of her breasts.

Back at Louie's, long before he had up-close-and-personal access, it wasn't those curves so much as it was the way she moved— it was the way she carried herself that had gotten his attention. His and everyone else's. And it was like she enjoyed the attention, enjoyed putting on a show, hiking her dress's skirt up to her thighs to take a shot while straddling the corner of the table. Every time she leaned over her pool cue, the strap of her dress slipped off her shoulder, the silky fabric allowing just a peek at her voluptuous breasts captured behind black lace.

Will shook his head and jammed the key into the ignition. It had been a hell of a night, one of the most passionate, erotic, exciting nights of his life. Instead of being angry, he should be patting himself on the back that Tess McGowan was letting him off with no strings attached. He was a lucky bastard. Hell, he hadn't been with another woman since he and Melissa had started seeing each other. And four years of sex with Melissa couldn't come close to one night with Tess.

He glanced up at the bedroom window again, and caught himself hoping Tess would be there. What was it about this woman that made him not want to leave? Was he simply imagining that there had been some connection, some special bond? Or had it just been sex?

He checked his wristwatch. He had a long trip back to Boston. He'd be pushing it to get there in time for dinner with Melissa and her visiting parents. It had been the only reason he had taken off a precious Monday from his brand-new job. And here he was, miles away from Boston and miles away from even thinking about Melissa.

Christ! How would Melissa not see the betrayal in his eyes? How fucking stupid was he to risk throwing away the last four years for one night of passion? So if it was such a mistake, why hadn't he left already? Why couldn't he get Tess's fragrance, the taste of her skin, the sounds of her passion...why couldn't he erase it all? Why did he want to go back up and do it all over again? That certainly didn't sound like a remorseful guy. What the hell was wrong with him?

He shifted the car into gear and peeled out of her driveway, letting his frustration squeal the tires. He swerved into the street and almost sideswiped a car parked at the opposite curb. Briefly the man behind the wheel glanced up at him. He wore sunglasses and had a map spread over the dash as though he was looking for directions. Tess's neighborhood was blocks away from any major thoroughfare. Immediately, Will wondered if the guy had been watching the house. Was it possible this was the owner of the expensive sapphire ring Tess wore on the wrong hand?

Will checked the rearview mirror and took one last look at the car. Then he noticed it had District of Columbia license plates instead of Virginia. Maybe because it was a little odd, maybe because he was a new assistant D.A.—hell, maybe it was just out of curiosity about the type of man who thought he owned Tess McGowan. Whatever the reason, Will committed the license number to memory, then headed back to Boston.

CHAPTER 19

The conference room went silent as soon as Maggie walked through the door. Without hesitating she continued to the front, disappointed to find the room arranged for a lecture. Chairs were set side by side, all facing the front of the room instead of at long, narrow tables as she had requested. She preferred more of a business setting where she could scatter crime scene photos in front of the participants. Where they felt more comfortable discussing rather than simply listening. However, the only table in the room was filled with coffee, juice, soft drinks and an assortment of pastries.

She felt her audience's stares as she pulled up a chair for her briefcase. Then, she began digging through the contents, pretending to search for something she had to have before she could start. Instead, she was waiting for her stomach to settle. She had eaten breakfast hours ago, and never got nauseated anymore before presentations. But her lack of sleep and several additional Scotches in her room last night, long after Turner and Delaney had left her, now punished her with a fuzzy head and a dry mouth. It was definitely not a good way to start a Monday.

"Good morning," she finally said, buttoning her double-breasted jacket. "I'm Special Agent Margaret O'Dell with the FBI. I'm a criminal profiler with the Investigative Support Unit at Quantico, which some of you may still refer to as the Behavioral Science Unit. This workshop focuses—"

"Wait a minute, ma'am," a man in the second row interrupted, shuffling uncomfortably in a chair that was too small to accommodate his considerable size. He wore tight trousers, a crisp, short-sleeved button-down shirt that stretched across his swollen belly, and scuffed shoes that refused to look new despite a fresh polish.

"Yes?"

"No disrespect intended, but what happened to the guy who was supposed to give this workshop?"

"Excuse me?"

"The program..." He looked around the room until he seemed to find encouragement from some of his comrades. "It said the guy wasn't just an FBI profiler, but an expert in tracking serial killers, a forensic psychologist with, like, nine or ten years' experience."

"Did the program actually say this person was a man?"

Now he looked puzzled. Someone beside him handed over a copy of the conference's program.

"Sorry to disappoint you," Maggie said, "but I'm him."

Most of the men simply stared at her. One woman in the group rolled her eyes in empathy when Maggie looked her way. Maggie recognized two men in the back. She had briefly met the Kansas City detectives Ford and Milhaven last night at the Westport bar and grill. Both men smiled as though they were in on her secret.

"Maybe they should say that in the program," the man persisted, trying to justify his objection. "They don't even use your name."

"Would it matter?"

"Yeah, to me it would've. I came here to learn some serious stuff, not listen to some desk jockey."

Her evening dosage of Scotch must have desensitized her emotions. Instead of feeling angry, his chauvinism simply made her feel more exhausted.

"Look, Officer—"

"Wait a minute. What makes you think I'm an officer? Maybe I'm a detective." He shot a smug grin to his buddies, giving himself away and reinforcing Maggie's initial assessment.

"Let me take a shot here," she said, walking to the center of the room, standing in front of him and crossing her arms. "You're a street cop in a metropolitan area, but not here in Kansas City. You're used to wearing a uniform and not business attire, not even business casual. Your wife packed your bag and picked out what you're wearing now, but you've gained some weight since she last bought anything for you. Except the shoes. You insisted on wearing your beat shoes."

Everyone including the officer shuffled in their chairs to get a look at his shoes. She failed to point out the subtle but permanent indentations in his close-cropped hair from too many hours spent wearing a hat.

"You're not able to carry your weapon at the conference, but you feel lost without your badge. It's inside your jacket pocket." She motioned to the tan jacket hidden by his hefty bulk and draped over the back of the chair. "Your wife also insisted on the jacket, but again you're not used to wearing one. Not like perhaps a detective might be used to wearing a jacket and tie."

Everyone waited as if watching a magic act, so the officer reluctantly twisted around, tugged at the jacket and brought out his badge to show them.

"All lucky guesses," he said to Maggie. "Whatcha expect from a roomful of cops?"

"You're right. You're absolutely right." Maggie nodded as eyes came back to her face, still waiting, still testing. "Most of what I said might be seen as obvious. There's a certain profile that goes along with being a cop. Just like there's a certain profile that goes along with being a serial killer. If you can pinpoint what those characteristics are and which ones apply—though some of them may seem obvious—you can use that information, that knowledge, as the beginning foundation for a profile."

Finally she had their attention, and with their minds diverted from what she looked like to what she was saying, her entire body began to relax, to access some auxiliary energy and override her initial fatigue.

"However, the tricky part is looking beyond the obvious, picking apart and examining small tidbits that might seem insignificant. Like, for instance, in this case—I'm sorry, Officer, would you mind telling me your name?"

"What? You mean you can't guess that?" He smirked, proud of what he considered a quick comeback and drawing a few laughs from the others.

Maggie smiled.

"No, I'm afraid my crystal ball leaves out names."

"It's Danzig, Norm Danzig."

"If I were to examine your profile, Officer Danzig, I'd try to break down everything I did know."

"Hey, you can examine me all you like." He continued to play with her, enjoying the attention, while looking at his buddies instead of Maggie.

"I'd wonder," she continued, ignoring his comment, "why your wife had bought clothes for you that were the wrong size."

Suddenly Officer Danzig sat still and quiet.

"I'd ask myself if there was a reason." From the rising color in his face, Maggie knew the reason was one he didn't care to expose. Her guess was that he and his wife had not shared a bed for some time. Perhaps there had even been a temporary separation, one that included Officer Danzig eating a few more fast-food meals. That could account for the extra pounds his wife hadn't expected when she purchased his clothes for the conference. Instead of embarrassing him with her theory, she simply said, "I'd guess your wife finally got fed up with you wearing the same outdated navy blue suit that you keep in the back of your closet."

The others laughed, and Officer Danzig looked around at them, smiling with relief. But when his eyes met Maggie's, she saw a hint of humbled awareness. His subtle show of appreciation was the slightest shift in his chair, crossing his arms, facing the front of the room as if finally ready to give her his full attention.

"It's also important not to get bogged down by the stereotypes." She began her ritual pacing. "There are a handful of stereotypes that seem to be perpetuated with serial killers. We should start by laying some of those to rest. Anyone care to guess what some of those stereotypes are?"

She waited out their silence. They were still summing her up. Finally, a young Hispanic man decided to take a shot.

"How about the idea that they're all crazy. They're total mental cases. That's not necessarily true, right?"

"Right. In fact, many serial killers are intelligent, well educated and as sane as you and I."

"Excuse me," a graying detective from the back of the room interrupted. "Son of Sam claiming a Rottweiler made him do it, that's not mental?"

"Actually it was a black Labrador named Harvey. But even Berkowitz later owned up to the hoax when profiler John Douglas interviewed him.

"I'm not saying some of these killers are not crazy, what I am saying is that it's a mistake to believe they have to be insane to do the things they do. When, in fact, killing for them is a conscious choice. They are masters of manipulation. Their crimes are all about dominating and controlling their victims. It's not usually because they hear orders to kill from a three-thousand-year-old demon living inside a black Lab.

"If they were simply nuts, it wouldn't be possible for them to carry out their elaborate murders over and over again—to perfect their methods and still avoid getting caught for months, sometimes years. It's important to recognize them not as deranged crazies, but for what they are. What they are is evil."

She needed to change the subject before she got carried away with a sermon on the effects of evil. How there was a shadow side to everyone's human nature; a shadow side that was capable of evil. But to discuss it always led to the question of what made some step over the line, while others dared not. After years of examining evil, Maggie hadn't a clue what that answer was.

"What about motive?" she asked instead. "What are some of the stereotypical motives?"

"Sex," a young man in the back said loudly, enjoying the sudden attention and laughs that the single word drew. "Don't most serial killers get some sexual gratification from killing, just like rapists?"

"Hold on," the one woman challenged. "Rape isn't about sex."

"Actually, that's not a true statement," Maggie said. "Rape is very much about sex."

Immediately there were a few sighs, some disgruntled shakes of heads as though they expected this from a woman.

"Rape is very much about sex," she repeated, ignoring their skepticism. "It's the one variable that distinguishes rape from any other violent crime. No, that's not to say that rapists rape simply for sexual gratification, but yes, they do use sex as one of their weapons to achieve their goals. So it's wrong to say rape isn't about sex when sex is definitely one of the weapons they use.

"In fact, rapists and serial killers use sex and violence in much the same way. Both are powerful weapons used to degrade the victim and gain control. Some serial killers even start out as serial rapists. But somewhere along the line they decide to take it a step further to achieve their gratification. They might begin by experimenting to reach different levels, starting with torture, working up to strangulation or stabbing. Sometimes that's not enough, so they begin different rituals with the dead body. That's when you see cases like the Pied Piper who sliced up his victims, made stew and fed it to his other captives.

She caught several of them grimacing. Skepticism seemed to be replaced by morbid curiosity.

"Or in Albert Stucky's case," she continued, "he began to experiment with different rituals of torture, slicing off victims' clitorises or nipples, just to hear them scream and plead with him."

She said these things calmly and casually, yet she could feel the tension in her muscles, an involuntary reflex as her body seemed to prepare for flight or fight anytime she thought of Stucky.

"Or you find more solemn rituals," she said, trying to expel Stucky from her mind. "Last fall in Nebraska, we tracked a killer who gave his young victims their last rites after he strangled and stabbed them to death."

"Hold on," Detective Ford interrupted. "Nebraska? You're the profiler who worked on that case with the dead little boys?"

Maggie cringed at the simplicity of his description.

"Yes, that was me."

"Morrelli was just telling us about that case last night."

"Sheriff Nick Morrelli?" An unexpected but pleasant flutter invaded her already tense body.

"Yeah, we all went out for ribs last night. But he's not Sheriff Morrelli anymore. Turned in his badge for a suit and tie. He's with the D.A.'s office in Boston."

Maggie retreated to the front of the room, hoping the distance would shield her and prevent them from witnessing her sudden discomfort. Five months ago, the cocky, small-town sheriff had been a thorn in her side from the day she arrived in Platte City, Nebraska. They had spent exactly one week chasing a killer and sharing an intimacy so palpable, just the thought of it was able to generate heat. Her class was staring at her, waiting. How was it possible for Nick Morrelli to dismantle her entire thought process by simply being in the same city?

CHAPTER 20

Tully reached under his glasses and tried to rub out the exhaustion. As though blaming them for lack of relief, he pulled the glasses off, tossing them onto one of the many piles on his desk. The glasses used to be for reading only. Now he found himself wearing them more often.

Ever since he'd hit forty three years ago, his body parts seemed to be failing him, one by one. Last year it was surgery on his knee, just a torn ligament, but it had put him out of commission for two weeks. Of course, it didn't help matters having a fourteen-year-old daughter telling him how "out of sync" he was. It seemed as if he couldn't do anything right as far as Emma was concerned.

Earlier she had been furious with him for having to spend another evening next door with Mrs. Lopez. Maybe that was part of the reason he was still here working, stalling, avoiding going home to his own daughter and the silence she wielded as punishment. Ironically, this was the same daughter he had fought so hard to keep near him.

Though it wasn't much of a fight once Caroline realized what kind of freedom she might have without the responsibility of a teenage daughter. This was the same woman who couldn't bear to be separated from her daughter and husband six or seven short years ago, when she took an account executive job at a national advertising firm. But as the high-profile clients rolled in and the promotions took her all the way to the top, somehow those expensive trips to New York City and London and Tokyo seemed to get a lot easier. By the final years of their marriage, she had become a stranger to him. A beautiful, sophisticated, ambitious woman, but a complete stranger.

Tully stretched back in his chair, lacing his fingers together behind his head. God, how he hated change! He glanced around the small fluorescent-lit room. He missed having an office with windows. In fact, if he even thought about being sixty feet under ground, he knew his claustrophobia would easily kick in. He had seriously considered turning down the position at Quantico, knowing the Investigative Support Unit was still located in what he considered the bowels of the training facility.

He was rubbing his eyes again when he heard the tap on his open door.

"Agent Tully, you're here late."

Assistant Director Cunningham wore shirtsleeves, but still carefully buttoned at the wrists and collar, whereas Tully's sleeves were rolled up in uneven folds and shoved above his elbows. Cunningham's tie was cinched tight at his neck, making Tully self-conscious about his own, now wrinkled and tossed aside somewhere on a file cabinet, leaving his collar unbuttoned and open.

"I was waiting for a phone call from the medical examiner," Tully explained. "From Dr. Holmes."

"And?"

The assistant director leaned against the door, and Tully wondered if he should clear off one of the chairs. Unlike his boss's immaculately neat office, Tully's looked like a storage closet, with piles of papers, scattered files and overflowing bookcases. He sorted through the stack of notes from his phone call, not wanting to depend on his memory, which at this time of night had shut down like a computer hard drive.

"The girl...the young woman had an incision in her left side that extended to the small of her back about four inches long. Dr. Holmes said it was very precise, almost as if he had performed surgery on her."

"Sounds like our boy."

"He removed her spleen."

"A spleen isn't very big, is it? It looked like there was much more in that pizza box."

Tully reached for the copy of *Gray's Anatomy* that he had borrowed from the library. He quickly thumbed to the place where he had used a gum wrapper as a bookmark. He grabbed his glasses.

"The spleen is about five inches in length, three inches in breadth and an inch or an inch and a half in thickness," he read out loud, then closed the book and set it aside. "The book says the spleen weighs about seven ounces, but that depends on what stage of digestion it's in. It can get much bigger. Our victim hadn't eaten much that day, so her spleen was fairly small. Dr. Holmes said that some of the pancreas was also attached."

"Were there fingerprints found anywhere at the scene?"

"Yes, we got two pretty good ones—a thumb and an index finger. But they're not matching Stucky's. It's possible they may have been made accidentally by someone on the scene, but it sure seems as though they were left behind on purpose. The entire rim of the Dumpster was wiped down, and then there are these two fingerprints right smack in the middle."

Cunningham frowned, his weathered brow creasing as if he remembered something. "Double-check Stucky's early file. Make sure the prints haven't been switched or altered or that there were any computer mistakes. If I remember correctly, Agent O'Dell was finally able to identify him because of a fingerprint Stucky left behind. He blatantly left it behind, too. But it took us a while to identify it at the time. Someone hacked into the county computer system and switched the prints on file."

"I'll double-check, sir, but we're not dealing with a county sheriff department's computer system here. We're checking these against the ones AFIS has on Stucky, prints they've taken directly off Stucky. And with all due respect, I don't think anyone can easily hack into the Bureau's system." AFIS (Automated Fingerprint Identification System) was the FBI's master database. Though it networked with local, state and federal agencies, dozens of precautions were in place against computer hackers.

Cunningham sighed and scratched his jaw. "You're probably right," he conceded with a fatigue Tully hadn't witnessed before.

"It may end up being a rookie cop's," he told his boss, as if hoping to relieve some of Cunningham's exhaustion. "If it is, we'll know in the next twenty-four hours. If they don't make a match to any law enforcement officers, then I'll have someone do a cold search."

Tully kept his glasses in place, feeling more alert with them on and needing to appear in control. "Sir, I haven't found anything that would suggest Stucky is trying to send some sort of message by which organ he extracts. I wonder if I'm missing something."

"No, you're not missing anything. Stucky does this for shock value and simply because he can," Cunningham said as he came farther into Tully's office, but remained standing.

"Did he study to be a surgeon at some point in his life?" Tully flipped through a file Agent O'Dell had put together on Stucky's past. In many ways it read like a résumé for a Fortune 500 executive.

"His father was a doctor." Cunningham wiped a hand over his jaw. Tully recognized the gesture as something his boss did when exhausted and trying to retrieve information from his vast memory bank. He took the opportunity to study his boss's face, which seemed thinner, the hollows in his cheeks and eyes darker in the fluorescent light. Even exhausted, his posture remained straight, no hunched shoulders as he now leaned against the bookcase. Everything about the man spoke of a quiet dignity.

Finally he continued, "If I remember correctly, Stucky and his partner started one of the first Internet, online stock-trading companies. Made millions and has it stashed in foreign banks."

"If we could track some of those accounts, maybe we could track him."

"The problem is we've never been able to find out how many different accounts he has or what names he uses. Stucky's sharp, Agent Tully. He's cunning, very intelligent and almost always in control. He's not quite like any of the others. He doesn't kill because he needs to, or because it's a mission or some urgency. Or even because he hears some inner voices. He kills for one major reason—because he enjoys it. It's a game for him to manipulate, to break down the human spirit, to shock people with what he's capable of doing, and also to thumb his nose at those of us who are trying to catch him."

"Certainly even Albert Stucky makes mistakes."

"Let's hope so. Have you found anything on where the victim may have been taken?"

Again, Tully dug out his notes from a variety of stacks, not wanting to depend on his fatigued memory. Immediately he found himself self-conscious and a bit embarrassed. His notes were scrawled on everything from a deli napkin to a brown paper towel from the men's rest room.

"We know she was taken before she finished her route. There were some customers who called complaining they hadn't received their pizzas. The manager is working on getting me a list of the addresses she was to deliver to."

"Why is that taking so long?"

"They write down the addresses in one place as the orders are phoned in. The delivery person takes the only copy."

"You're kidding," Cunningham sighed, and for the first time Tully thought he saw that it was an effort for him to confine his frustration. "Doesn't seem very efficient."

"It's probably never been a problem until now. The lab is trying to raise the addresses from the indentations on the notepad page underneath. Of course, our best bet is if we find the victim's car. Maybe the lists will have been left behind."

"Any luck finding the car?"

"Not yet. I got the make, model and plate number from DMV. Detective Rosen put out an APB. Nothing's shown up so far."

"Have Reagan National and Dulles airport security check their long-term parking lots."

"Good idea." Tully jotted another note to himself, this time using the cash-register receipt from his lunch. Why the hell didn't he have notepads like the rest of the world?

"He had to take her someplace," Cunningham said, staring over Tully's head, lost in thought. "Somewhere he could have plenty of uninterrupted time with her. I'm guessing he didn't go far from where he apprehended her. If we could get that list, we might be able to narrow down some possible locations."

"The thing is, sir, I've driven around within a ten-mile radius of where the body was found. The whole area is this picture-book community. We're not going to find any abandoned warehouses or condemned buildings."

"It's also easy to miss the most obvious place, Agent Tully. You can bet Stucky will be gambling on us doing just that. What else do you have?" he asked more brusquely now as he stood away from the bookcase, suddenly in a rush.

"There was a cellular phone recovered from the Dumpster. It was reported stolen a few days ago from a local shopping mall. I'm hoping once I get the phone record, maybe it'll lead us someplace, depending on what calls were placed."

"Good. Sounds like you've got everything under control." Cunningham started to leave. "Let me know what help you need. Unfortunately, I can't promise a whole task force again, but maybe I can pull a few people from other cases. Now, you need to go home, Agent Tully. Spend some time with your daughter."

He pointed to the photo Tully kept on the edge of his desk. It was the only one he had. It included the three of them, arms wrapped around each other and smiling for the camera. It couldn't have been taken that long ago, and yet he couldn't remember them being that happy. It was the first time Cunningham had referred to Tully's personal life. He was surprised his aloof boss remembered that his wife hadn't made the move with him.

"Sir?"

Cunningham stopped halfway into the hall.

Tully wasn't sure how to ask. "Should I give Agent O'Dell a call?"

"No." The answer was brisk and firm.

"You want to wait until we're sure it's Stucky?"

"I'm ninety-nine percent certain it is Stucky."

"Then shouldn't we at least tell Agent O'Dell?"

"No."

"But, sir, she might—"

"What part of my answer did you not understand, Agent Tully?" Again, his manner was firm without raising his voice. Then he turned and left.

CHAPTER 21

Once again, Turner and Delaney dragged Maggie from her hotel room to join them for dinner. This time their new Kansas City friends, Detectives Ford and Milhaven, treated them to what they claimed was the best barbecue place in the city, located not far from the bar and grill they had visited the night before.

Maggie had never seen two men put away more ribs than her FBI buddies. Their compulsion to compete with each other was ridiculous and getting old. Although Maggie recognized it was no longer for her benefit, but was now extended to their new friends. Ford and Milhaven encouraged Turner and Delaney's heartburn fest like spectators at a major sporting event. Ford had even placed a five-dollar bill on the table for the first man who would clean the current stack of ribs off his plate.

Maggie sat back, sipped her Scotch and tried to find something more interesting to watch through the dimly lit, smoke-filled restaurant. She found her eyes wandering to the entrance. She half expected to see Nick Morrelli walk in, and then realized she had no idea what she would do if he were to show up. Ford had told Maggie after class that he and Nick had gone to college together at the University of Nebraska. He said he had left a message at the hotel's front desk for Nick to join them at dinner. Now hours later, Nick obviously hadn't gotten the message or had other plans for the evening. Yet, Maggie found herself watching for him. It was ridiculous, but just knowing that he was at the conference had stirred up all those feelings she thought she had safely tucked away since the last time she had seen him.

That was over five months ago. To be more precise, it had been the Sunday after Halloween when she left Platte City, Nebraska, to go home to Virginia. She and Nick, who had been the county sheriff at the time, had spent exactly one week together, hunting a religious psychopath who had murdered four little boys. Two men had been captured and were awaiting trial, neither of whom Maggie was convinced was the real killer. Despite all the circumstantial evidence, Maggie still believed the real killer was a charismatic Catholic priest named Father Michael Keller. Only, Keller had disappeared somewhere in South America, and no one, not even the Catholic Church, seemed to know what had happened to him.

For the last five months, all Maggie had come up with were rumors of a handsome young priest who traveled from one small farming community to another, serving as their parish priest, though no assignment had officially been made. By the time Maggie tracked down the location, the elusive priest was gone, disappearing into the night with no explanation. Months later, the rumors would find him at another small parish, miles away. But again, by the time the location was narrowed down, Keller was gone. It was as though the communities protected him, keeping him safe like some fugitive unjustly accused. Or perhaps like some martyr.

The thought made Maggie sick to her stomach. That was what Maggie believed to be Keller's motive for murdering boys he thought were abused. He had hoped to make martyrs of them, as though he could administer a perfectly evil salvation. It seemed unfair that Keller would now be protected like a martyr, instead of executed for the evil monster he was. She wondered how long it would take before these poor farmers would start to find their little boys dead along some riverbank, strangled and stabbed to death but washed clean and given their last rites.

Would they be willing to see Keller punished then? There seemed to be a problem with punishing evil these days, an evil that gained strength by conspiring with other evil. Maggie knew Keller had been the one who had visited Albert Stucky in a Florida prison. Several guards had later identified Keller from a photograph. And though she had no proof, she also knew it had been Keller who had given Stucky the wooden crucifix. It was that dagger-like crucifix Stucky had used to cut himself free of his restraints and stab a transport guard.

She shook the thought from her mind and gulped the remainder of her Scotch. Turner and Delaney looked as though they were finally at a standstill. Delaney looked miserable. Turner's brown face had a greasy sheen to it, despite his efforts at wiping it clean. She was about to order another Scotch when Ford waved down the waitress for the check. Neither detective had allowed any of the FBI agents to pay. Maggie insisted on at least leaving the tip, which Ford did allow. Maybe he realized his detective's salary would never be able to keep up with Turner and Delaney's appetites.

Milhaven had driven them, but Maggie wished she could walk rather than be squashed once again into the Grand Am's back seat between her two bodyguards. The night was clear but crisp enough to provoke a shiver. Before they got to the parking lot, they noticed a gathering in the alley. One uniformed cop stood in front of a metal Dumpster and attempted to keep a small crowd of well-dressed onlookers at a distance.

Without a word, the detectives and FBI agents made their way to the scene.

"What's the problem here, Cooper?" Ford knew the frustrated officer.

"Let's move out of the way," Milhaven said to the onlookers as he and Delaney pushed them back into the parking lot that ran parallel to the alley.

The officer glanced at Maggie and Turner.

"It's okay," Ford reassured him. "They're FBI. Here for the conference. So what's going on?"

Officer Cooper pointed to the Dumpster behind him with a tilt of his head.

"Dishwasher at the Bistro took out the trash about a half hour ago. Noticed a hand sticking up out of the pile. Freaked. Called it in, but not before he announced it to the whole goddamn world."

Maggie felt the familiar knot in her stomach. Turner was already at the Dumpster, his six-foot-three frame allowing him to look over the edge without assistance. Maggie dragged an empty milk crate and joined him. Now she wished she hadn't drunk so much. She paused and waited for the brief spell of light-headedness to pass.

The first thing Maggie noticed was a red umbrella, its handle looped over the edge of the Dumpster as if the owner hadn't meant for it to be mistaken for trash. Or had it purposely been left as evidence?

"Officer Cooper." She waited for his attention. "You might mention to the detectives when they arrive that there's an umbrella here. It probably should be bagged and taken in for fingerprints."

"Will do."

Without disturbing anything, Maggie could see the woman was naked and lying on her back. The patch of red pubic hair was a stark contrast to the white skin. Immediately, Maggie knew the scene had been tampered with. Officer Cooper said the dishwasher had noticed only a hand sticking up out of the pile, yet the woman's entire torso was exposed. What looked like vegetable peels had been tossed onto her face. Her head was turned to the side, her brilliant red hair littered with pieces of leftovers.

Maggie could see the woman's mouth, partially opened as though something may have been shoved inside. Then she noticed a dot, a beauty mark above the upper lip. The knot in her stomach tightened. She leaned forward, stretched on tiptoe, sending the crate wobbling while she reached in.

"O'Dell, what the hell are you doing?" Turner scolded her as he watched.

Gently, she swiped at a potato peel and a clump of angel-hair pasta that was stuck to the side of the woman's face.

"It's Rita," she said, wishing she had been wrong.

"Rita? Rita who?"

Maggie waited, glanced at Turner and watched the recognition register on his face.

"Shit! You're right."

"You guys know her?" Ford asked as he looked over the top.

"She's a waitress from the bar and grill down the street," Maggie explained as her eyes continued to examine what she could of Rita's body.

Her throat had been slashed, so deep it had nearly decapitated her. The rest of her body had few bruises and no punctures except for her wrists, which showed ligature marks. Whatever the method of capture, the struggle had been minimal, suggesting that hopefully death had come quickly. Maggie found herself relieved and at the same time disparaged to be relieved by such a thing.

Then she saw the bloody incision in Rita's side underneath a mass of spaghetti. She shoved herself away from the Dumpster, half jumping, half falling off the crate. The light-headedness was quickly replaced by a dizzy buzz. She rushed a safe distance away before she wrapped her arms around herself to stop the wave of panic. Damn it! She never got sick at crime scenes anymore. But this was different. This was a mixture of dread and fear, not nausea.

"O'Dell, you okay?"

Turner was at her side. His large hand touched her shoulder, startling her. She avoided his eyes.

"Stucky did this," she said, keeping her voice steady and free of the quiver invading her lower lip.

"O'Dell, come on now."

"I thought I saw him when we were in the bar and grill last night."

"As I remember, we all had plenty to drink."

"No, Turner, you don't understand. Stucky must have seen her. He must have noticed us talking, joking with her. He chose her because of me."

"O'Dell, we're in Kansas City. You're not even on the conference roster. Stucky couldn't possibly know you're here."

"I know you and Delaney think I'm losing it. But this is exactly Stucky's M.O. We should start looking for a container, a take-out container, before someone else finds it."

"Look, O'Dell. You're just on edge."

"It's him, Turner. I know it. And whatever he sliced out of her is going to show up at some outdoor café table. Maybe even in front of this restaurant. We need to—"

"O'Dell, slow down," he whispered, looking around as if to make sure he was the only one witnessing her hysteria. "I know you're feeling like you need to be checking over your shoulder, thinking—"

"Damn it, Turner. This isn't my imagination."

He went to touch her shoulder again, and this time she jerked back just as she noticed a dark figure across the alley.

"O'Dell, relax."

The man stood at the edge of the crowd, a crowd that had doubled in only a few minutes. He was too far away, and it was too dark for her to be certain, but he wore a black leather jacket, like the man she had seen last night.

"I think he's here," she whispered, and positioned herself behind Turner so she could look without being obvious. Her pulse quickened.

"O'Dell." By the tone of his voice, she knew Turner was growing impatient.

"There's a man in the crowd," she explained, keeping her voice low, "tall, thin, dark, sharp features. From what I can see of his profile, it could be Stucky. My God, he's even carrying what looks like a take-out container."

"As are a whole bunch of others. Come on, O'Dell, this is a restaurant district."

"It could be Stucky, Turner."

"And it could be the mayor of Kansas City."

"Fine—" she let him hear her anger "—I'll just go talk to him myself."

She started around him, but Turner grabbed her arm.

"Stay put and stay cool," he said with an exaggerated sigh.

"What are you going to do?"

"I'm gonna talk to the man. Ask a few questions."

"If it's Stucky—"

"If it's Stucky, I'll recognize the bastard. If it's not, you're picking up the dinner tab tomorrow night. I'm thinking you better get your credit card ready for prime rib."

She watched Turner while trying not to be obvious about it. She positioned herself behind Delaney and Milhaven, who were deep in discussion about baseball. Neither man seemed to notice her. Through the space between them, Maggie could see Turner walk with his casual yet authoritarian gait toward the crowd. She knew he wasn't taking her seriously, and he wouldn't be prepared if it was, indeed, Stucky.

She reached inside her jacket and unsnapped the restraint on her holster, then kept her hand on the butt of the gun. Already her heart was pounding against her rib cage. All other motion, all other conversation stood still as she concentrated on the man in the black leather jacket. Could it really be Stucky? Could the bastard be so arrogant to kill in a city crawling with law enforcement officers from across the country, then stand back and watch? Yes, Stucky would love the challenge. He'd love to be able to thumb his nose at them all. A shiver slid down her back as a night breeze swirled around her, wet and cold.

Turner didn't reach the crowd before the man turned to leave.

"Hey, wait a minute." Turner yelled at the man loud enough for even Delaney and Milhaven to look. "I want to talk to you."

The man bolted and so did Turner. Delaney started to ask Maggie something, but she didn't wait to hear. She raced across the parking lot, gun drawn, its nose to the ground. The crowd scattered out of her way with gasps and one scream.

All Maggie could think was this time Albert Stucky would not escape.

CHAPTER 22

Maggie's heart slammed against her chest. Turner had disappeared around a corner and into another alley. She followed without slowing down and without hesitation. Halfway down, she made herself stop. The alley was unusually narrow, barely wide enough to accommodate a small vehicle. The tall brick buildings blocked out any streetlights. The moon was only a sliver, leaving dim bulbs to light the way, some cracked but most bare, hanging above rickety back doors.

She squinted, examining the shadows and trying to listen over the pounding in her ears. By now she was breathing much too hard from such a short run. Her skin felt clammy. Every nerve ending in her body seemed to be on alert. Her muscles tensed. Where the hell had they gone? She had been minutes, no, seconds, behind them.

Something rattled behind her. She spun around, her Smith & Wesson kept close to her body, but aimed and ready to blow to pieces the empty Burger King cup. She watched the breeze lift and push it down the alley as she tried to steady her nerves. Calm. She needed to stay calm, keep focused.

She turned, keeping her grip firm on the revolver. Again she strained to hear over the thunder in her ears. The cool night air sent a shiver down her back. She needed to breathe, to control the gasps. They were gasps caused by fear, not exhaustion. Damn it! She wouldn't let him do this to her. She needed to slow down. She needed to concentrate.

She took careful steps as she proceeded. The cobblestone street was old, with uneven and chipped bricks, some oddly spaced. It would be easy to twist an ankle, to stumble or trip, to become vulnerable. Still, she didn't look down. She kept her eyes moving, watching though it was difficult to see beyond fifty to a hundred feet. Was it getting darker, or was it simply her imagination? Her eyes darted over everything, checking stacks of boxes, black doorways, rusty fire escapes, anyplace Albert Stucky could hide behind or sneak into. He wouldn't trick her this time.

Where the hell was Turner? She wanted to call out, but couldn't risk it. Was it possible they had run another way? No, she was certain they had disappeared around this corner and into this alley.

Ahead she could see an open space where two cars were parked. A Dumpster blocked her view of the entire area. Behind her in the distance footsteps ran past, missing this narrow alley. From the open space she heard muffled voices. She pushed her body against the grimy brick wall and inched her way along. Her chest ached. Her knees felt mushy. Her palms were sweaty, but she gripped the gun's handle, keeping her finger on the trigger and the gun's nose down.

She came to the edge of the building and had nowhere else to go. She crouched and snuck behind the Dumpster. Where the hell were Delaney and Milhaven? By now they should have backtracked. Her eyes strained to see beyond the darkness to the end of the alley. Nothing. Now the voices ahead of her were more clear.

"Hold on a minute." She recognized Turner's voice. "What the hell do you have there?"

She waited, but there was no answer to his question. If Stucky had a knife, she'd never hear the damage until it was too late. She peeked out just enough to see the back of the leather jacket. Good. He was facing the opposite direction. He wouldn't see her. But how close was he to Turner?

She heard footsteps behind her, making their way noisily toward her over the cobblestone. From her hiding spot, she couldn't see them, couldn't wave them off, couldn't warn them. Damn it! In seconds Stucky would hear them, too, if he hadn't already. She needed to move now, take her chances.

In one quick motion, she jumped out from behind the Dumpster, scrambling to take a firm stance, legs apart, arms in front, aim focused on the back of the bastard's head. It wasn't until she cocked the gun's hammer that she saw Stucky flinch.

"Don't move an inch, or I'll blow your goddamn head off."

"O'Dell," she heard Turner say.

She could finally see him. He was standing close to the building, a shadow covering most of his face. With Stucky between them, Maggie couldn't see if Turner had his gun drawn. Instead, she concentrated on her target, not ten feet in front of her.

"O'Dell, it's okay," Turner told her, yet he still didn't move.

Did Stucky have a gun pointed at him?

"Drop whatever you're holding and put your hands up behind your head. Do it. Now!" she yelled, surprised at her own voice, amplified and bouncing off of the brick buildings.

The footsteps behind her had slowed, their echo making what Maggie knew to be only several men sound instead like a whole troop. She didn't turn. Her eyes never left the back of Stucky's head. He hadn't moved, but hadn't obeyed her command either.

"I said hands up. Now, goddamn it!"

"O'Dell, it's okay," Turner said again.

But there was still no movement, not from Stucky, not from Turner, not from the men keeping their distance behind her. Maggie inched closer. Perspiration trickled down her back. A breeze swept strands of damp hair off her forehead but whipped others into her face. Still, she didn't move, didn't flinch. Her finger remained firmly on the trigger, pressing, ready to squeeze. Her entire body had gone rigid, freezing much too stiffly, threatening to lock her muscles into position.

"Last time. Drop what you're holding and put your hands up behind your head, or I'll blow your skull wide open." This time the ultimatum came through clenched teeth. Maggie's head throbbed. Her hand began to ache from the effort it took not to squeeze the trigger.

Finally, his hands went up while something slapped and crunched against the cobblestone. She could feel it splatter her feet, and knew it was the plastic take-out container he had been carrying. But she refused to look down. She didn't want to see what part of Rita had been spread all over the ground. Instead, she kept her sights on where the nose of her gun pointed, in the middle of the tuft of black hair at the base of his skull. At this close range and at this angle, the bullet would drive through the skull and into the brain, shredding the cerebellum and ripping through the frontal lobe before it exited the top of his forehead. He'd be dead by the time his body hit the ground.

"Ease up, Maggie," she heard Delaney say, and suddenly he was beside her.

The others stayed behind them. Turner stepped out so she could see that he hadn't been injured. Silence filled the alley so completely, she wondered if they were all holding their breaths. Yet, she hadn't dropped her stance or lowered her weapon.

"Turn around," she ordered the back of Stucky's head.

"O'Dell, you can put away your gun," Turner said, but she didn't look at him. She wouldn't slip this time. She wouldn't let her guard down.

"I said turn around, damn it." Her stomach twisted into a series of knots. Would she be able to look him in the eyes?

He turned slowly. Her finger pressed tighter. All it would take was a minor adjustment, a split second for her to refocus between his eyes. Then one more second to squeeze the trigger. But she wanted him to see it coming. She wanted him to look at her. She wanted him to know what it felt like to know another person had total control over his life. She wanted him to feel fear, and yes, she wanted to see that fear in his eyes.

The man stared down at her with wide, frightened eyes, a thin, drawn face and shaking bony hands. He looked as if he'd faint from fear. It was the exact reaction Maggie had dreamed about. It was the exact revenge she had hoped for. Only the man was not Albert Stucky.

CHAPTER 23

Early Tuesday morning
March 31

Maggie opened her hotel-room door to Delaney. Without a word or an invitation, she turned and walked back into the room, leaving him there while she continued the pacing he had interrupted. Out of the corner of her eyes, she saw him hesitate. Even after coming in, he held on to the doorknob, looking as though he wished he could escape. She wondered how he and Turner had decided which of them would talk to her. Had Delaney lost the coin toss?

She ignored him as he walked across the room, careful to stay out of her path. He sat down at a small table that wobbled when he leaned his elbows on it. He picked up her empty plastic glass and fingered the miniature bottle of Scotch, giving both a sniff before replacing them. His shirtsleeves were rolled up. His collar button opened. His tie removed. He looked wrinkled and tired. During one of her turns, she saw him rub his hands over his bristled face and up through his thinning hair. She'd make him speak first. She was in no mood to talk. And certainly in no mood for a lecture. Why couldn't they just leave her alone?

"We're worried about you, Maggie."

So there it was. He'd have to start with a low blow, all that worrying-and-caring stuff. Plus, he was using her first name. This was serious stuff. She almost wished Turner had come instead. At least he would yell a little.

"There's no need to worry," she said calmly.

"Look at you. You're wound so tight you can't even sit still."

She shoved her hands into the pockets of her trousers, briefly alarmed, noticing for the first time how baggy the pants felt. When had she lost weight? She continued to pace, keeping her hands hidden in her pockets. No sense in showing Delaney how badly her hands had been shaking since she'd returned to her room.

"It was an honest mistake," she defended herself before he had a chance to make the obvious accusation.

"Of course it was."

"From the back he looked exactly like Stucky. And why the hell did he ignore my instructions three times?"

"Because he doesn't understand English."

She stopped and stared at him. The thought had never occurred to her. Of course it hadn't. She had been convinced it was Stucky. There had been no doubt in her mind.

"Then why did he run from Turner?"

"Who knows." Delaney dug his fingers into his eyes. "Maybe he's an illegal alien. Point is, Maggie, you not only made him splatter his veal capellini all over the pavement, you almost blew his frickin' head off."

"I did not almost blow his head off. I followed protocol. I couldn't see Turner. I couldn't see what this fucking idiot had in his hands, and he wasn't responding. What the hell would you have done, Delaney?"

His eyes met hers for the first time, and she held him there, despite his discomfort.

"I probably would have done the same thing." But his admission made him look away.

Maggie thought she saw a hint of embarrassment. There was more to this little visit than concern or a lecture. She braced herself and leaned against the chest of drawers, the only solid piece of furniture in the room.

"What's going on, Delaney?"

"I called Assistant Director Cunningham," he said, glancing up at her but avoiding her eyes. "I had to tell him what happened."

"Goddamn you, Delaney," she said under her breath, and began pacing once more to steady the brewing anger.

"We're worried about you, Maggie."

"Right."

"I saw the look in your eyes, Maggie, and it scared the hell out of me. I saw how much you wanted to pull the trigger."

"But I didn't, did I? Doesn't that count for anything? I didn't pull the goddamn trigger."

"No, not this time."

She stopped at the window and stared down at the lights of the plaza below. She bit her lower lip. The lights were beginning to blur. She would not cry. She closed her eyes tight against the urge. Behind her, Delaney remained still and quiet. She refused to give him anything other than her back.

"Cunningham wants you to return to Quantico," he said in a low, apologetic voice. "He's sending Stewart to finish your workshop. He'll be here in a couple of hours, so you don't need to worry about the morning session."

She watched several cars below as they glided through intersections. At this height, they reminded her of a slow-motion video game. Streetlights flickered, confused whether to stay on or shut off as the sky lightened in anticipation of sunrise. In less than an hour, Kansas City would be waking up, and she hadn't even been to bed yet.

"Did you, at least, tell Cunningham about Rita?"

"Yes."

When he offered nothing more, she turned to him, suddenly hopeful. She watched his face when she asked, "Does he believe it was Stucky?"

"I don't know. He didn't say, and I didn't ask."

"So maybe he wants me to return to finally help on the case?"

Again, Delaney looked away, staring at the tabletop. She knew without any response that she was wrong.

"Jesus! Cunningham thinks I'm losing it, too," she said quietly, and turned back to the window. She leaned her forehead against the cool glass, hoping it would steady her nerves. Why couldn't she just feel numb, instead of all this anger and now this sudden feeling of defeat?

After a long silence, she heard Delaney get up and start for the door.

"I already made arrangements for you. Your flight leaves a little before one this afternoon. I don't have any sessions today, so I can drive you to the airport."

"Don't bother. I'll take a cab," she said without moving.

She heard him waiting, fidgeting. She refused to give him her eyes. And she certainly would not give him the absolution she knew Delaney would feel guilty without. Down below, cars began to fill the video-game slots, black and red and white, stopping and going.

"Maggie, we're all just worried about you," he said again, as if it should be enough.

"Right." She didn't bother to disguise the hurt and anger.

She waited for the soft slap of the door to close behind him. Then she crossed the room and turned the dead bolt. She stood with her back leaning against the door, listening to her heart pound, waiting for the anger and disappointment to leave. Why couldn't she replace it with acceptance or, at least, complacency? She needed to go home to her new, huge Tudor house with her belongings stacked in cardboard boxes and her shiny new state-of-the-art security system. She needed to let this go, before she did slip so far over the edge there would be no return.

She waited, pressed against the door, staring at the ceiling and listening, if not for her heart to stop banging then at least for her common sense to return. Then making up her mind, she stomped to the middle of the room. She began stripping out of the clothes she had worn since yesterday morning. In minutes she was dressed in blue jeans, a sweatshirt and an old pair of Nikes. She slipped on her shoulder holster, shoved her badge into the back pocket of her jeans and wrestled into a navy FBI windbreaker.

Her forensic kit hadn't been used in months, but she still didn't leave home without it. She pulled out several pairs of latex gloves, some evidence bags and a surgical face mask, transferring the items to the pockets of her jacket.

It was almost 6:00 a.m. She had only six hours, but she wasn't leaving this city until she connected Albert Stucky to Rita's murder. And she didn't care if that meant checking every last Dumpster and every last discarded take-out container in Westport's market district. Suddenly feeling energized, she grabbed her room's key card and left.

CHAPTER 24

"Hey lady. What the hell you looking for?"

Maggie looked over her shoulder but didn't stop digging through the rubble. She was up to her knees in garbage. Her Nikes were stained with barbecue sauce, her gloved hands sticky. Her eyes stung from a smelly concoction of garlic, mothballs, spoiled food and general human crap.

"FBI," she finally shouted through the paper face mask, and turned just enough for him to see the yellow letters on the jacket's back.

"Shit! No kidding? Maybe I can help"

She glanced at him again, resisting the urge to swipe at the strands of hair in her face, instead waving at the flies who regarded her as an invader of their territory. The man was young, probably in his early twenties. A scar, still pink and swollen, ran along his jaw and a purple bend in his nose indicated a recent break. Maggie's eyes darted around the alley, wondering if the rest of his gang was close by.

"Actually, I have more help than I need. The KC cops are a couple of Dumpsters down" she lied, pleased when the kid immediately began a nervous dance. His head jerked in both directions. He shifted his weight from one foot to the other as if preparing to run.

"Yeah, well. Good luck then." Rather than decide which direction to risk, he found an unlocked door and disappeared into the back of a warehouse.

She tossed a bulging garbage bag to the side without opening it. Stucky would never leave it hidden inside a bag. In the past, his surprises had been left in plain sight, where they were easily discovered, often by unsuspecting citizens. Maybe she was wasting her time going through Dumpsters.

Just then she saw the corner of a white cardboard take-out container. Slowly, she stepped closer, lifting each leg high as if wading through water, ignoring the squish-squash sounds beneath her feet. The last two containers had yielded one green meatball sandwich and some moldy ribs. Yet, each time she spotted a new one her pulse quickened. She felt a surge of adrenaline as she swatted at flies and brushed off wilted lettuce, cigarette butts and wadded pieces of tinfoil.

She lifted the container carefully, keeping it level and setting it on the edge of the Dumpster. The box was about the size of a small cake or pie. It'd provide ample room for a kidney or a lung. Neither organ required much space. She had once found a lung from one of Stucky's victims stuffed inside a container no bigger than a sandwich.

Sweat trickled down her back, despite the morning being damp and chilly. By now, she imagined she reeked as bad as the garbage she stood in. She steadied her fingers and sucked in her breath. The surgical mask clung to her mouth and nose. She slipped off the container's tab and pulled open the lid. The smell made her turn her head and hold her breath. After a few seconds, she was able to look again. Who'd ever guess spoiled fettuccine Alfredo would curdle and stink like rotten eggs? At least that's what Maggie thought the contents had once been. It was difficult to tell without lifting the thin film of fuzzy green and gray scum off the top. She closed and secured the lid.

"Find anything interesting?"

The deep voice startled her. Had the young gangster changed his mind? She grasped the Dumpster's edge so she wouldn't slip and fall backward into the trash. When she turned, she found Detective Ford staring up at her. Only this morning she hardly recognized him. Like her, he was dressed in street clothes, blue jeans, a gray hooded sweatshirt and a blue Kansas City Royals baseball cap. He looked much younger without the suit and tie and without his older partner.

She tugged off the surgical mask and let it dangle at her neck.

"I'm finding that we waste entirely too much food in this country," she said, dropping the container and wading to the opposite side of the Dumpster where she had left a milk crate on the cobblestone to aid in her climb.

"I didn't realize the FBI was trying to police that sort of thing."

She checked to see if there would be a lecture. He smiled.

"So are you undercover or off duty?" she asked, pointing to the baseball cap as she peeled off the latex gloves.

"I should ask you the same thing."

"I had some free time this morning," she said, as if that should be explanation enough for her to be knee-deep, sifting through garbage.

"Hey, Ford, where the hell did you disappear?" a familiar voice called from around the corner.

"Over here," Detective Ford answered.

Even before he came into view, Maggie felt the annoying flutter in her stomach. Nick Morrelli looked just as handsome as she had remembered, tall and lean with a confident stride. He, too, wore blue jeans with a red Nebraska Cornhuskers sweatshirt. He was at Ford's side before he recognized her, and when he did, his smile revealed dimples in an otherwise strong, square jaw.

"Maggie?"

She tossed the sticky gloves and yanked off the surgical mask from around her neck, adding it to the garbage.

"Hi, Nick." She pretended to sound casual while wading the rest of the way out, suddenly acutely aware of flies now attracted and interested in her. She swatted at them and tucked wild strands of hair behind her ears and away from her face.

"That's right. I keep forgetting you two know each other." Ford was smiling, too. "Maggie had some free time this morning," he said to Nick.

"Jesus, it's good to see you, Maggie."

Immediately, she felt her face flush.

"It might not be so good to smell me," she said, needing to stop any sentimental reunion.

She gripped the edge of the Dumpster and swung a leg over the side. Her foot dangled, searching for the milk crate. Before she could find it, Nick's hands were on her waist to help. Her hip brushed against his chest on the way down. Despite being bombarded with smells all morning, she recognized the subtle scent of his cologne.

Once both her feet were on the ground, his hands lingered, but she avoided looking up at him. She avoided looking at either of them, needing the extra time to compose herself while waiting for the unexpected flutter to leave. Damn it! She wasn't some schoolgirl. Why the hell did her body respond like this?

She occupied herself wiping the sticking garbage from her pant legs and shoes. Unfortunately, when she did look up, both men were watching her. She continued to avoid Nick's eyes, remembering how they could look deep inside her and uncover vulnerabilities she had hidden even from herself.

"So," Ford finally said, glancing back into the Dumpster, "did you find anything interesting?"

She wondered how much Turner and Delaney had shared with Ford about her obsession with Stucky. Had Detective Ford seen how close to the edge she had come last night? And what had he discussed with Nick? She didn't think for a minute he had forgotten they knew each other. After all, Ford had invited Nick to have dinner with them last night, though there had never been an explanation as to why Nick hadn't joined them. Suddenly she was curious if Nick had simply wanted to avoid seeing her again. After all, if he was now living in Boston, why hadn't he called? She could feel his eyes taking her in, watching her, smiling at her, but thankfully not making a big deal of their reunion.

"No, I didn't find anything," she finally answered. She needed to change the subject before Detective Ford discovered it was body parts she had been rummaging for and not simply overlooked evidence. "Is this your case now?"

"Not officially. More than likely Milhaven and I will be putting in some hours on it. Today's supposed to be my day off. Nick and I were just about to get an early lunch."

"And you always take the alleys?"

Ford grinned and glanced at Nick.

"She doesn't let anybody get away with anything, does she?"

"No, she certainly doesn't." Nick's eyes caught hers, and she knew his simple statement had much deeper meaning, reminding her of the intimacies they had shared and those they had almost shared.

"So come on, Detective Ford." She needed to keep things light, capitalize on their jovial mood. She needed to keep Ford from realizing she had no business snooping around in his jurisdiction. She was already in enough trouble with Cunningham. "You're down here taking another look, too, right?"

"Okay, you caught me." He held up both hands as if in surrender. "I was telling Nick about last night."

Maggie cringed, and again she wondered what exactly had been discussed. Nick knew the whole story, all the gory details about her and Stucky. He had experienced firsthand her nightmares. Still, she kept her face impassive, pretending last night had been just another routine chase for her. Truth was, she didn't care if Ford thought she was losing it. But maybe she did care if Nick thought it. She waited and Ford continued.

"You sorta got my curiosity up last night, O'Dell."

Oh God, she thought, but instead said, "How is that?"

"All that talk about Albert Stucky sorta spooked me."

She glanced from Detective Ford to Nick, looking for some indication of whether or not they were taking her seriously. If this was Ford's way of patting her on the head and reassuring her how mistaken she was, she didn't need to waste her breath responding.

"You think I'm being paranoid?" She couldn't help it. The beginning anger slipped out. Nick noticed immediately and looked concerned. Ford looked genuinely confused.

"No, that's not at all what I meant.... Well, that's not exactly true. I guess I was thinking that last night."

"Albert Stucky has the financial wherewithal and the intelligence to go anywhere he wants, anytime he chooses. Don't think for a second Kansas City is safe, simply because he hasn't struck in the Midwest before." There it was. She hadn't meant to let the anger out. She hated how Stucky had such power over her emotions, triggering them with the mere mention of his name. Again she avoided Nick's eyes, and again she could feel them.

Ford stared at her, but there was no accusation on his face. Instead, he looked as though he was only waiting for her to finish her tirade.

"Can I talk now?"

"Be my guest." Maggie crossed her arms over her chest, bracing herself and yet doing her best to look defiant. It was a newly acquired talent.

"That was my way of thinking last night. Like, why in the world would this Stucky guy just happen to pick Kansas City instead of the East Coast? I know enough about serial killers to know they keep to familiar territory. But before I met Nick this morning, I sat in on the autopsy of your friend, Rita."

Detective Ford glanced at Nick, and it was obvious this was what the two of them had already discussed. He looked back at Maggie, waited until he had her full attention then said, "Seems our victim is missing her right kidney."

CHAPTER 25

Tully checked his watch. It wasn't like Assistant Director Cunningham to be late for a meeting. He sat back and waited. Maybe his watch was running fast again. According to Emma, it was ancient and uncool.

Tully stared at the huge map spread on the wall behind his boss's desk. It was Cunningham's personal log for his twenty years as head of the Investigative Support Unit. Each pushpin indicated a spot where a serial killer had struck. Each pushpin color designated a particular serial killer. Tully wondered how soon the assistant director would run out of colors. Already there were repeats: purple, light purple and translucent purple.

Tully knew his boss had worked on some of the most shocking cases, including John Wayne Gacy and the Green River Killer. By comparison, Tully was a rookie, with only six years' experience in profiling and most of that on paper, not in the field. He wondered how anyone lived day in, day out for decades examining such brutality without becoming jaded or cynical.

He glanced around the office again. Everything on the desk—a leather appointment book, two Bic pens with the caps intact (a talent Tully had not yet perfected), a plain memo pad with no doodles in the corners and a brass nameplate—all of it was organized in straight lines, perpendicular to one another, almost as if Cunningham used a T square every morning. It occurred to Tully that the tidy but stark office contained not one single personal item. There were no sweatshirts wadded in the corner, no miniature basketballs, not a single photo. In fact, Tully knew very little of who his boss was outside the office.

He had noticed a wedding band, yet Assistant Director Cunningham seemed to live at Quantico. There was never any rearranging of appointments for Little League games or school plays or visits to kids in college. Before this morning, he had never even been late for an appointment. No, Tully knew absolutely nothing about the quiet, soft-spoken man who had become one of the most respected men in the FBI. But at what cost? Tully wondered.

"Sorry to keep you waiting," Cunningham said as he breezed in, shedding his suit jacket and swinging it carefully over the back of his chair before sitting down. "What have you found out?"

In the beginning, that brisk, straight-to-the-point attitude had flustered Tully, who was accustomed to the courtesies of the Midwest. Now he appreciated getting down to business with no obligatory exchanges of chitchat or greetings. Though it also prevented the two men from knowing a single thing about each other's personal lives.

"I just received the files faxed over from the Kansas City police."

He pulled out the summary sheet from a group of folders he had brought along. He made certain it was the correct one and handed it across the desk. Cunningham pushed up his glasses.

Tully continued, "Early autopsy reports indicate a slashed throat as cause of death. No other defense wounds or injuries. There was one incision in the victim's right side through which the right kidney was extracted."

"Any sign of the organ?"

"No, not yet. But then the Kansas City cops weren't looking for it right away. It's quite possible someone found it, had no clue what it was and tossed it."

Tully waited patiently, watching his boss as he finished reading. He laid the report on the desk, sat back and rubbed a hand over his jaw.

"What's your perspective on this, Agent Tully?"

"The timing is off. It's much too soon after the delivery girl. And it's much too far away, entirely out of his territory. There was another latent fingerprint, a thumb. Again, it looks like it was deliberately left behind on an umbrella that belonged to the victim. Didn't even have the victim's fingerprints on it. It was definitely wiped down with the print left later. And again, it doesn't match Albert Stucky."

Cunningham frowned, squinting at the report and tapping his index finger to his lip. Tully thought the lines in his face seemed more pronounced this morning, his short hair peppered with more gray.

"So is it Stucky, or isn't it?"

"The M.O. definitely matches Stucky's," Tully said. "And there hasn't been enough in the news or even enough time for a copycat to get motivated. The print may belong to someone who came across the scene. A waiter found her. There's some speculation the scene had been contaminated. KC's faxing a copy of the print to the guys at CJIS in Clarksburg. We'll see if it matches the unidentified one left in Newburgh Heights. There's a good chance these belong to civilians coming across the scene after everything's been wiped clean."

"Okay, let's say that's the case. So what if it is Stucky?"

Tully knew exactly what Cunningham was thinking, but he evidently wanted or needed to hear it, to confirm what seemed to be the obvious.

"If it is Stucky, it's more than likely he followed O'Dell to Kansas City. He may be looking for a way to drag her into this again."

Cunningham glanced at his wristwatch. "She should be headed back right now."

"Actually, I checked, sir. I thought I'd meet her at the airport. She changed to a flight later tonight."

Cunningham shook his head and let out a sigh of frustration as he grabbed his phone and punched several buttons.

"Anita, do you have Special Agent Margaret O'Dell's hotel phone number in Kansas City?" He sat back while he waited.

Tully imagined the methodical Anita quickly accessing her records. Assistant Director Cunningham had kept the same secretary, inheriting her from his predecessor and yielding to her experience and expertise on important matters he couldn't saddle himself with. If such a thing was possible, Anita was even more meticulous than her boss.

"Good," Cunningham said into the phone. "Would you please get in touch with her even if it's through a message. Track her down if she's already checked out. I want to see her in my office tomorrow morning at eight."

He hesitated and listened as he rubbed the bridge of his nose under his glasses. "Oh yes, I forgot about that. Tell O'Dell nine o'clock then. Thanks, Anita."

He replaced the receiver and looked up at Tully, waiting.

"How long do you intend to keep her off this case?" Tully finally asked what he thought was the obvious question.

"For as long as is necessary."

Tully studied his boss's face, but had no clue how to read the composed and reserved expression. He respected the man tremendously, but he didn't know him well enough to know how far he could push him. He decided to take a chance anyway.

"You realize she's checking this one out on her own? That's more than likely why she's taking a later flight."

"All the more reason to get her back here." Cunningham held Tully's eyes, warning him to step carefully. "What else is happening in Newburgh Heights?"

"We found the pizza delivery girl's car. It was left in long-term parking at the airport, right next to a telephone company van that was reported stolen a couple of weeks ago."

"I knew it," Cunningham sat back and began drumming his fingers on the desk. "Stucky's done it before. He'll steal a vehicle, or sometimes only the license plates, from the airport's long-term parking. Chances are he has the plates or even the vehicle returned before the owner is back home. Has forensics impounded the van?"

Tully nodded, sorting through the information he had on both vehicles. "Not likely they'll find anything. It's pretty clean. However, we did find two delivery slips in the girl's car.

He dug in the folder, pulling out one torn piece of paper and another creased with fold lines. Both had been recovered from the floor of the girl's car. A red stain on one corner had tested as pizza sauce, not blood. Tully handed both over the desk. "The torn one is from her first route. Number four on the list is Agent O'Dell's new home address."

Cunningham sat forward, resting elbows on his desk. For the first time in Tully's three months of working at Quantico, he saw anger on his boss's face. The assistant director's dark eyes narrowed and his hands clenched the paper.

"So the damn bastard not only knows where she lives, but he's watching her."

"It looks that way. When I talked to Agent Delaney, he said the waitress in Kansas City had joked and talked with the three of them Sunday evening while she served them. He may be choosing women O'Dell comes in contact with in hopes of making her feel responsible."

"It's another of his goddamn games. He's still obsessed with O'Dell. I knew it. I knew he wouldn't let it go."

"It appears that way. May I say one more thing, sir?"

"Of course."

"You've offered me another agent to help on this case. You've also offered a forensic psychologist, which O'Dell is. You even suggested we have someone on hand to answer medical-related questions. If I'm not mistaken, Agent O'Dell has a premed background."

Tully hesitated, giving Cunningham a chance to cut him off. Instead, he only stared at Tully, his face back to its stoic expression as he simply waited.

"Rather than three or four people," Tully continued, "I'm officially requesting Agent O'Dell. If Stucky is targeting her, she may be the only one who can help us catch him."

Tully expected a flicker of anger or at least impatience. But Cunningham's face remained unchanged.

"I'll give your request careful consideration," he said. "Let me know what else you find out from Kansas City."

"Yes, sir," Tully said as he stood to leave, recognizing the signs of dismissal. Before he reached the door, Cunningham was on the phone again, and Tully couldn't help wondering if his request had also been dismissed.

CHAPTER 26

Maggie couldn't wait to peel off her damp, smelly clothes. Everyone in the hotel lobby had confirmed her suspicions—she reeked. Two people insisted on getting off the elevator, and the brave souls who continued the ride up with her looked as though they had held their breath for all twenty-three floors.

Detective Ford had dropped her and Nick at the front door then drove home to explain to his wife why he smelled like garbage on his day off. Nick's room was in the south tower of the huge hotel complex, explaining why they hadn't run into each other before. Which meant both banks of elevators would need disinfecting.

The three of them had spent several hours digging through Dumpsters, sifting through trash cans and looking for discarded containers on outdoor tables, window ledges, fire escapes and flower boxes. Maggie hadn't even noticed the thick, gray thunderheads that had rolled in until the rain came in sheets, forcing them to end their search and take shelter. She would have continued if she had been alone. The rain had felt good, slashing at her and perhaps peeling away the tension along with the rancid smells from her skin. But the cracks of thunder and flashes of lightning only made her more anxious and jumpy.

Detective Ford had assured her that Albert Stucky would, indeed, be considered a suspect in Rita's murder, despite their not finding the missing kidney. Maggie couldn't understand why Stucky would deviate from his game, or had some unsuspecting customer taken the container home? Was it possible someone could have placed it in his refrigerator without looking, without knowing what was inside? That seemed ridiculous, and Maggie didn't even want to think about it. The fact was, there wasn't anything more she could do.

As soon as she came into her room, she noticed the phone's red message light flashing. She grabbed the receiver and punched in the necessary numbers to retrieve her voice messages. She was used to getting emergency messages about her mother who attempted suicide as often as other women her age treated themselves to a manicure. But weren't her mother's new friends supposed to be taking care of her? Who could be calling? There was only one message, and it was, indeed, marked urgent.

"Agent O'Dell. This is Anita Glasco calling for Assistant Director Cunningham. He needs to see you in his office tomorrow morning at nine. Please call me back if you won't be able to make it. Thank you and have a safe trip home, Maggie."

Maggie smiled at Anita's soothing voice, though the message itself set her on edge. She listened to her options, punched the number to erase and hung up. She began pacing, trying to contain the anger before it grabbed hold of her. It was Cunningham's way of seeing to it that she returned immediately. He knew she would never blow off a request to meet with him. She wondered what he already knew about Rita's murder, or if he had even considered looking into it. After all, Delaney had probably made it sound as though she was losing her mind, simply imagining things.

She checked her wristwatch and scraped something dry and crusty from its face. She still had about six hours before her rescheduled evening flight. It was the last one to D.C. tonight. If she was to make the appointment with Cunningham in the morning, she couldn't afford another delay. But how the hell could she leave Kansas City knowing Albert Stucky was here, lurking somewhere in the city? Maybe looking for his next victim right this very minute.

She double-checked the door, making sure it was locked. She added the chain and rammed the back of the wooden desk chair up under the knob, kicking the legs until she was satisfied it was secure. Then she stripped down to her underwear and bra and tossed her smelly clothes and shoes into one of the plastic dry-cleaning bags in the closet. Still smelling them, she triple-bagged them, until the scent seemed to be contained.

She brought her Smith & Wesson with her to the bathroom, leaving it close by on the counter. She left the bathroom door open, slipped out of her bra and panties, then crawled into the shower.

The water beat and massaged her skin. She turned the temperature as hot as she could stand it. She wanted to be rid not only of the smells, but of that crawly feeling just under her skin. That infestation of maggots that invaded her system every time she knew Albert Stucky was nearby. She scrubbed at her skin until it was red and raw. She wanted her mind to be swept clean, and her body to forget the scars.

When she stepped out of the shower, she wiped at the foggy mirror. The brown eyes stared back at her with that damn vulnerability so close to the surface. And the scars were still there, too. Her body was becoming a scrapbook.

The scar began just beneath her breast. With the tip of her index finger, she forced herself to touch it. To trace its puckered line down across her abdomen.

"I could gut you in seconds," she remembered him telling her— no, promising, not telling. By then, she had resigned herself to death. He had already trapped her. He had already forced her to watch while he bludgeoned and gutted two women to death. He had threatened that if Maggie closed her eyes he would simply bring out another woman and start all over. And he had been true to his word.

There was still no escaping those images and sounds: bloodied breasts, the crack of bones, the hollow thud of a baseball bat against a skull. There had been so much blood from severed arteries and from knives sinking into flesh, into abdomens and vaginas—places where knives should never be allowed. No place was out of limits for Stucky. Nothing on a woman's body was sacred. He carved and sliced, pleased and encouraged by the screams.

After feeling the splatters of blood, the pieces of bone and brain, after hearing the mind-shattering cries for help and smacks of bloodied flesh, what more could he have done to her? Death would have been a relief. So instead, he left her with a constant reminder of himself, a scar.

Maggie snatched a T-shirt and wrestled into it, anxious to cover herself despite her skin being damp. She marched to the dresser and pulled out clean underwear and khakis. Her hair was still dripping as she rummaged through the service butler, relieved to find two new miniature bottles of Scotch. Thank God for the hotel staff's efficiency.

A soft tap on the door startled her. She stopped at the bathroom, retrieving her revolver. Before pulling the chair away, she checked the peephole. Nick's hair was damp and tousled. He wore clean blue jeans and a crisp oxford shirt with the sleeves rolled up.

She returned the chair to the desk and slipped the revolver into the back of her waistband. It wasn't until she opened the door and his eyes slid down her body that she realized she had nothing on underneath the thin T-shirt that now clung to her damp body.

"That was fast," she said, ignoring the flutter this man seemed to activate on sight.

"I was anxious to crawl out of those clothes." He returned to her face, a hint of embarrassment coloring his own. "I think I might need to throw out my shoes. There's gunk on them that I don't even want to know about."

They stared at each other. His presence, his scent seemed to dismantle her thought process. She felt hot and damp. She told herself it was from her shower and the extra-hot water she had used.

"I thought maybe we could get something to eat or drink," he finally said. "You do still have time before your flight?"

"I should...um...put something else on."

His eyes wouldn't let her go. Suddenly it unnerved her how much she wanted to touch him. She needed to close the door, get control of her senses, pull herself together. Instead, she heard herself saying, "Why don't you come in."

He hesitated, enough so that she could have taken back the invitation. Instead, she moved away from the door. She retreated to the dresser again, pulling things out at random, pretending to be searching while giving herself any excuse not to look up at him.

He came in and closed the door behind him.

"We seem to spend a lot of time in hotel rooms."

She glanced at him, immediately annoyed that the reminder brought a flush to her cheeks. In a small hotel room in Platte City, Nebraska, they had come dangerously close to making love. Five months later, she could still feel the same rush of heat. With all the emotions assaulting her over the past few days, how was it possible for Nick Morrelli to walk in and assault her with a whole new set?

She pulled out a white crew-neck sweater, the cotton knit cool but bulky and comfortable. She snatched a bra from the drawer as well.

"I'll just be a minute," she said as she disappeared into the steamy bathroom.

She changed quickly, avoiding any extra touches. She toweled the wetness out of her hair and brushed it back, grabbing the blow dryer, then deciding against it. She reached to remove her Smith & Wesson, hesitated, and left it in her waistband, pulling the loose sweater down and checking in the mirror to make sure it couldn't be seen. She knew she'd have to grab her badge on the way out.

Nick was at the window and watched as she tugged on socks and slipped on shoes. She noticed he had both miniature bottles of Scotch in his hand.

"Still having nightmares?" His eyes searched hers as he returned the bottles to the small table.

"Yes," she said quite simply, and gave him her back as she found her badge and some cash. She didn't need Nick Morrelli barging into her life and thinking he had any right to share or expose her vulnerabilities.

"Ready?" she asked as she headed for the door and opened it before looking back at him. She almost tripped over the room-service tray that sat on the floor outside her door. She stared down at the single dinner plate covered by a silver insulator. The two empty glasses and accompanying silverware sparkled on a crisp, white linen napkin.

"Did you order something from room service?" she turned to ask, but Nick was already by her side.

"No. And I didn't hear a knock, either."

He stepped over the tray and out into the hallway to look in both directions. Maggie listened. There were no slamming doors, no footsteps, no wisping elevators.

"Probably just a mistake," Nick said, but she could hear his tension.

Maggie kneeled next to the tray. Her pulse quickened. Carefully, she slipped the linen napkin out from under the silverware, using thumb and index finger. She unfolded it, then used it to grab the handle of the metal insulator. She lifted it slowly and immediately the smell filled the hall.

"Jesus," Nick said, jerking back a step.

In the middle of the shiny dinner plate lay a bloody glob Maggie knew was Rita's missing kidney.

CHAPTER 27

Within minutes, the hotel's lobby was filled with law enforcement officers from across the Midwest. All entrances and exits were guarded. Elevators were checked and watched. Stairwells were examined at all twenty-five levels. The hotel's room-service kitchen had been invaded and the staff questioned. Despite the overwhelming brigade of manpower, Maggie knew they would never find him.

Most criminals would consider it suicide to show up in a hotel where hundreds of cops, sheriffs, detectives and FBI agents were staying. For Albert Stucky it would simply be another challenge to his game. Maggie imagined him sitting somewhere, watching and amused by the commotion, the blunders, the unsuccessful attempts at catching him. That's why she was checking the most obvious places.

The second floor included an atrium overlooking the lobby. She stayed at the brass railing while her eyes searched down below— the line at the reservations counter, the man at the grand piano, the few diners at bistro tables in the glass-encased café the man behind the concierge desk, the cabdriver hauling out luggage. Stucky would blend in. He'd look as though he belonged. Even the room-service staff would not have noticed him had he walked into their kitchen in a white jacket and black tie.

"Any luck?"

Maggie jumped but managed to restrain herself from automatically reaching for her gun.

"Sorry." Nick looked genuinely concerned. "He'd be nuts to stick around. I'm guessing he's long gone."

"Stucky likes to watch. It isn't much fun if he doesn't get to see people's reactions. Half of these officers don't know what he looks like. If he plays it cool, they might never spot him. He has the uncanny ability to blend in."

Maggie continued searching, standing quietly and still. She could feel Nick examining her. She was tired of everyone watching for signs of some kind of mental meltdown, though she knew Nick was sincere.

"I'm fine," she said without looking at him, answering his unspoken question.

"I know you are. I still get to be concerned." He leaned over the railing, conducting his own search. His shoulder brushed against hers.

"Assistant Director Cunningham thinks he's protecting me by keeping me off the investigation."

"I wondered why you were teaching. John said there were rumors that you were burned out, losing your touch."

She had guessed as much, yet it felt like a slap in the face to hear it out loud. She avoided looking at him. She pushed strands of damp hair out of her eyes, tucking them behind her ears. She probably looked the part of the crazed FBI agent, with her tangled hair and baggy clothes.

"Is that what you think?" she asked, not certain she wanted to hear his answer.

They stood side by side, leaning against the railing, shoulders brushing while their eyes stayed safely ahead and away from each other. His silence lasted too long.

"I told John that the Maggie O'Dell I know is tough as nails. I saw you take a knife to the gut and still not give up."

Another of her scars. The mad child killer she and Nick had chased in Nebraska had stabbed her and left her for dead in a graveyard tunnel.

"Getting stabbed seems so much easier than what Stucky's doing to me."

"I know this isn't what you want to hear, Maggie, but I think Cunningham may be smart in keeping you out of this."

This time she turned to stare at him.

"How can you say that? It's obvious Stucky is playing with me again."

"Exactly. He wants to drag you into his little games. Why give him exactly what he wants?"

"But you don't understand, Nick." The anger bubbled too close to the surface. She tried to keep her voice calm and level. Talking about Stucky could bring her to the edge of sounding hysterical. "Stucky will continue to goad me whether I'm on the case or not. Cunningham can't protect me. Instead, he's keeping me from the one way I have to fight back."

"I'm guessing he must have told you he wants you on that flight back to D.C. tonight?"

"Agent Turner is escorting me." Why bother hiding her anger. "It's ridiculous, Nick. Albert Stucky is right here in Kansas City. I should stay here."

More silence. They were back to searching the crowd below, standing side by side, again leaning their elbows on the railing and again keeping their hands and eyes carefully away from each other. Nick moved closer as though purposely bringing their bodies in to contact. His shoulder no longer accidentally brushed hers. Now it stayed against her. She found a weird sense of comfort in this subtle touch, this slight contact, feeling perhaps that she wasn't in this alone.

"I still care about you, Maggie," he said quietly, without moving and still not looking at her. "I thought I didn't care anymore. I tried to stop. But when I saw you this morning, I realized I hadn't stopped caring at all."

"I don't want to have this conversation, Nick. I really can't. Not now." Her stomach churned with anticipation, with panic, with fear. She didn't need to feel anything more.

"I called you when I first moved to Boston," he continued as if he hadn't heard her.

She glanced at him. Was this some line? That boyish charm, that flirtatious reputation of his surely couldn't have disappeared so easily.

"I didn't get any message," she said, now curious and anxious to call him on his bluff if, in fact, that was what it turned out to be.

"Quantico wouldn't give me any information as to where you were, or when you'd be back. I even told them I was with the Suffolk County D.A.'s office." He glanced at her and smiled. "They weren't impressed."

It was a safe story. She wouldn't be able to confirm it or deny it. She concentrated on the lobby. Below, three men toted luggage behind a well-dressed woman with silver hair and a London Fog raincoat that didn't have a raindrop on it.

"I ended up calling Greg's law firm."

"You did what?"

She pushed herself away from the railing and waited until he did the same, giving her his attention and his eyes.

"Neither of you are listed in the Virginia telephone directory," he defended himself. "I figured the law office of Brackman, Harvey and Lowe might be more understanding. They might actually care about someone from a D.A.'s office getting in touch with one of their attorneys. Even if it was after hours."

"You talked to Greg?"

"I didn't mean to. I was hoping to catch you at home. I thought if Greg answered, I could tell him I needed to talk to you about unfinished business in Nebraska. After all, I knew you were still looking for Father Keller."

"But Greg didn't buy it."

"No." Nick looked embarrassed. He continued anyway. "He told me the two of you were working on your marriage. He asked me as a gentleman to respect that and stay away."

"Greg said that? About being a gentleman? As if he knew." She shook her head and returned to her perch, pretending to be distracted by the activity below. Greg had become so good at lying, Maggie wondered if he actually believed his own bullshit. "How long ago was this?"

"Couple months ago." He joined her again, but this time kept some distance.

"Months ago?" She couldn't believe Greg hadn't mentioned it, or that he hadn't let it slip out during one of their arguments.

"It was right after I moved, so it had to be around the last week of January. I got the impression the two of you were still living together."

"Greg and I both decided to stay at the condo, since neither of us were there that often. But I asked Greg for a divorce on New Year's Eve. That probably sounds heartless—I meant to wait." She watched as a maintenance crew pushed huge floor waxers into the lobby. "We were at his law firm's holiday party. He wanted us to masquerade as the happy couple."

The supervisor of the maintenance crew had a clipboard and wore shiny leather dress shoes. Maggie craned over the railing to get a glimpse of his face. Too young and too tall to be Stucky.

"People at the party kept congratulating me and welcoming me to the firm. They spoiled Greg's surprise. He had managed to get me a job as the head of their investigations department without even talking to me about it. Then he couldn't understand why I wouldn't jump at the chance to be digging through corporate files, looking for misappropriation of funds instead of digging through Dumpsters, looking for body parts."

"Right. Jesus, how silly of him."

She turned and rewarded his sarcasm with a smile.

"I am a pain in the ass, aren't I?" she said.

"An awfully beautiful pain in the ass."

She felt a blush and looked away, annoyed that he could make her feel sensual and alive while the world was going nuts around them.

"I finally moved into a house of my own last week. In a few weeks the divorce should be final."

"Maybe it would have been safer to stay at the condo. I mean as far as this thing with Stucky is concerned."

"Newburgh Heights is just outside D.C. It's probably one of the safest neighborhoods in Virginia."

"Yeah, but I hate thinking about you being all alone."

"I'd rather be alone when he comes for me. That way no one else gets hurt. Not this time."

"Jesus, Maggie! You *want* him to come after you?"

She avoided looking at him. She didn't need to see his concern. She couldn't take on the weight of it, the responsibility of it. So instead, she concentrated on the men in blue overalls wrestling with cords and mops. When she didn't answer, Nick reached for her hand, gently taking it. He intertwined her arm with his, bringing her hand to his chest and keeping it there, warm and tight against the pounding of his heart. Then they stood there while they watched the hotel lobby get its floors waxed.

CHAPTER 28

Washington, D.C.
Wednesday, April 1

He could feel Dr. Gwen Patterson staring at him while he stabbed at her furniture with his white cane, fumbling for a place to sit down. Nice stuff. The office even smelled expensive, fine leather and polished wood. But why would he expect anything less? She was a classy woman; sophisticated, cultured, wise and talented. Finally, a challenge to up the ante, so to speak.

He swiped his hand across her desktop, but there wasn't much to disturb—a phone, a Roledex, several legal pads and a daily calendar, flipped open to Wednesday, April 1. Only now did it occur to him that it was April Fools' Day. How ironically appropriate. He resisted the urge to smile, instead turning again and bumping into a credenza, barely missing an antique vase. The window above the credenza looked out over the Potomac River. In its reflection, he watched her grimace at his bold and reckless fumblings.

"The sofa is just to your left," she finally instructed, but stayed seated behind her desk. Though her voice sounded tight, restraining her impatience, she wouldn't embarrass him by coming to his rescue. Excellent. She had passed his first test.

He put his hand out and patted down the soft leather, feeling for the arm, and carefully sitting himself down.

"Would you like something to drink before we get started?"

"No," he snapped, being unnecessarily rude. Invalids could get away with shit like that. It was one of the few advantages he could look forward to. Then, to let her know he wasn't such a bad guy, he politely added, "I'd rather we just get started."

He set the cane by his side where he could find it easily. He bunched up his leather jacket and laid it in his lap. The room was dark, the blinds half-closed, and he wondered why she had bothered. He adjusted his sunglasses on the bridge of his nose. The lenses were extra dark so that no one could see his eyes. So that no one could catch him watching. It was a lovely twist to voyeurism. Everyone thought they were being the voyeurs, safe in staring at him, watching him, pitying him. No one seemed to question whether or not a blind guy could actually see. After all, why in the world would someone fake something like that?

Except that, ironically, the lie might be coming true. The drugs weren't working, and he couldn't deny that his eyesight was getting worse. He had lucked out so many times before, was his number finally up? No, he didn't believe in such a stupid thing as fate. So what if he needed a little extra help these days, a prop or two, or some assistance from an old friend to bring a little excitement into his life. Wasn't that what friends were for?

He cocked his head to one side, waiting, pretending to need to hear her before he could turn in her direction. In the meantime, he watched her. Through the dark lenses in the dark room, he found himself squinting. She was still staring at him, sitting back in her chair, looking comfortable and in control.

She stood and reached for her suit jacket on the back of her chair, but stopped, glanced over at him and left the jacket there. Then she came around to the front of the desk, leaning against the pristine top and standing directly in front of him. She looked soft and fragile, curves in all the right places, tight skin and few wrinkles for a woman in her late forties. She wore her strawberry-blond hair loose, letting it brush her jawline in delicate wisps. He wondered if it was her natural color, and he caught himself smiling. Maybe he would need to find out for himself.

He leaned back into the sofa, waiting, sniffing in her fragrance. God, she smelled good, though he couldn't name the fragrance. Usually he could narrow it down, but this scent was new. Her red silk blouse was thin enough to reveal small, round breasts and the slight pucker of nipples. He was glad she thought she didn't need the jacket. He tucked his hands into his lap, making sure his folded jacket covered the swelling bulge, pleased that his new diet of porn movies seemed to be helping his temporary lapses.

"As with all my patients, Mr. Harding," she said finally, "I'd like to know what your goals are. What you hope to accomplish in our sessions?"

He held back a smile. She was already accomplishing one of his goals. He tilted his head toward her and continued to stare at her breasts. Even if she could see his eyes, people accepted, they expected his eyes to be looking anywhere but in their own eyes.

"I'm not sure I understand the question." He had learned it was good to make women explain. It allowed them to feel in control, and he wanted her to believe she was in control.

"You told me on the phone," she began carefully as though measuring her words, "that you had some sexual issues you wanted to work on." She neither emphasized nor hesitated over the phrase "sexual issues." That was good, very good. "In order for me to help you, I need to know, more specifically, what you expect from me. What you'd like to see come out of these sessions."

It was time to see how easily she could be shocked.

"It really is quite simple. I want to be able to enjoy fucking a woman again."

She blinked and her light complexion flushed slightly, but she didn't move. It was a bit of a letdown. Maybe he should go ahead and add that he wanted to enjoy fucking a woman without wanting to fuck her to death. His new habit really wasn't much different than many of those in the animal and insect world. Perhaps he should compare his sexual habits to those of the female praying mantis who bites off her mate's head just as he is beginning to copulate.

Would she understand that the orgasm, the erotic surge was incredibly powerful when it included pain? Should he confess that seeing his women smeared in blood and screaming for mercy made him come in an orgasmic explosion like none he could achieve otherwise? Could she understand that this hideous thing inside threatened to take away the foundation of his being, his last primal instinct?

But no, he wouldn't share any of this with her—that would probably be a bit much. That was something Albert Stucky would do or say, and he needed to resist the urge to stoop to his old friend's level.

"Can you do that, Doc?" he asked, sticking his chin out and up as though he was listening for her movement, for her reaction.

"I can certainly try."

He looked over her shoulder, his body slightly turned to the side, despite her standing in front of him.

"You're blushing," he said, and allowed a curt smile.

The color in her cheeks deepened. Her hand went to her neck in the useless attempt to stop the blush.

"What makes you say that?"

Would she deny it? Would she disappoint him this soon and lie?

"I'm guessing," he said, letting his voice be soft and soothing, encouraging her to confide in him, hoping to gain access to her own vulnerabilities. If he was to accomplish his ultimate goal, he would need Dr. Gwen Patterson not to feel threatened. The good doctor had a reputation for delving into some of the most famous and devious of criminal minds. He wondered what she would think if she knew she was to be the guinea pig this time.

"Let me just say, I've been a psychologist quite a while." She tried to explain her reaction away casually, but he noticed the color remained in her cheeks. "I've heard many shocking things, much more so than your problem. You needn't worry about embarrassing me, Mr. Harding."

Okay, so she chose to play it safe and cool, refusing him access to her inner self. The idea of this excited him nevertheless. He did so enjoy a challenge.

"Perhaps," she continued, "we should start by you telling me why you no longer enjoy sex."

"Isn't that obvious?" He used the tone he had perfected. The one that sounded angry, offended, yet sad enough to invoke the right amount of pity. It usually worked.

"Of course it's not obvious."

He let one of his hands stray under the pile of leather. She was making this so easy. Playing right into his hands, so to speak. He cupped a palm over his erection.

"If you're thinking your—" she hesitated "—your handicap—"

"It's okay. You can call it what it is. I'm blind. I don't mind anyone saying the word."

"Okay, but your blindness certainly should not mean a loss of libido."

He liked the way she said "libido." Though her lips were thin and her mouth small, he liked the shape. He enjoyed watching the upper lip curl a bit at the corner. He detected a slight accent, but he couldn't place it—maybe upper New York? It made him anxious to hear her say "penis" and "fellatio," and he wondered how her lips would curl around those words.

"Is that what you're saying, Mr. Harding?" she interrupted his thoughts.

"That somehow your loss of sight has rendered you incapable of performing?"

"Men are highly visual creatures, especially when it comes to being sexually aroused."

"Very true," she said as she reached behind her and grabbed a file folder, his folder, his case history. "When did you begin losing your eyesight?"

"About four years ago. Do we have to talk about that?"

She looked up at him over the open file. She had shifted to the other end of the desk, but he kept his gaze on the spot where she had been.

"If it will help us deal with your current problem, then yes, I do think we should talk about it."

He liked her decisive manner, her direct tone. She wouldn't be pussyfooting around him. What a wonderful word—pussyfooting. He rubbed his hidden hand against his bulge.

"Do you have an objection to that, Mr. Harding? You certainly don't appear to be a man who runs away from a challenge."

He hesitated only because he didn't want to interrupt the sensation. It was okay. She'd think he simply needed a moment to think about it.

"I have no objection," he said, having some difficulty containing a smile. No, anyone who knew Walker Harding would never accuse him of running away from anything. But if he was to accept his new challenge, he'd need to depend on the master criminal mind that Dr. Patterson yet had the pleasure of examining. Yes, despite playing this new role, he would still need to depend on the genius of his old friend, Albert Stucky.

CHAPTER 29

Tully ripped off the latest fax that had just come in from the Kansas City Police Department. He scanned its contents while he gathered folders and notes and crime scene photos. In ten minutes he was meeting with Assistant Director Cunningham, and yet his mind was still preoccupied with the argument he'd had with his daughter less than an hour ago. Emma had waited until he was dropping her off at school to drop her bomb. Damn she was good. But then what did he expect? She had been schooled in the fine art of surprise attack by none other than the master, her own mother.

"Oh, by the way," she had announced in a matter-of-fact voice. "Josh Reynolds asked me to the junior/senior prom. It's a week from Friday, so I'll need to buy a new dress. Probably new shoes, too."

Immediately he had gotten angry. She was only a freshman. When had they decided she could date?

"Did I miss that conversation?" he had asked with enough sarcasm that he was now embarrassed in retrospect.

She had given him her best insulted, wounded look. How could he not trust her? She was "almost fifteen." Practically an old maid compared to her friends who, she assured him, had been dating for two or three years already. He passed on the opportunity to counter with the old argument that just because your friends jump off a bridge... Besides, the real problem was not that he didn't trust her. At forty-three, he could still remember how horny fifteen- and six-teen-year-old boys could get. He wished he could discuss it with Caroline, but he knew she'd side with Emma. Was he really just being an overprotective father?

He jammed the fax sheets into a file folder, adding it to the pile in his arms and headed down the hall. After talking to Kansas City Detective John Ford late last night, Tully was prepared for Cunningham to be in a foul mood. The waitress's murder looked more and more like the work of Albert Stucky. No one else would deliver the woman's kidney to Agent O'Dell's hotel room. Actually, Tully couldn't figure out why he wasn't on a plane to Kansas City to join O'Dell.

"Good morning, Anita," he greeted the gray-haired secretary who looked alert and impeccable at any hour of the day.

"Coffee, Agent Tully?"

"Yes, please. Cream but—"

"No sugar. I remember. I'll bring it in to you." She waved him by. Everyone knew not to set foot into the assistant director's office until Anita gave the signal.

Cunningham was on the phone, but nodded to Tully and pointed to one of the chairs in front of his desk.

"Yes, I understand," Cunningham said into the phone. "Of course I will." He hung up, as was his usual manner, without a goodbye. He adjusted his glasses, sipped coffee, then looked at Tully. Despite the crisp white shirt and perfectly knotted tie, his eyes betrayed him. Swollen from too little sleep, the red lines were magnified by the bifocal half of his glasses.

"Before we get started," he said, glancing at his watch, "do you have any information on Walker Harding?"

"Harding?" Tully had to think past horny high-school boys and pink prom dresses. "I'm sorry, sir, I don't recognize the name Walker Harding."

"He was Albert Stucky's business partner," a woman's voice answered from the open doorway.

Tully twisted in his chair to look at the young, dark-haired woman. She was attractive and wore a navy blue suit jacket with matching trousers.

"Agent O'Dell, please come in." Cunningham stood and pointed to the chair next to Tully.

Tully stared up at her, shuffling his files, awkwardly shoving them aside.

"Special Agent Margaret O'Dell, this is Special Agent R. J. Tully."

The chair wobbled as Tully stood and shook Agent O'Dell's outstretched hand. Immediately he was impressed with her firm grip and the way she looked directly into his eyes.

"I'm pleased to meet you, Agent Tully."

She was genuine. She was professional. There was no trace of what she must have gone through last night. This certainly didn't look like an agent who was on the verge of mental collapse.

"The pleasure is mine, Agent O'Dell. I've heard a great deal about you."

Tully could see Cunningham already growing impatient with all these pleasantries.

"Why were you asking about Walker Harding?" O'Dell asked as she sat down.

Tully picked up his files again. Okay, so she was used to the assistant director's style of getting right down to business. Now Tully wished he had spent some time preparing instead of agonizing over Emma's virginity. He honestly hadn't thought O'Dell would show up.

"For Agent Tully's benefit," Cunningham began explaining, "Walker Harding and Albert Stucky started an Internet stock-trading business, one of the first of its kind, in the early 1990s. They ended up making millions."

"I'm sorry, but I don't think I have any information on him," Tully said as he riffled through his files, double-checking.

"You probably don't." Cunningham sounded apologetic. "Harding was out of the picture long before Stucky took up his new hobby. He and Stucky sold their company, split their millions and went their separate ways. There was no reason for any of us to know about Walker Harding."

"I'm not sure I follow," Tully said, glancing at Agent O'Dell to see if he was the only one missing something. "Is there some reason why we should now?"

Anita interrupted, floating into the room and handing Tully a steaming mug.

"Thanks, Anita."

"Anything for you, Agent O'Dell? Coffee? Or perhaps your usual early-morning Diet Pepsi?"

Tully watched Agent O'Dell smile in a way that said the two women were quite familiar with each other.

"Thank you, Anita, but no, I'm fine."

The secretary squeezed the agent's shoulder in a gesture that looked more motherly than professional, and then she left, closing the door behind her.

Cunningham sat back and made a tent with his fingertips, picking up the conversation exactly where they had left off, as if there had been no interruption. "Walker Harding became a recluse after he and Stucky sold their business. Practically disappeared off the face of the earth. There seems to be virtually no records, no transactions, no sign of the man."

"Then what does this have to do with Albert Stucky?" Tully was puzzled.

"I checked the airline schedules within the last week for flights going from Dulles or Reagan National to Kansas City. Not that I expected to find Albert Stucky's name on any of the manifests." He looked from Tully to O'Dell. "I was looking for any of the aliases Stucky has used in the past. That's when I noticed that there was a ticket sold for a KC flight, Sunday afternoon out of Dulles, to a Walker Harding."

Cunningham waited, looking for some reaction. Tully watched, tapping his foot nervously but not impressed with the information.

"Excuse me, sir, for saying so, but that may not mean much. It may not even be the same man."

"Perhaps not. However, Agent Tully, I suggest you find out whatever you can about Walker Harding."

"Assistant Director Cunningham, why am I here?" Agent O'Dell asked politely but with enough candor to indicate she wasn't willing to continue without an answer.

Tully wanted to smile. Instead, he kept his eyes and his attention on Cunningham. It was hard not to like O'Dell. Out of the corner of his eye, he could see her shift in her chair, uncomfortable and restless but holding her tongue. She had been kept off this investigation since the beginning. Tully wondered if she was angry with having to sit and listen to these details if she couldn't be involved. Or had Cunningham changed his mind? Tully studied his face, but saw no clue as to what his boss was thinking.

When he didn't answer immediately, O'Dell must have seen it as an opportunity to proceed.

"I mean no disrespect, but the three of us are sitting here talking about a ticket that may or may not have been issued to a man who Albert Stucky may or may not have talked to for years. Yet, there is one thing that we can be certain of—Albert Stucky murdered a woman in Kansas City, and most likely he is still there."

Tully crossed his arms and waited, all the while wanting to applaud this woman he had heard was burned out and slipping over the edge. She certainly soared at the top of her game this morning.

Cunningham caved in his finger tent and sat forward, leaning elbows on his desk and looking as though he had been ambushed in a chess match. But now he was ready for his move, his turn.

"Saturday night about twenty miles from here, a young woman was found murdered, her body tossed into a Dumpster, her spleen surgically removed and placed inside a discarded pizza box."

"Saturday?" Agent O'Dell fidgeted while she calculated the unusually short time line. "Kansas City is not a copycat. He left the goddamn kidney at my door."

Tully winced. Forget chess. This would be more like a showdown at the OK Corral. Cunningham, however, didn't blink.

"The young woman was a pizza delivery person. She was taken while delivering her route."

Agent O'Dell became agitated, crossing her legs, then uncrossing them as if restraining her words. Tully knew she had to be exhausted.

Cunningham continued, "She had to have been taken somewhere close by. Perhaps in the neighborhood. He raped and sodomized her, slit her throat and removed her spleen."

"By sodomized are you saying he raped her himself from behind or with another item?"

Tully couldn't see a difference. Wasn't either hideous enough? Cunningham looked to him for the answer. This, unfortunately, he could answer without digging through a single file. The young girl had looked too much like Emma for him not to remember every detail. Whether he wanted them to be or not, they were stamped in his memory.

"There was no semen left behind, but the medical examiner seemed convinced it was penile stimulation. There were no traces or remnants that a foreign object might leave behind."

"Stucky's never done that before." O'Dell sat at the edge of her chair, suddenly animated. "He wouldn't do that. There would be no point. He likes to watch their faces. He enjoys seeing their fear. He wouldn't be able to see that from behind."

Cunningham tapped his fingertips on the desktop as if waiting for O'Dell to finish.

"The young woman delivered a pizza to your new home the night she was murdered."

The silence seemed amplified when the drumming of the fingertips stopped. Cunningham and Tully watched O'Dell. She sat back, looking from one to the other. Tully saw the realization in her eyes. He expected to see fear, maybe anger. It surprised him to find what looked like resignation. She rubbed a hand over her face and tucked strands of hair behind her ears. Otherwise, she sat quietly.

"That's why, Agent O'Dell, I'm guessing it didn't matter that you stayed in Kansas City. He'll follow you." Cunningham loosened his tie and rolled up his sleeves as though he was suddenly too warm. Both gestures seemed foreign. "Albert Stucky is pulling you into this, no matter what I do to keep you out of it."

"And by keeping me out of it, sir, you're taking away my only defense." O'Dell's voice had an undeniable quiver to it. Tully saw her bite down on her lower lip. Was it to restrain her words or control the quiver?

Cunningham glanced over at Tully, sat back and released his own sigh of resignation. "Agent Tully has requested that you assist him on the case."

O'Dell stared at Tully with surprise. He found himself a bit embarrassed and not sure why. It wasn't as if he had made the request to do her any favors. It could be putting her in even more danger. But the fact was, he needed her.

"I've decided to grant Agent Tully's request on two conditions, neither of which I'm willing to negotiate or compromise." Cunningham leaned forward again, elbows on his desktop, hands fisted together. "Number one, Agent Tully is to remain the lead on this investigation. I expect you to share all information and knowledge as soon as it becomes available to you. You will not—and I repeat, Agent O'Dell— you will not go off on a wild-goose chase or check on hunches without Agent Tully accompanying you. Is that understood?"

"Of course," she answered, her voice now strong and firm again.

"Number two. I want you to see the Bureau's psychologist."

"Sir, I really don't think—"

"Agent O'Dell, I said there will be no negotiating, no compromise. I'll leave it up to Dr. Kernan as to how many times he wants to see you each week."

"Dr. James Kernan?" O'Dell seemed appalled.

"That's right. I had Anita set up your first appointment. Check with her on your way out for the time. She's also setting up an office for you. Agent Tully occupies your old one. I saw no reason in moving both of you. Now, if the two of you will excuse me." He sat back, dismissing them. "I have another appointment."

Tully gathered his mess and waited for O'Dell at the door. For a woman who had just been given what she had wanted for the last five months, she looked more agitated than relieved.

CHAPTER 30

Tess looked forward to her morning appointment, although while she drove down the empty streets, the guilt crept over her for tip-toeing out of Daniel's house without waking him to say goodbye. She simply didn't have the energy for another battle. He would grumble about her leaving so early to run home and shower and change clothes, when she could do all that just as easily at his house. What he really wanted was for her to stay, because he was more easily aroused in the mornings, and he wanted to have sex.

Yet he would say ridiculous things like, "We have so little time for each other, we need those few extra minutes in the morning."

Each time she stayed over, it was the same thing, the same old argument—"How will we ever know if we're compatible, Tess, if we don't read the *New York Times* together or share breakfast in bed?"

He had actually given those examples. How could he believe any of that when he barely spoke to her over their dinners together? The mornings when he wanted her to stay for a quick fuck seemed to be the only time he was concerned about their compatibility.

Ninety-nine percent of the time, he could care less what was good for their relationship. Not that Tess had any clues about what made a successful relationship. Maybe it did include sharing the *New York Times* and breakfasts in bed. How would she know? She had never been in a relationship she could call a success, and she had never been in one with someone like Daniel Kassenbaum.

Daniel was sophisticated, intelligent, refined and cultured. My God, the man completed the *New York Times* crossword puzzle in ink. But unlike Daniel, she didn't kid herself about their relationship. She knew they had little in common. He certainly didn't consider her his equal, and often pointed out her deficiencies as if she were his Eliza Doolittle. Even the other night when she had asked him about investing her bonus money, she had felt as if he had patted her on the head with his "don't get into something you don't understand" comment.

However, the one area where Tess excelled, above and beyond Daniel, was sex. What Daniel lacked, Tess made up for. He had told her many times—though only in the heat of passion—that she was "phenomenally the best fuck" he had ever had. For some twisted reason, it pleased her to have this power over him, though it left her cold and hollow inside. Having sex with Daniel, despite being phenomenal for him, was neither enjoyable nor satisfying for Tess.

In fact, she had begun to wonder whether she was capable of feeling genuinely aroused—if she would ever feel the sort of passion she continuously faked with Daniel. Having Will Finley, a complete stranger, resurrect those feelings proved more unsettling and annoying than reassuring. And having those memories, still so fresh in her mind, of Will's hands and mouth knowing exactly how to touch her, made Daniel's inadequacies more pronounced. She almost wished that she had never been able to remember her night with Will, that the tequila could have erased her memory. Instead, she seemed able to think of nothing else. And those memories reeled over and over in her mind.

At one time she had been so good at blocking out memories. That was usually the purpose of the tequila. In the past, she used to drink too much. She danced and flirted and had sex with as many men as she wanted. She played and hustled pool, putting on wild, sexy shows for anyone interested in encouraging her. She used to believe that if her life ran constantly in fast-forward, she could forget the horrors of her childhood. After all, nothing she could do would be more shocking, more destructive, more frightening than what she had lived through as a child, right?

But in the process, all Tess had managed to do was create a life empty and hollow. Ironically, it had taken a fifth of vodka and a bottle of sleeping pills to wake her up. That was almost seven years ago. The last five years she had worked her ass off to re-create herself and leave not only her childhood behind, but those dark years spent covering it up and running away from it.

In order to do that, she had left the mad rush of D.C. and all its temptations of drugs, all-night clubs and congressmen's beds. Louie's had been a sort of halfway house for Tess. She took a job tending bar and found a tiny apartment by the river. When she finally felt ready, she went back to Blackwood, Virginia, and sold the family farm—the living hell—where she had lived with her aunt and uncle. They had died years before, her only notice coming by way of certified letter from an attorney. Somehow she had expected to automatically know when they died, as if the earth would sigh a relief. There had been no sigh, no relief.

Tess glanced up at herself in the rearview mirror, annoyed that the memories could still wrinkle her brow and clench her teeth. After her aunt's and uncle's deaths, she had let the farm sit empty, refusing to set foot on the property. Finally she had the courage to sell the place, but first destroying the house and all the dilapidated buildings. She had made certain that the storm cellar—her personal punishment chamber—had been bulldozed and filled in. Then, and only then, was she able to sell the place.

It had brought a decent price, supplying her with enough money to start a new life, which only seemed fair since it had taken away half her life in the first place. It was enough money for Tess to go back to school and get her real estate license, and to buy and furnish her brick cottage, in a nice neighborhood, in a quiet city, where no one knew her.

After getting the job at Heston Realty, she joined several business associations. Delores signed her on as a member at the Skyview Country Club. She had insisted it would be essential, allowing Tess to meet potential clients. Although Tess still had a problem seeing herself as a member of a country club. It was there she had met Daniel Kassenbaum. It had been a tremendous victory, proof of her successful new lifestyle. She would be able to do anything, go anywhere, if she was able to win someone as sophisticated, arrogant, well-bred and cultured as Daniel.

She reminded herself that Daniel was good for her. He was stable, ambitious, practical and most importantly, he was taken seriously. All things she wanted—no, needed in her life. That he didn't know or care how to touch her mattered very little in the larger scope of things. Besides, it wasn't as if she was in love with him. She preferred having no emotional investment. Love and emotions had never been key ingredients to a successful relationship. If anything, they had been ingredients for disaster.

Tess pulled the Miata in front of 5349 Archer Drive. Her eyes checked up and down the cul-de-sac, confirming that she had arrived too early. There was no sign of her 10:00 a.m. appointment. Actually, there were no signs of life. The neighborhood's residents had already left for their long commute, and those who were able to stay behind were probably still in bed. She decided to use the extra time to make certain the two-story colonial was in show condition.

She checked her reflection one more time. When had the lines around her mouth and eyes become so pronounced? For the first time in her life she was actually beginning to look her age. It had taken her years to get to where she was. Daniel was an important piece of the puzzle for her new professional persona. He lent credibility to her. She couldn't ruin it now. So why did she keep remembering Will Finley in that blue towel, looking so lean and handsome, and arousing senses she had buried long ago?

She shook her head and grabbed her briefcase, slamming her car door too hard and sending the echo throughout the quiet neighborhood. To make up for the noise, she walked slowly up the sidewalk, preventing her heels from clacking.

The house had been on the market for over eight months with little activity in the last three months. However, the sellers continued to stand firm on their selling price. Like so many of the houses on the outskirts of Newburgh Heights, money seemed to be no problem for the owners, which certainly made negotiations a problem.

Tess went to unlock the steel security door, but the key turned too easily. The dead bolt didn't click. The door wasn't locked, and now standing in the foyer, she could see the security system had also been disarmed.

CHAPTER 31

"Damn it!" Tess muttered, and flipped the light switch. Yes, the electricity was on, so there was no excuse for the alarm system not to be working.

She made a mental note to check on the last agent who had shown the house. Without even looking, she could guess it had been one of the imbeciles from Peterson Brothers. They were constantly forgetting things like this, and they had the professional ethics of pimps. There had been recent rumors about one of the Peterson brothers using empty client houses for sleazy sex parties.

Suddenly Tess remembered that this house had an extra-large master bedroom and bath with a skylight.

"There better not be a mess."

She checked her wristwatch. Only fifteen minutes left. She tossed her briefcase into a corner of the living room, pushed up the sleeves of her suit jacket, and started up the stairs, stopping to kick off her heels. She didn't need this crap, not this morning. Not when her patience and nerves had already been frayed and tested by her disappearing act from Daniel's bed. He'd be getting to his office right about now. Thankfully, she had left her cellular phone in the car, because knowing Daniel, he'd be calling to scold her.

She stomped up the stairs when halfway up she heard the front door open. He was early. Why did he have to be early? She shoved her sleeves back in place and searched for her leather pumps, slipping them on one by one as she found them. By the time she reached the bottom of the staircase, a tall, dark-haired man was wandering through the spacious living room. Without window treatments, sunlight cascaded in sheets of blinding light, surrounding him.

"Hello?"

"I know I'm a bit early."

"That's fine." Tess kept the annoyance from her voice, wishing she had been able to check the damn master bedroom first.

He turned, and only then did she notice the white cane. Immediately, she wondered how he had gotten here. She glanced out the window but saw no signs of another vehicle in the winding circular driveway.

She guessed he was around her age, middle to late thirties, though she found it hard to determine anyone's age when she couldn't see his eyes. His Ray-Ban sunglasses contained particularly dark lenses. She took notice of his designer silk shirt with the open collar, his expensive leather jacket and well-pressed chinos. She caught herself checking to see if everything matched. His features were handsome but sharp, with a chiseled jaw that was much too taut, thin but nicely curved lips and pronounced cheekbones. He had a bit of a widow's peak, but his dark hair was thick and close cropped.

"I'm Walker Harding," he said. "Are you the agent I spoke to on the phone?"

"Yes, I'm Tess McGowan." She offered her hand, then snatched it back quickly, embarrassed, when she realized he couldn't see it.

He hesitated and slowly removed his hand from his pocket. She noticed how strong and muscular it was as he held it out to her. He was a little off target, his fingers pointed to the side of her. She stepped in closer and shook it. Immediately she felt his large hand swallow hers. The long fingers wrapped all the way around her wrist, surprising her in what felt more like a caress than a handshake. She dismissed the thought and ignored her unexpected discomfort.

"I just arrived," she said, extracting her hand. "I didn't get a chance to make a quick run-through," she explained, wondering how in the world he would know the difference. How was she supposed to show him a house when he couldn't see a damn thing?

He left her and wandered without a word across the living room, tapping his cane in front of him and walking confidently. He stopped at the bay window that looked out over the backyard. He fumbled for the latch and opened it. Then he stood quietly, staring out as if transfixed by something in the yard.

"The sun feels wonderful," he finally said, tilting his head back and letting his face be warmed by the brilliant light. "I know it might seem silly, but I like lots of windows."

"No, it's not silly at all." She caught herself talking louder and immediately chastised herself. He was blind not deaf.

Tess studied his profile. The straight nose had a slight bend, and from this angle she could see a scar just below his jawline. She couldn't help wondering if his blindness had been caused by an accident of some kind. Despite his disability, he seemed to possess confidence. There was a self-assurance in his manner, the way he walked, the way he handled himself. However, his gestures seemed stiff, his hands constantly retreated to his pockets. Was he nervous, anxious?

"How big are the evergreens?" he asked, his voice startling her as though she had forgotten what they were here for.

"Excuse me?"

"I can smell evergreens. Are there a lot and are they big or small?"

She walked up beside him, keeping a safe distance without seeming rude and still being able to look out the window. The property lots here were huge, and the evergreens, mostly cedar and pine, created a natural border at the far edge. She couldn't smell them. But of course his other senses had probably become more refined.

"They're very large. Some cedar, some pine. There's a line of them that separates the properties."

"Good. I do like my privacy." He turned to her and smiled. "I hope you're not uncomfortable having to describe things to me."

"No, of course not," Tess said, hoping that she sounded convincing. "Where would you like to start your tour?"

"I was told there is a fabulous master bedroom. Could we start there?"

"Good choice," she told him. Damn it! She wished she had come earlier. That Peterson asshole better not have left a mess. "Do you prefer walking alone or would you like me to take your arm?"

"You smell quite lovely."

She stared at him, taken off guard.

"It's Chanel No. 5, right?"

"Yes, it is." Was he flirting with her?

"I'll follow your lovely scent. Just lead the way."

"Oh, yes. Okay."

She walked slowly, almost too slowly, causing his outstretched hand to bump into her once on the landing. He let it linger on her hip as though needing to get his bearings. Or at least that was what Tess told herself. She had experienced more outrageous come-ons and intentional gropes than this.

The master bedroom smelled of cleaning formula, and Tess's eyes darted around. Whoever had been here last had indeed cleaned up. Thankfully, the room looked in order. In fact, it smelled and looked freshly scrubbed. Tess found it odd that Mr. Harding, whose senses had been so keen downstairs, made no comment about these new overpowering scents.

"This room is about thirty by twenty," she proceeded casually. "There's another bay window on the south wall that looks out over the backyard. The floor is an oak parquet. There's a—"

"Excuse me, Ms. McGowan."

"Please, call me Tess."

"Tess, of course." He stopped and smiled. "I hope you won't find this offensive, but I like to have an idea of what the person I'm talking to looks like. May I touch your face?"

At first she thought she must have heard him wrong. She didn't know what to say. She remembered his touching her on the landing and now wondered if indeed it had been a grope and not a harmless miscalculation.

"I'm sorry. You're offended," he said apologetically, his voice low and soothing.

"No, of course not," she answered quickly. If she wasn't careful, her paranoia could lose her the sale. "I'm afraid I'm just not as prepared as I should be to help you."

"It's really quite painless," he told her as though he were explaining a surgical procedure. "I use only my fingertips. I assure you, I won't be pawing you." His lips curved into another smile, and Tess felt ridiculous making a fuss.

"Please, go ahead." She stepped closer, despite her apprehension.

He set the cane aside and started slowly, gently at her hair, using both hands, but only the tips of his fingers. She avoided looking up at him, staring off over his shoulder. His hands smelled faintly of ammonia, or was it simply the overpowering scent of the freshly scrubbed wooden floor? His fingers stroked her forehead and moved over her eyelids.

She tried to ignore their dampness, but glanced at his face for any indication that he was as uncomfortable as she was. No, he seemed calm and composed and his fingers began their descent on either side of her face, sliding down her cheeks. She dismissed what felt like a caress. But then his fingertips moved to her lips. His index finger lingered too long, rubbing back and forth. For a second it felt as though he might press it into her mouth. Startled by the sensation and the thought, Tess looked at his eyes. She tried to see beyond the dark lenses, and when she was successful, getting a glimpse of his black eyes, she saw that he was staring directly at her. Was that possible? No, of course not. She was simply being paranoid, an annoying tendency left over from her past life.

By now his fingers had wandered to her chin, tracing their way down to her neck. They briefly wisped beneath the neckline of her blouse, brushing her collarbone, hesitating as if he was testing her, as if asking how far she would let him go. She began to step back just when he wrapped his fingers around her throat.

"What are you doing?" Tess gasped and grabbed at his large hands.

Now he squeezed, choking her, his eyes definitely staring into hers, a twisted smile at his lips. She clawed at the fingers, steel vise grips clamped like the jaws of a pit bull. She struggled and twisted, but he shoved her back. Her head knocked into the wall with such a force she closed her eyes against the pain. She couldn't breathe. She couldn't think. God, he was so strong.

When she opened her eyes, she saw that he had released one of his hands. She was able to suck in air, her lungs aching and greedy. Before she could gather her strength, he shoved his arm up against her to hold her in place, stabbing his elbow into her throat and cutting off her air once again. That's when she saw the syringe in his free hand.

The terror spread through her quickly, her arms and legs flaying in defense. It was useless. He was much too strong. The needle poked through her jacket and sunk deep into the skin of her arm. She felt her entire body jerk. In seconds the room began to spin. Her hands, her knees, her muscles became limp, and then the room went black.

CHAPTER 32

The minute Maggie walked into Dr. James Kernan's office she felt like a nineteen-year-old college student again. The feelings of confusion, wonder and intimidation all came back to her in a rush of sights and smells. His office, set in the Wilmington Towers in Washington, D.C., and no longer on the University of Virginia's campus, still looked and smelled the same.

Immediately, her nostrils were accosted by stale cigar smoke, old leather and Ben-Gay rubbing ointment. The tiny space was littered with the same strange paraphernalia. A human brain's dissected frontal lobe bulged in a mason jar filled with formaldehyde. The jar acted as a makeshift bookend, ironically holding up such texts as *Explaining Hitler: The Search for the Origins of Evil*, Freud's *Interpretation of Dreams* and what Maggie knew to be a rare first edition of *Alice In Wonderland*. Of the three, the last seemed most appropriate for the professor of psychology who easily conjured up images of the Mad Hatter.

On the mahogany credenza across the room were antique instruments, their shapes and points intriguing until they were recognized as surgical instruments once used to perform lobotomies. On the wall behind the matching mahogany desk were black-and-white photographs of the procedure. Another equally disturbing photograph included a young woman undergoing shock treatment. The woman's empty eyes and resigned posture beneath the ominous iron equipment had always reminded Maggie more of an execution than a medical treatment. Sometimes she questioned how she could be involved in a profession that, at one time, could be so brutal while pretending to cure the ailments of the psyche.

Kernan, however, embraced the eccentricities of their profession. His office was simply an extension of the strange little man. A man as notorious for his crude jokes about "nutcases" as he was for his own version of shock treatment, which he had perfected on his students.

The man loved mind games and could lure and trick a person into them without warning. One moment he would drill an unprepared freshman with rapid-fire questions, not allowing the poor student to even answer. The next minute he'd be in a corner of the classroom, standing silently with his face to the wall. Then still later, he'd climb atop a desk and lecture while teetering from one desk to another, his small, stocky but aging body threatening to send him falling while he lectured and did a balancing act at the same time. Even the seniors in his classes had no idea what to expect of their odd professor. And this was the man the FBI trusted to determine her sanity?

Maggie heard the familiar clomp-squeak of his footsteps outside the office. Instinctively, she sat up straight and stopped her browsing. Even the man's footsteps transformed her into an incompetent college kid.

Dr. Kernan entered his office unceremoniously and shuffled to his desk without recognizing or acknowledging Maggie. He plopped down into the leather chair, sending it into a series of creaks. Maggie couldn't be sure that all the creaks came from the chair and not the old man's joints.

He began rummaging through stacks of papers. She watched quietly, her hands folded in her lap. Kernan looked as though he had shrunk since the last time she had seen him, over ten years ago.

Back then he had seemed ancient, but now his shoulders were hunched, his hands trembled and were speckled with brown spots. His hair, just as white as she remembered, was thin and feathery, revealing more brown spots on his forehead and the top of his head. Tufts of white hair protruded from his ears.

Finally he appeared to find what he had been so desperately in search of. He struggled to open the tin box of breath mints, took two without offering any to Maggie and snapped the container shut.

"O'Dell, Margaret," he said to himself, still not acknowledging her presence.

He sorted through the rubble again. "Class of 1990." He stopped and thumbed through a folder. Maggie glanced at the cover to see if he was reading her file, only to discover a label that read, Twenty-five Best Internet Porn Sites.

"I remember a Margaret O'Dell," he said without looking up at her, and in a voice that sounded like a senile old man talking to himself. "O'Dell, O'Dell, the farmer and the dell."

Maggie shifted in her chair, forcing herself to be patient, to be polite. Nothing had changed. Why was she surprised to find him treating patients the same way he had treated his students, playing silly word games, reducing names and identities to nursery rhymes? It was all part of his intimidation.

"Premed," he continued while riffling through the list of porn sites. Several times he stopped, smacking his lips together or hissing out a "tis, tis." "Sat in the back left corner of my classroom, taking very few notes. B student. Asked questions only about criminal behavior and hereditary traits."

Maggie hid her surprise. These could easily be odd little facts he may have noted and kept in a student file. And of course, he would have reviewed her file before she arrived, so as to have an advantage. Not that he needed an advantage. She waited, forcing her hands to keep still when they wanted to grip the arms of her chair. She wanted to dig her fingernails into the leather to steady herself and prevent her from storming out of this ridiculous inquisition.

"Got a master's in behavioral psychology," he went on in his droll tone. "Managed to land a forensic fellowship at Quantico." Finally he looked up at her, his pale blue eyes magnified and swimming behind the thick square glasses. Bushy white eyebrows stuck out in every direction. He rubbed his jaw and said, "Wonder what the hell you would have done if you'd been an A student." Then he stared at her, waiting.

As usual, he caught her off guard. She didn't know what to say. He had a talent for disarming people by making them feel invisible. Then suddenly he expected a response to what was never a question. Maggie remained silent and returned his steady gaze, vowing not to flinch. She hated that he could reduce her to an unsure, speechless teenager with only a few words and that goddamn look of his. This was certainly not her idea of therapy. Assistant Director Cunningham was way off base on this one. Sending her to see anyone was a waste of time. Sending her to see Kernan would only challenge her sanity further and would certainly not be a remedy.

"So, Margaret O'Dell, the quiet little bird in the corner, the B student who was so interested in criminals but didn't think she belonged in my classroom, is now Special Agent Margaret O'Dell, who wears a gun and a shiny badge and now doesn't think she belongs in my office."

He stared at her again, waiting for a response, still not asking a question. His elbows leaned on the wobbly stacks of paper as he laced his fingers together.

"That's true, isn't it? You don't think you should be here?"

"No, I don't," she answered, her voice strong and defiant despite the man's ability to intimidate the hell out of her.

"So your superiors are wrong? All those years of training. All that experience, and they're flat out wrong. Is that right?"

"I didn't say that."

"Really? That wasn't what you said?"

Word games, mind games, confusion—Kernan was a master. Maggie needed to concentrate. She couldn't let him twist her words. She wouldn't let him trap her.

"You asked me if I thought I should be here," she explained calmly. "I simply said no, I don't think that I should be here."

"Awwww," he said, drawing it out into a sigh as he sank back in his chair. He rested his hands on his thick chest, letting his wrinkled jacket fall open. "I'm so glad you clarified that for me, Margaret O'Dell."

She remembered that her one-on-one encounters with the man had always felt like an interrogation. It was disconcerting that this befuddled, little old man who looked as if he slept in his clothes, still possessed that same power. She refused to let him unnerve her. Instead, she stared at him and waited.

"So, tell me, Margaret O'Dell, who doesn't think she belongs in my office, do you enjoy this obsession you have with Albert Stucky?"

Suddenly she felt a knot in her stomach. Damn it! Leave it to Kernan to cut to the chase, to strike without warning.

"Of course I don't enjoy it." She kept her voice steady, her eyes level with his. She mustn't blink too many times. He would be counting the blinks. Despite those Coke-bottle glasses, Kernan wouldn't miss a twitch or a grimace.

"Then why do you continue to obsess?"

"Because I want him caught."

"And you're the only one who can catch him?"

"I know him better than anyone else."

"Oh yes, of course. Because he shared his little hobby with you. That's right. He left you with a little tattoo, a sort of brand to remember him by."

She had forgotten how cruel Kernan could be. Yet she forced herself to stay calm. She couldn't let him see the anger. That was exactly what he wanted.

"I spent two years tracking him. That's why I know him better than anyone else."

"I see," he said, tilting his head as if necessary to do so. "Then your obsession will end after you catch him?"

"Yes."

"And after he's punished?"

"Yes."

"Because he must be punished, right?"

"There is no punishment great enough for someone like Albert Stucky."

"Really? Putting him to death won't be punishment enough?"

She hesitated, well aware of his biting sarcasm and anticipating his trap. She proceeded anyway.

"No matter how many victims, no matter how many women Stucky kills, he can die only once."

"Ah yes, I see. And that wouldn't be a fitting punishment. What would be?"

She didn't answer. She wouldn't take his bait.

"You'd like to see him suffer, wouldn't you, Margaret O'Dell?"

She held his gaze. Don't flinch, she told herself. He was waiting for her to slip. He was setting her up, pushing her, forcing her to expose her anger.

"How would you choose to make him suffer? Pain? Excruciating, drawn-out pain?" He stared at her, waiting. She stared back, refusing to give him what he wanted.

"No, not pain," he said finally, as if her eyes had answered for her. "No. You prefer fear, don't you? You want him to suffer by feeling fear," he continued in a casual voice with neither accusation nor confrontation, inviting her to confide in him.

Her hands stayed in her lap. She continued to sit up straight, eyes never leaving his while the anger began churning in her stomach.

"You want him to experience the same fear, that same sense of helplessness that each of his victims felt." He sat forward in his chair, the creak amplified in the silence. "The same fear that you felt when he had you trapped. When he was cutting you. When his knife was slicing into your skin."

He paused, and she felt him examining her. The room had become hot, with very little air. Yet she kept her hands from wiping the strands of hair that had become damp on her forehead. She resisted the urge to bite down on her lower lip. Instead, she simply returned his stare.

"Is that it, Margaret O'Dell? You want to see Mr. Albert Stucky squirm, just like he made you squirm."

She hated that he referred to Stucky with the respect of using mister. How dare he?

"Seeing him squirm in the electric chair isn't enough for you, is it?" he continued to push.

Maggie's fingers started wringing in her lap. Her palms were sweaty. Why was it so damn hot in the room? Her cheeks were flushed. Her head began to throb.

"No, the electric chair isn't a punishment appropriate for his crimes, is it? You have a better punishment in mind, don't you? And how do you propose to administer this punishment, Margaret O'Dell?"

"By making him look directly at me when I shoot the goddamn bastard between his eyes," she blasted, no longer caring that she had just allowed herself to be swallowed whole into Dr. James Kernan's psychological trap.

CHAPTER 33

Tess McGowan tried to open her eyes, but her eyelids were too heavy. She managed a flutter, seeing a flash of light, then darkness. She was sitting up, but the earth was moving beneath her in a low rumble and steady vibration. Somewhere a soft, deep voice with a country twang was singing about hurting the ones you love.

Why couldn't she move? Her arms were limp, her legs like concrete. But the only restraint was across her shoulder, across her lap. A car. Yes, she was buckled into a car. That explained the movement, the vibration, the muffled sounds. It didn't explain why she couldn't open her eyes.

She tried again. Another flutter. Headlights flickered before her heavy eyelids fell closed. It was night. How could it be night? It had just been morning. Hadn't it?

She leaned against the headrest. She smelled jasmine, just a hint, soft and subtle. Yes, she remembered a few days ago she had bought a new sachet and stuck it under the passenger seat. So she was in her own car. The scent, the notion calmed her until she realized that if she wasn't driving, someone else was here with her. Was it Daniel? Why couldn't she remember? Why did her mind feel as though it was filled with cobwebs? Had she gone out drinking again? Oh dear God! Had she picked up another stranger?

She turned her head slightly to the side without removing it from the headrest. It took such effort to move, each inch as if in slow motion. One more time she attempted to open her eyes. Too dark, but there was movement. The eyelids dropped shut again.

She listened. She could hear someone breathing. She opened her mouth to speak. She would ask where they were going. It was a simple question, but nothing came out. There was a slight groan but even that hadn't come from her. Then the car began to slow, followed by a faint electric buzz. Tess felt a draft, smelled fresh tar and knew the window had opened. The car stopped, but the engine continued to hum. Gas fumes told her they were stalled in traffic. She tried once again to open her eyes.

"Good evening, Officer," a deep voice said from the seat next to her.

Was it Daniel? The voice sounded familiar.

"Good evening," another voice bellowed. "Oh, sorry," came a whisper. "Didn't see your wife sleeping."

"What seems to be the problem?"

Yes, Tess wanted to know, too. What was the problem? Why couldn't she move? Why couldn't she open her eyes? What wife was sleeping? Did the officer mean her?

"We've got an accident we're cleaning up on the other side of the toll bridge. A leftover from the rush-hour traffic. Be just a minute or two. Then we'll let you through."

"No hurry." the voice said much too calmly.

No. It wasn't Daniel. Daniel was always in a hurry. He'd be making the officer understand how important he was. He'd be causing a scene. Oh, how she hated when he did that. But it if wasn't Daniel beside her, then who?

A flutter of panic crawled over her. "No hurry?" Yes, the voice was familiar.

She began to remember.

"You smell quite lovely," that same voice had told her. It came to her in pieces. The house on Archer Drive. He wanted to see the master bedroom. "I hope you're not offended."

He wanted to see her face. "It's really quite painless." No, he wanted to feel her face. His hands, his fingers on her hair, her cheeks, her neck. Then wrapping those hands around her throat, tight and hard, the muscles squeezing. She couldn't breathe. She couldn't move. Dark eyes. And a smile. Yes, he had smiled while his fingers squeezed and wrung her neck. It hurt. Stop it. It hurt so bad. Her head hurt, and she could hear the smack of it hitting against the wall. She fought with fists and fingernails. God, he was strong.

Then she had felt it. A prick of the needle as it sunk deep into her arm. She remembered the rush of heat that flowed through her veins. She remembered the room spinning.

Now she tried to raise that same arm. It wouldn't move, but it ached. What had he given her? Who the hell was he? Where was he taking her? Even the fear felt trapped, a lump caught deep inside her throat, straining to be set free. She couldn't wave or swing her arms. She couldn't kick or run. My God, she couldn't even scream.

CHAPTER 34

Maggie had passed the exit for Quantico without a glance and had gone straight home after her meeting with Kernan. Meeting? That was a joke. She shook her head and now continued to pace in her living room. The hour-long drive from D.C. hadn't even begun to cool off her anger. What kind of psychologist left his patients wanting to slam fists through walls?

She noticed her bags at the bottom of the staircase, still packed from her Kansas City trip. Boxes remained stacked in the corners. Her nerves felt as if they had been rubbed raw. A knot tightened at the base of her neck and her head throbbed. She couldn't remember when she had last eaten. It had probably been on the flight last night.

She considered changing and going for a run. It was getting dark but that had never stopped her before. No, what did stop her was knowing Stucky could be watching. Had he returned from Kansas City? Was he out there somewhere hiding, waiting, watching? She paced from window to window, examining the street and then the woods behind her house, squinting to study the twilight shadows dancing behind the trees. She searched for anything out of the ordinary, anything that moved, but in the light breeze every rustle of a bush, every sway of a branch made her uneasy. She could already feel her muscles tightening, her nerves unraveling.

Earlier she had noticed a construction worker at the end of her street inspecting sewage grates and setting up pylons. His coveralls had been too clean, his shoes too polished. Maggie knew immediately that he had to be one of Cunningham's surveillance crew. How the hell did Cunningham expect to catch Stucky with such amateurish strategies? If Maggie had been able to see through the impostor, certainly Stucky, a professional chameleon, would find it laughable. Stucky took on identities and roles with such ease that surely he would spot someone doing the same thing, only doing it poorly.

She hated feeling like a caged animal in her own home. To make matters worse, the house was deathly quiet. Other than the clicking of her heels on the polished wood floor, Maggie heard nothing. No lawn mowers, no car engines, no children playing. But wasn't the peace and quiet, a piece of seclusion, exactly what she longed for when she bought this house? Hadn't that been her intention? What was that old saying—be careful what you wish for?

She unearthed her CD player, an inexpensive oversize boom box. She dug through the overflowing box of CDs. Some were in sealed wrappers, gifts from friends she hadn't taken time to open, let alone enjoy. Finally she decided on an early Jim Brickman, hoping the piano solos would soothe her agitated insides. The music barely began when Maggie noticed Susan Lyndell making her way up the circular drive. It looked as though there would be no stress relief.

She opened the door before Susan made it up the steps to the portico. Her eyes darted everywhere but at Susan, checking, double-checking.

"How was your trip?" Susan asked as though they were old friends.

"It was fine." Maggie grabbed the woman's elbow gently and quickly urged her into the foyer.

Susan stared at her, surprised. On her first visit Maggie had barely let the woman through the door, and now she was pulling her in.

"I got back late last night," Maggie continued, closing the door. All she could think about was Stucky watching. Stucky choosing his next victim.

"I tried to call but you're not listed yet."

"No, I'm not," she said with finality in case Susan expected she might tell her. "Did you speak with Detective Manx?"

"Actually, that's what I wanted to tell you. I think I was mistaken about what we discussed the other day."

"Why do think you were mistaken?" Maggie waited while her neighbor glanced around at her stacked cartons, taking in Maggie's living room and probably wondering how Maggie could ever afford such a house.

"I spoke with Sid," Susan told her, finally looking at Maggie, though she still seemed distracted by Maggie's things, or rather her lack of things.

"Mr. Endicott? What exactly did you speak to him about?"

"Sid's a good man. I hate to see him going through this all alone. I felt he had a right to know. Well, you know...about Rachel and that man."

"The telephone repairman?"

"Yes." Now Susan wouldn't meet Maggie's eyes, but it had nothing to do with the surroundings.

"What did you tell him?"

"Just that quite possibly she may have left with him."

"I see." She wondered why Susan Lyndell could so easily betray her friend. And why was it suddenly so easy to believe Rachel had left with some stranger who, only days ago, Susan thought might hurt her friend? "And what did Mr. Endicott say?"

"Oh, maybe you haven't heard. Rachel's car was not in the garage. The police initially saw Sid's Mercedes and didn't realize that Rachel's was gone. See, she usually drives Sid to the airport when he goes out of town so he won't need to leave the car in airport parking. Sid's always worried about his car. Anyway, I think Rachel must have taken off with this guy. She was certainly infatuated by him."

"What about the dog?"

"The dog?"

"We found her dog stabbed...injured under the bed."

Susan shrugged. "I have no idea about that," she said as if she couldn't be expected to figure out everything.

Maggie's cellular phone started ringing from inside her jacket pocket. She hesitated. Susan waved a birdlike hand at her to go ahead and get it as she backed away. "I won't keep you. Just wanted to fill you in." Before Maggie could protest, her neighbor was out the door and walking down the driveway in what Maggie thought looked almost like a skip. She definitely didn't seem like the same nervous, anxious woman she had met a few days ago.

Maggie quickly closed the door and took time to activate the alarm system while the phone continued to ring. Finished, she twisted the contraption out of her pocket.

"Maggie O'Dell."

"Jesus, finally. You need a better cell phone, Maggie. I think your battery must be low again."

Immediately, Maggie felt the tension return to her neck and shoulders. Greg's greetings always sounded like scoldings.

"My phone's been off. I've been out of town. You got my message." She went directly to the point, not wanting to encourage his attempt to chastise her for being unreachable.

"You should have some sort of messaging service," he persisted. "Your mother called me a couple of days ago. She didn't even know you moved. For Christ's sake, Maggie, you could at least call your mother and give her your new number."

"I did call her. Is she okay?"

"She sounded great. Said she was in Las Vegas."

"Las Vegas?" Her mother never left Richmond. And what a choice. Yes, Las Vegas was the perfect place for a suicidal alcoholic.

"She said she was with a Reverend Everett. You need to keep better tabs on her, Maggie. She is your mother."

Maggie leaned against the wall and took a deep breath. Greg had never understood the dynamics between Maggie and her mother. How could he? He came from a family that looked as if it had been special-ordered from a 1950s family catalog.

"Greg, did I leave a carton at the condo?"

"No, there's nothing here. You do realize that none of this would have happened if you had used United?"

Maggie ignored his I-told-you-so. "Are you sure? Look, I don't care if you've opened it or if you've gone through it."

"Listen to you. You don't trust or believe anybody anymore. Can't you see what this goddamn job is doing to you?"

She rubbed her neck and squeezed at the knot. Why did he have to make this so difficult?

"Did you check in the basement?" she asked, knowing there was no way it had ended up there, but giving him one last chance for a way out if he had, indeed, opened the box.

"No, there's nothing. What was in it? One of your precious guns? Are you not able to sleep at night without all three or four or however many of those things you have?"

"I have two, Greg. It's not unusual for an agent to have a backup."

"Right. Well, that's one too many for me."

"Would you just call me if the carton shows up?"

"It's not here."

"Okay, fine. Goodbye."

"Call your mom sometime soon," he said in place of a closing and hung up.

She leaned her head against the wall and shut her eyes. She tried to calm the throbbing in her head and neck and shoulders. The doorbell chimed, and she was grabbing for her revolver before she even realized it. Jesus! Maybe Greg was right. She did live in a crazy paranoid world.

Beside a lamppost in her driveway, she could see a van with Riley's Veterinary Clinic imprinted on the side. A man in white overalls and a baseball cap stood on the portico. Sitting patiently beside him with a blue collar and leash was a white Labrador retriever. Despite there being no massive bandage around the dog's chest and shoulder, Maggie recognized it as the dog she had helped rescue from the Endicotts' house. Nevertheless, she examined the man, making certain this wasn't a disguise. Finally she decided he was too short to be Stucky.

"The Endicotts live farther down the street," she said as soon as she opened the door.

"I know that," the man snapped. His jaw was taut, his face red, his forehead glistening with sweat as though he had run here instead of driving. "Mr. Endicott refuses to take the dog."

"He what?"

"He won't take the dog."

"Is that what he said?" Maggie thought the idea incredible after what the dog had been through.

"Well, his exact words were, it's his wife's frickin' dog—excuse my language, I'm just repeating what he said, but let me tell you, he didn't use 'frickin',' okay? Anyway, he said it's his wife's frickin' dog and if she took off and left the stupid dog, then he doesn't want him either."

Maggie glanced at the dog who cowered close to the ground, either from the man's raised voice or because he knew they were talking about him.

"I'm not sure what you expect me to do. I don't think my talking to Mr. Endicott will change his mind. I don't even know the man."

"Your name and address is on the release form you signed when you brought in the dog. Detective Manx told us to leave the dog with you."

"He did, did he?" Of all the nerve. It was Manx's one last dig. "And what if I refuse to take him? What will you do with him?"

"I have orders from Mr. Endicott to take him to the pound."

Maggie looked at the dog again, and as if on cue he stared up at her with sad, pathetic brown eyes. Damn it! What did she know about taking care of a dog? She wasn't home enough to take care of a dog. She couldn't have a dog. Her mother had never allowed her to have one while she was growing up. Greg was allergic to dogs and cats, or so he had said once when she had brought home a stray she had found while out running. Allergic or not, she knew he would never have been able to tolerate anything with four paws climbing on his precious leather furniture. Suddenly Maggie realized that seemed like a good enough reason.

"What's his name," she asked as she took the dog's leash from the man's hand.

"It's Harvey."

CHAPTER 35

Boston, Massachusetts
Thursday, April 2

William Finley couldn't sit still. He had been jumpy all morning. Now he roamed the halls of the county courthouse. He swiped a jerky hand over his face. Too much caffeine. That was his problem. That and very little sleep. It also didn't help matters that Tess McGowan hadn't returned any of his phone calls. Today was already Thursday. Since Monday, he had left messages on her answering machine and at her office. Or, at least, what he thought was her office. He had taken one of her business cards from the antique desk in her bedroom. Otherwise, he wouldn't have had her home phone number or known her last name. Hell, he had even tried leaving her messages at Louie's until the burly owner told him to "leave Tess alone and fuck off."

So why couldn't he leave her alone? Why did she consume his thoughts? He had never been obsessed with a woman before. Why this one? Even Melissa had noticed his preoccupation, but she had accepted his explanation of being overloaded at his new job and stressed out about all the last-minute wedding preparations.

It didn't help matters that he had avoided having sex with her since his night with Tess. Hell, it had only been three nights and yet he'd been afraid Melissa would notice, especially last night when she had hinted about spending the night at his place. He had practically shoved her out the door, using the lame excuse that he had to get some sleep for a big trial in the morning. What was his problem? Was he really afraid that Melissa would discover his betrayal somehow if he touched her differently? Or did he simply not want to erase the memories of having sex with Tess? Because he had played back that night over and over in his head so many times he could conjure it up at will.

Shit, he was fucked up!

As he turned the corner, heading to Records he ran into Nick Morrelli. The contents of Will's folder spilled across the floor, and he was on his knees before Nick had a chance to know what hit him.

"Hey, what's the hurry?" Nick said, joining Will on the floor.

Others stepped around them, not paying any attention as their heels smashed and crumpled the scattered papers.

Nick handed him the papers he had gathered while they stood up. But Will's eyes darted across the floor, making sure he had everything. That was all he needed—to lose some piece of paper that would give the defense an edge in whatever this trial was.

"So what's the rush?" Nick asked again, hands in his pockets, waiting.

"No rush." Will straightened the stack and raked his fingers through his hair. He wondered if Nick could see the slight tremor in his hand. Although the two men were new to the D.A.'s office, Nick had been one of Will's professors in law school back at the University of Nebraska. He still looked up to Nick as a mentor instead of a colleague. And he knew Nick had sort of taken him under his wing, helping a fellow Midwesterner adjust to the rush of big-city life in Boston.

"You look like shit." Nick looked concerned. "You feeling okay?"

"Yeah. Sure. I'm fine."

Nick didn't look convinced. He glanced at his watch. "It's almost lunchtime. How 'bout we get burgers down the street? I'm buying."

"Okay. Yeah, sure. If you're buying." Geez! Even his speech was jerky. "Let me drop this stuff at Records."

It was warm enough for shirtsleeves, but both men wore their jackets. Will realized he'd need to wear his jacket for the rest of the day if the pools under his arms were as obvious as they felt. Maybe all these physical reactions were simply cold feet. After all, the wedding was, what, three or four weeks away? Holy crap! How could it be that close?

Will filled the conversation with boring stuff about the trials Nick had missed while in Kansas City. It was the only way to ignore the concerned look in his ex-professor's eyes. Nick politely listened, then seemed to wait until Will's mouth was full of fries before he asked.

"So you ready to tell me what the hell's bugging you?"

Will wiped away the ketchup on the corner of his mouth and swallowed. He grabbed his Pepsi and washed down what threatened to stick in his throat.

"What makes you think something's wrong?"

"I didn't say wrong. I said what's bugging you?"

"Oh." He wiped his mouth again, buying time. Leave it to a lawyer to fuss over the wording.

"So what's wrong?"

Will shoved his plate aside. He had managed to wolf down half his burger and almost all his fries before Nick had taken a second bite of his burger. He could feel the heartburn tightening into a fist and settling in the middle of his chest. As if he needed one more physical discomfort.

"I think I fucked up big time."

Nick continued eating, waiting, examining him over the burger that he held with both hands. Finally he said, "It wasn't the Prucello case, was it?"

"No. No, it wasn't anything to do with work."

Nick looked relieved. Then his brow furrowed again. "You getting cold feet about the wedding?"

Will gulped his Pepsi. He waved at the waiter and pointed to his glass for another, wishing he could trade it for something stronger.

"Maybe. I don't know." Then he pulled in his chair and leaned across the table so he could keep his voice down despite the noisy lunch-hour crowd. Two of the tables next to them were filled with people he knew from the courthouse.

"Sunday night I met this woman. Christ, Nick! She was...incredible. I haven't been able to stop thinking about her."

Nick chewed and watched him as if contemplating what to say. If anyone would understand, surely it would be Nick Morrelli. Will knew that years ago, all the talk around campus about Nick and some of his own students, as well as several female professors, had not been idle rumor. Nick Morrelli had had his share of one-night stands. Even after he had left the university to take the position as sheriff of Platte City, the reputation and the activity had followed him.

"This woman," Nick said slowly, carefully, "was she a hooker?"

Will almost choked.

"No, hell no," he said, glancing around the small diner to make certain no one noticed he was agitated. "The guys—Mickey, Rob, Bennet—they sort of dared me into picking up this woman who was at the bar. She was incredible, sexy and so...I don't know, uninhibited. But no, she's no goddamn hooker." He stopped and lowered his voice, noticing two women at the next table staring at him. "She's older, probably about your age. Very attractive with this amazing...sensuality. But in a sophisticated sort of way, not, you know, cheap or anything like that. In fact, I think she's a real estate agent or something."

The waiter brought Will's refill. He slid back in his chair, grabbed the glass and gulped half of it. Nick continued eating, as if it was no big deal. Will started feeling anxious and a bit angry. Hell, he had just spilled his guts, and Nick seemed more interested in finishing his goddamn burger.

"So what you're really saying is that she's a pretty incredible fuck?"

"Jesus Christ, Nick!"

"Well? Isn't that what this is all about?"

"You know, man, I thought you of all people would understand this. But forget it. Forget I mentioned it." Will pulled his plate closer and started shoving French fries into his mouth, avoiding looking at Nick. One of the women at the next table smiled at him. Evidently she didn't know that he was an idiot.

"Come on, Will. Be sensible for one minute." Nick waited until he had Will's attention. "Are you willing to piss away three or four years with Melissa for one incredible fuck?"

"No. Of course not." Will slumped in his chair and wrestled with the knot in his tie. He looked up and met Nick's eyes. "I don't know what to think."

"Look, Will. I've been with a lot of women, incredible women. But you can't let one incredible fuck rule your life's decisions."

They sat in silence as Nick finished eating. Will sat up, leaned across the table again, only now noticing the sleeve of his jacket dripping with ketchup. Shit! These days he seemed to spend more money on dry cleaning than he did on food.

"It wasn't just the sex, Nick." He felt he needed to explain, but wasn't sure he understood it himself. "There was something else. I don't know what. Something about her. I can't get her out of my mind. I mean, here's this strong, passionate, sexy, independent woman, who could also be...oh, hell I don't know...vulnerable and sweet and funny and...and real. I know we both had too much to drink, and we know very little about each other, but...I can't stop thinking about her."

He watched Nick take out crisp bills and lay them on the plastic tray with the tab. Had it been a mistake to say any of this out loud? Should he have kept it to himself?

"Okay, so what do you want to do about it?"

"I don't know," Will said, giving in and fidgeting with the ketchup on his sleeve. "I guess maybe I want to see her again, just to talk, to see...hell, I don't know, Nick."

"So call her. What's stopping you?"

"I tried. She won't return my messages."

"Then stop by and see her, buy her lunch. Women like a guy taking action, not just talking."

"It's not that easy. It's a five-hour drive. She lives in this little town outside D.C.—Newton, Newberry, Newburgh. Yeah, Newburgh, I think."

"Wait a minute. Outside D.C.? Newburgh Heights? In Virginia?"

"Yeah. You know it?"

"I think a friend of mine bought a house there."

"Small world." Will watched Nick, whose mind suddenly seemed preoccupied. "You think they know each other?"

"I doubt it. Maggie's an FBI profiler."

"Hold on. Is this the same FBI Maggie who helped you on that case last fall?"

Nick nodded, but he didn't need to answer at all. Will could see it was the same woman. Will had noticed months ago that this woman couldn't be mentioned in general conversation without Nick getting all weirded out. Maybe this woman was Nick's obsession.

"So how come you've never called this Maggie or stopped by to see her?"

"Well, for one thing I didn't realize until a few days ago that she was getting a divorce."

"A few days ago? Wait a minute. Was she at the Kansas City thing?"

"Yes, she was at the Kansas City thing. She was one of the presenters."

"And?"

"And nothing."

Will noticed Nick's demeanor had changed to frustration with a hint of irritation. Yep, he was all weirded out again.

"But you saw her, right? You talked to her?"

"Yeah. We spent an afternoon digging through garbage together."

"Excuse me? Is that some new code for foreplay?"

"No, it isn't," Nick snapped, suddenly not in the mood for Will's attempt at humor. "Come on. Let's get back to work."

Nick stood, straightening his lopsided tie and buttoning his jacket, indicating that was the end of this conversation. Will decided to ignore it and press on.

"It sounds like this Maggie is your Tess."

"Jesus, kid. What the hell is that supposed to mean?" Nick shot him a look, and Will knew he was right.

"This Maggie drives you as crazy as Tess drives me. Maybe we both need to make a trip down to Newburgh Heights."

CHAPTER 36

Maggie was surprised to find that Agent Tully had managed to make her old office look smaller than it was. Books that didn't fit in the narrow floor-to-ceiling bookcase formed leaning towers in the corner. A chair intended for visitors was hidden under stacks of newspapers. On his desk, the in-tray was crushed under a pile of lop-sided documents and file folders. Strings of paper clips were left in odd places, a nervous habit of a man who needed to keep his fingers occupied. One lone mug teetered on a stack of legal pads and computer manuals. Peeking from behind the door, Maggie glimpsed gray running gear where normal people hung a trench coat or rain slicker.

The only thing in the office that held some prominence was a photo in a cheap wooden frame that sat on the right-hand corner of the desk. The entire corner had been cleared for its place of honor. Maggie immediately recognized Agent Tully, though the photo appeared to be several years old. The little blond girl had his dark eyes, but otherwise looked exactly like a younger version of her mother. The three of them looked so genuinely happy.

Maggie resisted the urge to take a closer look, as if doing so might expose their secret. What was it like to feel that completely happy? Had she ever felt that way, even for a brief period? Something about Agent Tully told her that happiness no longer existed for him. Not that she wanted to know. It had been years since she had worked with a partner, and the fact that Cunningham had made it one of the conditions of her return to the Stucky investigation was annoying. She felt as if he was still punishing her for the one stupid mistake of her career—going to that Miami warehouse alone. The warehouse where Stucky had been waiting for her. Where he had trapped her and made her watch.

Okay, so partly she knew Cunningham was doing it to protect her. Agents usually worked together to protect each other's backs, but profilers often worked alone and Maggie had grown accustomed to the solitude. Having Turner and Delaney hanging around had been stifling enough. Of course, she would abide by Cunningham's rules, but sometimes the best agents, the closest partners forgot to share every detail.

Agent Tully came in carrying two cartons, stacked so that he peered around the sides of them. Maggie helped him find a clear spot and unload his arms.

"I think these are the last of the old case files."

She wanted to tell him that every last copy she had made for herself had fit nicely into one box. But instead of pointing out what a little organization could do, she was anxious to see what had been added to the case in the last five months. She stood back and allowed Agent Tully to sort through the mess.

"May I see the most recent file?"

"I have the delivery girl on my desk." He jumped up from his squatting position next to the cartons and quickly riffled through several piles on his desk. "The Kansas City case is here, too. They've been faxing us stuff."

Maggie resisted the urge to help. She wanted to grab all his piles and make order of them. How the hell did this guy get anything done?

"Here's the file on the delivery girl."

He handed her a bulging folder with corners of papers and photos sticking out at odd angles. Immediately, Maggie opened it and started straightening and rearranging its contents before examining any of them.

"Is it okay if we use her name?"

"Excuse me?" Agent Tully continued to rummage over his messy desktop. Finally he found his wire-rimmed glasses, put them on and looked at her.

"The pizza delivery girl. Is it okay if we use her name when we refer to her?"

"Of course," he said, grabbing another file folder and shuffling through it.

Now he was a bit flustered, and Maggie knew he didn't know the girl's name without looking. It wasn't a matter of disrespect. It helped to disconnect. Profilers often referred to a body simply as "the victim" or "Jane Doe." Their first introduction to the victims came when they were bloody, tangled messes, often sharing little or no resemblance to their former selves. Maggie used to be the same, using general terms to disassociate, to disconnect. But then several months ago she met a little boy named Timmy Hamilton who took time to show her his bedroom and his baseball card collection just before he was abducted. Now it suddenly seemed important to Maggie to know this girl's name. This beautiful, young, blond woman who she remembered being so cheerful when she had delivered Maggie's pizza less than a week ago. And who was now dead simply because she had done so.

"Jessica," Agent Tully finally blurted out. "Her name was Jessica Beckwith."

Maggie realized she could have found the girl's name just as easily. The top document was the medical examiner's autopsy report, and the girl had already been identified at that point. She tried not to think of the parents. Some disconnection was necessary.

"Any trace recovered at the scene that could be used for DNA testing?"

"Nothing substantial. Some fingerprints, but they aren't matching Stucky's. Weird thing is, everything looked wiped clean except for this set of fingerprints—one index, one thumb. Chances are they belong to a rookie cop who touched stuff he wasn't supposed to touch and now he's afraid to admit it. AFIS hasn't come up with anything yet."

He sat on the edge of the desk, laying his folder open on a pile, leaving his fingers free to string more paper clips together.

"The weapon was not retrieved. Is that right?"

"Correct. Looks to be very thin, razor sharp and single edged. I'm thinking maybe even a scalpel, from the way he's able to slice and dice so easily."

Maggie winced at his choice of description, and he caught her.

"Sorry," he said. "That's the first thing that came to mind."

"Any saliva on the body? Any semen in the mouth?"

"No, which I know is different from Stucky's usual M.O."

"If it is Stucky."

She felt him staring at her but avoided his eyes and examined the autopsy report. Why would Stucky hold back or pull out early now? He certainly wouldn't go through the trouble of using a condom. After they had revealed his identity as being Albert Stucky, he had blatantly gone on to do whatever he wanted. And that usually meant showing off his sexual prowess by raping his victims several times, and often forcing them to perform oral sex on him. She wished she could take a second look at the girl's body. By now she knew what kinds of things to look for, otherwise insignificant physical evidence that telegraphed Stucky's patterns. Unfortunately, she saw at the bottom of the form that Jessica's body had already been released to her family. Even if she stopped the transfer, all the PE would be gone, washed away by a well-intentioned funeral director.

"We did find a stolen cellular phone in the Dumpster," Agent Tully said.

"But it was wiped clean?"

"Right. But the phone records show a call to the pizza place earlier that evening."

Maggie stopped and looked up at Agent Tully. My God, could it have been that easy? "That's how he abducted her? He simply ordered a pizza?"

"Initially that's what we were thinking," he explained. "We just found the delivery lists in her abandoned car. We've been running down the list, checking addresses and phone numbers. When Cunningham recognized Newburgh Heights as your new neighborhood, we checked for your address. Found it right away. Likewise, all the addresses are residential. But most of the people I've talked to so far were actually home and did receive their pizza. I have only a few left that I can't reach by phone, but I plan to drive to Newburgh Heights and check them out."

He handed her two photocopies of what looked like pieces of paper torn from a spiral notebook. The copier had even picked up the frayed edges. There were almost a dozen addresses on both lists. Hers was close to the top of the list labeled "#1." She leaned against the wall. The exhaustion from the night before was catching up with her. Of course, she had spent most of last night pacing from window to window, watching and waiting. The only sleep she had gotten had been on the flight back from Kansas City, and how could anyone get any rest while bobbing thirty-eight thousand feet above control? Now she couldn't even remember how long ago that was.

"Where did you find her car?"

"The airport's long-term parking lot. Also found a telephone company van parked alongside it that was reported stolen a couple of weeks ago."

"Any trace inside Jessica's car?" she asked as she glanced over the list of addresses.

"There was some mud on the accelerator. Not much else. Her blood and some blond hair—also hers—were recovered from the trunk. He must have used her own car to dump her body. No signs of a struggle inside the car, though, if that's what you're thinking. He had to have taken her someplace where he could take his time with her. Problem is, there aren't many abandoned warehouses or condemned properties in Newburgh Heights. I was thinking he might have given a business address, knowing the offices would be empty at night. But nothing commercial shows up on either list."

Suddenly Maggie recognized an address on one of the lists. She stood up straight and away from the wall. No, it couldn't be this easy. She reread the address.

"Actually, he may have had someplace much more luxurious in mind."

"Did you find something?" Agent Tully was at her side, staring at the list that he must have examined over and over himself. But of course, he wouldn't have seen it. How could he?

"This address," Maggie pointed halfway down the page. "The house is for sale. It's empty."

"You're kidding? Are you sure? If I remember correctly, the phone is still connected to a voice messaging service."

"The owners may be forwarding their phone calls. Yes, I'm sure it's for sale. My real estate agent showed it to me about two weeks ago."

She no longer cared about the rest of the file, which she had tucked under her arm. She was almost out the door before Agent Tully stopped her.

"Hold on," he said, grabbing his wrinkled jacket from the chair behind his desk. As he did so, he stumbled over a worn pair of sneakers Maggie hadn't noticed. Agent Tully reached for the corner of his desk to catch his balance and one of the piles gave way, scattering papers and photos across the floor. When he waved off her help, Maggie leaned against the doorjamb and waited. It was bad enough Cunningham was making her see Dr. James Kernan, but saddling her with her Dudley DoRight seemed almost laughable.

CHAPTER 37

Maggie tried to wait patiently while Delores Heston of Heston Realty attempted to find the right key. The sun was sinking behind the ridge of trees. She couldn't believe how much time they had wasted trying to track down Tess McGowan. And although Ms. Heston had been more than accommodating, Maggie felt agitated, on edge and overly anxious. She knew this was where Albert Stucky had killed Jessica Beckwith. She could feel it. She could sense it. It was so easy, so simple, so very much like Stucky.

Ms. Heston dug out another bundle of keys and Maggie fidgeted, shifting her weight from one foot to the other. Ms. Heston noticed.

"I don't know where Tess is. I'm sure she probably just decided to take a couple of days off."

It was the same explanation the woman had given Maggie over the phone, but again Maggie could hear the concern.

"One of these has to work."

"I would think you'd have them labeled." Maggie tried to contain her irritation. She knew Ms. Heston was doing them a favor by letting them take a look after their bogus explanation about investigating possible break-ins. Since when did the FBI get involved in local burglaries? Luckily, Ms. Heston didn't question them.

"Actually, these are the spare keys. We do keep a labeled set, but Tess must have forgotten to return it after she showed the house yesterday."

"Yesterday? She showed the house to someone yesterday?"

Ms. Heston stopped and gave Maggie a nervous glance over her shoulder. Maggie realized her voice must have sounded too shrill, too alarmed.

"Yes, I'm sure it was yesterday. I checked the show schedule before I left the office tonight—Wednesday, April 1. Is there a problem? Do you think the house may have been broken into before that?"

"I really can't say," Maggie said, trying to sound indifferent when she wanted to kick in the door. "Do you know who she showed the house to?"

"No, we keep the names off the schedule for confidentiality reasons."

"You don't have the name of the person written down anywhere?"

Ms. Heston shot her another concerned look over her shoulder. The woman's flawless deep brown skin now had worry lines in her forehead and around her mouth. "Tess would have it written down somewhere. I trust my agents. No need for them to have me standing over their shoulder." Concern was quickly turning to frustration.

Maggie hadn't meant to make the woman defensive. She simply wanted the goddamn door opened.

She glanced around and saw Agent Tully finally emerge from the house across the street. He had been inside a long time, and Maggie wondered if the blonde in spandex who had answered the door simply found him charming, or if she really had some information to share. Judging by the woman's smile and wave, Maggie guessed it to be the former. She watched the tall, lanky agent hurry across the street. Out here, he moved with a confident, long-legged gait. In his dark suit, sunglasses and closely cropped hair, he looked like standard government-issue FBI, except that Agent Tully was too polite, too friendly and much too accommodating. If he hadn't told her he was from Cleveland, she would have guessed the Midwest. Maybe it was something in Ohio's water.

"This house has a security system." Ms. Heston was still trying to find the right key. "Oh, here we go. Finally."

The lock clicked as Agent Tully bounded up the steps. Ms. Heston turned, startled by his sudden appearance.

Ms. Heston, this is Special Agent R. J. Tully.

"Oh my. This must be important."

"Just routine, ma'am. We tend to travel in pairs these days," Tully said with a smile that relaxed the woman and immediately reminded Maggie of Sergeant Joe Friday.

She wanted to ask him if he had learned anything from the neighbor, but knew she'd have to wait for a more appropriate time. She hated waiting.

As soon as they entered the foyer, Maggie noticed the security system had been disarmed. None of the regular lights flashed or blinked.

"Are you certain the service has been continued?" Maggie asked as she pointed out the silent box. By now it should have been buzzing incessantly, screeching for the correct code to be entered.

"Yes, I'm quite certain. It's in our contract with the owners." Heston punched several buttons and the box came alive. "I don't understand this. Surely Tess wouldn't have forgotten to set it."

Maggie remembered Tess McGowan being very careful about deactivating and reactivating the alarm systems of the houses she had shown Maggie, this one included. Security systems had been one of Maggie's priorities, and she knew this one had not been anything out of the ordinary. She remembered it as being sufficient for the regular home owner. Most people didn't need to barricade themselves in at night away from serial killers.

"Mind if we look around?" Agent Tully asked, but Maggie was already halfway up the open staircase. She reached the first landing when she heard Ms. Heston's panicked voice.

"Oh, good Lord!"

Maggie leaned over the oak railing to see Ms. Heston pointing to a briefcase she had discovered in the corner of the living room.

"This belongs to Tess." Up until now, the woman had been incredibly professional. Now her sudden panic was unnerving.

By the time Maggie came down the steps, Agent Tully had taken the briefcase and started carefully extracting its contents with a white handkerchief.

"No way that girl's gonna leave this and not come back for it." The panic rushed her words, reducing her previous crisp dialect to a slang version she obviously found more comfortable. "There's her appointment book, her pocketbook...good Lord, something's just not right here."

Maggie watched as Agent Tully brought out the last item—a labeled set of keys. Without getting a closer look, Maggie knew they were the keys for this house. Suddenly she felt nauseated. Tess McGowan may have shown this house yesterday, but she certainly didn't leave of her own free will.

CHAPTER 38

"We don't know that Stucky had anything to do with this." Tully tried to sound convincing, but he wasn't sure he believed his own words.

It was obvious he needed to be the objective one. Ever since Ms. Heston left them, Agent O'Dell seemed to be coming apart at the seams. The calm, controlled professional now paced, quick long steps, back and forth. She ran her fingers through her short dark hair too many times, tucking strands behind her ears, tousling it with her fingers and tucking it in again. Her voice was clipped, and possessed an edge that hadn't existed before. Tully thought he heard it quiver several times.

He felt as if he was watching from the sidelines as she passed by him. She didn't seem to know what to do with her hands. They ducked into her trouser pockets, then a quick swipe through her hair again. Several times they slipped into her jacket, and he knew she was checking her revolver. Tully wasn't sure what to do with her. This was so unlike the woman he had spent most of the day with.

It had gotten dark, and Agent O'Dell had gone through the entire two-story house, turning on lights and pulling closed what few draperies there were, but only after staring out into the night at each window. Was she expecting him to be there?

She was doing a second check downstairs now. Tully decided they needed to leave. The house was spotless. Though the master bedroom smelled strongly of a recent dousing of ammonia, there was no trace that anything had occurred in the house. Least of all, a brutal murder and a violent kidnapping.

"There's no evidence that anything suspicious happened here," he tried again. "I think it's time we leave." He glanced at his watch and cringed when he saw that it was after nine. Emma would be furious with him for having to spend the entire evening with Mrs. Lopez.

"Tess McGowan was the real estate agent who sold me my house," O'Dell repeated. It was the most she had said to him in the last several hours. "Don't you see? Don't you get it?"

He knew exactly what she was thinking. It was the same thing he was thinking. Albert Stucky would have known too, especially since he must be spending a good deal of time watching Agent O'Dell. He would have seen the two of them together, just the way he saw the pizza girl and the Kansas City waitress. But the truth was, they had absolutely no evidence that McGowan was even missing, other than a forgotten briefcase, and that was hardly proof. He refused to fuel O'Dell's panic.

"Right now there's nothing substantial to prove Ms. McGowan was abducted. And there's nothing more we can do here. We need to call it a night. Maybe we can track down Ms. McGowan tomorrow."

"We won't track her down. He's taken her." The quiver was there though she did her best to hide it. "He's added her to his collection. She may be dead already." Her hands reached for her holster then disappeared into her pockets. "Or if she's not dead, she may be wishing she was," she added in almost a whisper.

Tully rubbed his eyes. He had removed his glasses hours ago. O'Dell was starting to spook him. He didn't want to think about the fact that Albert Stucky may have added to his collection. Back on his desk, buried under manuals and documents, he had a bulging file of missing women from across the country. Women who had disappeared without a trace in the last five months since Stucky's escape.

The volume wasn't that unusual. It happened all the time. Some of the women left and didn't want to be found. Others had been abused by husbands and lovers and chose to disappear. But too many were gone without any explanation, and Tully knew enough about Stucky's games to pray that none of them in his file folder were actually in Stucky's new collection.

"Look, there's nothing more we can do tonight."

"We need to do a luminol test. We can have Keith Ganza bring it and the Lumi-Light, so we can go over the master bedroom."

"There's nothing here. There's absolutely no reason to believe anything happened in this house, Agent O'Dell."

"The Lumi-Light might show any latent prints. And the luminol will show any blood left in the cracks, any stains we can't see. He obviously tried to clean things up, but you can't clean enough to get rid of blood." It was almost as if she didn't hear him. As though he wasn't there and she was talking to herself.

"We can't do anything more tonight. I'm exhausted. You must be exhausted." When she started for the stairs again, he gently grabbed her arm. "Agent O'Dell."

She wrenched her arm away, turning on him with eyes flashing anger. She stood solidly, firmly in place, staring at him as though challenging him to a dual. Then without warning she turned on her heel and marched to the door, snapping off lights in her path.

Tully followed her cue before she changed her mind. He ran upstairs and shut off those lights, and when he returned, O'Dell was in the foyer, activating the security system. It wasn't until he locked the front door and walked alongside her to his car that he saw her revolver in her hand, dropped at her side but in a tight grip.

Suddenly Tully realized that the hysteria, the frustration, the anger he had witnessed was actually fear. How stupid of him not to have seen it before now. Special Agent Maggie O'Dell was scared to death, not just for Tess McGowan, but for herself, too.

CHAPTER 39

Tess jerked awake. Her throat felt like sandpaper, so dry it hurt to swallow. Her eyelids felt like lead shutters. Her chest ached as though some massive weight had pressed against her. There was nothing on top of her now. She lay on what appeared to be a narrow, lumpy cot. The room was dimly lit, forcing her to squint. The smell of mildew surrounded her. A draft made her pull the scratchy blanket up under her chin.

She remembered feeling paralyzed. In a mad panic, she lifted both her arms, grateful to find no restraints but quickly disappointed to find her limbs heavy, movement awkward. They felt detached and unresponsive. But at least she could move and at least she was not tied down.

She started to sit up, and immediately her muscles protested. The room began to spin. Her head throbbed and nausea washed over her so sudden and so strong, she lay back. She was used to hangovers, but this was much worse. Something had been injected into her bloodstream. Then she remembered the dark-haired man and the needle. Dear God, where the hell had he taken her? And where was he?

Her eyes darted around the small space. The nausea forced her to keep her head on the pillow as she twisted and turned her neck to examine her accommodations. She was inside some sort of wooden shack. Rotted wood allowed faint light to seep in between the slats. That was the only light. From what Tess could tell, it was cloudy or else too early or late for sunshine. Either way, she'd only be able to guess. There were no windows, or at least not anymore. One wall had boards nailed over a small area that may have been a window at one time. Other than the cot, there was nothing else except a tall plastic bucket in the corner.

Tess's eyes searched and found what looked like a door. It was difficult to tell. The wood blended in with the rest of the shack. Only a couple of rusted hinges and a keyhole gave it away. Of course, it would be locked, maybe even bolted from the outside, but she needed to make an attempt.

She sat up slowly and waited. Again, the nausea sent her head to the pillow.

"Damn it!" she shouted, and immediately regretted it. What if he was watching, listening?

She needed to concentrate. She could do this. After all, how many hangovers had she survived? But her surroundings only added to her vulnerability. Why was he doing this? What did he want from her? Had he mistaken her for someone else? A fresh panic began to crawl in her stomach. She couldn't think about his intentions now or about him. She couldn't think about how she got here. She wouldn't think about any of it or it would immobilize her exactly like the contents of that syringe.

She rolled onto her side to assuage the nausea. A sharp pain pierced her side, and for a brief moment she thought she had rolled onto a spike. But there was nothing there, only the hard, lumpy mattress. She moved her fingers up under her blouse, noticing the hem had already been pulled out from her trouser's waistband. A button was missing and the rest were off a buttonhole.

"No, stop it," she scolded herself in a whispered rush.

She had to focus. She couldn't think about what he may have done while she had been unconscious. She needed to check and see if she was okay.

Her fingers found no open wound, no sticky blood, but she was almost certain one of her ribs had been broken or badly bruised. Unfortunately, her past afforded her the knowledge of what broken ribs felt like. Carefully, her fingers probed the area under her breasts while she bit down on her lower lip. Despite the stabbing pain, she guessed bruised, not broken. That was good. She could function just fine with bruised ribs. Broken could sometimes puncture a lung. Another piece of trivia she wished she didn't know firsthand.

She slipped a foot out from under the covers and dangled it close to the floor. She was barefoot. What had he done with her shoes and stockings? Again, she glanced around the room. Her eyes had adjusted to the dim light, though her vision remained a bit off focus and her contact lenses felt gritty. It didn't matter. There was nothing more to see in the shack.

She let her toes and the ball of her foot touch the floor. It was colder than she expected, but she kept the foot there, forcing her body to grow accustomed to the change in temperature before she tried to stand up. The air in the shack felt damp and chilly.

Then she heard the beginning tap-tap-tap, soft against the roof. The sound of rain had usually been a comfort to her. Now she frantically wondered how badly the rotted roof leaked and felt a new chill. She knew the bucket in the corner hadn't been placed there for leaks. Instead, it was meant to accommodate her. He obviously intended to keep her here for a while. The thought reawakened the fear.

She pushed herself out of the cot and stood with both feet flat on the cold floorboards while she bent at the waist and held on to the bed. Again, she bit her lip, ignoring the taste of blood, fighting the urge to vomit and waiting for the room to stop spinning.

Her pulse quickened. The sound inside her head hummed like wind in a tunnel. She tried to concentrate on the tap-tap-tapping of the rain. Maybe she could find some level of comfort, some level of sanity, in the rain's natural and familiar rhythm. A sudden rumble of thunder startled her like a gunshot, and she spun around to the door as though expecting to see him there. When her heart settled back in her chest, she almost burst out laughing. It was only thunder. A little bit of thunder. That's all.

Slowly she tested her feet, coaxing her stomach to behave, trying to ignore the pain in her side and the panic from strangling her. Only now did she realize that her breathing came in gasps. A lump obstructed her throat, and it threatened to come out screaming. It took a conscious effort to prevent it from doing so.

Her body began shivering. She grabbed the wool blanket, wrapped it around her shoulders and tied two ends together in a knot at her neck, keeping her hands free. She checked under the cot, hoping to find something, anything to aid in her escape, or at least her shoes. There was nothing, not even furballs or dust. Which meant he had prepared this place for her, and recently. If only he hadn't taken her shoes and stockings. Then she remembered she had worn panty hose under her trousers.

Oh God! He had undressed her, after all. She mustn't think about it. She had to concentrate on other things. Stop remembering. Stop feeling aches and bruises in places that might remind her of what he had done. No, she couldn't, she wouldn't remember. Not now. She needed to focus all her energies on getting out of here.

Again she listened to the rain. Again she waited for its rhythm to calm her, to regulate her raspy breathing.

When she could walk without the threat of nausea crippling her, she carefully made her way to the door. The handle was nothing more than a rusted latch. One more time, she looked around to see if she had missed anything that could be used to help pry open the door. Even the corners had been swept clean. Then she saw a rusted nail swept into a groove in the floor. She pried it out with her fingernails and began examining the keyhole. The door was indeed locked, but was it bolted as well?

She steadied her fingers and inserted the nail into the keyhole, slipping it in and out, jingling and twisting it expertly. Another talent acquired in her not so illustrious past. But it had been years, and she was out of practice. The lock groaned in rusted protest. Oh, dear God, if only—something gave way with a metallic click.

Tess grabbed the latch and gave it a yank. The door swung open freely, almost knocking her over in her surprise. No force had been necessary. It hadn't been bolted. She waited, staring at the open doorway. This was too easy. Was it a blessing or another trap?

CHAPTER 40

Friday, April 3

Tully drove with one hand on the steering wheel and the other fumbling with the plastic lid of his coffee container. Why did fast-food places have to make the contraptions like child-protective caps? His finger punched at the uncooperative triangular perforation, cracking the plastic and splashing hot coffee onto his lap.

"Damn it!" he yelled as he swerved to the side of the road and screeched on the brakes, splattering more coffee onto the fabric of his car seat. He grabbed napkins to sop it up, but already the brown stain spread deep into the cream color. As an afterthought, he checked the rearview mirror, relieved no one was behind him.

He shoved the car's gearshift into park and released his foot from the brake pedal, only now realizing how tense and rigid his body had become in response to the stress. He sat back and rubbed a hand over his jaw, immediately feeling the nicks he had inflicted earlier with his razor. It had been one day and already Agent O'Dell had him feeling as if he was on the rim of her personal cliff, and he was straddling the ledge while pieces of rock crumbled at his feet.

Maybe it had been a mistake asking Assistant Director Cunningham to let O'Dell help on the Stucky case. Last night may have been proof that she simply couldn't handle the pressure. But then her phone message this morning telling him to meet her back at the Archer Drive house made Tully realize that he was in for an even more difficult task.

They had found nothing at the house to warrant a further search. Yet O'Dell had told him she had written permission from Ms. Heston and the owners to do so. Now he wondered if she had gotten them out of bed. How else had she been able to obtain written permission between last night and early this morning? And how the hell would he make her see that she was being irrational and paranoid and possibly wasting precious time?

After last night, Tully knew O'Dell was wound so tight, that controlling her could be impossible, and trying to restrain her could make matters worse. But he wouldn't talk to Cunningham. He couldn't. Not yet. He needed to handle this. He needed to settle O'Dell down so they could move forward.

He sipped what coffee was left and glanced at his watch. Today the damn thing was slow, according to the car's digital clock. It wasn't even seven o'clock. O'Dell had left the message on his machine at about six while he was in the shower. He wondered if she had gone to bed at all last night.

He put the coffee container safely into a cup holder, massaged the tension in his neck and then shifted into drive. He had only three blocks to go. When he turned onto the street, his tension turned to anger. Parked in the driveway were O'Dell's red Toyota and a navy blue panel van, the kind the forensic lab used. She hadn't wasted any time nor bothered to wait for his okay. What was the use of being lead in an investigation if no one paid any goddamn attention? He needed to put a stop to this now.

As he walked toward the front door, lampposts along the driveway blinked, trying to decide whether to stay on or shut off. They needed rain. Each time it looked like spring showers, the rains dumped on the shoreline or just offshore before rolling inland. But this morning thick clouds smudged out the sunrise. A low rumble could be heard in the distance. It suited Tully's mood, and he caught himself making fists as he got closer to the door. He hated confrontation. If he couldn't get his own daughter to obey him, then how the hell did he expect to get Agent O'Dell to?

The front door was unlocked, the security system silent. He followed the voices upstairs to the master bedroom. Keith Ganza wore a short white lab coat, and Tully wondered if the man even owned an ordinary sports jacket.

"Agent Tully," O'Dell said, coming from the master bathroom, wearing latex gloves and carrying jugs of liquid. "We're almost ready. We just finished mixing the luminol."

She set the jugs on the floor in the corner where Ganza had set up shop.

"You two know each other, right?" O'Dell asked as though she thought that was the reason for Tully's frown.

"Yes," he answered, trying to restrain his anger and maintain his professionalism.

Ganza simply nodded at Tully and continued loading and preparing a video camera. A Will comm camera on a tripod stood in the center of the room, already assembled. Several duffel bags, more jugs and four or five spray bottles were carefully set on the floor. A black case leaned against the wall. Tully recognized it as the Lumi-Light. Each of the windows were covered with some kind of black film taped to the frames so that light couldn't filter in from the outside. Even now the room required the ceiling light. The bathroom lights were on too, and Tully wondered what, if anything, they had used to block out the skylight. This was ridiculous.

Agent O'Dell began filling spray bottles with the luminol, using a funnel and steady hands. There seemed to be no sign of the jumpy, nervous, frazzled woman he had seen last night.

"Agent O'Dell. We need to talk."

"Of course, go ahead." Except she didn't look up at him and continued to pour.

Ganza appeared oblivious to Tully's anger, and he wanted to keep it that way.

"We need to talk in private."

Both O'Dell and Ganza looked up at him. Yet neither stopped what they were doing. O'Dell screwed the spray top onto the bottle she had filled. Tully expected her to see his anger. He expected her to be concerned or at least somewhat apologetic.

"Once we have the luminol mixed, we need to use it immediately," she explained, and began filling another spray bottle.

"I realize that," Tully said through clenched teeth.

"I have written permission," she continued without interrupting her pouring. "The luminol is odorless, and it leaves little residue. Nothing more than a sprinkle of white power when it dries. Hardly noticeable."

"I know that, too," Tully snapped at her, though her tone was not at all condescending. This time O'Dell and Ganza stopped and stared at him. How had he suddenly become the hysterical one, the irrational one?

"Then what seems to be the problem, Agent Tully?" She stood to face him, but again there was nothing challenging in her manner, which only made it worse.

Even the expression on Ganza's lined and haggard face was one of impatience. They continued to stare at him, waiting as though he was holding up the process unreasonably.

"I thought we decided last night that there was nothing here."

"No, we decided there was nothing more we could do last night. Although it would have been much better to do this last night. Hopefully, it'll be dark enough. We lucked out with it being so cloudy."

Ganza nodded. They both waited. Suddenly all of Tully's objections—which seemed completely logical minutes ago—now sounded immature and arrogant. There was nothing here. It was a ridiculous waste of time and effort. But rather than telling O'Dell that, perhaps it was better for her to see for herself. Maybe only then would she be satisfied.

"Let's get this over with," he finally said. "What do you want me to do?"

"Close the door and stay there next to the light switch." Ganza motioned to him while he picked up the video camera. "I'll let you know when to flip it off and on again. Maggie, grab a couple of spray bottles. You spritz. I'll be right beside you filming."

Tully got into position, no longer bothering to hide his reluctance or his impatience. However, he could see that anything he did would be wasted on O'Dell and Ganza. They were so involved in the task at hand, they barely noticed him except as a utility.

He watched O'Dell load both her hands with spray bottles, holding them like revolvers, her index fingers ready on the triggers.

"Let's start at the wall closest to the door and move toward the bathroom," Ganza instructed in his monotone. He reminded Tully of Icabod Crane. The man's voice never showed emotion—a perfect match for his tall, slumped appearance and deliberate and precise movements.

"Maggie, you remember the drill. Start on the walls, top to bottom. Then the floor, wall to center," Ganza went on. "Let's keep a steady spray going all the way to the bathroom. We'll stop at the bathroom door. You'll probably need to reload with luminol by then."

"Gotcha."

Tully just then realized that O'Dell and Ganza had done this as a team before. They seemed comfortable with each other, knowing each other's roles. And O'Dell had managed to get Ganza here at the break of dawn, despite the man's overloaded schedule.

Tully manned his post, waiting with arms crossed over his chest and his shoulder leaning against the closed door. He caught himself tapping his foot, an unconscious nervous habit that Emma accused him of when he was being "close-minded." Where the hell did she come up with stuff like that? Nevertheless, he stopped his foot from tapping.

"We're ready, Agent Tully. Go ahead and hit the lights," Ganza told him.

Tully flipped the switch and immediately felt swallowed by the pitch black. Not a hint of light squeezed in past the film on the windows. In fact, Tully could no longer tell where the windows were.

"This is excellent," he heard Ganza say.

Then Tully heard a faint electronic whine and a tiny red dot appeared where he imagined the video camera was in Ganza's hands.

"Ready when you are, Maggie," Ganza said as the red dot bobbed up.

Tully heard the spritz of liquid, steady and insistent. It sounded as if she was dousing the entire wall. Tully wondered how many bottles, how many jugs of luminol it would take for her to realize that there was nothing here. Suddenly the wall began to glow. Tully stood up straight, and so did the hairs on the back of his neck and arms.

"Jesus Christ," he gasped, staring in disbelief at the streaks, the smudges and handprints that smeared the entire wall and now glowed like fluorescent paint.

CHAPTER 41

Maggie stepped back, giving Keith room. It was worse than she expected. The smears stretched, reached, clawed and swiped with the undeniable motion of someone desperate and terrified. The handprints were small, almost child-size. She remembered Jessica Beckwith's delicate hands holding out the pizza box for her.

"Jesus, I can't believe this."

She heard Tully's voice again come out of the black. She knew he had believed they wouldn't find a thing, that nothing had taken place here. There was no victory in proving him wrong. Instead, she found herself light-headed and nauseated. Suddenly it was too hot in the room. What the hell was the matter with her? She hadn't been sick at crime scenes since the early days, those first years of initiation. Now for a second time in less than a week, her stomach attempted to revolt against her.

"Keith, what are the chances of this being a cleaning solution? The house is for sale. It still smells like someone has given it a recent scrubbing."

"Oh, it's been scrubbed all right. Someone was trying to get rid of this."

"But luminol can be sensitive to bleach," she continued. "Maybe a residential-cleaning company scrubbed down everything including the walls." After a fitful, sleepless night of anticipating, of knowing what they'd discover, why did she not want to believe it? Why did she find herself wanting to believe the streaks and swipes in front of her were simply an overzealous maid?

"In the linen closet there's a bunch of cleaning supplies. Mop, bucket, sponges and liquid cleaners. Smells like the same stuff that was used. None of it contains bleach," Ganza countered. "I checked. Besides, no one cleans and leaves handprints like that."

She forced herself to stare at the prints before they faded. The small fingers were elongated as they had grabbed and clawed and slid. She closed her eyes against the images her mind was trained to concoct. With little coaxing, she knew she could see it all in slow motion as if visualizing a scene from a movie, a horror movie.

"Ready, Maggie?" Keith's voice made her jump. He was right beside her again as the room started to return to darkness. "Let's get the floor from here to the bathroom."

She felt her fingers shaking as she repositioned them on the spray bottles. Gratefully, neither Keith nor Tully could see them. She steadied herself and tried to remember exactly what direction and how far it was to the bathroom. Once she felt back in control, she began spritzing, keeping the mist away from her feet as she slowly walked sideways. Maggie hadn't reached the bathroom door when the floor began lighting up like a runway, long skid marks following her.

"Oh my God!" She heard Tully mutter from his dark perch, and she wanted to tell him to shut up. His shock unnerved her and worse, reminded her of her own.

Ganza pointed the red dot to the floor, following the trail that had once been bloody feet dragged across the parquet floor. Maggie pushed back strands of hair and swiped at the perspiration on her forehead. Was Jessica unconscious by the time he got her to the bathroom? The girl would have lost a lot of blood putting up a fight like the one smeared on the wall. Maggie wondered if she was conscious when Stucky lifted her into the whirlpool bath. When he told her all the horrible things he would do to her. Was she dead or alive when he started cutting?

"Let's take a break here," Keith said. "Agent Tully, go ahead and switch the lights back on."

Maggie blinked against the burst of light, relieved at the interruption of her mind's descent into the depths of hell. If she tried, she would be able to hear Jessica's screams, her pleas for help. Maggie's memory bank seemed filled with audio clips of what sheer terror sounded like. It was something she'd never forget, no matter how many years went by.

"Agent O'Dell?"

Tully startled her, suddenly standing in front of her. She looked around to see Keith busy in the corner, and only now did she notice that he had taken the spray bottles from her hands and was filling them.

"Agent O'Dell, I owe you an apology," Agent Tully was saying. At some point he had removed his jacket and rolled up his shirtsleeves in haphazard and uneven folds. He unbuttoned his collar and twisted the knot of his tie loose. "I really thought there was nothing here. I feel like such an asshole."

Maggie stared at him and tried to remember the last time anyone, especially in law enforcement, had apologized to her, let alone admitted to making a mistake. Was this guy for real? Instead of looking embarrassed, he genuinely looked sorry.

"I have to admit, Agent Tully, I was simply acting on gut instinct."

"Maggie, we should remember to pull the drain from the whirlpool bath," Ganza interrupted without looking up. "I'm betting that's where he cut her open. We may find some leftovers."

Agent Tully's face grew paler, and she saw him wince.

"One thing we didn't check last night, Agent Tully, was the garbage cans outside," she told him, offering to save him. "Since the house is for sale and empty, the garbage collectors may have skipped it."

He seemed grateful for the chance to escape. "I'll go check."

As he left, Maggie realized he could possibly find something equally shocking in the garbage. Perhaps she wasn't saving him at all. She pulled out a fresh pair of latex gloves from her forensic kit and tossed out the ones she had contaminated with luminol. Keith unpacked a wrench, screwdriver and several evidence bags.

"You're being awfully nice to the new guy," he said.

She glanced at him. Though he kept his eyes on the items he was unearthing from his bag, she could see the corner of his mouth caught in a smile.

"I can be nice. It's not like it's an impossibility."

"Didn't say that it was." He dug out Q-Tips, several brushes, forceps and small brown bottles, lining everything up as if taking inventory. "Don't worry, Maggie, I won't tell anyone. Wouldn't want to ruin your reputation." This time he gave her his eyes, light blue behind hooded, heavy lids that Maggie knew in the last thirty years had seen more horror and evil than any one person should ever be allowed to see. Yet now they were smiling at her.

"Keith, what do you know about Agent Tully?"

"I've heard nothing but good things."

"Of course there are nothing but good things. He looks like a cross between Mr. Rogers and Fox Mulder."

"Fox Mulder?" He raised his eyebrows at her.

"You know, from the TV show *The X-Files?*"

"Oh, I know who he is. I'm just surprised you know who he is." She found herself blushing as though he'd discovered some secret.

"I've caught a couple of episodes. What things have you heard? About Tully?" She quickly returned to the subject.

"He's here from Cleveland at Cunningham's request, so the guy has to be good, right? Someone said he's able to look at crime scene photos alone and come up with a profile that nine times out of ten is on target."

"Crime scene photos. That explains why he's so squeamish with the real thing."

"I don't think he's been with the Bureau long—five, six years. Probably slipped in right at the age limit."

"What did he do before? Please don't tell me he's a lawyer."

"Something wrong with lawyers?" Agent Tully interrupted from the doorway.

Maggie checked his eyes to see if he was angry with them. Keith went back to his task, leaving Maggie feeling as though she was the one who needed to explain.

"I was just curious," she said without apology.

"You could just ask me."

Yes, he was angry, but she saw him pretending not to be. Did he always make certain his emotions were so carefully kept in check?

"Okay. So what did you do before you joined the Bureau?"

He held up a black garbage bag in one hand.

"I was an insurance fraud investigator." In his other latex-gloved hand he held up a wad of what looked like candy bar wrappers. "And I'd say our boy has a serious sweet tooth."

CHAPTER 42

Maggie gripped the revolver and aimed at the dark figure in front of her. Her right hand shook. She could feel her jaw clench and her muscles tense.

"Goddamn it!" she yelled though no one could hear her in the empty firearms target alley. She had come in just as Agent Ballato, the firearms instructor, had ended his class. This late on a Friday, she would have the place to herself.

She relaxed her stance once again, dropping her arms and rolling her shoulders, flexing her neck. Why the hell couldn't she relax? Why did she feel wound so tight? Like something would explode inside her at any minute?

She pushed her goggles up on top of her head and leaned against the half wall of her galley. After she and Agent Tully had left the house on Archer Drive she had called Detective Ford in Kansas City. She had listened to him describe the details of Rita's murder, of her blood-soaked apartment, the semen-stained sheets and the remnants of skin and tissue the KC forensic team had found in

Rita's bathtub. It wasn't that different from what they had found in the whirlpool bath at Archer Drive. Only, Stucky didn't bother to clean up after himself in Rita's apartment. Why did he clean up at Archer Drive after killing Jessica? Was it because he needed to use the house again? Did he lure Tess McGowan there and take her for later? And if he did take her, where the hell was he keeping her?

Maggie closed her eyes and wished the tightness in her chest would let up. She needed to focus. She needed to relax. It was too easy to conjure up the images. It was what she had been trained to do, but this time she wished she could shove them away. Her mind wouldn't listen. Despite her effort to stop the images, they came anyway. She could see Jessica Beckwith's small hands passing her the pizza box. Then she could see those same hands clawing and grabbing at the walls of the empty bedroom. Why hadn't anyone heard her screams when they seemed so loud and vivid in Maggie's head?

She set the gun aside and rubbed her eyes with both hands. It didn't help. She could remember Rita's face, the waitress's fatigued but friendly smile as she had served the three of them Sunday evening in the smoke-filled bar and grill. And then, without effort or warning, came the images of Rita's garbage-riddled body, her slashed throat and the glob that once was her kidney lying on a shiny dinner plate. Both women were dead only because they had had the misfortune of meeting her. And now Maggie was certain that two more women had been taken for the same reason; they had met her.

She wanted to yell and scream. She wanted the throbbing to go away. She wanted her goddamn hand to stop shaking. Ever since Tully found that handful of candy bar wrappers, Maggie kept wondering about Rachel Endicott. Was it possible she was simply jumping to conclusions, trying too hard to connect Rachel's disappearance with Tess's?

There had been mud on the steps in Rachel's house. Mud with some odd metallic substance. Tully had said that a sparkling dirt had been found on Jessica's car accelerator. Could it be the same? There was something else that Tully had told her. She couldn't remember what it was. It nagged at Maggie, but she couldn't remember. Maybe something in the police report?

"Goddamn it!" Why couldn't she remember?

Lately she felt as if her mind was unraveling, pieces shredding and peeling away. Her nerves felt raw, her muscles exhausted from constantly being on alert. And the worst part, the most infuriating part, was that she seemed to have absolutely no control over any of it.

Albert Stucky had her right where he wanted her, clinging to some imaginary mental ledge. He had made her an accomplice to his evil. He had made her his partner by letting her choose who his next victim would be. He wanted her to share the responsibility. He wanted her to understand the power of evil. By doing so, did he also expect to unleash some evil beast from inside her?

She picked up the Smith & Wesson, letting her hands stroke the cool metal, wrapping her fingers around the handle with care, almost reverence. She ignored the earplugs dangling around her neck and left the goggles perched on top of her head. She raised her right arm, keeping the elbow bent, just a little. Her left hand crisscrossed her right, adding strength and reinforcement. She stared down the front sight, willing it, commanding it not to move, not to quiver. Then without further hesitation, she squeezed the trigger, firing in rapid succession until all six bullets were spent and the scent of the discharge filled her nostrils.

Her ears were ringing when she allowed her arm to relax and drop to her side. Her heart pounded as she punched the button on the wall, flinching at the screech of the pulley as it wheeled the target toward her. The dark figure, the silhouette of her pretend assailant stopped in front of her with a rustle of paper and a clank of metal. Maggie saw that her aim had been right on target. She took a deep breath and sighed. She should have been relieved at her precision. Instead, she felt that ledge getting closer and crumbling beneath her. Because the six bullets she had just fired had expertly and intentionally been placed right between the eyes of her target.

CHAPTER 43

Tess skidded to a stop. Her bare feet were caked with mud. She could smell it and looked to find mud stuck to her hands, her trousers, her skinned elbows. She didn't remember ripping her blouse, yet both elbows showed through, the flesh scraped and bloody, and now dirty with rancid mud. The rain had stopped without her noticing, but she knew it would be temporary because the clouds had darkened and the fog became a thicker gray, wisping around her like unsettled spirits rising from the ground. Dear God, she couldn't think of such things. She shouldn't think at all, just run.

Instead, she leaned against a tree, trying to catch her breath. She had followed the only path she could find in the dense woods, hoping it would lead to freedom. Her nerves were frayed. The terror raced inside her, completely beyond her control. She expected him to step out and grab her at any second.

Dry burrs and broken twigs poked through her blanket cape. It had been caught many times, yanking her backward like hands gripping her neck. It was a constant reminder of the painful bruises his fingers had left. Yet she refused to let it go, as if it was a flimsy shield, a makeshift security blanket. She was soaked from the rain and her own perspiration, wet strands of hair plastered against her face. Her silk blouse clung to her like a second skin.

The thick fog added to the dampness. In less than an hour darkness would enshroud these endless woods. The thought brought fresh panic. She could hardly see through the damp haze. Twice she had slid down a ridge, almost tumbling into the body of water that had seemed like a gray mist when seen from above. The dark would make further movement impossible.

He had taken her wristwatch, for obvious reasons, though he had left the sapphire ring and earrings. She'd gladly trade the three-thousand-dollar ring for her Timex. She hated not knowing the time. Did she know what day it was? Could it still be Wednesday? No. She remembered it being dark when she was in the car. Yes, there had been oncoming headlights. Which meant she had slept most of Thursday. Suddenly it occurred to her that she really had no idea how long she had been unconscious. It may have been days.

Her breathing became labored again as the fear crawled through her insides. Calm. She needed to stay calm. She needed to figure out what to do for the night. She would take this moment by moment. Despite the instinct to continue running, it was more important that she find someplace to wait out the night. Now she wondered if she should have stayed in the shack. Had she really accomplished anything by leaving it? At least it had been dry, and that lumpy cot now sounded wonderful. Instead, she had no idea where she was. It certainly didn't feel as if she had gotten any closer to escaping this endless wooded prison, though she must have covered several miles.

She crouched down, her back pressed against the rough bark. Her legs begged to sit, but she needed to stay alert and ready to run. Black crows screeched down at her. They startled her, but she remained still and quiet, too tired, too weak to move out of their way. The crows were settling in the treetops for the night. Hundreds of them flapped overhead, coming from all directions, their rude caws a warning as they claimed their evening roost.

Suddenly it occurred to Tess that these birds wouldn't settle here if they didn't perceive it to be somewhat safe. And if there was danger sometime during the night, they would probably react better than an alarm system.

Her eyes began searching the area for a safe resting place. There were plenty of fallen leaves and pine needles, bits and pieces left over from last fall. However, everything was damp from the rain and fog. She shivered just thinking about lying on the cold ground.

The crows' squawks continued. She looked up and began examining branches. She hadn't climbed a tree since she was a kid. Back then it had been a survival tactic, one more way to hide from her aunt and uncle. Her aching muscles reminded her how foolish the thought of climbing anything was right now. Foolish or not, it would be the safest place to be. He'd never look for her up above, not to mention other nightly predators. Dear God, she hadn't even thought of other animals.

The tree beside her had a perfect Y to accommodate her. Immediately, she pushed herself into action and began dragging logs and branches. She stacked them, crisscrossing the larger ones to construct a crude stepladder. If she could reach the lower branches, she might be able to swing her feet up into the Y.

She tried to ignore her fatigue, tried to pretend her feet weren't already cut and stinging. With every load of branches or lift of a log, her muscles screamed out for her to stop. But she could feel a new surge of energy. Her heart pounded in her ears, only this time with excitement.

Overhead the crows had gone silent, as if watching and interested in her frantic work. Or did they hear something else? She stopped. Her arms were full. Her breathing rasped. She couldn't hear over the pounding of her heart. She held her breath as best she could and listened. It was as if the entire woods had gone silent, as if the impending dark had swallowed every sound, every movement.

Then she heard it.

At first it sounded like a wounded animal, a muffled cry, a high-pitched hum. Tess turned slowly, her eyes squinting against the fog and into the dark. A sudden breeze created night shadows. Swaying branches became waving arms. Rustling leaves sounded like footsteps.

Tess unloaded her arms while her eyes continued to dart around her. Could she get into the tree without building her makeshift ladder? Her fingers clawed into the bark. Her feet tested the pile's strength and structure. She pulled herself up and grabbed onto the closest branch. It creaked under her weight, but didn't break. Her fingers clung to the branch despite loose bark falling into her eyes. She was ready to swing her feet up into the Y when the muffled cry transformed into words.

"Help me. Please, help me."

The words, drifting with the breeze, were crisp and clear. Tess froze. She hung from the branch, her toes barely reaching the pile. Maybe she was hearing things. Maybe it was simply exhaustion playing tricks on her.

Her arms ached. Her fingers felt numb. If she was going to make it up into the tree, she needed to use this last surge of energy.

The words came again, floating over her as if a part of the fog.

"Please, someone help me."

It was a woman's voice, and it was close by.

Tess dropped to the ground. By now she could see only a foot or two into the thickening darkness. She walked slowly, following the path, silently counting her steps with arms stretched out in front of her. Twigs grabbed at her hair and unseen branches reached for her. She moved in the direction of the voice, still afraid to call, afraid to give away her presence. She stepped carefully, continuing her count so she could turn around and hopefully find her tree sanctuary.

Twenty-two, twenty-three. Then suddenly the ground opened beneath her. Tess fell and the earth swallowed her.

CHAPTER 44

Tess lay at the bottom of the pit. Her head roared. Her side burned as if on fire. Her breathing came in gasps and quick bursts as the terror swept through her veins. Mud oozed up around her, sucking at her arms and legs like quicksand. Her right ankle twisted under her. Even without attempting to move it, she knew she would have trouble doing so.

The smell of mud and decay gagged her. The black dark squeezed around her. She couldn't see in any direction. Above her she could barely make out a few shadows of branches, but the fog and the night had already begun devouring the twilight. What shadows she could see were only enough to reveal how deep her earthly tomb was. It had to be at least fifteen feet to the top. Dear God, she'd never be able to climb out.

She struggled to stand, falling when the ankle refused to hold her up. A fresh wave of panic sent her to her feet again. This time she clawed and scratched at the dirt to hold herself up. She ripped at the wall with fingers digging and searching for a ledge that didn't exist. Chunks of damp earth came off in her hands. She could feel the worms slithering through her fingers. She flung them off. They reminded her of snakes. And dear God, how she hated snakes. The thought alone unleashed a new terror.

Suddenly her bare feet and hands slashed and pounded, climbed and slid. The wind tunnel in her head continued to roar. Her heart slammed against her rib cage. She couldn't breathe. That's when she realized she was screaming. It wasn't the sound that alarmed her as much as her raw throat and her aching lungs. When she stopped, the screaming continued. Surely she was losing her mind. The scream transformed into a whine, then a low moan that emanated from the black corner of the hole.

A shiver slid down Tess's mud and sweat-drenched back. She remembered the voice. The voice that had led her to this hellhole. Had it all been a trap?

"Who are you?" she whispered into the dark.

The moans became muffled sobs.

Tess waited. She slid along the wall, ignoring her throbbing ankle and refusing to sit back down. She needed to be alert. She needed to be ready. She glanced up, expecting her captor to be smiling down at her. Instead, there was a flicker of light she recognized as lightning. A low rumble in the distance confirmed it.

"Who are you?" she shouted this time, giving in to the raw emotion that squeezed her chest and made it difficult to breathe. "And what the hell are you doing here?" She wasn't sure she wanted or needed an answer to her second question.

"He...did this." The voice came with effort, high-pitched and quaking. "Awful things..." she continued. "He did...this. I tried to stop him. I couldn't. I wasn't strong enough." She started moaning again.

The woman's fear was palpable. It grabbed Tess by the throat and crawled under her skin. She couldn't afford to take on this woman's terror, too.

"He had a knife," the woman said between sobs. "He...he cut me."

"Are you hurt? Are you bleeding?" But Tess stayed against the wall, unable to move. Her eyes tried to adjust to the dark, but she could see nothing but a huddled shadow only six or seven feet away from her.

"He said...he told me he'd kill me."

"When did he put you down here? Do you remember?"

"He tied my wrists."

"I can help you untie—"

"He tied my ankles. I couldn't move."

"I can—"

"He ripped my clothes, then he took off my blindfold. He said...he told me he wanted me to watch. He...wanted me to see. Then he...then he raped me."

Tess wiped at her face, replacing tears with mud. She remembered her own clothes, the misbuttoned blouse, the missing panty hose. She felt nauseated. She couldn't think about it. She didn't want to remember. Not now.

"He cut me when I screamed." The woman was still confessing, her voice rambling now out of control. "He wanted me to scream. I couldn't fight him. He was so strong. He got on top of me. So heavy. My chest...he crushed my chest, sitting there on top of me. He was so heavy. My arms were pinned under his legs. He sat on top of me so he could stick...so that he could...he shoved himself down my throat. I gagged. He shoved farther. I couldn't breathe. I couldn't move. He kept—"

"Shut up!" Tess yelled, surprising herself. She didn't recognize her own voice, frightened by the shrillness of it. "Please just shut up!"

Immediately there was silence. No moans. No sobs. Tess listened over the pounding of her heart. Her body shook beyond her control. A liquid cold invaded her veins. Air continued to leak out, replaced by more of the rancid smell of death.

Thunder grew closer, vibrating the earth against her back. The flashes of lightning lit up the world above, but didn't make it down into the black pit. Tess leaned her head against the dirt wall and stared up at the branches, eerie skeletal arms waving down at her in the flickering light. Her entire body hurt from trying to control the convulsions threatening to take over.

She wrapped her arms around herself, determined to ward off those childhood memories, those childhood fears she had worked so hard to destroy. She could feel them crashing through her carefully constructed barriers. She could feel them seeping into her veins, a poison infecting her entire body. She couldn't...she wouldn't allow them to return and render her helpless. Oh dear God! It had taken years to lock them away. And several more years to erase them. No, she couldn't let them back in. Please, dear Lord, not now. Not when she was already feeling so vulnerable, so completely helpless.

The rain began, and Tess let her body slide down against the wall until she felt the mud sucking at her again. Her body began rocking back and forth. She hugged herself tight against the cold and against the memories, but both broke through anyway. As though it had been only yesterday, she remembered what it felt like. She remembered being six years old and being buried alive.

CHAPTER 45

"I think Stucky may have taken my neighbor, too."

"Come on, Maggie. Now you're just sounding paranoid." Gwen sat in Maggie's recliner, sipping wine and petting Harvey's huge head, which filled her lap. The two had become instant pals. "By the way, this wine is very nice. You're getting good at this. See, there are things other than Scotch."

However, Maggie's glass of wine remained full to the rim. She rummaged through the files Tully had given her on Jessica's and Rita's murders. Besides, she hadn't waited for Gwen to arrive before she drank just enough Scotch to settle the restlessness that seemed to have taken up permanent residence inside her. She had hoped target practice would have helped dislodge it. But even the Scotch had not done its usual job of anesthetizing it. Still she was having trouble reading her own handwriting through the blur. She was pleased, though, that she had finally been able to choose a wine that Gwen liked.

A gourmet cook, Gwen enjoyed fine food and wine. When she

had called earlier, offering to bring over dinner, Maggie had rushed out to Shep's Liquor Mart to search the aisles. The clerk, an attractive but overly enthusiastic brunette named Hannah, had told Maggie that the Bolla Sauve was "a delicious semi-dry white wine with touches of floral spiciness and apricot." Hannah assured her that it would complement the chicken and asparagus en papillote that Gwen had promised.

Wine was much too complex. With Scotch she didn't need to choose from merlot, chardonnay, chablis, blush, red or white. All she needed to remember was Scotch, neat. Simple. And it certainly did the job. Though not this evening. The tension strangled her muscles and tightened her rib cage, squeezing and causing her chest to ache.

"What do the police say about Rachel's disappearance?"

"I'm not sure." Maggie flipped through a file folder with newspaper clippings, but still couldn't find what she was looking for. "The lead detective called Cunningham and complained about me barging in on his territory, so it's not like I can just call him up and say, 'Hey, I think I know what happened with that case you want me to keep my nose out of.' But my other neighbor gave me the impression everyone, including the husband, is treating it as though Rachel just decided to leave."

"That seems odd. Has she done this sort of thing before?"

"I have no clue. But doesn't it seem odder that the husband wouldn't want the dog?"

"Not if he thinks she ran off with someone. It's one of the few ways he has left to punish her."

"It doesn't explain why we found the dog in the condition we did. There was a lot of blood, and I'm still not convinced it was all Harvey's." Maggie noticed Gwen stroking Harvey's head as though administering therapy. "Who names a dog Harvey?"

He looked up at Maggie's mention of his name, but didn't budge.

"It's a perfectly good name," Gwen declared as she continued her generous strokes.

"It was the name of the black Lab that David Berkowitz believed was possessed."

Gwen rolled her eyes. "Now, why is it that you think of that immediately? Maybe Rachel is a Jimmy Stewart fan or a classic-movie buff, and named him after Harvey the six-foot invisible rabbit."

"Oh, right. Why didn't I think of that?" It was Maggie's turn for sarcasm. The truth was, she didn't want to think of Harvey's owner and what she believed may have happened to her, or was still happening to her. She returned her attention to the folders. She wished she could remember exactly what it was that Agent Tully had said. There was something nagging at her. Something that connected Rachel's disappearance to Jessica's murder. Not just the mud. Yet she couldn't remember what it was that made her think that. She was hoping one of the police reports would trigger her memory.

"Why the hell isn't the husband the prime suspect?" Gwen suddenly sounded irritated. "That would be a logical explanation to me."

"You'd need to meet Detective Manx to understand. He doesn't seem to be approaching any of this logically."

"I'm not so sure he's the only one. The husband does seem to be the logical suspect, and yet here you are jumping to the conclusion that Stucky kidnapped her because...let me get this straight. You think Stucky kidnapped Rachel Endicott because you're sure he killed this pizza delivery girl and you found candy bar wrappers at both scenes."

"And mud. Don't forget the mud." Maggie checked the lab's report on Jessica's car. The mud recovered from the accelerator contained some sort of metallic residue that Keith was now going to break down. Again she remembered the mud with sparkling flecks on Rachel Endicott's stairs. But what if Manx hadn't bothered to collect it? And even if he had, how would she be able to compare the two? It wasn't like Manx would easily hand over a sample.

"Okay," Gwen said. "The mud I can understand, if you can make a match. But finding candy bar wrappers at both houses? I'm sorry, Maggie, that's a bit of a stretch."

"Stucky leaves body parts in take-out containers just for fun, to toy with people. Why wouldn't he leave candy bar wrappers, sort of his way of thumbing his nose at us? Like he was able to commit this inconceivably horrible murder and then have a snack afterward."

"So the wrappers are part of the game?"

"Yes." She glanced up. Gwen didn't buy it. "Why is that so hard to believe?"

"Did you ever consider they could be a necessity? Maybe the killer or even the victims have an insulin deficiency. Sometimes people with diabetes keep candy bars to prevent fluctuations in their insulin intake. Fluctuations possibly caused by stress or an injection of too much insulin."

"Stucky's not diabetic."

"You know that for sure?"

"Yes," Maggie said, quite certain, then realized their lab analysis of Stucky's blood and DNA had never been tested for the disease.

"How can you be so certain?" Gwen persisted. "About a third of people with Type 2 diabetes don't even know they have it. It's not something that's routinely checked unless there are symptoms or some family history. And I have to tell you, the symptoms, especially the early ones, are very subtle."

She knew Gwen was right. But she would know if Stucky had diabetes. They had his blood and DNA on file. Unless this was some recent development. No, she couldn't imagine Albert Stucky being susceptible to anything other than silver bullets or maybe a wooden stake through his heart.

"How about the victims?" Gwen suggested. "Maybe the candy bars belonged to the victims. Any chance they're diabetic?"

"Too much of a coincidence. I don't believe in coincidences."

"No, you'd much rather believe that Albert Stucky has kidnapped your neighbor, who by the way wasn't your neighbor yet, *and* took a real estate agent simply because you bought a house from her. I have to tell you, Maggie, it all sounds a bit ridiculous. You have absolutely no proof that either of these women are even missing, let alone that Stucky has them."

"Gwen, it's no coincidence that the waitress in Kansas City and the pizza delivery girl had both come in contact with me only hours before they were murdered in the same manner. I'm the only link. Don't you think I want to believe that neither Rachel nor Tess were taken by Stucky? Don't you think I'd rather believe they are both on some secluded beach sipping piña coladas with their lovers?"

She hated that her voice could get so shrill, that her hands could shake and her heart pound in her ears. She went back to the pile, shuffling through the folders and trying to make sense of Tully's attempt at order, or rather his disorder. She could feel Gwen's eyes examining her. Maybe Gwen was right. Perhaps the paranoia skewed her rationality. What if she was blowing all this out of proportion? What if she was slipping over some mental edge? It certainly felt like that.

"If that's true, then it would mean Stucky is watching you, following you."

"Yes," Maggie said, trying to sound as matter-of-fact as possible.

"If he's choosing women he sees you with, then why hasn't he chosen me?"

Maggie looked up at her friend, startled by the flicker of fear she thought she saw in the otherwise strong and confident eyes. "He only targets women I come in contact with, not women I know. It makes his next move less predictable. He wants me to feel like an accomplice. I don't think he wants to destroy me. And hurting you would destroy me."

She went back to her search, wanting to close the subject and dismiss the possibility. Fact was, she had thought about Stucky moving on to those who were close to her. Nothing would stop him from doing so if he wanted to up the ante.

"Have you talked to Agent Tully about any of this?"

"You're my friend, and you think I'm nuts. Why in the world would I share any of it with him?"

"Because he's your partner, and the two of you should be working through this mess together, no matter how crazy every tidbit appears to be. Promise me you won't be checking out stuff on your own."

Maggie found a new set of documents and began flipping through the pages. Was it possible she was only imagining that there was something else that linked Rachel Endicott to Stucky?

"Maggie, did you hear me?"

She glanced up to find Gwen's normally smooth forehead wrinkled with concern, her warm green eyes filled with worry.

"Promise me you won't go off on your own again," Gwen demanded.

"I won't go off on my own again." She dug out a brown manila envelope and started extracting its contents.

"Maggie, I mean it."

She stopped and looked up at her friend. Even Harvey stared at her with sad, brown eyes. This from the same dog who had spent the last two nights going back and forth, checking the front door and each of the windows, looking for and waiting for his master to pick him up as though he couldn't stand to spend one more moment with Maggie.

"Please, don't worry, Gwen. I promise I won't do anything stupid." She unfolded several copies and immediately found what she had been searching for. It was the report from the airport authority and a police impound notice for a white Ford van. "Here it is. This is it. This is what's been nagging at me."

"What is it?"

Maggie stood and began pacing.

"Susan Lyndell told me that the man Rachel Endicott may have run off with was a telephone repairman."

"So what's your proof? Her phone bill?" Gwen sounded impatient.

"This is an impound notice. When the police found Jessica Beckwith's car at the airport, they found a van parked alongside it. The van had been stolen about two weeks ago."

"I'm sorry, Maggie, but I'm lost. So Stucky stole a van and abandoned it when he was finished with it. What does that have to do with your missing neighbor?"

"The van that was recovered belonged to Northeastern Bell Telephone Company." Maggie waited for Gwen's reaction, and when it was less than satisfactory, she continued, "Okay, it's a long shot, but you have to admit, it's too much of a coincidence and—"

"I know, I know." Gwen raised her hand to stop her. "And you don't believe in coincidences."

CHAPTER 46

Tess couldn't remember a night so long and dark and brutal, despite having a repertoire of many in her childhood. She sat curled in a corner, hugging her knees and trying not to think about her bare, swollen feet buried in the rancid mud. The rain had finally stopped although she heard thunder in the distance, a low rumble like a boulder rolling overhead. Was it the clouds that were preventing the sun from rising or had the madman made a deal with the devil?

At times she could hear the woman moaning quietly to herself. Her breaths, her gasps were so close. Thankfully, the sobs and the high-pitched whine had stopped. As the sky lightened, the huddled form began to take shape.

Tess closed her eyes against the gritty, burning sensation. Why had she been so stubborn and refused the ever-wear contact lenses? She wanted to rub and dig at her eyes. Soon she'd need to make a choice about taking the contacts out or leaving them in. When she opened her eyes again, she blinked several times. She couldn't believe what she was seeing. In the dim light she saw the woman across from her was completely naked. She had twisted herself into a fetal position, her skin slathered in mud and what looked and smelled like blood and feces.

"Oh dear God," Tess mumbled. "Why didn't you tell me you had nothing on?"

Tess struggled to her feet. Her ankle rebelled, sending her to her knees. Now her pain seemed minor. She forced herself up again, putting all the weight on her other foot. Her fingers frantically pulled at the knot keeping her blanket cape around her shoulders. The woman's body shivered. No, she wasn't just shivering. Her muscles looked to be in some sort of convulsions. Her teeth chattered and her lower lip was bleeding where she must have bitten herself repeatedly.

"Are you in pain?" Tess asked, realizing how stupid the question sounded. Of course she was in pain.

She ripped the blanket off and draped it carefully around the woman. It was damp but the wool had somehow kept her own body heat from escaping all night long. Hopefully it wouldn't make matters worse. How could it possibly make things worse?

Tess kept a safe distance as she examined the horrible bruises, the raw cuts and torn flesh left from what looked like bites—human bites.

"Dear God. We need to get you to a hospital." Another ridiculous thing to say. If she couldn't get out of this pit, how could she get her to a hospital?

The woman didn't seem to hear Tess. Though her eyes were wide and open, they stared at the mud wall in front of her. Her tangled hair stuck to her face. Tess reached down and wiped a clump away from her cheek. The woman didn't even blink. She was in shock, and Tess wondered if her mind had retreated inside herself, into a deep, unreachable cavern. It was exactly what Tess had done so many times as a child. It had been her only defense in combating the long stays of punishment that had exiled her to the dark storm cellar, sometimes for days at a time.

She caressed the woman's cheek, wiping mud and hair from her face and neck. Her stomach lurched when she saw the bruises and bite marks that covered her neck and breast. A raw gash also circled her neck. It looked like an indentation left from a rope or cord pulled so tight it had dug into the flesh.

"Are you able to move?" Tess asked, but got no response.

She looked up to survey the depths of their hell now that light seeped down to them. It was not as deep as she had initially thought—twelve, maybe fifteen feet at the most, about five feet wide and ten feet long. It looked to be an old trench, partially caved in with uneven sides. Tree roots snaked out and rocks jutted out in places. But there were fresh spade marks that told her he intended for this to be a trap.

What kind of monster did this to a woman and then threw her into a pit? She couldn't think about him. She couldn't wonder or imagine, or it would completely paralyze her. Instead, she needed to concentrate on getting them out of here. But how the hell could she do that?

She kneeled next to the woman. The blanket seemed to reduce the convulsions. She'd need to examine her for broken bones. There were enough gashes in the walls and jutting rocks that they could climb their way out, but she'd never be able to pull or carry the woman.

Just as Tess reached to touch the woman's shoulder, she saw what it was that the woman's eyes were focused on so intently. Startled, she jumped back. Slowly she forced herself closer for a better look, despite her amazement, despite her revulsion. Directly in front of her, buried in the dirt wall and partially unearthed by the rain was a human skull, the empty eye sockets staring out at them. And then, Tess realized. This wasn't a trap, at all. It was a grave. It was their grave.

CHAPTER 47

Saturday, April 4

She wore another red silk blouse. She looked good in red. It emphasized her strawberry-blond hair. It had become a habit for her to leave off her jacket and stand in front of her desk, half sitting on the corner. Today, she didn't bother to pull down the skirt hem that hiked up just enough to reveal shapely smooth thighs. Lovely, tender thighs that made him wonder what it would feel like to sink his teeth into them.

She waited for him to talk while she scribbled in her notepad, probably not even taking notes on him. If the notes were about him, he wasn't the least bit curious about what they said. He was more interested in what her moans would sound like when he finally stuck himself inside her, thrusting deep and hard until she was screaming. He so enjoyed it when they screamed, especially when he was inside them. The vibration felt like shock waves, like he was causing a fucking earthquake.

It was one of many things he had in common with his old friend, his old partner. At least it was one thing he didn't need to fake. He pushed the sunglasses up on the bridge of his nose and realized she was waiting.

"Mr. Harding," she interrupted his thoughts. "You never answered my question."

He couldn't remember what the fucking question had been. He cocked his head to the side and jutted out his chin in that pathetic gesture that said, "Forgive me, I'm blind."

"I asked if any of the exercises I suggested have helped."

Sure enough. If he waited, people always made it easy, supplying the answer, repeating themselves or getting up and doing whatever it was they had wanted him to do. He was getting good at this. Probably a good thing, in case it became permanent.

"Mr. Harding?"

She didn't have much patience today. He wanted to ask how long it had been since she had been fucked. That was, no doubt, the problem. Or perhaps she needed a few porn movies from his new private collection.

He knew from his personal research that she was divorced, for almost twenty-five years now. It had been a short, two-year marriage, a youthful indiscretion. Certainly there must have been several lovers since, though, of course, those details weren't easily accessible on the Internet.

Now he could see her impatience growing in the way she crossed her arms. Finally, he said politely, "The exercises worked quite well, but that doesn't prove or help anything."

"Why do you say that?"

"What good does it do to get myself...well, excuse the expression...to get my little general all hot, hard and bothered when I'm alone?"

She smiled, the first she had surrendered since they had met.

"We need to start somewhere."

"Okay, but I'm afraid I must object if you suggest I move on to blow-up dolls."

Another smile. He was on a roll. Should he tell her he'd like her to be his blow-up doll? He wondered how good a blow job she could give with that sweet, sexy little mouth of hers. He was certain he could fill it quite nicely.

"No, I won't make any more suggestions for the time being," she said, detecting none of what went through his mind. "However, I would encourage you to continue with the exercises. The idea is to have a—excuse the expression—surefire method of arousal to fall back on should you find yourself wanting to perform with a woman but not able to."

She was idly swinging her left foot as she sat on the corner of the desk. Her black leather pump teetered at the end of her toes as she played with it. He wished the shoe would fall off. He wanted to see if she had painted her toenails. He loved red painted toenails.

"Whether we want to believe it or not, many of our preconceived notions about sex," she continued, though he paid little attention, "come from our parents. Boys especially find themselves imitating their fathers' behaviors. What was your father like, Mr. Harding?"

"He certainly had no problems when it came to women," he snapped, and immediately regretted letting her see that the subject was a touchy one. Now she wouldn't leave it alone. She'd insist they poke and probe through it until she found a way to bring his mother into it as well. Unless...unless he turned it around somehow and embarrassed her away from the subject entirely.

"My father brought women home quite frequently. He even let me watch. Sometimes the women let me join in. What other thirteen-year-old boy can say he got his cock sucked by a woman while his dad fucked the shit out of her from behind?"

There it was—that look of utter shock. Soon it would be followed by the pity look. Funny how the truth possessed such remarkable power. A knock at the door made her jump. He stared off into oblivion like a good little blind fucker.

"Sorry to interrupt," her secretary called from the door. "That phone call you've been waiting for is on line three."

"I need to take this call, Mr. Harding."

"That's fine." He stood and fumbled for his cane. "Perhaps we can end early today."

"Are you sure? This really will take but a minute or two."

"No, I'm exhausted. Besides, I think you more than earned your money today." He rewarded her with a smile so that she wouldn't continue to object. He found the door before she could offer to call his make-believe driver. As he waited for the elevator, the anger began to churn inside his guts. He hated thinking about his parents. She had no right bringing them into this. She had overstepped her bounds. Yes, today, Dr. Gwen Patterson had gone too far.

CHAPTER 48

Assistant Director Cunningham had commandeered a small conference room for them on the first level. Tully was so excited about having windows—two that looked into the woods at the edge of the training field—he didn't care that he had to walk up and down stairs, clear to the other end of the building to bring stuff from his cramped office.

He spread out everything they had gathered in the last five months, while O'Dell followed behind him, insisting on putting it all in neat little stacks, lining it up on the long conference table so that it flowed from left to right in chronological order. Instead of being irritated by her anal-retentive process, he found himself amused. So they approached puzzles differently. She liked to start by finding all the corner pieces and lining them up, while he liked to scatter all the pieces in the center, picking and choosing random sections to piece together. Neither way was right or wrong. It was simply a matter of preference, although he doubted that O'Dell would agree with that assessment.

They had tacked up a map of the United States, marking the recent murders in Newburgh Heights and Kansas City with red pushpins. Blue pins marked each of the other seventeen areas where Stucky had left victims before his capture last August. At least those were the ones they knew about. The women Stucky kept for his collection were often buried in remote wooded areas. It was believed there could be as many as a dozen more, hidden and waiting to be discovered by hikers or fishermen or hunters. All this, Stucky had accomplished in less than three years. Tully hated to think what the madman may have done in the last five months.

Tully continued to examine the map and left O'Dell to her housekeeping. For the most part, Stucky had stayed on the eastern edge of the United States from as far north as Boston to as far south as Miami. The Virginia shoreline seemed to be a fertile ground for him. Kansas City appeared to be the only anomaly. If Tess McGowan was, in fact, missing, that meant Stucky really was playing with O'Dell again, bringing her in, making her a part of his crimes. And by choosing only women who she came in contact with, rather than friends or family members, he made it virtually impossible for them to know who might be next. After all, what could they do? Lock O'Dell up until they caught Stucky? Cunningham already had several agents watching her house and following her. Tully was surprised O'Dell hadn't objected.

Saturday morning and she was already digging in as if it were any other weekday. After the week she had, anyone else would still be at home in bed. Although this morning he did notice that she hadn't bothered to use makeup to conceal the dark, puffy lines under her eyes. She wore an old pair of Nike running shoes, a chambray shirt with the sleeves rolled up to the elbows and the tails neatly tucked into the waistband of faded jeans. Though they were in a secured facility, she kept her shoulder harness on, her Smith & Wesson .38 ready at her side. Compared to O'Dell, he felt overdressed, except when Assistant Director Cunningham stopped by, looking as crisp, spotless and wrinkle-free as usual. That was when Tully noticed the coffee stains on his own white shirt and his loosened and lopsided tie.

Tully checked his watch. He had promised Emma lunch and a

total discussion of this prom thing. He had already decided to stand firm on the matter. Emma could call it being close-minded if she wanted to, but he simply didn't want to start thinking about her as being old enough to date. At least not yet. Maybe next year.

He glanced over at O'Dell who stood over the reports they had received earlier from Keith Ganza. Without looking up at him, she asked, "Any luck with airport security?"

"No, but now that Delores Heston has filed a missing-person's report, we can get an APB out on the car. A black Miata can't be that hard to miss. I don't know, though. What if McGowan just decided to take off for a couple of days?"

"Then we ruin her vacation. What about the boyfriend?"

"The guy has a house and business in D.C., and another house and office in Newburgh Heights. I finally tracked down Mr. Daniel Kassenbaum last night at his country club. He didn't sound very concerned. In fact, he told me he suspected McGowan might be cheating on him. Then he quickly added that their relationship was a no-strings sort of thing. That's what he called it. So, I guess if his suspicions are true, maybe she simply took off with some secret lover."

O'Dell looked up at him. "If the boyfriend thought she was cheating on him, can we be certain he didn't have something to do with her disappearance?"

"I honestly don't think the guy cares, not as long as he was getting what he wanted." O'Dell looked puzzled. Tully felt a surge of emotion and knew this was a touchy subject with him. Kassenbaum reminded him too much of the asshole Caroline had left him for. Still, he continued, "He told me the last time he saw her was when she stayed over at his house in Newburgh Heights Tuesday night. Now, if the guy thinks she's cheating on him, why is he still having her stay overnight at his house?"

O'Dell shrugged. "I give up. Why?"

He wasn't sure if she was serious or being sarcastic. "Why? Because he's an arrogant asshole who doesn't care about anyone other than himself. So as long as he's getting his jollies serviced, what does he care?" She was staring at him. He should have known when to quit. "What do women see in guys like that?"

"Getting his jollies serviced? Is that what you call it in Ohio?"

Tully felt his face grow red, and O'Dell smiled. She went back to the reports, letting him off the hook, and evidently not realizing how hot the subject made him. Last night, Daniel Kassenbaum had treated him like some servant he didn't have time for, scolding Tully for interrupting his dinner. Like the guy didn't think maybe Tully was interrupting his own dinner by looking for his girlfriend? Maybe Tess McGowan really did take off with some secret lover. Good for her.

He stood facing the map again. They had circled possible sites, mostly remote wooded areas. There were way too many to check. The only clue they had was the sparkling dirt found in Jessica Beckwith's car and in Rachel Endicott's house. Keith Ganza had narrowed down the chemical concoction that made up the metallic substance, but even that didn't narrow down the sites. In fact, it made Tully wonder if they were looking in the wrong places. Maybe they should be checking out deserted industrial sites instead of wooded areas. After all, Stucky had used a condemned warehouse in Miami to hide his collection until O'Dell found him.

"What about an industrial site?" He decided to try out his theory on O'Dell.

She stopped what she was doing and came beside him, studying the map.

"You're thinking of the chemicals Keith found in the mud?"

"I know it doesn't follow his pattern, but neither did the warehouse down in Miami." As soon as he said it, he glanced at O'Dell, realizing the subject may still be a touchy one. If it was, she made no indication.

"Wherever he's hiding, it can't be far. I'm guessing an hour, maybe an hour and a half at most." She traced the area with her index finger, a fifty-to-seventy-mile radius, with her home in Newburgh Heights at the center. "He couldn't drive too far and still keep watch over me."

Tully watched her out of the corner of his eyes, again looking for any signs of the frenzy, the terror he had witnessed the other night. He wasn't surprised to find it masked. O'Dell wouldn't be the first FBI agent he knew who could compartmentalize her emotions. With O'Dell, however, he could see it was an effort. He wondered just how long she could contain them without cracking at the seams again.

"The map may not show old industrial sites that have been closed. I'll check with the State Department and see if they have anything."

"Don't forget Maryland and D.C."

Tully jotted notes on the McDonald's brown paper sack that had held his breakfast; a sausage biscuit and hash browns. For a brief moment he tried to remember the last meal he had eaten that hadn't come from a bag. Maybe he'd take Emma somewhere nice for lunch. No fast food. Somewhere with tablecloths.

When he turned back, O'Dell was back at the table. He looked over her shoulder at the crime scene photos she had sorted. Without looking at him, she said in almost a whisper, "We need to find them, Agent Tully. We need to find them very soon or it'll be too late."

He didn't need to ask who she meant. She was talking about the McGowan woman, and also her neighbor, Rachel Endicott. Tully still wasn't convinced either woman was missing, let alone taken by Stucky. He didn't share his doubts with O'Dell, nor did he share with her that he had talked to Detective Manx in Newburgh Heights. With any luck Manx would find it in his stubborn, isolationist pig head to share whatever evidence he recovered from the Endicott house. Though Tully didn't expect much. Detective Manx had told him the case was nothing more than a bored housewife running off with a telephone repairman.

He hated to think Manx might be right. Tully shook his head. What was it with married women these days? He didn't like being reminded of Caroline for the second time that morning.

"If you are right about Tess McGowan and the Endicott woman," Tully said, careful to keep his own doubts aside, "that means Stucky has killed two women and taken two others in a span of only one week. Are you sure Stucky could pull that off?"

"It would be tough but not impossible. He would have had to take Rachel Endicott early last Friday. Then come back to Newburgh Heights, watch Jessica deliver my pizza, lure her to the house on Archer Drive and kill her late Friday evening or early Saturday morning."

"Doesn't that seem like a bit much?"

"Yes," she admitted, "but not for Stucky."

"Then somehow he finds out that you'd be in KC. Even finds out where you're staying. Again, he watches you, Delaney and Turner with the waitress—"

"Rita."

"Right, Rita. That was what, Sunday night?"

"Around midnight...actually early Monday morning. If Delores Heston is correct, Tess showed the house on Archer Drive Wednesday." She avoided Tully's eyes. "I know it sounds like a lot, but keep in mind what he's done in the past."

She started sorting through the photos again. "It's never been easy to track. Some of the bodies were found much later, long after they were reported missing. Most of them were so badly decomposed we could only guess at the time of deaths. But the spring before we caught him, we estimated that he killed two women, leaving them in Dumpsters, and that he had taken five others for his collection. That was all in the span of two or three weeks. At least that's the time frame that the women were first discovered missing. We didn't find those five bodies until months later, and they were all in one mass grave. The women had been tortured and killed at different intervals. There were signs that he may have even hunted down a couple of them. We found evidence that he may have used a crossbow and arrows."

Tully recognized the photos. O'Dell had laid out a series of Poloraids that chronicled one victim's wounds. If the photos hadn't been marked, it would be difficult to tell that they were all the same woman. This was one of those five victims who had been found in that mass grave. The corpse was one of the rare ones found before decomposition or before animals had ravaged it. It was one of the few that was intact and whole.

"This was Helen Kreski," O'Dell said without looking up the name. "She was one of the five. Stucky choked and stabbed her repeatedly. Her left nipple had been bitten off. Her right arm and wrist were broken. There was a puncture through her left calf with a broken arrow still intact." O'Dell's voice was calm, too calm, as though she had resolved herself to something beyond her control. "We found dirt in her lungs. She was still alive when he buried her."

"Christ, this is one sick son of a bitch."

"We need to stop him, Agent Tully. We need to do it before he crawls back into a hole someplace. Before he runs off and hides and starts playing with his new collection."

"And we'll do that. We just need to find out where the hell he's hiding." He didn't want to notice that she had used the word *stop* instead of *catch*.

He left her side and checked his watch again.

"I need to leave around eleven. I promised my daughter we'd have lunch together." O'Dell had moved back to the reports they had received from Ganza. She had the fingerprint analysis and was reading it over for the third time. He wondered if she had even heard him. "Hey, why don't you join us?"

She glanced up, surprised by his invitation.

"I still think the print was left by someone who looked at the house earlier," he said, referring to the fingerprint report and taking her off the hook if she really didn't want to accept his invitation.

"He wiped down everything in the bathroom," she said, "but he missed two clean and whole fingerprints. No, he wanted us to find these. He's done it before. It was how we finally confirmed who he was."

He watched her rub her eyes as if the memory brought on a whole new fatigue.

"At that time, we had no name, no idea who The Collector was," she continued. "Stucky evidently thought we were taking too long to figure it out. I think he left us a print on purpose. It was so blatant, so careless, it had to be on purpose."

"Well, if this one was on purpose, why bother to clean up the place at all? He never seemed to care before."

"Maybe he cleaned up because he wanted to use the house again."

"For McGowan?"

"Yes."

"Okay. But why bother to leave us a print that doesn't even belong to him? Just like on the Dumpster behind the pizza place and on the umbrella in Kansas City."

O'Dell hesitated, stopping her hands from shuffling papers and looking at him as if wondering whether or not to tell him something. "Keith hasn't been able to find a match for those prints in AFIS. But he says he's almost certain all three sets of prints belong to the same person."

"You're kidding. He knows that for sure? If that's the case, maybe these murders aren't Stucky, after all."

He stared at her, waiting for some kind of reaction. Her face remained impassive, just like her voice when she said, "Jessica's murder and Rita's in Kansas City are awfully close together. I know I just said that Stucky could pull it off, but the anal penetration with Jessica is not Stucky's M.O. Also, she's much younger than any of his other victims."

"So what are you saying, O'Dell. You think this one was a copycat?"

"Or an accomplice."

"What? That's crazy!"

She buried her eyes in the files again. He could see she was having a difficult time with the theory herself. O'Dell was used to working and brainstorming alone. Suddenly he realized that it probably took a good deal of trust for her to share this idea with him.

"Look, I know you're serious, but why would Stucky take on an accomplice? You have to admit, that's out of character for any serial killer."

In reply, O'Dell pulled out several photocopied pages that looked like magazine and newspaper articles and handed them to Tully.

"Remember Cunningham said he found the name Walker Harding, Stucky's old business partner, on an airline manifest?"

Tully nodded and began sorting through the articles.

"Some of those go back several years," she told him.

They were articles from *Forbes,* the *Wall Street Journal, PC World* and several other business and trade periodicals. The *Forbes* article included a picture. Though the grainy black-and-white copy had obliterated most of the men's features, the two of them could have passed for brothers. Both had dark hair, narrow faces and sharp features. Tully recognized Albert Stucky's piercing black eyes, which he knew to be void of color despite the poor reproduction. The younger man smiled while Stucky's face remained stoic and serious.

"I'm guessing this must be the partner?"

"Yes. A couple of the articles mention how much the two men had in common and how competitive they were with each other. However, they seemed to have ended their partnership amicably. I wonder if they might still be in contact with each other. Maybe still in competition with each other, only with a new game."

"But why now after all these years? If they were to do something like this, why not when Stucky first started his game?"

O'Dell sat down and tucked strands of hair behind her ears. She looked exhausted. As if reading his thoughts, she sipped her Diet Pepsi, which he had noticed was her coffee substitute. This was her third one of the morning.

"Stucky has always been a loner," she explained. "I haven't done any research on Harding except for these articles, but for Stucky to have chosen anyone as a business partner is remarkable. I've never thought about it before, but perhaps the two men had, and still have, some strong connection, a connection Stucky didn't realize until recently. Or perhaps there's some other reason he decided he needed his old friend."

Tully shook his head. "I think you're grasping at straws, O'Dell. You know as well as I do that statistically, serial killers don't take on partners or accomplices."

"But Stucky is far from fitting any of the statistics. I'm having Keith run a check to see if Harding has ever been fingerprinted. Then we can see if we have a match to the fingerprints being left at the crime scenes."

Tully looked over the articles, scanning the text until something caught his eye.

"Looks like there's a slight problem with your theory, O'Dell."

"What's that?"

"There's a footnote to this *Wall Street Journal* article. Stucky and Harding ended their partnership after Harding was diagnosed with some medical problem."

"Right. I saw that."

"But did you finish reading it? This part is blurred at the bottom from the copier. Unless Walker Harding found some miracle cure, he can't be Stucky's accomplice. It says here he was going blind."

CHAPTER 49

Maggie waited until Tully left to meet his daughter. Then she began unearthing every scrap of information she could find on Walker Harding. She pounded the computer's keys, searching the FBI's files and other Internet sites and directories. The man had virtually disappeared after announcing his ambiguous medical problem almost four years ago. Now she realized Keith Ganza might never find a fingerprint record, either. Perhaps it was simply a gut instinct, but she felt certain Harding was still connected to Stucky, helping him somehow, continuing to work with him.

From what little she had read, she knew Harding had been the brains of their business, a whiz with computers. But Stucky had been the one who had taken all the financial risk, investing a hundred thousand dollars of his own money; money he had joked about winning one weekend in Atlantic City. Maggie couldn't help noticing that the investment capital and the start-up of the business happened the same year Stucky's father died in a freak boating accident. Stucky had never been charged though he had been questioned in what looked like a routine investigation, and only because Stucky had been the sole beneficiary of his father's estate, an estate that made that hundred thousand dollars look like pocket change.

Harding appeared to have been reclusive long before his business venture with Stucky. Maggie could find nothing about his childhood, except that he—like Stucky—had been raised by a single, overbearing father. One directory listed him as a 1985 graduate of MIT, which made him about three years younger than Stucky. The state of Virginia listed no marriage license, driver's license or property owned by a Walker Harding. She had begun a search of Maryland's records when Thea Johnson from down the hall knocked on the open conference-room door.

"Agent O'Dell, there's a phone call for Agent Tully. I know he left for a while, but this sounds important. Do you want to take the call?"

"Sure." Maggie didn't hesitate and reached behind her for the phone. "What line?"

"Line five. It's a detective from Newburgh Heights. I believe he said his name was Manx."

Immediately, Maggie's stomach took a dive. She sucked in a deep breath and punched line five.

"Detective Manx, Agent Tully is at lunch. This is his partner, Agent Margaret O'Dell."

She waited for the name to register. Even after a sigh, there was a pause.

"Agent O'Dell. Barge in on any crime scenes lately?"

"Funny thing, Detective Manx, but here at the FBI we usually don't wait for engraved invitations." She didn't care if he heard the irritation in her voice. If he was calling Tully, he wanted something from them. Besides, what was he going to do? Go tell Cunningham she was mean to him again?

"When's Tully gonna be back?"

So that was the way he wanted to play.

"Gee, you know, I don't remember if he told me. He might not be back until Monday."

She waited out his silence and imagined the scowl on his face. He was probably swiping a frustrated hand over that new buzz hairdo of his.

"Look, Tully talked to me last night about this McGowan woman down here in Newburgh Heights that's supposedly missing."

"She is missing, Detective Manx. Seems you have a problem with women disappearing in your jurisdiction. What's up with that?" She was enjoying this too much. She needed to back off.

"I thought he should know that we checked out her house this morning and found a guy snooping around."

"What?" Maggie sat up and gripped the phone.

"This guy said he was a friend and was worried about her. He had a screen off a back window and looked like he was getting ready to break in. We brought him in for questioning. Just thought Tully might like to know."

"You haven't released him yet, have you?"

"No, the boys are still chatting with him. I think we got him pretty damn scared. First thing, he insisted on calling his fucking lawyer. Makes me think he's guilty of something."

"Don't release him until Agent Tully and I have a chance to talk to him. We'll be there in about a half hour."

"Sure, no problem. Lookin' forward to seeing you again, O'Dell."

She hung up, grabbed her jacket and was almost out the door before she realized she should probably call Tully. She patted her jacket down until she felt the cellular phone in the pocket. She'd call him from the road. No, of course, this wasn't a matter of her running off on her own. It wasn't breaking any of Cunningham's new rules. She simply didn't want to ruin Agent Tully's lunch with his daughter.

That was what she told herself. The fact was, she wanted to check this out on her own. If Manx had Albert Stucky or even Walker Harding, Maggie wanted him all to herself.

CHAPTER 50

As the sun moved overhead and more light seeped down, Tess could see the hellhole for what it was. The skull that stared out from the earth wall was not the only human remains that surrounded them. Other bones glistened, washed white by the rains, protruding at odd angles from the uneven walls and the muddy floor.

At first Tess told herself it was some ancient burial ground, maybe a mass grave from a Civil War battle. Then she found a black underwire bra and a woman's leather pump with a broken heel sticking out of the ground. Neither looked old enough or deteriorated enough to have been there much longer than weeks, maybe months.

Dirt had been recently thrown into one of the corners. The mound looked fresh despite the rain packing it down. She stared at it, but didn't dare go near it, staying away as if the pile would crumble and reveal some new horror. If that was at all possible.

The rays of sunshine felt wonderful, though they wouldn't last long. She managed to gently drag the woman to the center, so she could be warmed directly. Even the wool blanket had begun to dry. Tess stretched it out across some rocks, leaving the woman naked but bathed in sunlight.

Tess was getting used to the rancid smell of the woman. She could stay close without the urge to vomit. The woman had defecated in her corner several times and had accidentally rolled in it. Tess wished she had some water to clean her. The thought reminded her how dry and raw her mouth and throat were. Surely the woman was already in a state of dehydration. Her convulsions had calmed to a mild shiver and her teeth had stopped chattering. Even her breathing seemed to return to normal. Now with the sunlight on her skin, Tess noticed she had closed her eyes, as though finally able to rest. Or had she finally decided to die?

Tess sat on a broken branch and examined the pit again. She knew she could climb out. She had tried twice, reaching the top both times. Each time she peered over the edge, the relief and satisfaction overwhelming her to tears. But each time, she lowered herself back down, carefully easing the pressure on her swollen ankle.

Though she didn't want to think about the madman, she realized there could be safety in this pit. He must have dumped the woman here, expecting her to die from her wounds and exposure. Eventually, he would return to throw some dirt over her and create yet another mound. When he discovered Tess was gone from the shack, he might not think to look for her down here.

That didn't mean she wanted to stay. She hated feeling trapped. And this hellhole reminded her too much of the dark storm cellar her aunt and uncle had used as punishment for her. As a child, being buried beneath the ground for an hour was terrifying. One or two days, unimaginable. Even as an adult, she could never remember what she had done to deserve such punishment. Instead, she had readily believed her aunt when she called her an evil child and dragged her down to the damp torture chamber. Each time, Tess had screamed how sorry she was and pleaded for forgiveness.

"No apologies accepted," her uncle would always say, laughing.

In the dark, Tess would pray over and over for her mother to come and rescue her, remembering her mother's last words, "I'll be right back, Tessy." But she never came back to rescue Tess. She never returned at all. How could her mother leave her with such evil people?

As Tess grew older and stronger, her aunt was no longer a match for her. That's when her uncle took over. Only, her uncle's form of punishment came late at night when he let himself into her bedroom. When she tried to lock him out, he removed the door to her room. At first she screamed, knowing her aunt could now hear without the door to muffle the sounds. It didn't take long for her to realize that her aunt had always heard, had always known. She just didn't care.

Tess ran away to D.C. when she was fifteen. Quickly, she had learned that she could make quite a bit of money doing what her uncle had taught her for free. Fifteen years old, and she was fucking congressmen and four-star generals. That was almost twenty years ago, and yet she had only recently found her escape from that life. She had finally begun a life that was her own. And she sure as hell would not end it here. Not now. Not in this remote grave where no one would ever notice.

She got to her feet and approached the woman. She squatted next to her and put a gentle hand on her shoulder.

"I don't know if you can hear me. My name is Tess. I want you to know I'm going to get us out of here. I'm not going to leave you here to die."

Tess pulled a branch closer so she could sit next to the woman in the sunlight. She needed to rest her ankle. She buried her toes into the mud. Despite the slimy earthworms against her skin, the mud did soothe the cracks and cuts and bruises on her feet.

She surveyed the jutting rocks and tree roots, trying to come up with a plan. Just when she began to think it would be impossible, the woman moved slightly to her side. Without opening her eyes, she said, "My name's Rachel."

CHAPTER 51

Maggie wasn't sure what she expected. Could Albert Stucky or Walker Harding be stupid enough to get caught by the Newburgh Heights Police Department? Yet, when Manx showed her into the interrogation room, her heart sank. The handsome young man looked more like a college student than the hardened criminal Manx had described when he had insisted the man was guilty of something.

The kid even stood up when she entered the room, not able to stifle his good manners despite the situation.

"There's been a huge misunderstanding," he told her as if she was the new face of reason.

He wore khakis and a crew-neck sweater. Maybe this was what Manx expected burglars to wear in Newburgh Heights.

"Sit the hell down, kid," Manx snapped at him as though he was jumping up to attack her.

Maggie walked around Manx and sat down at the table opposite the young man. He slid back into his chair, wringing his hands in front of him on the table, his eyes darting from Manx to the other two uniformed officers already in the room.

"I'm Special Agent Margaret O'Dell with the FBI." She waited for his eyes to settle on hers.

"FBI?" He looked worried and fidgeted in his chair. "Something's happened to Tess, hasn't it?"

"I know you may have already explained all this, but how do you know Ms. McGowan, Mr.—"

"Finley. My name's Will Finley. I met Tess last weekend."

"Last weekend? So you haven't been friends for very long. Did she show you a piece of real estate?"

"Excuse me?"

"Ms. McGowan is a real estate agent. Did she show you a house last weekend?"

"No. We met at a bar. We...we spent the night together."

Maggie wondered if it was a lie. Tess McGowan hadn't looked like the barfly type. Plus, she guessed Tess to be close to her own age. She couldn't imagine Tess giving this college kid a second glance. Unless she had been trying to get back at her big-shot, country-club boyfriend. Of course, she also couldn't imagine Tess McGowan with the guy who Agent Tully called an arrogant asshole. But then she realized she really hadn't taken time to get to know anything about Tess McGowan. Nevertheless, she was certain Will Finley had nothing to do with Tess's disappearance. Now she was glad she hadn't dragged Tully away from lunch with his daughter for this.

"What's happened to Tess?" Will Finley wanted to know. He looked genuinely concerned.

"Maybe you ought to be tellin' us," Manx said from behind Maggie.

"How many times do I have to tell you? I didn't do anything to her. I haven't seen her since Monday morning. She hasn't returned any of my phone calls. I was worried about her." He scraped a shaking hand over his face.

Maggie wondered how long they had kept him here. He looked

exhausted, his nerves frayed. She knew after enough hours of the same questions, in the same room, sitting in the same position, that the most innocent of men could break down.

"Will." She waited again for his eyes. "We're not sure what happened to Tess, but she is missing. I'm hoping you might be able to help us find her."

He stared at her as though he wasn't sure whether to believe her or if this was a trick.

"Is there anything you can remember?" she continued, keeping her voice calm and steady, unlike Manx's. "Anything you might be able to tell us that could help us find her?"

"I'm not sure. I mean, I really don't know her very well."

"Well enough to fuck her, though, right?" Manx said, insisting on playing out his role as the bad cop.

Maggie ignored him, though Will Finley stared at him and fidgeted with the appropriate amount of guilt. Manx was right about the kid hiding something. It was the illicitness of the affair, not that he had hurt Tess.

"Where did you spend the night together?"

"Look, I know my rights, and I know I don't have to answer these questions." He sounded defensive now. Maggie didn't blame him, especially since Manx treated him like a suspect.

"No, you don't need to answer any of my questions. I just thought you might want to help us find her." Maggie gently tried to persuade him.

"I don't see how knowing where or when or how or what we did that night is going to help."

"Hey, kid, you banged an older woman. You should be jumping at the chance to share the details."

Maggie stood and faced Manx, trying to maintain her calm and bridle her impatience.

"Detective Manx, do you mind if I have a word with Mr. Finley alone?"

"I don't think that's a good idea."

"And why is that?"

"Well..." Manx hesitated while he manufactured a reason. She could practically hear his rusty gears grinding. "Might not be safe to leave you alone with him."

"I'm an experienced FBI agent, Detective Manx."

"You sure don't dress like one, Agent O'Dell," he said as he purposely let his eyes slide slowly over her body.

"Tell you what. I'll take my chances with Mr. Finley." She glanced over at the officers. "You gentleman can verify that I said that."

Manx stalled, then finally waved the two officers out of the room. He followed but not before shooting a warning look in Finley's direction.

"I'd apologize for Detective Manx, but that would mean I was trying to excuse his behavior, and quite honestly, there is no excuse for his behavior."

She sat back down with a sigh and an absent rub at her eyes. When she looked up at Will Finley, he was smiling.

"I just realized who you are."

"Excuse me?" Maggie asked.

"You and I have a mutual friend."

The door opened again, and Maggie jumped to her feet, ready to snap at Manx. It was, instead, one of the other officers. His entire face seemed to be apologetic.

"Sorry, but the kid's lawyer just got here. He's insisting on seeing him before any more questioning is—"

"You shouldn't be questioning him at all," a voice from the hall interrupted. "At least not without his attorney present." Nick Morrelli pushed past the officer and into the room. Immediately, his eyes found Maggie's and his anger gave in to a smile. "Jesus, Maggie. We have to stop meeting like this."

CHAPTER 52

Harvey greeted Nick at the door with an impressive growl, teeth bared and his upper lip curled back. Maggie smiled at Nick's surprise even though she had warned him.

"I told you I have my own private bodyguard. Down, Harvey. Actually, we're temporary roommates." She petted the dog's head, and his entire hind end started wagging. "Harvey, this is Nick. He's one of the good guys."

Nick extended an apprehensive hand for the dog to sniff. In seconds, Harvey decided Nick deserved the royal treatment, and the dog stuck his snout in Nick's crotch. Maggie laughed and pulled back on Harvey's collar. Nick seemed more amused than embarrassed.

"So I see you have him checking out other things for you as well."

His comment caught her off guard. She led Harvey into the living room, hoping Nick didn't notice.

"I just moved in last week. I don't have a lot of furniture yet. I barely got some of the blinds up late last night."

"It's an incredible house, Maggie," he said, wandering into the sunroom and looking out at the backyard. "Pretty secluded. How safe is it?"

She looked up from the alarm system she was resetting. "About as safe as I would be anywhere. Cunningham has me under twenty-four-hour surveillance. Didn't you notice the cable TV van down the street? He says it's so we can catch Stucky, but I know he thinks it'll protect me."

"You don't sound convinced."

She opened her jacket to show him her revolver in her shoulder harness.

"This is the only thing that I find convincing these days."

He smiled. "Geez, I get so turned on when you show me your gun."

She found herself blushing from his innocent flirting. Immediately, she looked away. Damn it! She hated that he could get her pulse racing by his simple presence. Had it been a mistake to invite him here? Maybe she should have sent him back home to Boston with Will.

"I'm going to check if dinner is possible. I only have the very basics." She retreated to the kitchen, wondering what she would do if he went beyond flirting. Would she remember to act sensibly? "Would you mind taking Harvey out in the backyard?"

"No, not at all."

"His leash is by the back door. Press the green flashing button on the security system."

"It's a little like living in a fort." He motioned to the sensors and the alarm boxes. "Are you okay with all this?"

"I don't have much of a choice, do I?"

He shrugged and met her eyes. She realized he was feeling helpless, as though there must be something he should be able to do.

"It's part of the job, Nick. A lot of profilers live in gated communities or houses with elaborate alarm systems. After a while you get used to having an unpublished phone number and making certain your address isn't listed in any directory. It's all a part of my life, the part Greg didn't want to deal with. Maybe he shouldn't have had to deal with it. Maybe no one should."

"Well, Greg was a fool," he said as he snapped the leash onto Harvey's collar. Harvey licked Nick's hand in advanced appreciation. "But then, I sorta see Greg's loss as my gain." He smiled at her, then pushed the green button and let Harvey pull him into the backyard.

Maggie watched them, wondering what was it about this man and that lean body and those charming dimples that could so easily stir up feeling and emotions she hadn't accessed in years? Was it just a physical attraction? Did he simply set off her hormones? Nothing more?

When she met Nick last fall in Platte City he was a cocky, arrogant sheriff with a playboy reputation. Immediately, she had been annoyed with herself for being attracted to his charm and classic good looks. But over the course of that terrifying, exhausting week, she had the opportunity to see a sensitive, caring man who truly wanted to do the right thing.

Before she left Nebraska, he had told her that he loved her. She wrote it off with all the other confusing emotions people think they feel after being thrown together during a crisis. In Kansas City, he said he still cared about her. Now that he knew she was divorcing Greg, she wondered what Nick's intentions were. Did he really care about her, or was she only one more notch he wanted to carve in his bedpost?

It didn't matter. She didn't have the energy to entertain such thoughts. She needed to remain focused. She needed to start listening to her head and her gut, not her heart. And more importantly, she didn't want to care about someone who Stucky could take away from her in a split second.

What Gwen had said last night about Stucky coming after her stayed with Maggie, gnawing at her. Although she honestly didn't believe Gwen needed to worry. They all believed Stucky had chosen women who were mere acquaintances of hers, in order to make it impossible to predict who his next target might be. But the fact of the matter was, Maggie had few people she allowed into her life. Gwen claimed it was because she wasn't over the loss of her father. What a bunch of psychobabble that was. Gwen believed that

Maggie purposely made herself off-limits, emotionally, to her friends and co-workers. What Maggie called professional distancing, Gwen called fear of intimacy.

"If you don't let people in, they can't hurt you," Gwen had lectured in her motherly tone. "But if you don't let people in, they can't love you either."

Nick and Harvey were coming back, Harvey carrying the bone Maggie had bought him. She thought he had taken it out and buried it because he didn't want it. Instead, the fresh hole under the dogwood was merely for safe storage. She certainly had a lot to learn about her new roommate.

As soon as Nick unleashed Harvey, he bounded up the stairs.

"He looks like a guy with a mission." Nick watched.

"He'll plop down in the corner of my bedroom and gnaw on that thing for hours."

"The two of you seem to be getting attached to each other."

"No way. The smelly brute goes home as soon as they find his mom." Or at least, that's what she kept telling herself. Fact was, she would feel horribly betrayed when Rachel Endicott showed up and Harvey ran to her without so much as a glance in Maggie's direction. The thought alone felt like a stab. Okay, maybe not a stab—a poke or a pinch.

The point was, Gwen was full of crap. Letting anyone in, including a goddamn dog, usually ended up hurting like hell. So she protected herself. It was one of the few things in her twisted life she could protect herself from. One of the last things she could have control over.

She realized Nick was leaning against the kitchen counter, watching her, concern clouding his crystal blue eyes.

"Maggie, are you okay?"

"I'm fine," she answered, and his smile told her she had hesitated much too long to convince him.

"You know what?" he said as he walked slowly across the kitchen toward her, stopping directly in front of her, his eyes holding hers. "Why don't you let me take care of you for one evening?"

His fingertips stroked her cheek. The familiar current of electricity raced through her, and she knew exactly what he meant by saying he wanted to take care of her.

"Nick, I can't."

She felt his breath in her hair. His lips didn't pay attention to her words as they traced where his fingers had been. Her breathing was already uneven by the time his lips brushed hers. But instead of kissing her, he moved to her other cheek. His lips moved over her eyelids and nose and forehead and hair.

"Nick," she tried again, only she wondered if the word was audible. Her own heart beat so noisily in her ears, she couldn't hear herself think. Not that her thought process was in any kind of working condition. Instead of concentrating on what his hands and lips were doing, she kept thinking about the edge of countertop that was cutting into the small of her back as if that would allow her to hang on to reality and not be swept away.

Finally, Nick stopped, his eyes meeting hers, his face still so close. God, she could easily get lost in his eyes, the warm blue oceans. His hands caressed and massaged her shoulders. His fingers strayed inside her collar to gently touch her throat and then the nape of her neck.

"I just want to make you feel good, Maggie."

"Nick, I really can't do this," she heard herself say while the flutter in her stomach disagreed with her words, screaming at her to take them back.

Nick smiled, and his fingers caressed her cheek again.

"I know," he said, taking a deep breath. There was no disappointment or hurt, only resignation, almost as if her response had been a foregone conclusion. "I know you're not ready. It's too soon after Greg."

It was great that he understood, because Maggie wasn't sure she did. How could she explain it to him?

"With Greg, it was so comfortable." It was the wrong thing to say. She saw the wounded look in his eyes.

"And it's not comfortable with me?"

"With you, it's..." His fingers were distracting her, still exploring, making her breathing uneven. Was he trying to change her mind? Did he realize how easy it could be to change her mind? "With you," she tried to continue, "it's so intense, it scares me." There, she said it. She had admitted it out loud.

"And it scares you because you might lose control." He looked into her eyes.

"God, you know me well, Morrelli."

"Tell you what. When you're ready, and I'm emphasizing when. No ifs," he said, his eyes not letting her go, his fingers still touching her. "I'll let you have all the control you want. But tonight, Maggie, I just want to make you feel good."

The flutter reawakened, immediately kicking into overdrive.

"Nick—"

"Actually, I was thinking maybe I could fix you dinner."

Her shoulders relaxed immediately, and she sighed with a smile. "I didn't realize you knew how to cook."

"There are a lot of things I know how to do that I haven't shown you...yet." And this time, he smiled.

CHAPTER 53

Maggie couldn't believe such delicious aromas were coming from her kitchen. Even Harvey had come down for a look and a closer sniff.

"Where did you learn to cook like this?"

"Hey, I'm Italian." Nick faked an accent that sounded nothing like Italian as he stirred the tomato sauce. "Don't tell Christine, okay?"

"Afraid you might ruin your reputation?"

"No, I don't want her free dinner invitations to stop."

"Is this enough garlic?" She stopped chopping and mincing long enough for him to examine her progress.

"One more clove."

"How are Christine and Timmy?" Maggie had grown attached to Nick's sister and his nephew in the short time she had spent in Nebraska.

"They're good. Really good. Bruce has taken an apartment in Platte City. Christine's making him earn his way back into their lives. I think she wants to make sure his philandering days are completely over. Here, taste this." He held the wooden spoon out to her, keeping an open palm underneath to catch any drips.

She took a careful lick. "A little more salt and definitely more garlic."

"So can you tell me anything about this Tess who Will is so crazy about? Any idea what happened to her?"

Maggie wasn't sure where to begin, or how much she wanted to share. All of it was still speculation. She watched him take salt in the palm of his hand, make a fist and sprinkle it into the simmering pot. She liked the way he moved around her kitchen, as though he had been fixing her dinners for years. Already Harvey followed him, anointing Nick the new master of the house.

"Tess was my real estate agent. She sold me this house, then less than a week later, she disappeared."

She waited, wondering if it would sink in, if he would make the connection on his own. Or was she the only one who could see that connection so clearly? He came over to the island where she sat on a bar stool and minced garlic. He poured more wine into both their glasses and took a sip. Finally, he looked at her.

"You think Stucky's murdered her?" He said it calmly and frankly.

"Yes. Or if he hasn't murdered her, she may be wishing he had."

She avoided his eyes and pretended to concentrate on the pieces of garlic. She didn't want to think about Stucky carving up Tess McGowan or playing his little torture games with her mind and body. Now Maggie's mincing had turned into vicious chops and hacks. She stopped herself and waited for the beginning fury to settle back down. She handed the cutting board to Nick.

Thankfully, he took it without commenting on the slight tremor in her hands. He scraped the garlic bits into the steaming sauce and immediately the new aroma filled the kitchen.

"Will told me there was a car parked outside Tess's house that morning he left."

"Manx ran the license-plate number through the DMV." It was one of the few things Manx had grudgingly shared with her. "The number belongs to Daniel Kassenbaum, Tess's boyfriend."

Nick glanced over his shoulder. "The boyfriend? Did anyone question him?"

"My partner did, briefly. Manx promised he would question him in more detail."

"If he saw Will leaving her house, then he should be pissed. Maybe Stucky doesn't have anything to do with her disappearing."

"I don't think it's that simple, Nick. Apparently, the boyfriend doesn't much care that Tess is missing or that she may have been cheating on him. My gut tells me Stucky has everything to do with this."

Maggie's cellular phone rang, startling both of them. She grabbed her jacket and searched until she found it in the breast pocket.

"Maggie O'Dell."

"Agent O'Dell, it's Tully."

Damn it! She had forgotten all about Tully. She hadn't called him, hadn't even left him a message.

"Agent Tully." She probably owed him an apology or at least an explanation.

Before she had a chance to say anything he said, "We've got another body."

CHAPTER 54

At first, Tully had been relieved when he heard the body wasn't in Newburgh Heights. The call came from the Virginia State Patrol. The state patrolman told Tully that a trucker had grabbed a take-out container from the counter of a small café. On the phone, he explained with a quaking voice how the truck driver hadn't made it back to his truck before he discovered the container was leaking. What he thought was his leftover chicken-fried steak was suddenly dripping blood.

Tully remembered the truck stop, just north of Stafford, off Interstate 95 but it wasn't until he pulled into the café's parking lot that he realized this was probably Agent O'Dell's route home from Quantico. His relief quickly dissipated. If this wasn't Tess McGowan, chances were, O'Dell would still recognize the body.

Tully cursed when he saw the media vans and strobe lights already set up for the TV cameras. They had been lucky up to this point. Only local media had taken the time to be interested. Now he could see the national players were here. A group was crowded around a large, bearded man who Tully guessed was the truck driver.

Thank God, the State Patrol had had enough sense to confiscate the take-out container, and restrict the area behind the café. That's where a battered gray, metal trash bin rested against a chain-link fence. The trash bin was one of the extra-large commercial ones. Tully estimated it to be at least six feet tall. How the hell did Stucky dump the body? Never mind that, how had he gone undetected, with the gas pumps and the café open twenty-four hours a day, seven days a week?

He flashed his badge at a couple of uniforms keeping the media behind the sawhorses and yellow crime scene tape. His long legs allowed him to step over the ribbon without much effort. The Stafford County detective Tully had previously met behind the pizza place was already on the scene, directing the commotion. Tully couldn't remember his name, but as soon as the detective saw him, he waved him over.

"She's still in the Dumpster," he said, wasting no time. "Doc Holmes is on his way. We're trying to figure out how the hell to get her out of there."

"How did you find her?"

The detective took out a pack of gum. He unwrapped a piece and popped it into his mouth. The pack was in his pocket before he thought to offer Tully a piece. He started grabbing for it again, but Tully shook his head. He couldn't imagine having an appetite for anything, even gum.

"Probably wouldn't have found her," the detective finally said, "if not for that snack pack he left behind."

Tully grimaced. He wondered how many years it would take before he could refer to body parts in such a nonchalant way.

The detective didn't notice and continued, "Least not until the trash truck dumped this sucker. But you know, these big ones hold a lot. We might never've found her. Not like anyone would complain about the smell. This stuff always smells. So it looks like this guy's on a roll again."

"It appears so."

"I was working in Boston the last time."

Tully would have guessed the accent had the detective not told him. He was keeping an eye on the reporters near the ribbon, constantly looking over Tully's shoulder. Tully had the impression not much got past this guy. Without knowing anything more, he decided he liked him. But whether Tully liked him or not probably would matter little to the detective. And Tully liked that about him, too.

"Yeah, I remember the last time when they found that councilwoman's body in the woods. Bite marks, skin ripped off, cuts in places you don't need to see cuts."

"Stucky's one sick bastard, that's for sure." Tully remembered the photos of Stucky's collection that O'Dell had laid out on the conference-room table. Side by side they looked like a savage pack of wolves had ripped up the bodies and left them for the vultures.

"Wasn't he playing games with one of your agents back then? I remember reading something. That he was messin' with her head, sending her notes and stuff?"

"Yes, yes he was."

"Whatever happened to that agent?"

"If I'm not mistaken, that's her red car pulling into the parking lot."

"Fuck, no kidding? She's still working on this case?"

"She doesn't have much choice."

"She's got some balls."

"I guess you could say that," Tully said, now distracted. "More than likely, Agent O'Dell will be able to identify the victim for us."

He watched O'Dell. Her badge was getting her across the barriers but not without a lot of glances and long looks. He had worked with other attractive women in law enforcement and in the Bureau, but none quite like O'Dell. There was no discomfort and certainly no preening. Instead, she seemed oblivious to the stares, almost as if she had no clue they were aimed at her.

Tully didn't see it until O'Dell was closer to them. She carried a small black bag, not a purse but a case. They couldn't touch the body until the medical examiner got to the scene. He hoped O'Dell didn't have other plans.

Her eyes met his as her only greeting. He could see the exhaustion, the nervous anticipation.

"Detective—" Tully again realized he didn't know the man's name "—this is Special Agent Maggie O'Dell."

She offered him her hand, and immediately Tully could see the detective's tough exterior softening.

"Sam Rosen," he said, more than willing to fill in the blank for Tully.

"Detective Rosen." O'Dell gave him her polite and professional greeting.

"Call me Sam."

Tully resisted the urge to roll his eyes.

"Sam here—" Tully tried to keep the sarcasm to a minimum "—is with the Stafford County Sheriff's Department. He was at the first crime scene with the pizza delivery...with Jessica Beckwith."

"Is the victim still in the Dumpster?" O'Dell appeared anxious and unwilling, or unable, to hide her anticipation.

"We're waiting for Doc Holmes," Sam told her.

"Is there any way I can take a look without disturbing the scene?" She was already taking out a pair of latex gloves from her black case.

"Probably not a good idea," Tully said, knowing that O'Dell wanted to see if she recognized the victim. He saw her eyeing the trash bin. The thing was almost a foot taller than her. She brushed past them for a closer look.

"How were your men able to look inside?"

"We pulled a cruiser alongside. Davis crawled up on the roof. He took a couple of Polaroids. Want me to get them for you?" Sam looked as if he'd do just about anything she asked. Tully couldn't help being amazed. And even more amazing was how oblivious O'Dell seemed to it all.

"Actually, Sam, would you mind pulling the cruiser alongside it again?"

Or maybe she wasn't entirely oblivious. Without hesitation, Detective Rosen shouted at one of the uniforms holding back the reporters. He left them to meet the officer halfway and started telling him what he wanted, with hands gesturing as quickly as he talked.

"There's a chance it might not be her," Tully said while Detective Rosen was still busy giving directions. He knew she was expecting this to be the missing real estate agent.

"I want to assist with the autopsy. Do you think we can convince Dr. Holmes to do it tonight?" She avoided looking at him and kept her eyes on Rosen.

It was the first time she had asked anything of him, and he could tell it was not an easy thing for her to do.

"We'll insist he do it tonight," he promised.

She nodded, still keeping her eyes from him. They stood quietly, side by side, watching the police cruiser drive up as close as possible to the metal trash bin. He heard her take a deep breath as she set down the black case and threw the pair of gloves she had extracted on top. Detective Rosen met her at the bumper, offering her a hand, but she waved it off. She kicked out of her shoes and crawled up on the trunk with bare feet and little effort.

She paused, almost as if preparing herself mentally. Then she carefully stepped up on top of the roof and stood upright, able to stare down into the trash bin.

"Does anyone have a flashlight?" she called out.

One of the officers from the group who had gathered around to watch hurried to the cruiser to hand her a long-handled flashlight. O'Dell shone a stream of light into the bin, and Tully watched her face. She took her time, sweeping the inside, back and forth. He knew she was trying to examine as much of the scene as she could with her eyes since she couldn't use her hands. Her face remained composed, indifferent, and he couldn't tell whether she recognized the victim as the McGowan woman or not.

Finally she crawled down. She handed back the flashlight, tapped the cruiser's window to thank the driver and then found her shoes.

"Well?" Tully asked, still watching her closely.

"It's not Tess McGowan."

"That's a relief," he sighed.

"Not really a relief at all."

Now under a lamppost, he could see she looked agitated, her face tight with tension, the exhaustion clouding her eyes.

"It's not Tess, but I do recognize her."

Tully felt the knot winding around his stomach. He couldn't begin to imagine what O'Dell was feeling.

"Who is she?"

"Her name's Hannah. She's a clerk at Shep's Liquor Mart. She helped me pick out a bottle of wine last night."

She rubbed a hand over her face, and Tully saw the slight tremor in the fingers.

"We need to stop this goddamn son of a bitch," she said, and Tully heard that the tremor had also invaded her normally calm voice.

CHAPTER 55

Tess felt the panic seeping into her system as the last bit of light turned everything into shadows. She tried to ignore the little voice in the back of her mind that kept telling her to crawl out of this tomb, to run as far away as possible. It didn't matter what direction or where she ended up, at least she would be out of this hell pit, this grave of mutilated bones and lost souls.

She sat next to the woman named Rachel, close enough to hear her ragged breathing. Soon she wouldn't be able to see, but she had made certain the blanket covered her. The woman would not spend another cold night exposed to the elements.

Tess wasn't sure why she had returned. Why hadn't she just left for good? She knew it would be best for Rachel if she went for help. But after an afternoon of roaming the endless woods, she knew help was not close by. She had barely found her way back, trying to leave herself a trail of pinecones. Now she wondered if it had been a mistake to come back. If by doing so, she might be guaranteeing her own death. But for some reason, she couldn't bring herself to leave this woman. She wasn't certain whether she was being gallant or just selfish, because she couldn't bear to spend an entire night out here alone.

Tess had managed to bring back a shoeful of water, using the broken-heeled leather pump she had unearthed. Rachel had to be incredibly thirsty, yet she drank little, most of it dribbling out of her cut and swollen lips and trickling down her bruised chin.

She had said little since uttering her name. Sometimes she answered Tess's questions with a simple yes or no. Most of the time she remained silent as though breathing took all her effort. And Tess had noticed that the woman's breathing had become more raspy, more labored. She had a fever and her muscles went into spasms for long periods racking her entire body, no matter what Tess tried to do to help her.

After hours of analyzing the area, and examining every possible rock step, dirt ledge and sturdy root, Tess had resigned herself to the fact that she could not pull or carry or drag Rachel out. And no amount of rest would cure or repair the damage already done to her body.

Tess leaned her head against the dirt wall, no longer caring that pieces crumbled inside her collar and down her back. She closed her eyes and tried to think of something or somewhere pleasant. A difficult task, considering her empty reservoir of pleasant experiences. Without much effort, Will Finley came to mind. His face, his body, his hands, his voice were all so easily retrieved from her memory bank. He had touched her so gently, so lovingly, despite his urgency and his insatiable passion. It was as though he genuinely felt something deeper than pleasure. And he seemed so intent on pleasing her, as though it truly mattered that she feel what he was feeling.

In all her many experiences with men and sex, she had never thought to associate sex with love. Oh sure, she knew that was the way it was supposed to be, but it had certainly never been a part of her experiences. Even with Daniel, she felt nothing remotely close to love. But she had never expected to—she had never promised or lied to herself that it would ever happen.

She didn't know Will Finley, so how was it possible to feel something remotely close to love? He was a stranger, a one-night stand. How could that be any different than any of the many johns she had serviced? Yet, even here—especially here—she couldn't lie to herself. Will Finley and their one night together had been different. She wouldn't turn it into something cheap and dirty. Not when it could be the closest she may ever get to feeling real love. And not now, when she needed it most. So she tried to remember. She remembered his soft lips, his gentle exploring hands, his hard body, his whispers, his energy, his warmth.

It worked for a short while, carrying her away from the smell of decay and the feel of mud. She thought perhaps she might even sleep. Then suddenly Tess noticed how quiet it was. She held her breath and listened. When the realization came, it swept over her like ice water being injected into her veins. The panic rushed through her, squeezing her heart. Her breathing resumed in quick bursts, frantic gasps. Her body began shaking uncontrollably, and she wrapped her arms tightly around herself, rocking back and forth.

"Oh dear God. Oh God, no," she mumbled over and over like a madwoman. When she could get her body to keep still for a moment, she listened again, straining over the pounding of her heart, straining to hear, willing the truth to be untrue. It was no use. The silence couldn't lie. She knew Rachel was dead.

Tess curled into the damp corner and then allowed herself to do something she hadn't done since she was a child. She cried out loud, releasing years of welled-up sobs and letting them rack her entire body in hysterical convulsions over which she had absolutely no control. The sound pierced the silent darkness. At first she didn't recognize it as something coming out of her, coming up from some deep well inside herself. But there was no stopping, no confining it. And so, she surrendered herself to it.

CHAPTER 56

Maggie watched from across the metal table as Dr. Holmes sliced into the woman's chest, making a precise Y incision that curved under the woman's breasts. Though she had gowned up, her gloved hands ready, she restrained herself from taking part. Instead, she waited for his permission, participating only when asked, trying to confine her impatience when things took too long. She reminded herself that she should be grateful the medical examiner had agreed to do the autopsy on a Saturday night rather than waiting for Monday morning.

He had allowed her to do the busywork; helping insert the body block, scraping behind the woman's nails, taking the external measurements and then the samples of hair, saliva and body fluids. Maggie couldn't stop thinking that Hannah had put up the fight of her life. Bruises covered her body, the one to her hip and thigh suggesting she had fallen down some stairs in the process.

Now, as Maggie watched Dr. Holmes, she found herself going through the woman's brutal murder, step by step, from the telltale signs her body telegraphed. Hannah had scratched and clawed as

Jessica had, only Hannah managed to get pieces of Stucky under her nails. Why had her death not been simple and swift? Why wasn't he able to tie her up, rape her and slit her throat as he had with Jessica and Rita? Had Stucky not been prepared for this challenge?

Maggie wanted to shove her sleeves up. The plastic apron was making her sweat. God, it was hot. Why wasn't there better ventilation?

The county morgue was larger than she had expected, with dingy gray walls and the overpowering scent of Lysol. The counters were a dull yellow Formica rather than stainless steel. The overhead fluorescent lighting unit hung low over the table, almost brushing the tops of their heads when they stood up straight. Dr. Holmes was not much taller than Maggie, but she noticed he had grown accustomed to the light fixture, ducking automatically each time he came underneath it.

Her forensic and premed background had allowed her to perform many autopsies on her own and assist in plenty of others. Maybe it was her exhaustion or perhaps it was simply the stress of this case, but for some reason she was having difficulty disconnecting from the body on the metal table in front of her. Her face felt hot from the hovering light. The windowless room was threatening to suffocate her, though a hidden fan circulated the stale air in the room. She resisted the urge to swipe at the strands of hair that stuck to her damp forehead. The tension in her neck had spread to her shoulders, and was now knotting its way down to take control of her lower back.

Ever since she had recognized the woman, Maggie couldn't help feeling responsible for her death. Had she simply not asked for help in choosing a bottle of wine, the woman would still be alive. Maggie knew the thoughts were counterproductive. They were exactly what Stucky wanted her to be thinking, to be feeling. But she couldn't shut them off. She couldn't stop the growing hysteria that gnawed at her insides, the exploding anger that whispered promises of revenge. She couldn't control the brewing desire of wanting to put a bullet between Albert Stucky's eyes. This anger, this need for revenge was beginning to scare her more than anything Albert Stucky could do to her.

"She hasn't been dead for very long," Dr. Holmes said, his voice bringing her mind back to where it needed to be. "Internal temperature indicates less than twenty-four hours."

Maggie knew this already, but also realized he was saying this for the tape recorder on the stand next to them, and not for her benefit.

"There appears to be no signs of livor mortis, so she was definitely murdered somewhere else and moved within the span of two or three hours." Again, he said this in a matter-of-fact tone for the recorder.

Maggie appreciated his casual manner, his conversational style. She had worked with other M.E.'s whose hushed reverence or clinically cold methods acted as a constant reminder of the brutality and violence that had brought them to their task. Maggie preferred to view an autopsy only as a fact-finding mission, the soul or spirit long gone by the time the body lay on the cold metal table. The best thing for the victim at this stage was a search for evidence that could help catch whoever had committed such an act. Although this time, she knew there would be little Hannah could tell them that would bring them any closer to finding Albert Stucky.

"I heard you ended up with the dog."

It took Maggie a minute to realize Dr. Holmes was talking to her and not speaking for the recorder. When she didn't answer immediately, he looked up and smiled.

"He seemed like a good dog. Tough son of a bitch to survive whoever stabbed him."

"Yes, he is."

How could she have forgotten about Harvey? Already she wasn't a very good dog owner. Greg had been right about her. She had no room for anything or anyone else in her life.

"That reminds me. May I use your phone?"

"Over in the corner, on the wall."

She had to stop and try to remember what her new phone number was. Before she dialed, she took off her latex gloves and wiped her forehead with the sleeve of the borrowed gown. Even the telephone receiver smelled of Lysol. She punched in the numbers and listened to it ring, feeling guilty that she had completely forgotten. She certainly wouldn't blame Nick if he had been angry enough to leave. She checked her wristwatch. It was a quarter past ten.

"Hello?"

"Nick? It's Maggie."

"Hey, are you all right?"

He sounded concerned, not a hint of anger. Maybe she shouldn't expect his reactions and responses to be similar to Greg's.

"I'm okay. It wasn't Tess."

"Good. I was kinda worried that Will would flip out if it was."

"I'm at the county morgue, assisting with the autopsy." She paused, waiting to hear some sign of anger. "Nick, I'm really sorry."

"It's okay, Maggie."

"I might be a couple more hours." Again, she paused. "I know I ruined our plans...your dinner."

"Maggie, it's not your fault. This is what you do. Harvey and I went ahead and ate. We saved you some. It'll warm up fine in your microwave whenever you're ready for it."

He was being so understanding. Why was he being so understanding? She didn't know how to respond to this.

"Maggie? Are you sure you're okay?"

She'd left too much of a pause.

"Just very tired. And I am sorry I missed having dinner with you."

"Me too. Do you want me to stay with Harvey until you get back?"

"I can't ask you to do that, Nick. I don't even know for sure how late I'll be."

"I carry around an old sleeping bag in my trunk. Would you mind if I crashed here for the night?"

For some reason the thought of Nick Morrelli sleeping in her huge and empty house brought an incredible feeling of comfort.

"Maybe it's not such a good idea," he added quickly, misreading her hesitation.

"No, it's a good idea. Harvey would really like that." She had done it again, disguising her true emotions—careful not to reveal a thing. It had become habit. "I'd really like it, too," she said, surprising herself.

"Be careful driving home."

"I will. Oh, and Nick."

"Yeah?"

"Don't forget to always reset the alarm system after you've taken Harvey out. And there's a Glock 40 caliber in the bottom desk drawer. Remember to shut the blinds. If you need—"

"Maggie. I'll be just fine. You concentrate on taking care of you, okay?"

"Okay."

"I'll see you when you get back."

She hung up the phone and leaned back against the wall, closing her eyes and feeling the exhaustion and a chill seep into her bones. She needed to ignore the strong urge to leave now. To go home and curl up with Nick in front of a warm, crackling fire. She could still remember what it had felt like to fall asleep in his arms, though it had happened only once and that was over five months ago. He had comforted her and tried to shield her from her nightmares. And for a few hours, it had worked. But there was nothing Nick Morrelli could do to help her escape Stucky. These days Albert Stucky seemed to be in everything she touched and everyplace she went.

She looked back at the metal table with the woman's gray body splayed open. Dr. Holmes was now removing organs, one by one, weighing and measuring them like a butcher preparing different cuts of meat. She tucked her hair behind her ears, pulled on a fresh pair of gloves and joined him.

"Not easy having a life of your own in this business, is it?" He didn't look up as he continued to cut.

"It's certainly not a life for a dog. I'm never home. Poor Harvey."

"Well, he's still better off with you. From what I understand, Sidney Endicott is an idiot. It wouldn't surprise me if he had murdered his wife and stashed her body somewhere so we'll never find it."

"Is that the direction Manx is going?"

"I have no idea. Take a look at the muscle tissue here and here." He pointed to the layers he had cut through.

Maggie only glanced at the area. She was wondering if the medical examiner realized that what he said regarding Mr. Endicott would be caught on tape. But what if he was right? Maybe Stucky hadn't taken Rachel Endicott. Perhaps her husband did have something to do with her disappearance, although it seemed much too easy. Suddenly she realized Dr. Holmes was staring at her over the bifocals that had slipped down to the tip of his nose.

"I'm sorry, what was it you were looking at?"

He pointed again, and immediately she could see that there was hemorrhage in the muscle tissue. She leaned against the counter behind her and felt the anger swelling up inside her again.

"If there's this much hemorrhage in the muscle tissue it has to mean—"

"Yes, I know," she stopped him. "It means she was still alive when he started cutting her."

He nodded and returned to his task, quickly and expertly tying string to each of the arteries as he cut, leaving generous lengths for the local mortician who would later use these same arteries when he or she injected the embalming fluids. Then with both hands, Dr. Holmes carefully scooped out the woman's heart and set it on the scale. "Heart looks to be in good condition," he said for the recorder. "Weight is 8.3 ounces."

While he dunked the organ in a container of formaldehyde, Maggie forced herself to take a closer look at the incision Stucky had made. Now that she could look into the body cavity, she could follow the path. His precision continued to amaze her. He had extracted the woman's uterus and ovaries as though it had been a surgical procedure. On the counter at the other end of the room lay his handiwork, still enclosed in the plastic take-out container that the truck driver had had the misfortune of picking up.

Dr. Holmes looked at what had drawn her attention. On his way back from the sink, he brought the container with him and set it on the table with their instruments. He flipped open the lid and began examining the contents.

The intercom on the wall buzzed, and Maggie jumped.

"It's probably Detective Rosen. He said he'd stop by if they found anything." He headed for the door, removing his gloves.

"Wait, are you sure?" She couldn't believe he'd open the door without checking first. "It's pretty late, isn't it?"

"Yep, it sure is," he said, stopping and looking at her over his shoulder. "But in case you didn't notice earlier, I think Rosen has developed a crush on you."

"Excuse me?"

"No, I didn't think you noticed." He smiled but didn't wait to explain, instead turning the dead bolt without hesitation or caution.

Maggie's fingers dug into her gown, groping to get at her holster and her gun, but Dr. Holmes was already opening the door.

"Evening, Sam."

"Hey, Doc." Detective Rosen's eyes found Maggie without even noticing the corpse. He held up a couple of evidence bags with what looked like dirt in them. "Agent O'Dell, I think we found something kinda interesting."

After Dr. Holmes's comment, she wondered if Sam had really discovered something at the scene or if he would try to pass off dirt as evidence in order to justify his stop. She was being ridiculous. Maybe Greg had been right about that, too. She didn't trust anyone.

He handed her one of the Ziploc bags over the table. This time he glanced down at the body. It didn't seem to bother him. She guessed that Detective Rosen had seen his share of autopsies, which meant he hadn't always belonged to the Stafford County Sheriff's Department.

She took and inspected the bag of dirt and immediately recognized it. She held the bag up to the light. Yes, there were bits of silver and yellow that sparkled under the bright fluorescent.

"Where did you find this?"

"On the side of the trash bin closest to the chain-link fence. There's actually some metal rails, sorta like steps. We found muddy prints from shoes or boots. That's probably how he was able to climb up and toss in her body. It faces away from the parking lot. No one would see him there."

Rosen seemed excited with the discovery, and she wondered why. "Did you show this to Agent Tully?"

"Nope, not yet. But I figure this has gotta be a big break. It should lead us to where this guy has been hiding out."

Maggie waited for the detective to explain. Now he seemed to be distracted by Dr. Holmes, or rather the bloody glob in the take-out container that Dr. Holmes was examining.

"Detective Rosen," Maggie waited for his attention. "Why do think this will lead us anywhere?"

"For one thing, it's mud." He stated the obvious as though he had uncovered a secret. When he realized she didn't see the significance, he continued, "Well, it hasn't rained for quite a while. It's looked like it several times, but nothing. Not around here anyway. Always offshore."

She drummed her fingers on the counter, waiting for something more than this weather report. He noticed her impatience, quickly opened one of the bags and pinched some of the dirt between his fingers, bringing it out and showing her.

"It's a thick, sticky clay. Even smells a bit moldy. Again, nothing like we have around here."

She could put an end to all of this by simply admitting she had seen the stuff before, that they had actually analyzed and broken it down. Instead, she let him go on.

"A couple of the guys who've lived here all their lives said they haven't seen anything like this stuff before. Take a close look. It's unusual, with bits of reddish rock, and that yellow and silvery crap is pretty weird...maybe even man-made."

Finally, she confessed, "We have found similar dirt at two other crime scenes, Detective Rosen, but—"

"Sam."

"Excuse me?"

"Call me Sam."

Maggie brushed annoying, damp strands off her forehead. Had Dr. Holmes been right about Detective...Sam? Was he really only here to flirt and try to impress her?

"Sam, we have analyzed this stuff. It may be from a closed-down industrial site. We do have several people trying to find a possible location."

"Well, I think I can save you some time."

She stared at him, growing more impatient with his cocky smile. He was wasting their time with this grandstanding.

"I think I know where this came from," he said, pleased with himself despite Maggie's look of skepticism. "I went fishing a couple of weekends ago. A little spot about fifty miles from here on the other side of the toll bridge. I was supposed to meet a buddy, but I still don't know this area very well. I ended up getting lost in this isolated wooded area. When I got home I noticed this sticky mud covering my boots. Took me almost two hours to clean them. The mud looked just like this crap. Couldn't figure out what the hell that silver dust was."

Now he had Maggie's full attention. She could feel her pulse begin to race. The area sounded exactly like someplace Stucky would hole up. Detective Rosen was right. This could be their big break.

"Well, I hope this pans out," Dr. Holmes interrupted, only now looking up from the contents of the plastic container. "This guy is one sick bastard. I think this woman may have confessed to him, tried appealing to him, hoping he had one ounce of human dignity in him."

"What are you talking about?" Maggie watched the medical examiner wipe his forehead, suddenly not caring that he smeared blood from his gloves to his face. The calm, experienced professional seemed visibly shaken by his discovery.

"What is it?" she tried again.

"Might not be a coincidence that he chose to extract her uterus." He stepped back from the table and shook his head. "This woman was pregnant."

CHAPTER 57

Detective Rosen had called and filled in the Newburgh Heights Police Department when they realized Hannah Messinger may have been taken from the downtown liquor store. O'Dell had anxiously accompanied Dr. Holmes, and Rosen had stayed behind at the truck stop, gathering evidence, so Tully decided to accompany Manx and his men. After talking to Detective Manx earlier in the week and not being impressed with his foot-dragging tactics on the Tess McGowan case, Tully knew he should be here if any evidence showed up.

As he waited for one of Manx's officers to jimmy the lock on the back door, he found himself wondering if Detective Manx had been called away from some nightclub. He was dressed in chinos and a bright orange jacket with a blue tie. Okay, maybe the jacket could pass for brown. It was difficult to tell under the street lamps. But he was certain the tie had little dolphins on it. He took a sidelong look at Manx. He looked to be about his age. His buzz cut emphasized his square features, but Tully supposed women probably found Manx attractive in a brutish sort of way. Actually, he had no clue what women found attractive anymore.

From this position in the alley, Tully recognized the back of Mama Mia's Pizza Place on the corner. A shiny new Dumpster replaced the one they had found Jessica Beckwith in. Perhaps it was the owner's way of getting rid of any and all memories. What would they think when they found out that another woman had been taken and murdered only several stores away?

He pulled up the collar of his jacket against the sudden chill of the night. Or perhaps the chill came simply from the memory of that beautiful young woman tangled unceremoniously in a web of garbage. Thinking of young Jessica Beckwith reminded Tully of Emma. How could he ever make Emma understand he only wanted to protect her? That he wasn't simply being mean. Not that she wanted any explanation. And of course, now she wasn't even talking to him since he had prevented her from going to the prom with Josh Reynolds.

"We tried to get hold of the owner," Manx interrupted Tully's thoughts. "He's out of town, won't be able to get back until late tomorrow. His wife said Messinger was taking care of things."

Tully reached for his eyeglasses and noticed the officer was making a mess of the door's lock. Finally something clicked just as the door handle came loose and fell off.

Manx found a light switch and not only did the back storeroom brighten, but the entire shop lit up, aisle by aisle. It didn't take much time to inspect the small shop and realize nothing seemed to be out of place. The cash register had been shut down and locked up. Even the Closed sign had been turned on. There was no indication of forced entrance.

"He may have grabbed her while she was walking to her car," Manx said, scratching his head, reminding Tully of one of the Three Stooges.

An officer took off out the door to check the alley, while the other started rummaging through the storeroom.

"Rosen filled me in, told me about O'Dell."

Tully stopped and glanced over at Manx from behind the counter. The detective's bulldog features softened. He actually looked sympathetic, if that was possible. Tully decided the jacket was definitely orange. In the bright light of the store there was no doubt.

"Now maybe you'll understand," Tully said, "why she's been overly anxious about your investigation of the McGowan woman's disappearance."

"Well, I figure there might be a reason to rethink the Endicott case, too." Manx hesitated as though making a major concession. "I've got copies of the case file for you in my car."

"Detective," the officer from the storeroom called out. He appeared at the door, his face pale and his eyes wide. "There's a wine cellar below the storeroom. I think you better take a look."

Tully followed Manx. They started down the narrow steps, only a bare lightbulb above to guide the way. But Tully didn't need to see anything to know they had found the murder site. No farther than the third or fourth step, he could smell the blood, and he knew his stomach was not ready for what was below.

CHAPTER 58

He couldn't believe that she had escaped. How had she been able to unlock the door so easily? He should have felt disappointment rather than exhilaration. But even his fatigue would not deprive him of the thrill and challenge of a good hunt.

The night goggles seemed to make little difference. Sure they helped him see, but there was nothing to see. Where could that little cunt have wandered off to? He shouldn't have left her unattended for so long, but he had been distracted with the cute brunette. She had been so thoughtful, just as she had been with Agent Maggie. She had taken her time, helping him pick out a nice bottle of wine, not minding that it was closing time. In fact, she had already shut off the Open sign and was locking the front door, when he hurried in. Yes, she had been most helpful, insisting he try the crisp, white Italian for his special occasion, all the while not realizing that she herself would be the denouement of his special occasion.

But his little detour had taken its toll on him. He should have simply taken his prize and left her body in the cellar of the liquor store. At least then his muscles wouldn't be aching. His eyes were having problems focusing. The red lines were appearing more frequently, or were the night goggles malfunctioning? He hated to think that his eyesight had gotten worse in less than a week. He hated the idea of depending on someone else. But he would do whatever was necessary to accomplish his goal, to finish this game.

He wandered through the dark woods, annoyed that his feet kept tripping over tree roots and slipping on the mud. He had fallen once, but not again. He bet she hadn't wandered far from the shed. They never did. Sometimes they even came back, afraid of the dark or wanting to get out of the cold or the rain. Stupid bitches, so gullible, so naive. Usually they followed the same path, hoping the worn trail would lead them to freedom. Never thinking it might lead them, instead, to another trap.

He had to hand it to Tess McGowan. She had managed to hide herself quite nicely. But it wouldn't last. He knew these woods like the back of his hand. There was no way for her to escape unless she was willing to swim. Funny, he thought as he adjusted the goggles to a different setting, none of them ever attempted that. But then, not many of them had had the opportunity. Tess was lucky he had been held up—even luckier that she had found a way to escape from the shack. He should have been angry with her, but her talents excited him. He did so love a challenge. It would make it all the sweeter to finally take her down, to possess her—mind, body and soul.

As he climbed the ridge he hoped he wouldn't find her with a broken neck at the bottom of some ravine. That would be a total waste. He was hoping she would make up for his disappointment in Rachel. She hadn't lived up to his expectations at all. She had been such a flirt as long as she thought he was a lowly utility worker she could tease and control. She seemed to have so much energy and vibrancy, yet she had whimpered like a helpless child when he was fucking her, the fight driven out of her so easily it was pathetic. To make matters worse, she lasted less than a half hour when he released her into the woods. What a shame.

He grabbed onto the vines and pulled himself up to the top of the ridge. Here he'd be able to look down and see for quite a distance. Nothing registered. There was no mass of heat that lit up his goggles. Where the hell had she gone?

He reached under the contraption to rub his eyes. Maybe he needed sleep more than he needed to punish Tess McGowan with a good fuck. With the familiar lethargy taking over his body, he didn't need the added disappointment if he did find her and wasn't able to...fuck her. He didn't even want to think about that. No, he'd start again in the morning, when he had the energy and could enjoy a good hunt. Yes, he'd start bright and early. He looped the rope over his shoulder, picked up the crossbow and headed back. Maybe he'd open that nice bottle of Italian wine that Hannah had promised would delight him.

CHAPTER 59

Maggie felt numb. It took all her effort to keep her eyes open. She didn't realize until she pulled into her driveway that she had been functioning on autopilot. She couldn't remember leaving the interstate nor winding along Highway 6 with its sharp curves and steep ditches. It was a wonder she had found her way in the dark of night and through the fog of her mind.

Nick had left the light on in the portico for her. His Jeep remained where he had parked it earlier. She pulled up next to it, surprised to find the sight of its dusty sides and huge rugged tires supplied her with a wave of comfort. Now she was glad Detective Rosen had convinced her to wait until morning. How could she have thought to go hunting for Stucky in strange, dark woods in the middle of the night? Yet it had made plenty of sense only an hour ago. She had been prepared to stage a sneak attack, forgetting so quickly that she had lost the last one to Stucky. Why was it so easy for Albert Stucky to destroy all her common sense with a sweep of a hand, or rather a cut of his knife?

She knew Dr. Holmes was right, despite the probability that they would never be able to confirm it. She knew the liquor store clerk must have pleaded with Stucky. Maggie could hear it in her head— it came without warning and she couldn't seem to turn it off.

She could hear Hannah pleading, and when she realized Stucky didn't care, she must have begged for her unborn baby's life. He would have laughed at her. It would not have made any difference to him. But she would have continued to beg and cry. Was that why he started cutting while she was still alive? Had he attempted to show her the unborn fetus? It would have been a new challenge to add to his repertoire of horror. It seemed grotesquely inconceivable, but, for Stucky, she knew it was not.

Maggie tried to shut out the images. She unlocked the door, and she tried to be as quiet as possible. It had been a long time since she had come home to anyone or anything other than a dark, empty house. Even before she and Greg had begun avoiding each other, their schedules conflicted more often than not. In the last several years they had become nothing more than roommates who left behind notes for each other. Or at least there had been notes in the beginning. Gradually, the only signs of double occupancy had been the empty milk cartons in the frig and unrecognizable socks and underwear in the laundry room.

The alarm system beeped only once before Maggie punched in the correct code. Immediately, she felt Harvey's cold nose sniffing her from behind. She reached out a hand in the dark, and his tongue found it.

Though the foyer was dark, the living room was bathed in moonlight. Nick hadn't closed any of the blinds, and she was glad he hadn't. She liked the blue glow that made the room seem magical. She saw him stretched out on the floor, his long body only halfway encased in the sleeping bag. He was bare-chested and the sight of his skin, his knotted arms, his tight stomach brought a flutter to her stomach. And just when she thought she was too tired to feel anything more.

She set down her forensic kit, took off her jacket and began peeling off her shoulder holster, when she heard the sleeping bag rustle. Harvey had returned to Nick's side, laying his head on the bundle of legs.

"Don't get too comfortable here," she told Harvey.

"Too late," Nick said, rubbing a hand over his face and lifting himself up onto one elbow.

"I meant Harvey." She smiled.

"Ah. Good."

He ran his fingers through his short hair, causing it to stick up in places. Suddenly Maggie had an incredible urge to smooth it down for him, to run her own fingers through his hair and along that strong, square jawline.

"How are you holding up?" Even in the blue light, she could see the concern in his eyes.

"I honestly don't know, Nick. Maybe not so good." She leaned against the wall and rubbed her eyes. She didn't want to remember the dead clerk's eyes. She didn't want to see the shriveled-up fetus still clinging to the wall of its mother's uterus.

"Hey," Nick said quietly, "why don't you join Harvey and me." He pulled back the top of the sleeping bag, inviting her inside. In doing so, he also revealed tight jockey shorts and muscular thighs.

Again, the stirrings of arousal surprised her. Her face felt hot, and she was a bit embarrassed by her reaction, because she knew Nick didn't mean the invitation as anything more than to curl up next to him. But now, however, he seemed to be reading her thoughts.

"I promise I'll let you have as much control as you want." His eyes were serious, and she knew he had managed to zoom in on her feelings. Was she that transparent?

All she wanted was to feel something other than the frayed nerves, the exhaustion, the emotions that had rubbed her mentally raw. She could no longer remember what it felt like to feel warm and safe. Earlier, in her kitchen, Nick's presence had reminded her just how few times in the past several years she had felt any stirrings of passion and desire. Ironically, the only times she could remember were when she and Nick had been together back in Nebraska.

Without a word, she slipped off her shoes and started undoing her jeans. She met his eyes and saw a bit of surprise mixed with anticipation. He looked as though he wasn't sure what to expect. She had no idea herself.

She left on her chambray shirt. Her underpants were already damp before she climbed in next to him. Harvey stood up, turned around three times and flopped down with his back up against Nick. They both laughed, and Maggie was grateful for the release of tension.

They lay facing each other, each braced up on an elbow. His eyes held her, but he kept his hands away. She realized he was serious about letting her have control. He looked anxious to see what she might do with him. She touched his face with her fingertips, stroking his cheek, his bristled jaw and lingering at his lips. He kissed the tips of her fingers, his mouth warm and wet and inviting.

She moved down to the scar, the slight pucker of white on his chin. Then, to his throat, watching him swallow hard as though trying to contain his emotions. Her eyes stayed with his as her fingers caressed the muscles of his chest and traced a path over his hard, flat stomach. His breathing was already uneven by the time her fingers made it to the bulge in his jockey shorts. As soon as she touched him, he sucked in air like a man no longer able to stifle himself.

"Jesus, Maggie," he managed breathlessly. "If I'd known this was what it would be like to give you control—"

She didn't let him finish. She kissed him lightly on the lips while her hand slipped into his waistband. His entire body quivered. Then his mouth urged her on. Each of her nerve endings seemed to come alive, though he still touched her nowhere except her lips. She knew she had him close to the edge, but he was holding back. She brought the length of her body against his. The kisses had become deep and urgent, but she left his mouth and moved her lips to his ear. She let her tongue run along his outer ear and then slip inside, rewarded immediately by a groan. She whispered, "Don't hold back, Nick."

It didn't take long and his breathing came in gasps through clenched teeth. Moments later, her hand was wet and sticky. Nick collapsed onto his back, his eyes closed, waiting to gain control over his body again. Maggie's own body was still a live wire, tingling without any stimulation other than in reaction to Nick. How was it possible for this man to make her feel so alive, so whole and full of electricity without even touching her? As she watched him, she realized she had never before felt so sensual or so completely satisfied.

He put his hands behind his neck. Sweat glistened on his forehead. His breathing had almost returned to normal. He was looking up at her now, as if trying to read her thoughts, maybe even wondering what was next. He glanced over at Harvey who had moved to the sunroom.

"Is he giving us some privacy, or is he tired of us waking him up?"

She smiled but didn't answer. She braced herself up on her elbow again, lying on her side and watching him. Why was she suddenly not exhausted anymore?

Nick reached up and touched her hair, pushing back a strand and letting his fingers caress her cheek. She closed her eyes and absorbed the lovely sensation being sent through her body. When she opened her eyes again, he was on his side, leaning so close she could feel his breath. Yet he kept their bodies from touching while his hand gently made its way down her neck and into the collar of her shirt. He unbuttoned her shirt, hesitating at each button to give her time to protest. Instead, she lay back, inviting his touch. He was going slowly, cautiously, as if that would give her control. As if that would reduce the intensity. It only made her ache.

He sensed her urgency and let his mouth replace his fingers, gently kissing her. He tugged open the rest of her shirt and his mouth wandered, taking his time moving down her body. Suddenly he stopped. She was breathing too hard to notice at first. Then she felt his fingertips on her stomach, lightly tracing the scar that ran across her abdomen. The hideous scar that Albert Stucky had left. How could she have forgotten it?

She sat up abruptly and disentangled herself from the sleeping bag, escaping before Nick could react. In her rush, she almost tripped over poor Harvey. Now, she stood looking out over the backyard, the front of her shirt gathered into a fist. She heard him come up behind her. She realized she was shivering though she wasn't cold. Nick wrapped his arms around her, and she leaned into his warm body, resting her head back against his chest.

"You gotta know by now, Maggie," he whispered into her hair, "there isn't anything you can say or show me that's gonna scare me away."

"You sure about that?"

"Positive."

"It's just that he's with me all the time, Nick." Her voice was hushed, and there was an annoying catch in it. "I can't seem to get away from him. I should have known that there would be some way for him to ruin even this."

He tightened his hug and nuzzled her neck. But he didn't say anything. He didn't try to persuade her that she was wrong. He didn't try to contradict her just to make her feel better. Instead, he just held her.

CHAPTER 60

Maggie got up before dawn. She left Nick a scrawled note, apologizing for last night and giving him brief instructions for setting the alarm. He had said that he needed to get back to Boston to prepare for a trial, but she knew as he was telling her that he was trying to figure a way out of it. She told him she didn't want him to jeopardize his new job. What she left out was that she didn't want him close by for Albert Stucky to hurt.

She called Agent Tully from the road, but when he answered his door he didn't look as if he expected her. He wore jeans and a white T-shirt and was barefoot. He hadn't shaved yet, and his short hair stuck up. He let her in without much of a greeting and gathered up a scattered edition of the *Washington Post*. He grabbed a coffee mug from the top of the TV.

"I'm brewing coffee. Would you like a cup?"

"No, thanks." She wanted to tell him there was no time for coffee. Why did he not feel the same urgency she was feeling?

He disappeared into what she thought must be the kitchen. Instead of following, she sat down on a stiff sofa that looked and smelled brand-new. The house was small with very little furniture, and most of it looked like hand-me-downs. It reminded her of the apartment she and Greg had right out of college—with milk crates for a TV stand, and concrete blocks and stained two-by-sixes for bookshelves. The only thing missing was a lime green beanbag chair. The sofa and a black halogen floor lamp were the only two new pieces.

A girl wandered into the room rubbing her eyes and not bothering to acknowledge Maggie. She wore only a short nightshirt. Her long blond hair was tangled and her steps were those of a sleepwalker. Maggie recognized the teenager as the little girl in the photo Tully paid homage to on his office desk. The girl plopped into an oversize chair facing the TV, found a remote between the cushions and turned the TV on, flipping through the channels but not paying much attention. Maggie hated feeling that she had gotten the entire household out of bed as if it was the middle of the night instead of morning.

The girl stopped her channel surfing in the middle of a local news report. With the volume muted, Maggie still recognized the truck stop behind the handsome, young reporter who gestured to the gray trash bin cordoned off with yellow crime scene tape.

"Emma, shut the TV off, please," Tully instructed after only a glance at the screen. His coffee mug was filled to the brim and the aroma filtered in with him. He handed Maggie a cold can of Diet Pepsi.

"What's this?" she asked, taken by surprise.

"I remembered Pepsi is sorta your version of morning coffee."

She stared at him, amazed that he would have noticed. No one except Anita ever remembered.

"Did I get it wrong? Is it regular and not diet?"

"No, it's diet," she said, finally taking the can. "Thanks."

"Emma, this is Special Agent Maggie O'Dell. Agent O'Dell, this is my ill-mannered daughter, Emma."

"Hi, Emma."

The girl looked up and manufactured a smile that looked neither genuine nor comfortable.

"Emma, if you're up for the morning, please put on some regular clothes."

"Yeah, sure. Whatever." She pulled herself out of the chair and wandered out of the room.

"Sorry about that," he said while he skidded the chair Emma had vacated around to face Maggie and the sofa rather than the TV. "Sometimes I feel like aliens abducted my real daughter and transplanted this impostor."

Maggie smiled and popped open the Diet Pepsi.

"You have any kids, Agent O'Dell?"

"No." The answer seemed simple enough, but she noticed Tully still staring at her as though an explanation should follow. "Having a family is a little bit tougher to accomplish when you're a woman in the FBI than when you're a man in the FBI."

He nodded as though it was some new revelation, as though he had never considered it before.

"I hope I didn't wake your wife, too."

"You'd have to be pretty noisy to do that."

"Excuse me?"

"My wife lives in Cleveland...my ex-wife, that is."

It was still a touchy subject. Maggie could see it in the way he suddenly avoided making eye contact. He sipped his coffee, wrapping both hands around the mug and taking his time. Then, as though he remembered why they were here in his living room on a Sunday morning, he stood up abruptly, set down the mug on the overflowing coffee table and started digging through the piles. Maggie couldn't help wondering if there was any part of Agent Tully's life that he kept organized.

He pulled out a map and started unfolding and spreading it out over the surface of uneven piles.

"From what you told me on the phone, I'm figuring this is the area we're talking about."

She took a close look at the spot he had highlighted on the map in fluorescent yellow. Here she had thought he wasn't even listening to her when she had called and woken him.

He continued, "If Rosen was lost, it's hard telling exactly where he was, but if you cross the Potomac using this toll bridge, there is this piece of land about five miles wide and fifteen miles long that hangs out into the river sort of like a peninsula. The toll bridge passes over the top half. The map shows no roads, not even unpaved ones down in the peninsula part. In fact, it looks like it's all woods, rocks, probably ravines. Pretty tough terrain. In other words, a great place to hide out."

"And a difficult place to escape from." Maggie sat forward, hardly able to contain her excitement. This was it. This was where Stucky was hiding out and keeping his collection. "So when do we leave?"

"Hold on," Tully sat down and reached for his coffee. "We're doing this by the book, O'Dell."

"Stucky strikes hard and fast and then disappears." She let him hear her anger and urgency. "He's already killed three women and possibly kidnapped two others in a week. And those are just the ones we know about."

"I know," he said much too calmly.

Was she the only one who seemed to understand this madman?

"He could pick up and leave any day, any minute. We can't wait for court orders and county police cooperation or whatever the hell you think we need to wait for."

He sipped his coffee, watching her over the rim. "Are you finished?"

She crossed her arms over her chest and sat back. She should never have called Tully. She knew she could talk Rosen into assembling a search team, though the area in question was across the river, which meant not only a different jurisdiction but also a different state.

"First of all, Assistant Director Cunningham is getting in touch with the Maryland officials."

"Cunningham? You called Cunningham? Oh wonderful."

"I've been trying to find out who owns the property." He ignored her and went on. "It used to be owned by the government, which may account for that weird chemical concoction in the dirt. Probably something they were testing. It was purchased by a private corporation about four years ago, something called WH Enterprises. I can't seem to find out anything about it, no managing CEO, no trustees, nothing."

"Since when does the FBI need permission to hunt down a serial killer?"

"We're operating on hunches, Agent O'Dell. We can't send in a SWAT team when we don't know what's there. Even the mud simply means that Stucky may have been in this area. Doesn't prove he's still there."

"Goddamn it, Tully!" She stood up and paced his living room. "This is the only lead we have as to where he might be, and you need to analyze it to death when we could just go find out!"

"Don't you want to know what you might be walking into this time, Agent O'Dell?" He emphasized "this time," and she knew he was referring to last August when she went running off to find Albert Stucky in an abandoned Miami warehouse. She hadn't told anyone else. She had been following up on a hunch then, too. Only Stucky had been expecting her, waiting for her with a trap. Was it possible he'd be waiting for her again?

"So what do you suggest?"

"We wait," Tully said as though waiting was no big deal. "We find out what's there. The Maryland authorities and their resource people can fill us in. We find out who owns the property. Who knows? We certainly don't want to go onto private property if there's some white supremacist group holed up with an arsenal that could blow us off the planet."

"How long are we talking?"

"It's tough getting in touch with everyone we need on a Sunday."

"How long, Agent Tully?"

"A day. Two at the most."

She stared at him, the anger clawing to reveal itself.

"By now you should know what Albert Stucky can do in a day or two." She calmly walked to the door and left, allowing the slamming door to enunciate what she thought about waiting.

CHAPTER 61

Tully sank into the chair and laid his head back against the cushion. He listened to O'Dell slam her car door and then gun the engine, squealing the tires—taking out her anger on his driveway. He could understand her frustration. Hell, he was frustrated, too. He wanted Stucky caught just as badly as O'Dell. But he knew this was personal for O'Dell. He couldn't imagine what she must be feeling. Three women, all of them acquaintances of hers, all of them brutally murdered simply because they had the misfortune of meeting Maggie O'Dell.

When he looked up, Emma stood in the door to the hallway, leaning against the wall and watching him. She hadn't changed or combed her hair. He was suddenly too tired to remind her. She continued to stare at him, and he remembered that she still wasn't talking to him. Well, fine. He wasn't talking to her either. He laid his head back again.

"Was that your new partner?"

He glanced at her without moving from his comfortable position, trying to keep the surprise of her sudden armistice to himself in case she had temporarily forgotten.

"Yeah, O'Dell's my new partner."

"She sounded really pissed at you."

"Yeah, I think she is. I guess I really have a way with women, don't I?"

Surprisingly, Emma smiled. He smiled back and then she laughed. In two steps she came to him and crawled into his lap the way she used to do when she was a little girl. He wrapped his arms around her and held her tight against him before she could change her mind. She tucked her head under his chin and settled in.

"Do you like her?"

"Who?" Tully forgot what they were talking about. It felt so good to hold his little girl again.

"O'Dell, your new partner."

"Yeah, I guess I like her. She's a smart, tough lady."

"She's really pretty."

He hesitated, wondering if Emma was concerned he would run off with one of his co-workers just as her mother had done.

"Maggie O'Dell and I are only partners at work, Emma. There isn't anything else going on between us."

She sat quietly, and he wished she'd talk to him about any fears she might have.

"She did seem really pissed at you," she finally said with a bit of a giggle.

"She'll get over it. I'm more concerned about you."

"Me?" She twisted around to look at him.

"Yeah. You seemed really pissed at me, too."

"Oh, that," she said, settling in against him again. "I'm over that."

"Really?"

"I was thinking if we don't spend all that money it'd cost me to go to the prom, I thought maybe I could get a really cool CD Walkman, instead?"

"Oh, really?" Tully smiled. Yes, he was quite certain he'd never understand women.

"Don't have a cow. I have enough of my own money saved." She wiggled out of his arms and out of his lap. Now she stood in front of him, arms crossed, waiting for his response and looking more like the teenager he remembered. "Can we go pick one out today?"

Was this any way to raise a teenage daughter, teaching her that she would receive some material thing for good behavior? Instead of analyzing it, he simply said, "Sure. Let's go this afternoon."

"All right!"

He watched her practically skip back to her room while he got up and wandered over to the coffee table. He found the file folder and slid it out from under one of the piles. He flipped it open and started going through the file: a police report, a copy from a DNA lab, a plastic bag with a pinch of metallic-flecked dirt stapled to an evidence document, a medical release form from Riley's Veterinary Clinic.

Last night Detective Manx had given him the file marked Rachel Endicott, the missing neighbor O'Dell suspected Stucky had taken. Now, from the looks of the evidence and a recent DNA lab report, even the arrogant, stubborn Manx had been able to figure out that Ms. Endicott may have indeed been kidnapped. After seeing how close to the edge O'Dell was this morning, Tully wondered whether or not he should show her the file. Because according to the lab's DNA test, Albert Stucky had not only been in Rachel Endicott's house, but he'd helped himself to a sandwich and several candy bars. And now there was no doubt in Tully's mind that Stucky had also helped himself to Ms. Endicott.

CHAPTER 62

Maggie drove without a destination, hoping only to burn off the mounting anger. After an hour, she pulled into the busy parking lot of a pancake house, thinking some food might settle her nerves and her stomach. She was at the door of the restaurant, her hand on the door handle when she spun around, almost bumping into two customers before hurrying back to the car. She didn't dare have breakfast. How could she possibly risk another waitress's life?

Back on the road, Maggie's eyes darted all around her, checking the rearview mirror and every car alongside her. She pulled off the interstate, drove several miles down a deserted two-lane highway, then returned to the interstate. Several miles later, she exited at a rest stop, circled around, parked, waited, then headed back onto the interstate.

"Come on, Stucky," she said to the rearview mirror. "Where the hell are you? Are you out there? Are you following me?"

She used her cellular phone and tried to call Nick, but he must have already left for Boston. Desperate for a distraction, any distraction, she dialed her mother's phone number. Maybe she could drive down to Richmond. That would certainly take her mind off Stucky. Her mother's answering machine picked up on the fourth ring.

"I can't come to the phone right now," a cheerful voice answered, and Maggie immediately thought she had dialed the wrong number. "Please call back another time, and remember, God watches out for those who can't watch out for themselves."

Maggie snapped the phone shut. Oh God, she thought, wishing the voice had not been her mother's, and that she indeed had the wrong number. However, she recognized the raspy, cigarette-smoking tone despite the false cheerfulness. Then she remembered what Greg had said about her mother being out of town. Of course, she was with Reverend Everett—whoever the hell he was. They were in Las Vegas. Where else would manic-depressed alcoholics go to find God?

She noticed the gas tank getting low so she pulled off the interstate and found an Amoco station. She had the gas cap off when she realized the pumps were not set up for credit cards and a pay-at-the-pumps. She glanced over at the station's shop. As soon as Maggie saw the female clerk's blond curls, she replaced the gas cap and got back into the car.

It took two more attempts and about twenty more miles before she found a pay-at-the-pumps station. By now her nerves were rubbed raw. Her head hurt and the nausea had left her feeling hollow and sick to her stomach. There was nowhere she could go. Running away would not solve anything. Nor could she coax Stucky into coming after her. Unless he was already waiting for her. She decided to take her chances and return home.

CHAPTER 63

Tess ran, her ankle throbbing. Her feet ached and were now bleeding despite her attempt to wrap them with what once were the sleeves of her blouse. She had no idea where she was headed. The sky had clouded up again, bulging gray and ready to burst. Twice she had come to a ledge that overlooked water. If only she had learned to swim, she wouldn't have cared how far away the other side appeared to be. Why couldn't she escape this eternal prison of trees and vines and steep ridges?

She had spent the morning eating wild strawberries or, at least, that's what she thought they were. Then she drank from the muddy bank of the river, not caring what algae also slipped into her cupped hands. Her reflection had frightened her at first. The tangled hair, the shredded clothes, the scratches and cuts made her look like a madwoman. But wasn't that exactly what she had been reduced to? In fact, she couldn't think of Rachel without feeling something raw and primitive ripping at her insides.

She couldn't be sure how much time had gone by while she

cringed in a corner of the hole. She had cried and rocked, hugging herself with her forehead pressed against the wall of dirt. At times she had felt herself slipping into some other dimension, hearing her aunt shouting down at her from the top of the hole. She could swear she had seen her aunt's pinched face scowling at her and waving a bony finger, cursing her. She had no clue whether she had spent one night or two or three. Time had lost all meaning.

She did remember what had brought her out of her stupor. She had felt a presence, someone or something rustling above at the ledge of the hole. She had expected to look up and see him like a raptor, perched and ready to jump down on her. She didn't care. She wanted it to end. But it wasn't the madman, or a predator. Instead, it was a deer looking into the hole. A young, beautiful doe curiously staring down at her. And Tess found herself wondering how something so lovely and innocent could exist on this devil's island.

That's when she pulled herself together, when she decided once again that she would not die, not here, not in this hellhole. She had covered her temporary companion as best she could with branches from a pine tree, the soft needles like a blanket on the battered, gray skin. And then she crawled out into the open. However, there had been no sense of relief in leaving the earthly tomb that, ironically, had become a sanctuary of sorts. Now after running and walking for miles, she felt farther away from safety than she had felt inside that musty grave.

Suddenly she saw something white up on the ridge and through the trees. She climbed with new energy, pulling herself up with tree roots, ignoring the cuts in her palms that she hadn't noticed before. Finally on level ground again, she was gasping for air, but she had a better view. Hidden by huge pine trees was a huge white, wooden frame house.

Tess's pulse quickened. She blinked, hoping the mirage would not disappear. An incredible wave of relief swept over her as she noticed a wisp of smoke coming from the chimney. She could even smell the wood from the fireplace. She heard a wind chime and immediately saw it hanging from the porch. Along the house, daffodils and tulips were in full bloom. She felt like Little Red Riding Hood finding her way through the woods to her grandmother's warm and inviting house. Then she realized the analogy might prove more real than fantasy. An alarm seemed to go off in her head. The panic raced through her veins. She turned to run and slammed right into him. He gripped both her wrists and smiled down at her, looking exactly like a wolf.

"I was looking for you, Tess," he said calmly while she pulled and twisted against his strength. "I'm so glad you found your way."

CHAPTER 64

Washington, D.C.
Monday, April 6

Maggie couldn't believe Cunningham had insisted she keep her Monday-morning appointment with Dr. Kernan. It was bad enough that they had to wait for some kind of unofficial permission from the Maryland authorities. How could they be sure Stucky wouldn't find out? If any of the information leaked, they wouldn't need to worry about Stucky setting another trap. No, this time he'd be long gone. It would be another five or six months before they heard from him again.

She had made the trip, angry and on edge—an hour's drive in D.C.'s early-morning rush. And now she had to wait some more. Once again Kernan was late. He shuffled in, smelling of cigar smoke and looking as though he had just crawled out of bed. His cheap brown suit was wrinkled, his shoes scuffed, with one shoe-string untied and dragging behind him. He had plastered down his thin white hair with some foul-smelling gel. Or maybe it was the Ben-Gay assaulting her nostrils. The man looked like a poster model for homeless mental patients.

Again, he didn't acknowledge her as he shifted and creaked in his chair, back and forth, until he decided he was comfortable. This time Maggie felt too restless and angry to be intimidated. She didn't care what strange insights he might probe from her psyche. Nothing Kernan could do or say would reduce or heal the chaotic storm ticking away inside her chest like some time bomb ready to explode without warning.

She tapped her foot and drummed her fingertips on the arm of the chair. She watched him sift through his mess. God, she was sick of everyone's messes. First Tully's, now Kernan's. How did these people function?

She sighed, and he scowled at her over his thick glasses. He smacked his lips together in a "tis, tis," as if to scold her. She continued to stare at him, letting him see her contempt, her anger, her impatience. Letting him see it all, and not giving a damn what he thought.

"Are we in a hurry, Special Agent Margaret O'Dell?" he asked as he thumbed through a magazine.

She glanced at his fingers and caught a glimpse of the magazine's cover. It was a copy of *Vogue,* for God's sake.

"Yes, I am in a hurry, Dr. Kernan. There's an important investigation I'd like to get back to."

"So you think you've found him?"

She looked up, surprised, checking to see if he knew. But he appeared engrossed in the magazine's pages. Was it possible Cunningham had told him? How else would he know?

"We may have," she said, careful not to reveal anything more.

"But everyone is making you wait, is that it? Your partner, your supervisor, me. And we all know how much Margaret O'Dell hates to wait."

She didn't have time for his stupid games.

"Could we please just get on with this?"

He looked up at her again over his glasses, this time surprised. "What would you like to get on with? Would you like some special absolution, perhaps? Some sort of permission to go racing after him?"

He put the magazine aside, sat back and brought his hands together over his chest. He stared at her as if waiting for an answer, an explanation. She refused to give him any of what he wanted. Instead, she simply stared back.

"You'd like us all to get out of your way," he continued. "Is that it, Special Agent Margaret O'Dell?" He paused. She pursed her lips, denying him a response, and so he continued, "You want to go after him all by yourself again, because you're the only one who can capture him. Oh no, excuse me. You're the only one who can stop him. Perhaps you think stopping him this time will absolve *you* of his crimes?"

"If I was looking for absolution, Dr. Kernan, I'd be in a church and certainly not sitting here in your office."

He smiled, a thin-lipped smile. Maggie realized it was the first time she had ever seen the man smile.

"Will you be looking for absolution after you shoot Albert Stucky between the eyes?"

She winced, remembering their last session and how out of control she had been. It reminded her that she still felt out of control, only now the anger gave her a false sense of how close the ledge really was. If she remained angry, perhaps she wouldn't see the ledge at all. Would she even feel herself slipping or would the fall be abrupt and sudden when it happened?

"Maybe I've been around evil too long to care about what I need to do to destroy it." She was no longer concerned with what she told him. He couldn't use any of it to hurt her. No one could hurt her more than Stucky already had. "Maybe," she continued, letting the anger drive her, "maybe I need to be as evil as Albert Stucky in order to stop him."

He stared at her, but this time it was different. He was contemplating what she had said. Would he have some smart-ass response? Would he try his reverse psychology on her? She wasn't one of his naive students anymore. She could play at his game. After all, she had played with someone ten times as twisted as him. If she could play at Albert Stucky's game, then Dr. James Kernan's would be nothing more than child's play.

She stared him down, without flinching, without fidgeting. Had she rendered the old man speechless?

Finally he sat forward, elbows on his messy desk, fingers constructing a tent of bent and misshapen digits.

"So that's what concerns you, Margaret O'Dell?"

She had no idea what he was talking about, but she kept the question from her face.

"You're concerned," he said slowly, as if approaching a delicate subject. It was an unfamiliar gesture, one that immediately made Maggie suspicious. Was it another of Kernan's famous tricks or was he genuinely concerned? She hoped for a trick. That, she could handle. The concern, she wasn't too sure about.

"You're worried," he began again, "that you may be capable of the same sort of evil Albert Stucky is capable of."

"Aren't we all, Dr. Kernan?" She paused for his reaction. "Isn't that what Jung meant when he said we all have a shadow side?" She watched him closely, wanting to see how it felt to have one of his students contradict him with his own teachings. "Evil men do what good men only dream of doing. Isn't that true, Dr. Kernan?"

He shifted in his chair. She should have counted the succession of eye blinks. She wanted to smile, because she had him on the ropes, so to speak. But there was no victory in this truth.

"I believe—" he hesitated to clear his throat "—I believe Jung said that evil is as essential a component of human behavior as good. That we must learn to acknowledge and accept that it exists within all of us. But no, that doesn't mean we're all capable of the same kind of evil as someone like Albert Stucky. There's a difference, my dear Agent O'Dell, between stepping into evil and getting your shoes muddy, and choosing to dive in and wallow in it."

"But how do you stop from falling in headfirst?" She felt an annoying catch in her throat as the inner frenzy threatened to reveal itself. Her thoughts of revenge were black and evil and very real. Had she already dived in?

"I'm going to tell you something, Maggie O'Dell, and I want you to listen very closely." He leaned forward, his face serious, his magnified eyes pinning her to the chair with their unfamiliar concern. "I don't give a rat's ass about Jung or Freud when it comes to this evil crap. Remember this and only this, Margaret O'Dell. The decisions we make in a split second will always reveal our true nature, our true self. Whether we like it or not. When that split second comes, don't think, don't analyze, don't feel and never second-guess—just react. Trust. Trust in yourself. You do that—just that—and I'm willing to bet you end up with nothing more than a little mud on your shoes."

CHAPTER 65

Tully punched at the laptop's keyboard. He knew the computer down in his office was much faster, but he couldn't leave the conference room. Not now that he had had all the calls forwarded, and every last file on the case was spread out over the tabletop. Agent O'Dell would be furious about the mess. Though he doubted she could get much angrier. He hadn't seen or talked to her since she had stormed out of his house yesterday.

Assistant Director Cunningham had informed him that O'Dell would be spending the morning in D.C. at a previously scheduled appointment. He didn't elaborate, but Tully knew the appointment was with the Bureau psychologist. Maybe it would help calm her down. She needed to keep things in perspective. She needed to realize that everything that could be done, was being done, and as quickly as possible. She needed to get past her own fear. She couldn't keep seeing the bogeyman in every corner and expect to handle it by running after him with guns blazing.

Although Tully had to admit, he was also having a tough time waiting. The Maryland authorities were hesitant to go storming onto private property without just cause. And no government department seemed willing to admit or confirm that the metallic mud could have come from the recently closed and sold government property. All they had was Detective Rosen's fishing story, and now that Tully had repeated it over and over to top government officials it was beginning to sound more and more just like a fish story.

It might be different if the property in question wasn't miles and miles of trees and rocks. They could drive down the road and check things out. But from what he understood, this property had no road, at least not a public one. The only dirt road available included an electronic gate, a leftover from when the government owned the property and had allowed no unauthorized access. So Tully searched for the new property owners, hoping to find something that would tell him who or what WH Enterprises was.

He decided to use a new search engine and keyed in "WH Enterprises" again. Then he sat, elbows on the desk, his chin resting on his hand as he watched the line crawl along the bottom of the screen...3% of document transferred...4%...5%... This would take forever.

The phone rescued him. He wheeled his chair around and grabbed the receiver.

"Tully."

"Agent Tully, this is Keith Ganza—over in forensics. They told me Agent O'Dell was out this morning."

"That's right."

"Any chance I could get hold of her? Maybe her cell phone? I was wondering if you had the number."

"Sounds important."

"Don't really know for sure, but I figure that's up to Maggie to determine."

Tully sat up straight. Ganza's voice was a constant monotone, but the fact that he didn't want to talk to him alarmed Tully. Had O'Dell and Ganza been on to something that she wasn't letting him in on?

"Does this have anything to do with the luminol tests you did? You know Agent O'Dell and I are working on the Stucky case together, Keith."

There was a pause. So he was right. There was something.

"Actually, it's a couple of things," he finally said. "I spent so much time analyzing the chemicals in the dirt and then the fingerprints that, well, I'm just getting to that bag of trash you found."

"It didn't look too unusual except for all the candy bar wrappers."

"I might have an explanation for those."

"The candy wrappers?" He couldn't believe Ganza would waste his time with those.

"I discovered a small vial and a syringe at the bottom of the trash bag. It was insulin. Now, it could be that one of the previous owners of the house has diabetes, but then we should have found more. Also, most diabetics I know are fairly conscientious about properly disposing of their used syringes."

"So what exactly are you saying, Keith?"

"Just telling you what I found. That's what I meant about Maggie determining whether or not it was important."

"You said there were a couple of things?"

"Oh yeah..." Ganza hesitated again. "Maggie asked me to do a search of prints for a Walker Harding, but it's been taking me a while. The guy has no criminal record, never registered a handgun."

Tully was surprised Maggie hadn't stopped Ganza after they had read the article and discovered that Harding was going blind. He couldn't possibly be a suspect. "Save yourself the time," he told Ganza. "Looks like we don't need to check."

"I didn't say I wasn't able to find anything. The cold search just took a bit longer. The guy had a civil servant job about ten years ago, so his prints are on file after all."

"Keith, I'm sorry you went through all that trouble." Tully only half listened to Ganza as he watched the computer screen. The search engine must be accessing something on WH Enterprises if it was taking this long. He started tapping his fingers.

"Hopefully, it was worth the trouble," Ganza went on. "The prints I lifted from the whirlpool bath were an exact match."

Tully's fingers stopped. His other hand gripped the phone's receiver. "What the hell did you just say?"

The fingerprints I lifted off the bathtub at the house on Archer

Drive...they matched this Walker Harding guy. It's an exact match. No doubt about it."

The pieces of the puzzle were falling into place, but Tully didn't like the picture they were forming. On an obscure Web site designed to look like some clearinghouse run by the Confederacy, he found computer video games for sale. All were wholesale priced, and the search could be completed by clicking on the tiny Confederate-flag icons. The games were available though a company called WH Enterprises. Most of them guaranteed graphic violence and others promised to be of pornographic nature. These were not the types of games kids could pick up at Best Buys or Kids "R" Us.

The sample that could be viewed with a simple click of the mouse included a naked woman being gang-raped, with the player being able to gun down all the assailants, only to be rewarded by raping the woman himself. Despite the animation, the video clip was all too real. Tully found himself sick to his stomach. He wondered if any of Emma's friends were into this sort of garbage.

One of the Web site's features was the "Lil' General's Top Ten List," including a note from the CEO of WH Enterprises. Tully knew what he'd find before he scrolled down to see the message ending with, "Happy hunting, General Walker Harding."

Tully paced the conference room, walking from window to window. Walker Harding may have been going blind, but he sure as hell could see now. How else could he run a computer business like this one? How else could he be at each crime scene, helping his old pal, Albert Stucky?

"Son of a bitch," Tully said out loud. O'Dell had been right. The two men were working together. Maybe they were still competing in some new game of horror. Whatever it was, there was no denying the evidence. Walker Harding's fingerprints matched those found on the Dumpster with Jessica Beckwith's body. They matched the umbrella in Kansas City, and they matched the prints left on the whirlpool bath at the house on Archer Drive.

Earlier, the Maryland authorities had finally confirmed that there was a large two-story house and several wooden shacks on the property. All government buildings had been bulldozed before the sale. The rest of the property, Tully was informed, was surrounded on three sides by water and covered with trees and rock. There were no roads except a dirt path that led to the house. No electrical lines or telephone cables had been brought in from the outside. The new owner used a large generator system left behind by the government. The place sounded like a recluse's dream come true and a madman's paradise. Why hadn't he realized sooner that, of course, WH Enterprises would belong to Walker Harding?

Tully checked his wristwatch. He needed to make some phone calls. He needed to concentrate. He took several deep breaths, dug the exhaustion out from under his glasses and picked up the phone. The waiting was over, but he dreaded telling Agent O'Dell. Would this be the final thread to unravel her already frayed mental state?

CHAPTER 66

Tess woke slowly, painfully. Her body ached. Her head throbbed. Something held her down. She couldn't move. Couldn't open her eyes again, the lids were too heavy. Her mouth felt dry, her throat was raw on the inside as well as the outside. She was thirsty and ran her tongue over her lips, alarmed when she tasted blood.

She forced her eyes open and strained against the shackles that clamped her wrists and ankles to the small cot. She recognized the inside of the shack, could feel its dampness and smell its musty odor. She twisted, trying to free herself. She felt a scratchy blanket beneath her and that's when she realized she was naked. Panic rushed through her insides, shoving against the walls of her body. A scream stuck in her throat, but nothing came out except a gasp of air. That was enough, however, to send a scrape of pain down her throat as though she were swallowing razor blades.

She settled down, trying to calm herself, trying to think before terror took control of her mind. She no longer had control over her body, but no one would control her mind. It was a painful lesson she had learned from her aunt and uncle. No matter what they did to her body, no matter how many times her aunt had banished her to the dark cellar or how many times her uncle had shoved himself inside her, she had retained control over her mind. It was the ultimate defense. It was her only defense.

Yet, when she heard the locks to the door clicking open, Tess felt the terror clawing at the flimsy barricades to her mind.

CHAPTER 67

Maggie swerved around slower-moving traffic, trying to keep her foot from pushing the accelerator to the floor. Her heart hadn't stopped ramming against her chest since Tully's phone call. All the anger she had accessed in Kernan's office had been converted to sheer panic. It no longer ticked quietly like a time bomb. Instead, it pressed against her rib cage like some heavy weight being lowered, little by little, threatening to crush her.

She knew Walker Harding was involved. It made sense that Stucky would call on his old pal. Though she still had a difficult time believing Stucky would allow anyone to help, even his ex-partner—unless the two men were competing at some bizarre game. And from Tully's description of Harding's new entrepreneurial venture, it seemed more than possible that he was capable of the same sort of twisted, perverted evil as Stucky was.

She tucked her hair behind her ears and rolled down the window. The breeze whipped through the car's interior, bringing with it the fumes of exhaust and the scent of pine trees.

Dr. Kernan had said she shouldn't think so much—just trust. All her life she had felt as if she was the only person she could trust. There was no one else. Did he understand how incredibly frustrating, how...hell, why not admit it?—how frightening it was to think she could no longer trust the one person she had trusted her whole life? That she could no longer trust herself?

She had a B.A. in criminal psychology, and a master's in behavioral psychology. She knew all about the shadow side, and she knew it existed in everyone. There were plenty of experts who debated the fine line between good and evil and they all hoped to explain why some people choose evil, while others choose good. What was the determining factor? Did anyone really know?

"Trust in yourself," Kernan had told her. And that the decisions she made in a split second would somehow reveal her true self.

What kind of psychobabble was that? What if her true self really was her shadow side? What if her true self was capable of Stucky's blend of evil? She couldn't help thinking that all it would take was a split second for her to aim and fire one bullet right between those black eyes. She no longer wanted to capture him, to stop Albert Stucky. She wanted him to pay. She wanted—no, she needed—to see fear in those evil eyes. The same kind of fear she felt in that Miami warehouse when he cut her abdomen. The same fear she felt every night when darkness came and sleep would not.

Stucky had made this a personal war between the two of them. He had made her an accomplice to his murders, making her feel as though she had handpicked each woman for his disposal. If he had somehow managed to coerce Walker Harding into his game of horror, then there were now two of them who needed to be destroyed.

She glanced at the map spread out on the passenger seat. The toll bridge was about fifty miles from Quantico. Tully was still making arrangements. It would take several hours before he had everything ready according to his careful, by-the-book standards. There would be more waiting. They'd be lucky to make it to Harding's property by nightfall. Tully was expecting her back at Quantico in the next ten to fifteen minutes. Up ahead a sign indicated that her exit was just ten miles away.

She pulled out her cell phone and slowed the car to the speed limit, allowing her to maneuver more easily with one hand on the steering wheel. She punched in the number and waited.

"Dr. Gwen Patterson."

"Gwen, it's Maggie."

"You sound like you're on the road."

"Yes, I am. Just coming back from D.C. Can you hear me okay?"

"Little bit of static, but not bad. You were in D.C.? You should have stopped in. We could have done lunch."

"Sorry, no time. Look, Gwen, you know how you're always saying I never ask anything of my friends? Well, I need a favor."

"Wait a minute. Who did you say this was?"

"Very funny." Maggie smiled, surprised she was able to amidst all the internal tension. "I know it's out of your way, but could you check on Harvey this evening—let him out, feed him...all those dog things that a real dog owner normally does?"

"You're off fighting serial killers, and you're still worried about Harvey. I'd say you already sound like a dog owner. Yes, I will stop and spend some quality time with Harvey. Actually, that's the best offer I've had in a long time as far as spending an evening with a male companion goes."

"Thanks. I really appreciate it."

"Does this mean you're simply working late or have you found him?"

Maggie wondered how long it had been since her friends and co-workers could simply ask her about "him" and automatically mean Albert Stucky.

"I don't know yet, but it's the best lead we've had so far. You may have been right about the candy bar wrappers."

"Wonderful. Only I don't remember what it was I said."

"We dismissed Stucky's old business partner as an accomplice because the guy was supposedly going blind due to some medical condition. Now the evidence suggests that the condition could be diabetes. Which means the blindness may not have been sudden or complete. In fact, he could be hoping to control it with insulin injections."

"Why would Stucky be working with an accomplice? Are you sure that makes sense, Maggie?"

"No, I'm not sure it makes sense. But we keep finding finger-prints at the scenes that don't belong to Stucky. This morning we found out the prints are a perfect match with Stucky's old business partner, Walker Harding. The two sold their business about four years ago and supposedly went their separate ways, but they might be working together again. We also discovered a remote piece of land just across the river registered to Harding. This place sounds like the perfect hideout."

Maggie glanced down at the map again. The exit to Quantico was getting closer. Soon she'd need to make a decision. She knew a shortcut to the toll bridge. She could be there in less than an hour. Suddenly she realized that Gwen's pause had lasted too long. Had she lost the call?

"Gwen, are you still there?"

"Did you say the partner's name is Walker Harding?"

"Yes, that's right."

"Maggie, last week I started seeing a new patient who is blind. His name is Walker Harding."

CHAPTER 68

Tully ripped off the fax and began piecing the four sheets together. The Maryland Parks Commission had faxed an aerial view of Harding's property. In black and white not much could be seen through the acres of treetops. The first thing Tully noticed was that, from above, the area looked like an island except for a sliver that connected it to the mainland. The property jutted out into the water with the Potomac River on two sides and a tributary river on the third.

"The SWAT team is assembled and ready to go," Cunningham said as he entered the conference room. "Maryland State Patrol will meet you on the other side of the toll bridge. Are those any help?" He came around the table and looked at the map Tully had just finished taping together.

"Can't see any buildings. Too many trees."

Cunningham pushed his glasses up the bridge of his nose and bent down to examine the map. "From what I understand, the facility housing the generator is in the upper northwest corner." He ran his index finger over the spot that resembled a black-and-gray mass. "I would think the house would need to be close by. Any idea how long Harding has lived here?"

"At least four years. Which means he's settled and knows the area. It wouldn't surprise me if he had a bunker somewhere on the property."

"That seems a bit paranoid, doesn't it?" Cunningham raised his eyebrows.

"The guy was a recluse long before he and Stucky started their business. Some of the computer video games he sells are his own creations. The guy may be a computer genius, but he's weirder than hell. A lot of the games are antigovernment, white supremacist garbage. He even has one called 'Waco's Revenge.' Lots of Armageddon-type stuff, too. Probably sold truckloads of it in 1999, so it wouldn't surprise me if he's well prepared."

"What are you saying, Agent Tully? You mean we might have more problems on our hands than busting a couple of serial killers? You think Harding may have an arsenal in there, or worse, have the property booby-trapped?"

"I don't have any proof, sir. I just think we should be prepared."

"But be prepared for what? A stand-off?"

"Anything. I'm just saying if Harding is as extreme as his games would suggest, he could freak out with the FBI showing up on his doorstep."

"Wonderful." Cunningham stretched his back and walked over to the bulletin board where Tully had tacked up printouts of Harding's Web site next to photos of the crime scenes.

"When is Agent O'Dell scheduled to be here?"

Tully glanced at his watch. She was already a half hour late. He knew what Cunningham was thinking.

"She should be here any minute now, sir," Tully said without indicating he thought that she might not show up. "I think we have everything we need. Is there anything I'm forgetting?"

"I want to brief the SWAT team. We should let them in on your suspicions," Cunningham said, looking at his own watch now. "What time did Agent O'Dell leave D.C.?"

"I'm not really sure. Will they need any extra preparations?" He avoided his boss's eyes, just in case he could see that Tully was stalling and changing the subject.

"No extra preparations. But it is important they know what they're in for."

When Tully looked up, Cunningham was staring at him with his brow furrowed.

"You're sure Agent O'Dell is on her way here?"

"Of course, sir. Where else would she be headed?"

"Sorry, I'm late," O'Dell came in as if on cue.

Tully restrained the deep sigh of relief he felt.

"You're just in time," he told her.

"I need a few minutes with the SWAT team, and then you're on your way." Cunningham headed out the room.

As soon as it was safe, Tully asked, "So how close to the toll bridge did you get before you turned back?"

O'Dell stared at him in surprise.

"How did you know?"

"Lucky guess."

"Does Cunningham know?" Suddenly she seemed more angry than concerned.

"Why would I tell Cunningham?" He pretended to look wounded. "There are some secrets only partners should share." He grabbed a bundle from the corner, handed her a bulletproof vest and waited for her at the door. "Coming?"

CHAPTER 69

"We have to stay back and let them attempt to serve the search warrant," Tully instructed. He wasn't sure that O'Dell was even listening. He could hear her heart pounding. Or was that his own heart? The thumping seemed indistinguishable from the rumble of thunder in the distance.

They had left their vehicles far back on the other side of the electronic gate that blocked the road. Not much of a road, really. Tully had seen cow paths that were more easily accessible. Now as he and O'Dell crouched in the brush and mud, he regretted wearing his good shoes. A crazy thing to be thinking about when they were this close to capturing Stucky and Harding.

The Maryland State Patrol had supplied them with a half-dozen officers—officially for the sole purpose of serving the search warrant to the owner or occupants of the house. If no one responded, the FBI SWAT team would secure the area and accompany Tully and O'Dell in a search of the house and grounds. Tully was quick to notice that all the members of the SWAT team wore sturdy boots. At least O'Dell had remembered the FBI windbreakers. He was sweating under the weight of the bulletproof vest, but that didn't protect him from the wind. Out here in the woods the wind swirled around the trees, crisp and cold. If the thunder was any indication, they would also be wet before the night was over. Night would come quickly in these woods, and with the thick cloud cover they would soon be in the pitch black. Already the twilight was providing eerie shadows that grew darker by the minute.

"There's smoke coming out of the chimney," O'Dell whispered. "Someone must be here."

A faint light appeared in one of the windows, but it could easily be set to a timer. The smoke, however, was a little more difficult to manufacture without someone stoking a fire in the fireplace.

Two of the state patrol officers approached the front door as several of the SWAT team members moved in behind the bushes along the cobblestone path that led to the door. Tully watched, hoping he was wrong about Harding's paranoia and hoping that the patrolmen would not simply be easy targets. He pulled out his own revolver and started scanning the windows of the house, looking for gun barrels peeking through. The house sat nestled in the woods like something out of a fairy tale. There was a porch swing and Tully could hear a wind chime. He couldn't help noticing that there were way too many windows for a man who was going blind.

No one was answering the patrolman's knock. He tried again while everyone else waited quietly. Tully wiped his forehead and suddenly realized that all the chirping birds and rustling forest creatures had also gone silent. Maybe they knew something their human counterparts did not. Even the wind had settled down. The thunder rumbled closer and flashes of lightning streaked across the horizon beyond the wall of trees.

"Perfect," Tully whispered to no one in particular. "Isn't it bad enough that this place already looks like something out of *Dark Shadows?*"

"Dark Shadows?" O'Dell whispered back.

"Yeah, the old TV show." He glanced at her, only now she had a blank look on her face. "You know, with Barnabus Collins and

The Hand?" There was still no glint of recognition. "Forget it. You're too young."

"Doesn't sound like I missed much."

"Hey, watch it. *Dark Shadows* was a classic."

The two patrolmen looked over their shoulders and into the bushes. Not very discreet. One shrugged. The other put an ear to the door. Then he knocked one last time. For some reason he tried the doorknob, then again looked over to the bushes, pointing and indicating that the door was unlocked. Of course, Tully found himself thinking, why the hell would anyone lock the door out here?

Agent Alvando, who was heading the SWAT team, hurried over to Tully and O'Dell.

"We're ready to go in. Give us a few minutes. I'll come back out and give an all-clear sign."

"Okay," Tully said, but O'Dell was up, looking as if she was ready to go in with the SWAT team.

"Come on, Agent Alvando," O'Dell began to argue, and Tully wanted to pull her back down into the brush. "We're trained agents, too. It's not like you're here to protect us."

She looked to Tully as if for reassurance. He wanted to disagree, but she was right. The SWAT team was here for backup, here to help with the search-and-arrest mission, not to protect them.

"We'll go on in with you, Victor," he reluctantly told Agent Alvando.

There was barely enough light to see inside the house. The entry included a hallway down the middle with a great room to the left and an open staircase over to the right. The second-floor landing was visible, separated only by a balcony railing. The team split up with half of them going upstairs, and the other half covering the main floor. Tully followed Agent O'Dell up the stairs. Before they got to the landing, they noticed the SWAT team members had stopped at the end of the hall. Tully could hear what sounded like a voice on the other side of the door where the three men hesitated. They motioned to each other, getting into position. Tully followed O'Dell's lead and pressed himself against the wall. One of the men kicked the door open, and they stormed the room without a word to each other.

O'Dell looked disappointed when they got to the door and discovered the voice came from one of the half-dozen computers lined up along the wall.

"Click twice for confirmation," the electronic voice said. "Speak into the microphone when ready."

From another computer, an electronic voice gave different instructions. "That order has been shipped. Please check the status in twenty-four hours."

"What the fuck is this?" one of the SWAT team asked.

O'Dell was taking a closer look while the rest of them stayed next to the door watching their backs.

"It's a whole computer system set up to be voice activated." She walked from one computer to the next, examining the screens without touching anything. "Looks like it reports the status of his video-game business."

"Why would anyone want a voice-activated system?" Agent Alvando was at the door.

O'Dell looked back at Tully, and he knew what she was thinking. Why, indeed, unless that person was blind—not just partially, but totally blind.

CHAPTER 70

Tess squeezed her eyes shut. She could do this. She could pretend she was somewhere else. After all, she had done it many times before. There wasn't much difference really. She needed to convince herself of that. What did it matter whether a paying john fucked her or some madman?

She needed to relax or it would only hurt more. She needed to stop feeling his thrusts, stop thinking about his hands fondling her breasts, stop hearing his groans. She could do this. She could survive this.

"Open your eyes," he grunted between clenched teeth.

She squeezed them tighter.

"Open your goddamn eyes. I want you to watch."

She refused. He hit her across the mouth, whipping her head so violently to the side that she heard her neck crack. Immediately, she tasted blood. She kept her eyes closed.

"Goddamn you, bitch. Open your fucking eyes."

He was gasping, rocking back and forth with such force she thought he'd crack her insides open as well. She felt his hot breath on her neck and suddenly his teeth sank into her skin. His hands clamped down on her breasts, and he was hanging on to her, riding her, every part of him scraping, rubbing and thrusting at her, devouring her like a rabid dog.

She bit down on her lower lip. She forced her eyes to remain shut. Not much longer. She could do this. He would come, and then it would be over. Why the hell didn't he come already? It wouldn't be much longer. It couldn't be. She twisted her head as far away as possible and kept her eyelids closed tight.

Finally, his body jerked, his teeth let go, his hands gave a final squeeze and he relaxed. He crawled off her, jamming his knee into her stomach and slamming his elbow against her head. Finally, it was over. She lay still, swallowing blood and pretending not to feel the sticky mess between her legs. Instead, she reminded herself that she had survived.

He was so quiet, she wondered if he had gone. She opened her eyes to find him standing over her. The yellow glow of the lantern he had brought with him created a halo behind him. When she met his eyes, he twisted his lips into a smile. He looked as calm and composed as he had when he entered the shack. How was it possible? She had hoped that he would be exhausted, spent and ready to leave. But he showed no signs of fatigue.

"This part you will watch," he promised. "Even if I need to cut your fucking eyelids off." He held up a shiny scalpel for her to see.

Her weak, muffled scream made it past the raw pain in her throat.

"Scream all you want." He laughed. "No one can hear you. And quite frankly, I like it."

Oh dear God. The terror rushed through her veins and exploded in her head. She pulled and shoved against the restraints. Then suddenly she noticed him backing away, his head cocked to the side, as though he was listening to something outside the shack.

Tess strained to hear over the pounding in her head and chest. She lay still, watching him, and then she heard it. Unless she had gone mad, it sounded like voices.

CHAPTER 71

Maggie wondered if they were too late. Had Stucky and Harding escaped into the woods? She looked out the window and watched as Agent Alvando and his men combed the area, disappearing into the woods. Soon they wouldn't be able to see anything without flashlights and strobes, things they hated to use, because the lights made them easy targets for snipers. As much as she wanted to be out there looking with them, she knew Alvando was right. She and Tully weren't equipped or trained to participate in a SWAT team sweep of the woods.

The rain had started softly with a pitter-patter on the metal gutters. The sound was almost comforting, except that the approaching roar of thunder promised a storm. Maggie was grateful the house depended on a generator and not electricity that could easily be knocked out.

"Could we have been wrong about this place?" Agent Tully asked from the other side of the room. He had pulled out some of the cartons from under the computer desks, and with latex gloves on he sifted through what looked like ledgers, mail orders and other business documents.

"All of this could simply be preparation for him losing his sight entirely. I'm not sure what to think." Perhaps it was the impending storm and the electrical current thick in the air. Whatever it was, she couldn't shake the feeling of dread and restlessness. "Maybe we should go check and see if they got that room opened in the basement."

"Alvando told us to stay put." Tully shot her a warning look.

"It could be a torture chamber, not some bunker."

"I'm only guessing it's a bunker. We won't know for sure until Alvando's men can get it opened."

She glanced around the room. It looked like a typical home office except for the talking computers. What a disappointment. What a letdown. She had psyched herself up for a showdown with Albert Stucky, and he was nowhere to be found.

"O'Dell?" Tully was hunched over another of the cartons he had unearthed. "Take a look at this."

She looked over his shoulder expecting to see more X-rated computer software and videos. Instead, she found herself staring at newspaper clippings about her father's death.

"Where the hell do you suppose he got this?" Tully asked.

She was wondering the same thing until she saw her appointment book and childhood photo album. It was her missing carton from the move. She had completely forgotten about it. So Greg had been telling the truth. The carton hadn't been left at the condo. Somehow Stucky had been watching and had managed to take it from the movers. A shiver slid down her back as she thought about him handling her personal possessions.

"Maggie?" Tully stared up at her, concern in his eyes. "Do you think he broke into your house without you knowing?"

"No, I've been missing it since the day I moved in. He must have stolen the box before it made it into the house."

The rage began in the pit of her stomach. She left Tully to dig through the other cartons while she paced the room from window to window.

"That means Stucky has been here," Tully said without looking up.

She kept her eyes on the windows as she walked back and forth. The lightning struck closer, igniting the sky and making the trees look like skeleton soldiers standing at attention. Suddenly she saw a reflection of someone in the hallway walking past the door. She spun around, her revolver gripped firmly, outstretched in front of her. Tully jumped to his feet and had his gun out in seconds.

"What is it, O'Dell?" He kept his eyes ahead watching the doorway. She moved slowly across the room, gun aimed, hammer cocked.

"I saw someone walk by," she finally explained.

"Are any of the SWAT team still in the house?"

"They were finished up here," she whispered. Her heart slammed against her chest. Her breathing was already coming too quickly. "They wouldn't come back up and not announce themselves, right?"

"Do you smell something?" Tully was sniffing the air.

She smelled it, too, and the terror that had begun to crawl up from her stomach started to explode.

"It smells like gasoline," Tully said.

All Maggie could think was that it smelled like gasoline and smoke. It smelled like fire. The thought grabbed hold of her, and suddenly she couldn't breathe. She couldn't think. She couldn't walk the rest of the distance to the door—her knees had locked. Her throat plugged up, threatening to strangle her.

Tully ran to the door and carefully peeked out, his gun ready.

"Holy crap," he yelled, looking out into the hallway in both directions without stepping out. "We've got flames on both sides. There's no way we're getting out the way we came in."

He returned his gun to his holster and hurried to the windows, trying to open one while Maggie stood paralyzed in the middle of the room. Her hands shook so badly she could barely grip her revolver. She stared at her hands as though they belonged to someone else. Her breathing was out of control, and she worried she might start to hyperventilate.

The smell alone sparked images from her childhood nightmares: flames engulfing her father and scorching her fingers every time she reached for him. She could never save him, because her fear immobilized her.

"Damn it!" She heard Tully struggling behind her.

She turned toward him, but her feet wouldn't move. He seemed so far away, and she knew she was losing visual perception. The room began to tilt. She could feel the motion, though she knew it couldn't possibly be real. Then she saw him again, a reflection in the window. She twisted around, but it felt as if she was moving in slow motion. Albert Stucky stood tall and dark in the doorway, dressed in a black leather jacket and pointing a gun directly at her.

She tried to raise her own gun, but it was too heavy. Her hand wouldn't obey the command. The room had tilted to the other side, and she felt herself slipping. He was smiling at her and seemed to be oblivious to the flames shooting up behind him. Was he real? Had her panic, her terror, brought on hallucinations?

"This damn thing is stuck," she heard Tully yell somewhere far off in the distance.

She opened her mouth to warn Tully, but nothing came out. She expected the bullet to hit her squarely in the heart. That's where he was aiming. Everything in slow motion. Was it a dream? A nightmare? He was pulling back the hammer. She could hear wood creaking, giving way in crashes outside the room. She pulled at her arm one more time as she saw Stucky begin to squeeze the trigger.

"Tully," she managed to yell, and just then Stucky slid his aim to the right of her and pulled the trigger. The explosion jolted her like an electrical shock. But she wasn't hit. He hadn't shot her. She looked down. She wasn't bleeding anywhere. It was an effort to move her arm, but she raised it, ready to fire at the now-empty doorway. Stucky was gone. Had it all been her imagination? There was a groan behind her, and before she turned to look, she remembered Tully.

He gripped his bloody thigh with both hands and stared at it as though he couldn't believe what he was seeing. The smoke had entered the room and burned their eyes. She ripped off her windbreaker. She could do this. She had to be able to do this. She ran to the door, forcing herself not to think of the heat and the flames. She slammed the door shut, wadded up her jacket and shoved it into the crack under the door.

She came back to Tully and kneeled next to him. His eyes were wide and beginning to glaze over. He was going into shock.

"You're gonna be okay, Tully. Breathe but not too deeply." Already the smoke was seeping in between the cracks.

She pulled at his necktie, undoing the knot and removing it. Gently she moved his hands away from the wound. She tied the necktie around his thigh, just above the bullet hole, tightening it and wincing when he shouted out in pain.

Smoke was filling the room. The crashing of beams sounded closer. She could hear a commotion of voices outside. Tully hadn't managed to make either window budge. Maggie crawled to her feet, trying to focus only on Tully and getting them out of the room, out of the house. She would not think of the flames on the other side of the door. She would not imagine the hellish heat licking at the floorboards beneath them

She grabbed one of the computer monitors, yanking the cords and cables until they became unplugged.

"Tully, cover your face."

He only stared at her.

"Goddamn it, Tully, cover your face and head. Now!"

He pulled up his windbreaker and turned to face the wall. Maggie felt her arms weakening under the weight of the monitor. Her eyes burned, and her lungs screamed. She hurled the monitor through the window, and then quickly kicked out the chunks of glass. She grabbed Tully under the arms.

"Come on, Tully. You're going to have to help me."

Somehow she managed to drag him out the window and onto the roof of the porch. Agent Alvando and two other men were down below. It wasn't a great distance to the ground, but with a bullet in his thigh, she couldn't expect Agent Tully to jump. She held on to his arms as he lowered his body over the edge and waited for the men below to grab him. The entire time, his eyes held hers. But there wasn't shock now. There wasn't fear. Instead, what she saw in Agent Tully's eyes surprised her even more. The only thing she saw was trust.

CHAPTER 72

Tully's leg hurt like hell. Most of the flames were out. He sat a safe distance away, but the heat actually felt good. Someone had thrown a blanket around his shoulders. He didn't remember it happening. He also didn't remember that it was raining until he discovered his clothing wet and his hair plastered to his forehead. Somehow Agent Alvando had managed to get the ambulance past the electronic gate and all the way to the burning house.

"Your ride is here." Agent O'Dell appeared from behind him.

"Let them take the McGowan woman first. I can wait."

She studied him as if she would be the judge of whether he waited or not.

"Are you sure? They might be able to fit both of you."

He looked past O'Dell to examine Tess McGowan himself. She was sitting in one of the SWAT team's trucks. From what he could see of her, she looked to be in bad shape. Her hair was tangled and wild like Medusa. Her body, now wrapped in a blanket, had been covered with bloody cuts and bruises. She could barely stand. Alvando's men had found her locked in a wooden shack not far from the house. She had been shackled to a cot, gagged and naked. She had told them that the madman had left only seconds before they found her.

"I'm not bleeding anymore," Tully said. "She's been through God knows what. Get her out of here and into a nice warm bed somewhere."

O'Dell turned and caught one of the men's attention, then waved to him. He seemed to know exactly what she meant and went directly to the truck to escort Ms. McGowan to the ambulance.

"Besides," Tully said, "I want to be here when they bring them out."

The men had found a fire hydrant in back, probably a leftover from when the property had been occupied by the government. They were dousing the entire house with thick streams of water that were much more efficient than the light rainfall. Firefighters from some neighboring community had stomped their way to the scene about an hour ago, but only after their truck had gotten stuck in the mud about a mile from the entrance. Now they ventured into the burned-out hull of the house as though on a mission. They had discovered two dead and burned bodies in the basement bunker.

Tully rubbed the soot from his face and eyes. O'Dell sat down on the ground next to him. She pulled her knees up to her chest, wrapping her arms around her legs and resting her chin on the tops of her knees.

"We don't know for sure that it's them," she said without looking at him.

"No, but who else would it be?"

"Stucky doesn't seem like the suicidal type."

"He may have thought the bunker was fireproof."

She glanced over at him, not moving from her position. "I never thought of that." She looked almost convinced. Almost.

The firefighters came out of the wreckage, hauling a body on a gurney. It was draped with a black canvas. Two more followed with another gurney. O'Dell sat up straight. Tully heard her suck in air, and he thought she was holding her breath as she watched. The second gurney approached the FBI's truck, when suddenly the dead man's arm slipped out from under the canvas. The arm slipped off the gurney, hanging down, clothed in what looked like a leather jacket. He felt O'Dell stiffen. Then finally, he heard her breathe a deep sigh of relief.

CHAPTER 73

If it hadn't been so late, Maggie would have offered to take Gwen out for dinner. However, she had spent too much time at the hospital making sure Tess was comfortable and that Agent Tully had no permanent damage to his leg.

Though she should have been completely exhausted, for the first time in a very long time she felt like celebrating. So she searched and discovered a Chinese place that was still open on the north side of Newburgh Heights. She could finally stop by a restaurant again without worrying the waitress would end up in a Dumpster the next day. She picked up kung pao chicken, sweet-and-sour pork and plenty of fried rice. She asked for extra fortune cookies and wondered whether Harvey liked egg rolls.

Maggie arrived home to find the two of them curled up in the recliner watching Jay Leno on the portable TV. The cartons reminded her once again of the carton Stucky had stolen, now gone forever, literally up in flames. The photo album had contained the only pictures she had possessed of her father. She didn't want to think about it right now. Not now when she was enjoying what felt like some sort of liberation.

Gwen saw the bags of takeout and smiled. "Thank God! I'm starved."

She had called Gwen from the road, filling her in on most of the details. Her friend had sounded relieved not only for Maggie but for herself as well. At least she wouldn't have to worry about Walker Harding ever again.

"Why don't you spend the night here?" Maggie suggested over a forkful of chicken.

"I have an early-morning appointment. I'd rather drive tonight. I'm worthless in the morning." She was examining Maggie while she scooped out more rice. "How are you? Honestly?"

"Honestly? I'm fine."

Gwen frowned at her as though that was too easy an answer.

"I came close to getting Tully and myself killed," she said, now serious. "I panicked with the fire. I couldn't move. I couldn't breathe. But you know what?" She smiled. "I survived. And I got us out of there."

"Very good. Sounds like you passed some major personal test, Maggie."

Harvey shoved his nose under Maggie's arm, insisting on another egg roll. She gave him a half-eaten roll and patted his back.

"I don't think you're supposed to feed dogs egg rolls, Maggie."

"And how would I know that? Is there a book with all these rules?"

"I'm sure there are several. I'll pick one up for you."

"Might not be a bad idea since it looks like Harvey and I are going to be permanent roommates."

"Does that mean you were right about his owner?"

"Tess told us there was another woman. A woman named Rachel who's dead in a pit somewhere on the property. Of course we don't know yet, but I feel certain it's Rachel Endicott." She noticed Gwen's grimace. "They'll continue to search for her tomorrow. Tess said there were other bodies, bones, skulls. Stucky and Harding may have been using this property for years."

"What do you suppose Harding had planned for me?"

"Don't, Gwen," Maggie snapped at her, and immediately she apologized. "I'm sorry, I just don't want to think about it, okay?"

"I suppose it makes sense that the two of them would have eventually moved on to women you knew more intimately. Friends, relatives...oh, speaking of intimately—" she smiled "—that reminds me. You had a phone call earlier. That hunky ex-quarterback from Nebraska."

"Nick?"

"What, you know more than one hunky ex-quarterback?" Gwen looked as if she was enjoying Maggie's annoying blush.

"Did he want me to call him back tonight?"

"Actually, he said he was headed for the airport. I took a message." Gwen pulled herself up off the floor. "You need to shop for a table, Maggie. I'm getting too old to be eating on the floor." She found the note she had left on the desk. She read the message, squinting as though someone else had written it. "He said his dad had a heart attack."

"Oh Jesus." Now Maggie wished she had talked to him. Nick and his father had a complex relationship, one in which Nick had only recently been able to get away from. "Is he going to be okay? He's not dead, is he?"

"No, but I think Nick said they were talking about surgery as soon as possible." Gwen scrunched up her face as she continued to decipher her notes.

"This is something that I didn't understand. He said his dad had received a letter, and that's what they think may have caused the heart attack. But unless I'm mistaken, I could swear Nick said the letter was from South America."

Maggie felt sick to her stomach. Had Father Michael Keller sent Antonio Morrelli some sort of confession? Maggie seemed to be the only one who believed the charismatic young priest was the one who had killed four boys in Platte City, Nebraska. But he had left the country before she had been able to prove it. The last she knew, he was still in South America.

"That's it," Gwen said. "Does any of that makes sense to you?"

The phone startled both of them.

"Maybe this is Nick." Maggie untangled herself out of the cross-legged position on the floor and grabbed the phone. "Maggie O'Dell."

"Agent O'Dell. It's Assistant Director Cunningham."

She checked her watch. It was late, and she had just seen him at the hospital a couple of hours ago.

"Is Tully okay?" It was the first thing that came to mind.

"He's fine. I'm with Dr. Holmes. He was good enough to do the autopsies tonight."

"Dr. Holmes has had his share of autopsies in the past two weeks."

"There's a problem, Agent O'Dell." Cunningham didn't waste any time.

"What kind of problem?" Maggie prepared herself, leaning against the desk and gripping the phone. Gwen watched from her perch on the recliner.

"Walker Harding died of a gunshot wound to the back of his head. He was shot with a .22, execution style. Not only that, but his organs are in an extremely advanced state of decomposition. Dr. Holmes is guessing he's been dead for several weeks."

"Several weeks? That's impossible, sir. We found his fingerprints at three of the crime scenes."

"I think we might have an explanation for that. Several of his fingers are missing, cut off, including his thumb. I'm guessing Stucky did it. Took the fingers with him. Preserved them and used them at the crime scenes to throw us off."

"But Gwen has had two sessions with Harding." She glanced at Gwen and her friend's face showed concern and alarm. Even Harvey started pacing in the sunroom, tilting his head, listening.

"Dr. Patterson has never seen Albert Stucky," Cunningham said, keeping his cool professional tone and ignoring the frantic edge to Maggie's. "If we ask her to describe the man she had the sessions with, I'm guessing she'll describe Stucky. I've only seen one or two photos of Harding, but if I remember correctly, there was an uncanny resemblance between the two men. Stucky must have been using Harding's identity for some time now, pretending to be him. That probably also explains the airline ticket in Harding's name."

"Jesus." Maggie couldn't believe it. Though it all made sense. She wasn't sure she had completely believed Stucky would allow anyone, even Harding, in on his game. "So he had the perfect disguise and the perfect hiding place."

"There's more, Agent O'Dell. The other body has been dead for several weeks, too, and it's not Albert Stucky."

Maggie sat down before her knees gave out from under her. "No, this can't be happening. He can *not* have escaped again."

"We're not sure who it is. Maybe a friend or caretaker of Harding's. Harding was definitely blind. Dr. Holmes says both his retinas were detached, and there were no signs of diabetes."

Maggie was barely listening anymore. She could hardly hear him over the pounding of her heart as she glanced frantically around the room. She noticed Harvey sniffing at the back door, now agitated. Where the hell had she left her Smith & Wesson? She opened the desk drawer. The Glock was gone.

"I've sent several agents back to watch your house," Cunningham said as if that would be enough. "I suggest you not leave tonight. Stay put. If he comes after you, we'll be ready."

If he comes after me, I'll be a sitting duck, but she kept the thought to herself.

She met Gwen's questioning eyes. The fear began invading Maggie's system like cold liquid injected into her veins. Still, she held herself up and pushed away from the solid security of her father's rolltop desk.

"Stucky wouldn't dare come after me again."

CHAPTER 74

He crawled through the bushes, staying low to the ground. The damn bushes had prickly branches that kept grabbing his sweatshirt. This sort of thing would never happen with his leather jacket. He missed it already, though it had been a worthy sacrifice to see Special Agent Maggie O'Dell's look of relief and know it to be false. He had fooled them all, slipping in and out of hiding places he had specifically prepared for just such an occasion.

He rubbed at his eyes. Fuck, it was dark! He wished the red lines would go away. Pop, pop—no, he wouldn't think of the fucking blood vessels rupturing in his eyes. The insulin stabilized his body, but there seemed to be nothing to stop the exploding blood vessels in his eyes.

He could still hear Walker's tinny laugh, telling him, "You'll be a blind fucker just like me, Al." Walker was still laughing when he put the .22 at the base of his head and pulled the trigger—pop, pop.

The lights were completely out now. He had seen her moving

back and forth in what he knew to be the bedroom. He wished he could see her face, relaxed and unsuspecting, but the curtains were drawn and not sheer enough.

He had already intercepted and dismantled the security system with a handheld gadget that Walker had invented for him a few months ago. Blind as a bat, but the man had been an electronics genius. He didn't even know how the thing worked. But he had tested it on the house on Archer Drive, and it did, indeed, work.

He started up the trellis that was hidden by vines and more bushes. He hoped it was sturdier than it looked. Actually, all of this seemed too easy, not much of a challenge. But then, she would be the challenge. He knew she wouldn't disappoint him.

He thought of the scalpel in its thin sheath, tucked safely inside his boot. He'd take his time with her. The anticipation aroused his senses so intensely he needed to stifle what sounded like panting. Yes, this would be well worth the effort.

CHAPTER 75

Maggie sat in the dark corner. Her back pressed against the wall of the bedroom, her outstretched arms leaning on her knees. Her hands gripped her Smith & Wesson, her finger on the trigger. She was ready for him this time. She knew he had been watching. She knew he would come. Yet, when she heard him at the foot of the trellis, her pulse began to race. Her heart slammed against her chest. Sweat trickled down her back.

In a matter of minutes, he was at the window. She saw his shadow hovering, a black vulture. Then his face was at the glass, startling her and almost making her jump. Don't move. Don't flinch. Stay calm. Steady. Yet the terror hammered away at her, raw and unyielding to any of her mental commands. A slight tremor threatened her aim. She knew she was safe in the dark corner. Besides, he would be looking at the curled-up bundle of pillows he would mistake for his sleeping victim.

Would he be surprised that she had gotten so good at his game? Would he be disappointed that she could predict his moves? Certainly he wouldn't expect that they had already discovered the second body to not be his. He must have realized they would and soon, because he was wasting no time coming after his ultimate victim, his ultimate blow to his nemesis. This would be his grand finale, his final scar to leave Maggie with before the diabetes left him completely blind.

She tightened her grip. Instead of the terror, she concentrated on the faces of his victims, the litany of names, now adding Jessica, Rita and Rachel to the list. How dare he make her an accomplice to his evil. She let the anger seep into her veins, hoping it would replace the crawly feeling that invaded her insides.

He eased the window up, gently, quietly, and before he stepped into the room, she could smell him, the scent of smoke and sweat. She waited until he got to the edge of the bed. She waited for him to draw the scalpel from his boot.

"You won't be needing that," she said calmly, not moving a muscle.

He spun around, holding the scalpel. With his free hand he stripped off the bedcovers, then grabbed for the lamp on the nightstand. The yellow glow filled the room, and when he turned toward her, she thought she saw a flash of surprise in his colorless eyes. He quickly composed himself, standing straight and tall, replacing the surprise with one of his twisted smiles.

"Why, Maggie O'Dell. I wasn't expecting you."

"Gwen isn't here. In fact, she's back at my house. I hope you don't mind me taking her place?" Stucky hadn't dared come for her. That would have been too easy. Just like in that Miami warehouse eight months ago. It would have been easier to kill her. Instead, he left her with a scar, a constant reminder of him. So this time, why wouldn't he do it again? No, Stucky didn't intend to kill her. He simply wanted to destroy her. It would be his ultimate blow, to hurt a woman Maggie knew, one she cared about and loved.

"You're good at our little game." He seemed pleased.

Without warning, she squeezed the trigger, and his hand flew back, the scalpel clinking to the floor. He stared at his bloodied hand. His eyes met hers. This time she saw more than alarm. Was that the beginning of fear?

"How does it feel?" she asked, trying to keep the quiver out of her voice. "How does it feel to have me beating you at your own game?"

There was that smile again, a cocky smirk that she wanted to shoot off his face.

"No, I should be asking you, Maggie. How does it feel to play at my game?"

She felt the hairs on the back of her neck stand up. She could do this. She would not let him win. Not this time.

"It's over," she managed to say. Could he see her hand tremble?

"You like seeing me bleeding. Admit it." He raised his hand to show her the blood dripping down his sleeve. "It's a powerful feeling, isn't it, Maggie?"

"Is it a powerful feeling to kill your best friend, Stucky? Is that why you did it?"

She thought she saw him grimace. Maybe she had finally found his Achilles' heel.

"Why did you do it? Why did you kill the one man, the only person who could stomach being your friend?"

"He had something I needed. Something I couldn't get anywhere else," he said, holding up his chin and looking away from the light.

"What could a blind Walker Harding possibly have that was worth killing him for?"

"You're a smart lady. You already know the answer to that. His identity. I needed to become him." Now he laughed and squinted.

Maggie watched his eyes. The light was bothering him. Yes, she was right. Whether it was diabetes or something else, Stucky was losing his eyesight.

"Not like Walker was doing much with his identity anyway," Stucky continued. "Sitting in that house in the boonies with his cyberlife. Jacking off to porn videos instead of enjoying the real thing." His lips curled into a snarl as he added, "He was pathetic. Never would I become what he was, at least, not without a fight."

He reached for the lamp again to turn it off. Maggie pulled the trigger. This time the bullet shattered his wrist. He grabbed at his hand, the anger and pain distorting his face while he tried to keep it composed.

"Are your eyes giving you a little trouble?" she taunted him, despite the panic sliding down into her legs and paralyzing her. She couldn't run. She needed to stay put. She couldn't let him see her fear.

He managed another smile, his face void of the pain that had to be shooting up his arm. He started walking toward her. Maggie pulled back the hammer and squeezed the trigger again. This time the bullet ripped into his left kneecap, knocking him to the floor. He stared at his knee in disbelief, but he didn't wince or cry out in pain.

"You like this, don't you? Have you ever felt such power before, Maggie?"

His voice began to unnerve her. What was he doing? If she wasn't mistaken, he was the one taunting her. He wanted her to continue.

"It's over, Stucky. This is where it ends." But she heard the quiver in her voice. Then a new fear rushed through her when she realized that he had heard it, too. Damn it! This wasn't working.

He crawled back to his feet. Suddenly her previous plan seemed ridiculous. How could she incapacitate him enough to bring him down, let alone bring him in? Was it possible to harness someone as evil as Stucky? As he started toward her again, she wondered if it was possible to even destroy him. He barely limped from his shattered kneecap, and now she could see that he had retrieved the scalpel while he had been down on the floor. How many bullets did she have left in the chamber? Had she fired twice or three times? Why the hell could she suddenly not remember?

He held up the scalpel for her to see, flipping it around and getting a better grip on it in his good hand.

"I was hoping to leave your good friend Gwen's heart on your doorstep. Seemed kind of poetic, don't you think? But now I guess I'll have to settle for taking out yours instead."

"Put it down, Stucky. It's over," but even she wasn't convinced by her words. How could she be with her hands shaking like this?

"The game ends only when I say it ends," he hissed at her.

She took aim, trying to steady her hands, concentrating on her target—that space between his eyes. Her finger twitched as she kept it pressed against the trigger. He wouldn't win this time. She forced herself to stare into his black eyes, the evil holding her there, pinning her against the wall. She couldn't let it dismantle her. But as he continued slowly toward her, she felt the wall of fear blocking her, the raw hysteria strangling her and blurring her vision. Before she could squeeze the trigger, the door to the room flew open.

"Agent O'Dell," Cunningham yelled, rushing in with his revolver drawn.

He stopped when he saw the two of them, stunned, hesitating. Maggie was startled, looking away for a split second. Just long enough for Stucky to dive at her, the scalpel plunging down. Gunfire exploded in the small bedroom, in rapid succession—the echoes bouncing off the walls.

Finally, the sound stopped as suddenly as it had started.

Albert Stucky lay slumped over Maggie's knees, his body jerking, blood spraying her. She wasn't sure whether or not some of it was hers. The scalpel stuck into the wall, so close she felt it against her side, so close it had ripped the side of her shirt open. She couldn't move. Was he dead? Her heart and lungs slammed against each other, making it difficult to breathe. Her hand shook uncontrollably as she still gripped the warm revolver. She knew without checking that its cylinder was empty.

Cunningham shoved Stucky's body off her, a thud with no sound of life. Suddenly Maggie grabbed Stucky's shoulder, desperate to see his face. She rolled him over. Bullets riddled his body. His lifeless eyes stared up at her, but she wanted to cry out in relief. With all the holes in his body, there was *not* a single one between his eyes.

CHAPTER 76

Tess leaned against the glass. Now she realized she should have taken the wheelchair that the Nurse Ratched look-alike had recommended. Her feet burned and the stitches pinched and pulled with little provocation. Her chest ached, and it was still difficult to breathe. She had been wrong about the ribs, two cracked, two bruised. The other cuts and bruises would heal. In time she would forget about the madman they called Albert Stucky. She would forget his cold, black eyes pinning her to the table like the leather shackles that had held her wrists and ankles. She would forget his hot breath on her face, his hands and body violating her in ways she thought were not possible.

She gathered the front of the thin robe in her fist, warding off the shiver, the icy fingers that could still strangle her whenever she thought about him. Why fool herself? She knew she would never forget. It was one more chapter to try to erase. She was so very tired of rewriting her past in order to survive her future. Now she struggled to find a reason why she should even bother. Perhaps that was what had brought her here.

She looked past her battered reflection in the window and watched the wrinkled red faces. Little chunky fists batted at the air. She listened to the newborns' persistent cries and coos. Tess smiled. What a cliché to come here looking for the answers.

"Girlfriend, what are you doing out of bed?"

Tess glanced over her shoulder to find Delores Heston in a bright red suit, lighting up the sterile white corridor as she marched toward her. She wrapped her arms around Tess, carefully and gently hugging her. When she pulled away, the hard-nosed business owner had tears in her eyes.

"Oh mercy, I promised myself I wouldn't do this." Delores swiped at her eyes and the running mascara. "How are you feeling, Tess?"

"I'm fine," she lied, and tried to smile. Her jaw hurt where he had punched her. She found herself checking over her teeth again with the tip of her tongue. It amazed her that none of them had been chipped or broken.

She realized Delores was studying her, examining for herself whether Tess was fine. She lifted Tess's chin with her soft hand, taking a closer look at the bite marks on her neck. She didn't want to see the horror and pity in Delores's face so she looked away. Without a word, Delores wrapped her arms around her again, this time holding her, stroking her hair and rubbing her back.

"I'm making it my job to take care of you, Tess," she said emphatically as she pulled away. "And I don't want a single argument, you hear me?"

Tess had never had anyone make her such an offer. She wasn't sure what the correct response was. But of all her choices, tears did not seem appropriate. Not now. Delores took out a tissue and dabbed at Tess's cheeks, smiling at her like a mother preparing her child for school.

"You have a handsome visitor waiting for you in your room."

Tess's insides clenched. Oh God, she couldn't handle facing Daniel. Not like this.

"Could you tell him I'll call later and thank him for the roses?"

"Roses?" Delores looked confused. "Looked like a bunch of purple violets he was clutching. He's squeezing those flowers so tight, they're probably potpourri by now."

"Violets?"

She looked over Delores's shoulder, and Tess could see Will Finley, watching, hesitating at the end of the corridor. He looked incredibly handsome in dark trousers, a blue shirt and, if her blurred vision served her correctly, a bunch of violets in his left hand.

Maybe there were a few new chapters in her life that needed writing, after all.

EPILOGUE

One week later

Maggie wasn't sure why she had come. Perhaps she simply needed to see him lowered into the ground. Maybe she needed to be certain that this time Albert Stucky would not escape.

She stood back, close to the trees, looking at the few mourners and recognizing most of them as reporters. The religious entourage from St. Patrick's outnumbered the mourners. There were several priests and just as many altar boys carrying incense and candles. How could they justify sending off someone like Stucky with all the same ceremony given an ordinary sinner? It didn't make sense. It certainly didn't seem fair.

But it didn't matter. She was finally free. And in more ways than one. Stucky had not won. And neither had her own shadow side. In a split second, she had chosen to defend herself, but had not given in to true evil.

Harvey nudged her hand, suddenly impatient and probably wondering what use it was to be out in the open if they were not going to walk and enjoy it. She watched the procession make its way from the grave down the hill.

Albert Stucky was finally gone, soon to be buried six feet under like his victims.

Maggie petted Harvey's soft fur and felt an incredible sense of relief. They could go home. She could feel safe again. The first thing she wanted to do was sleep.